DEAD COORDINATES

By **Monsuta**

Autopsy Notes
An imprint of Ink Beyond

Monsuta

Dead Coordinates
First Edition – May 2026
Printed in the United States of America

ISBN: 978-1-969141-07-2

Published by Autopsy Notes
An imprint of Ink Beyond Publishing

DEDICATION

For Stacy,

On July 3, 2012, after work one evening, I asked you if you wanted to try something new with me. Neither of us really knew what a geocache was. It sounded simple enough, maybe even a little strange, but we decided to give it a try anyway.

When we found that first cache together, something clicked. What started as a small experiment quickly became so much bigger. Before long we were planning trips, chasing coordinates through forests, along lakes, down trails, and into places we never would have discovered otherwise. Geocaches became our adventures.

Over the years we spent countless hours exploring together, sometimes hiking miles into the woods, sometimes searching city streets while pretending not to look suspicious. We found caches tucked under bridges, hidden in hollow logs, and disguised in ways that blew our minds. Every find came with its own story, and those stories became a collection of memories we still talk about today.

One of my favorites will always be the day we chased our very first First to Find. The cache was on a tiny island in the middle of a lake, and the only way to reach it was to swim. Most people probably would have turned around and called it a day. Instead, we looked at each other, shrugged, and jumped in, fully clothed. By the time we climbed onto that island and signed the logbook, soaking wet and laughing, I knew that caching had become something special for us.

What started as a simple hobby turned into years of adventure, exploration, and shared stories that still make us smile. More than anything else, it became a reason to get outside and to see what waited just around the next bend in the trail.

Thank you for saying yes that day. Thank you for every mile, every search, and every adventure we've shared since.

Monsuta

This story may be fiction, but the memories that inspired it are real. And they're some of my favorite ones with you. TFTC, Lover.

"Not all those who wander are lost."
~ **J.R.R. Tolkien**, *The Fellowship of the Ring*

"Adventure is worthwhile in itself."
~ **Amelia Earhart**

"The real voyage of discovery consists not in seeking new landscapes, but in having new eyes."
~ **Marcel Proust**

"Somewhere, something incredible is waiting to be known."
~ **Carl Sagan**

Dead Coordinates

A Note on finding geocaches

Caching is a real-world scavenger hunt played using GPS coordinates. Participants, known as geocachers, search for hidden containers called geocaches (or simply caches) that have been placed by other players. Inside, they may find small logbooks, trinkets, or clues that lead to additional locations.

The game can be whatever you want it to be, a hobby for the whole family, an excuse to spend time outdoors with friends, a way to meet others in the community, or simply an opportunity to explore new places and enjoy the quiet of the world around you.

The hobby is generally safe as long as participants approach it with the same awareness and preparation they would bring to any outdoor activity. Cachers are encouraged to respect their surroundings and practice a simple ethic: leave the cache site in the same condition, or better, than how they found it.

Caches may be hidden deep in forests, under bridges, inside hollow logs, or tucked into the overlooked corners of cities. Some containers are simple, an ammo can or a small film canister, while others involve complex puzzles or multi-stage adventures where one set of coordinates leads to the next until the final cache is discovered.

When cachers locate a cache, they sign the logbook inside and later record the find online through one of the geocache websites. Some enthusiasts also chase a small badge of honor known as an FTF, or First to Find, awarded to the first person who signs the log after a new cache is published.

For millions of people around the world, the game is a simple reason to step outside, follow the coordinates, and see where the trail leads.

Chapter 1: First To Find

The phone screen illuminates the dark, giving the night a ghostly life. Fir silhouettes crowd the Pacific Northwest sky, their tips obscured by a blanket of fog. Moist air grips the throat with the earthy taste of moss and a hint of sap. Off-trail in the Yacolt Burn Forest, the ground softens, each step pressing the forest a little deeper into silence.

The GPS chirps once at forty-two feet before the sound dies into the hush of the river echoing through the forest. A figure eases through sword ferns and blown-down limbs, careful and deliberate, boots brushing the wet curl of a cedar branch, causing water flecks to bead and vanish. The pre-dawn is awake with quiet friction, cloth on bark, and a monitored breath.

The ammo can is set at the base of a bigleaf maple between two massive roots, encasing the metal container like bones caging a heart. The latch gives with a muffled click. Inside are the usual relics of the game, plastic trinkets slick with condensation, a number two pencil and disposable pen, and the sanctified empty space kept for whatever trinkets are left here. A gloved hand slides a fresh logbook into the can and places a Polaroid onto the pile. The woman in the photo is smiling, but it feels forced, required. The lid closes and is snapped shut.

Wind lifts and moves the crown of the oak in a single shudder and the air smells as though the rain is turning to snow somewhere higher than this valley will ever see. A plane rumbles far off and never appears.

The figure adjusts the can until the latch faces north. Details matter, lines lie if they aren't true. A few yards back sits a blind made of fallen limbs and moss, the kind you'd miss unless you'd built it with your own hands. The watcher settles there, knees loose, back set, breath slowing until the pulse in the neck matches the river's steady rhythm. Minutes lengthen into the early morning when the forest begins to awaken and small animals become active.

A branch cracks in the distance. Down the path, footsteps find rhythm in gravel, then loam. The sound is the cautious stutter of someone leaving the trail, looking for something out of sight, moving toward where a compass arrow told them to. The watcher listens to the space between sounds the way hunters do, the way surveyors do when they're measuring an absence. The prey is right on time.

At 5:14 a.m., Erin's phone rattles on the nightstand, using the vibration to find the ledge. She was already awake, floating just above the surface of sleep, waiting for another sound from her phone, an alarm. The hour between sleep and day still feels like stolen light to her. She catches the phone just before it dives and checks the notification. A new cache was published: Hidden Hollow.

The coordinates are tucked deep into the Yacolt forest she remembers by smell. Strangely though, there is no owner's name linked to the cache. She rubs her eyes and dismisses it, figuring the new cache might need time for details to populate.

She chews a mint on the way to the closet because it keeps her nerves steady when the pin drops. The mint tastes like toothpaste and medicine. She slides on a pair of thermals before her jeans, feeling her bones already aching from the onset of autumn. Next, she grabs a pair of socks that lie about staying dry.

A new cache posting means the site will be swarming with players eager to capture the prestigious but meaningless bragging rights of being the first to find. Erin doesn't have time to mosey out the door if she wants to rob others of their find.

The rest of her apartment smells like wet wool and citrus cleaner not fully wiped. The corkboard next to the fridge catches her phone's light, revealing printouts, a stained map with a grid overlay, and colored pins. She tries not to get distracted, but fails, and looks anyway. She smirks, each pin is her own first-to-find map of success, and she plans on planting a new pin when she gets home.

She grabs a sticky note from the corner of the frame and writes Hidden Hollow, *5:14 a.m.* without thinking, indulging a quiet superstition she's carried for years. If anything ever happened to her chasing a cache alone, at least someone would know when she walked out the door, not that anyone was around anymore to see the note. She presses the new pin with the note into the board, then pats the map before moving into the kitchen to pour yesterday's coffee into a travel mug without heating it up. On her way out, the mirror in the entry throws back a damp-haired woman with ink on her thumb from grading papers all night. She pauses to pull her hair up, then rushes out, locking the door behind her.

She drives, leaving the phone face down in the cup holder. The roads are mostly empty in the pre-dawn twilight, which she's thankful for as the needle on her speedometer has gone past the speed limit and has stayed there since she left the city. The minutes pass and Erin knows the longer she takes, the chances of capturing those FTF bragging rights disappear.

The highway is a dark ribbon with no color yet, just suggestions and reflective lines. Streetlamps make the wet asphalt look newer than it is, hiding the cracks and divots. By the time the valley chokes the road down into two lanes framed by cedar and alder, fog sits knee-high over the ferns, and every low beam turns the forest into breath.

Erin speeds through the Larch Mountain roads, feeling her stomach drop each time she crests a hill. She reaches her dirt road turn-off and continues straight to the trailhead, where she kills the engine. Silence hammers in the dark while she collects her gear from the passenger seat, thankful there are no other vehicles in the lot. When she gets out of her car, a disturbed raven clacks once from somewhere she can't place.

The trail's signboard is slick with a film of rain and hints of mold. A *Know Before You Go* banner smiles above a missing-person flyer that has survived three seasons on the same board, probably longer than the person in the photo. Erin touches the paper's corner without thinking. For a moment, it clings to her glove, almost as though it is begging to be taken with her.

The GPS on her phone app glows and the digital arrow spins before finding position. 1.37 miles, bearing northeast. Hidden Hollow is listed as difficulty 2.5 and a terrain 3. The part of her brain that tracks numbers does the math, this should be an easy find. The other part, the one that's been hungry for weeks, leans in closer to the trail map on the signboard, looking at the other entry points and lot locations. She recognizes she's the first at this lot, but others may still provide access for seasoned cachers. She knows her FTF isn't yet guaranteed, so her feet hit the trail.

The path becomes a thin stretch of crushed needles and exposed roots. She jogs half a mile before finding the evidence of a fresh trail of padded down foliage off to the right. She steps off trail where the arrow wants, and the moss gives. This is the right direction, she can feel it.

The canopy dims the morning into something akin to a chapel

with no priests and many pews. Sword ferns drip, prehistoric and patient while alder trunks lean together like gossipers. A banana slug the size of her hand slides along the pressed reeds, minding its own for its entire life.

Her GPS calls each cautious step, counting down forty-five feet, thirty-seven feet. At thirty, she puts her device away so her eyes can do the real work. Her body clocks the shift without question, her stomach tightens, and her breath shortens. The forest matches energy every time she inhales.

The approach is the part of this game that she loves. The not-yet, but almost. How a search squeezes every other worry into a thread she can pocket and forget about. She slows and lets her eyes work, finding patterns and signs from every other cache she's ever found. She scans for fallen logs with fresh breaks, anthropic rocks, or an unnatural corner where this place prefers curves.

Her pocket buzzes and she knows she is within a twenty-foot radius. Barring a weak signal, she knows it's close, and her skin tingles with anticipation. A scan into the forest tells her no competition has arrived yet, so she hones in, looking for a loose pile of sticks or fallen bark that has been put back into place.

A bigleaf maple grips a hunk of ground with roots webbed in lichen. Between two of them, she spots a shade of green that doesn't occur here naturally. She goes still, not in the way prey does, more like a diver right before meeting the water. The can is exactly where it should be, but also exactly where it shouldn't.

Erin navigates a diagonal approach, careful to disturb as little of the forest floor as her body will allow. The latch of the box has the dull sheen of something well-used but not abused. The paint is scuffed at the corners, and a fine tooth of rust runs along the hinge.

She sets her gloved palm on the lid and takes in the feel of cold metal, she holds without completely knowing why. Sometimes its superstition dressed as caution, sometimes the shape of being watched tries to become a thought. She looks over her shoulder and sees trees, a ferny slope, and listens to the babbling of water, but no trace of human activity. The forest isn't an audience, but it feels like one at times.

She takes her hand away, flexes, and reaches again, this time to open the container. The latch makes that tiny throat-click that always sounds louder in a forest than it would in a living room.

Something moves twenty yards off, some sort of weight-shift making a fern quiver. It's not wind and doesn't sound like deer. If it's a person, they're good at being present without saying they are. She freezes and listens, but the creek speaks louder to cover it. Erin quits looking, she's getting this FTF. She opens the can, quickly snatching the logbook.

Along the same ridge, the watcher surveys the cacher.

The figure in the blind has not moved since Erin's been hunting for the cache and had been still for the hour before human feet have disrupted the silence of the forest. A disciplined body learns this trick, how to be a shape that doesn't interrupt itself. A finger rests on the rim of the view hole, centering and grounding. Breath comes slow enough to not let ghosts leave the mouth.

Erin's headlamp throws a dull silver across the roots, the beam is as careful as someone touching a stranger's wrist. The watcher takes the small measurement every maker takes when work is about to be judged, admiring the angle, distance, approach, and the moment hands will meet what was made.

Surveying the scene, the figure notes what matters, how Erin didn't turn the box, where she spared the moss, and how she bends with weight on the outside of her left foot, a knee favoring some old story she won't tell. The forest keeps stories like that, and the river tells the stories further downstream, even when nobody asks it to.

The lid is open and for Erin, the moment is small and large all at once. The second before the Polaroid becomes a fact is longer than time knows, long enough to imagine the expression, long enough to decide whether this player earns the next point or only the knowledge of having touched what they shouldn't.

Then comes the sound, the one the figure came for, something to be witnessed from twenty yards. Not the click, not the breath, but the cacher learning something she didn't want to know.

The watcher allows one breath to crest and fall, before settling into stillness again, complete as snowfall. The moment is right on time.

Erin doesn't remember lifting her phone. The shutter sound of the camera is obscene here, but the image taken is already a copy of a copy. The Polaroid is glossy and damp, but not old. The woman in the photograph sits against a disused structure, a background that could be any shed. Her smile is the problem. Her lips are curled under pressure, and her eyes are alive with something quite the opposite of joy, something more aligned with terror.

Erin's brain attempts to rationalize the photo with logic. The cache owner left a Halloween photo. It is a still from a student film. Someone visiting a haunted house piece. She questions the photo out loud, but the forest denies her a reply, choosing instead to observe in silence.

She slides the Polaroid back and her fingers feel too big for such a soft move. She grabs the small notebook with the black cover and a strip of orange tape half-peeled along the spine. She opens it to the first page and signs the empty log with the date, time, and her geocache handle. The letters look like someone else's handwriting but leaving it unsigned would make the moment feel dirty, like hiding.

She closes the can and covers it just as she found it, letting her hand rest a heartbeat longer than needed. When she straightens, her knees pop.

On the way back to the old trail, she catches sight of a fresh scuff that cuts the moss where her feet never touched, maybe the pivot of a heel. It is the kind of mark someone leaves when they change their mind about being seen. She looks behind her, then further up the trail, but each direction is empty.

Pins run up Erin's spine, and she sprints through the morning fog. The plank bridge near the trailhead complains when she races across, and somewhere in the dense greens, the raven laughs with a ruined voice. The lot comes into view, showing its usual rude geometry, but is now brightening from oncoming headlights.

A truck swings across and settles two spaces down, then idles. The engine cuts to silence and the driver steps out with his hood up and hands visible as a peace offering to Erin, the lone jogger.

She stops for a moment, taking in the activity, before realizing she recognizes both the truck and the hoodie. Mark. They know each other the way geocachers do; at caching events, through trail banter, and that smug FTF once that he lorded over her for exactly two minutes too long. He's friendly enough to nod at across a room, but not generally friendly enough to call at dawn for a ghost hunt.

He doesn't cross the painted line between spaces. "You beat me," he says.

"I wish I hadn't," Erin says between breaths. She reaches her car and stops, resting her hand on the hood to steady her heart.

His playful smile crumples into concern. "Why, did something happen?"

She shakes her head. "There was a photo in the cache."

"Yeah? I don't see the big deal about a photo." He glances down the trail, half expecting to see someone chasing her.

"It didn't feel right." She coughs once and clears her throat. "It looked like someone was in trouble."

He nods once, filing a thought she can't see. He continues with questions rather than offer comfort. "Was it PostmarkPilgrim? I know he leaves photos in caches all the time."

"No. It wasn't like that." Erin opens her car door and fetches her cold coffee, then takes a swig. "This wasn't some historical photo, it was new, recent. The girl looked like she was in real danger."

She walks to the front of her car again and sets the cup down on the hood. Mark walks to the empty parking stall between their vehicles and she notices mud freckles below his knees, down his pant legs. He follows her glance down, too casual. "I was nearby," he says. "Saw the publish and headed this way."

"Were you looking for this cache? I was the first to sign." The sensation of pins return, tracing her spine.

"I was planning to find it, but realized I was too far away, in the wrong lot." He lets it sit. "Figured I'd come over here and check from this side."

She watches him the way she watches a river crossing for the rock that's going to roll underfoot. "But you were in the area?"

They are silent for a moment, deciding whether two people become allies or evidence. She glances back at the still-dark trail, tracing her steps and imagining if he has made any on the same path this morning. He tips his chin at her phone. "Did you mark it as found?"

Her grip tightens on the phone, debating if she could dial for help without being noticed, the internal struggle feels longer in the fog. She pulls the phone into her view, the blue light illuminates her fear, and Mark takes a step toward her. She catches his movement and dials the non-emergency line she memorized after the incident with her leg.

The speaker crackles. "Clark County Dispatch. What's the address or location of your emergency?"

Mark freezes in his step and Erin looks at him over the phone. "My name is Erin Caldwell. I'm at Yacolt Burn, off the 2000 Road near the spur to the old plank bridge, in lot three. I was hiking out here and found something disturbing at a geocache, a photo of a girl.

I think she's in trouble."

Mark steps back, glancing again down the trail, then to his truck. He doesn't move any farther. The speaker on her phone buzzes with a response, "Are you safe right now? Are you alone?"

Erin's eyes stay settled on Mark and she responds, her voice shaky. "No, there's another cacher here. I was the first one at the site, though. I took a picture of the photo."

"Okay, stay at your car with the doors locked. Do not go back to the container and don't handle it further. Can you give me your callback number and vehicle description?"

She gives them the details. Mark hasn't moved off his stripe the entire time.

"We're sending a deputy to check the site," the dispatcher says. "Someone should arrive shortly. We can't receive images at this line, so please be ready to show the photo when the deputy arrives."

"Will do."

"If anything changes, if anyone approaches you or you feel unsafe, call back immediately. Stay on scene unless it becomes unsafe."

The line goes quiet except for Erin's breath and the lot's damp hum. Mark nods as she puts the phone in her pocket and grabs her cup. "You did the right thing."

"I'm going to wait in my car," she says, but her tone isn't as convincing as her words.

He chuckles and kicks at the gravel. "Of course, that also means…" His sentence trails off and he shakes his head.

Erin moves to her driver door, fishing for her car keys. "What? What does that mean?"

"It's stupid." He shifts in place. "Now I can't log this find until the cops clear it."

"Then you can wait too. When they're done, you can have it." She gets in, locks the doors, and brings the photo up on her screen, examining the girl's expression before watching both Mark and the sunrise over the tree line.

Chapter 2: Thanks For The Cache

Erin sits in her car, watching the coffee shop from across the street while the engine rumbles. She questions whether she should even attend a caching meetup so soon after her experience outside of Yacolt, feeling like she's doing something wrong, like she's being disrespectful. She stares at the call history on her phone, the unknown number that turned out to be a police detective, feeling like she would do best to skip this event and head directly to the meeting with law enforcement in forty-five minutes. She looks up again at the coffee shop windows which are sweating from the heat inside while rain needles the glass storefront. She sighs and cuts the engine, "Might as well kill some time."

Erin steps just inside the door long enough to let her eyes adjust to the brightness. She takes in the smells of espresso and the sugary aroma of pastries that usually promise more in the case than they deliver in the mouth. A green board is propped up near the register that reads *TFTC ~ Thanks For The Coffee* in chalk. She huffs quietly, "Somebody thinks they're clever."

Jackets dry on chair backs and backpacks slouch in empty seats, abandoned by owners too excited to mingle than track their belongings. GPS units and cheap hiking gear pepper tables.

"Caching and Coffee," a man near the sign-in table proclaims and raises his drink to toast. A ring of paper cups lifts with a cheer, then damp cardboard and milky froth meet lips. Laughter that sounds staged is shared throughout the small space.

Erin notices Mark is already here, but not with the group holding court. He's in the corner that lets a person see the door and the back exit at the same time. He lifts two fingers in something that isn't a wave and isn't not. She acknowledges him, then scans the rest of the cachers.

TrailWolf has brought his own weather, capturing people in the storm of his personality. Each person he visits shares conversation with him and ends up in a picture from his phone which he has a case color-coordinated with his signature coat and backpack combo. Bright rope is coiled too neatly on his pack for a night that doesn't need rope. He claps a guy on the shoulder and laughs for the lens. "FTF hounds," he grins, and the phone snaps a picture of the two sharing a side embrace.

Jessa and Colt arrive late with a gust of apology and his camera on a tripod. He has the broadcast voice that comes out when recording lights blink. She chews gum like it's keeping the bills paid. "We're doing a little segment," Colt says to the crowd. "Local caching celebs." He means himself and Jessa. He pans the phone across the shop without asking. People lean out of frame and then remember they're here for community and lean back in.

The barista leans over the counter. "If you're filming, keep it to your group, please. Not everyone is part of your event." His nod is dismissive more than acknowledgment.

A man with a red headlamp looped around his wrist hovers near the pastry case as if the muffins might be nocturnal and easier to approach at dusk. His gray stubble works hard to hold up eyes that might otherwise slide off his face and stick to the floor. The hum he makes under his breath finds the note of the refrigerator and joins it. Someone whispers GhostLogger the way you say a campfire name to spook a kid. He flinches and pretends he didn't hear, preferring the company of a pastry than of a person.

Somebody near the event table announces, too loud, "Hidden Hollow got archived." The murmur that follows is the sound of gossip putting on a lab coat. "Owner deleted," another says. "Profile gone." "Told you it was a plant," someone else adds, triumphant with having predicted nothing. Erin glances at Mark who is watching her without giving the courtesy of pretending he isn't.

"Looks like that's one geocache most of us will never get to find." He casually proclaims to the room. "Seems like it was a crime scene." His comment adds new fuel to the current buzz.

Erin breathes through the coil of anger his comment sparked and chooses not to be its leash. She orders a coffee she will most likely not finish. She pays with cash and the money smells like damp leather. While her focus is getting her caffeine, the weight of Mark's stare rests heavy on her, though not as heavy as the picture of the Polaroid on her phone. The only evidence that Hidden Hollow was ever a live cache. She still debates if having it is somehow illegal, if she's in possession of evidence she shouldn't have. The thought still makes her queasy, but saving the image feels like an alibi.

Colt hears the words *crime scene* and *archived,* so he leans into inspiration. "This is, like, story fuel," he says softly. We should interview, I heard TrailSister was the one who found it."

Jessa's gum slows. She touches his elbow and doesn't remove her hand. "Maybe we don't," she says.

He turns the livestreaming camera onto himself. "We absolutely do," he says.

Mark catches Colt's intent and appears at Erin's elbow without notice. "Walk?" he asks her while giving Colt the dead-eye. She nods, but detours to the table where the regulars have laid out trackables and signature swag like an altar. Someone's geocoin glints next to a bright enamel compass rose tracking code which has been taped onto the table to prevent armchair thieves. The table is a small religion. She scans homemade iron-on patches with phrases like, *Trade up, not down* and *leave a place better than you found it*. She wants the world to work like that even when it doesn't.

Her phone buzzes, but not from a call, and not just hers, a chorus of buzzes answers around the room, like a startled hornet's nest. A new cache has been published, *Lamppost Lament*. The owner is listed as *Overlook Lane Crew*. A glance at any phone in the room shows the coordinates are a mere two blocks away.

The notification does the old magic. Chairs scrape in excitement while voices sharpen with anticipation. As jackets wrap across shoulders, someone warns "beware the muggles."

TrailWolf's grin becomes a blade. He pats his chest to check for his pen, for tweezers, for his stamp. "On your six," he says to no one and everyone, already moving.

Colt is talking simultaneously to his camera, to Jessa, and to the door. "Spontaneous urban run," he narrates. "Let's go, let's go." Jessa rolls her eyes at Erin and that tiny solidarity makes Erin like her for two seconds in a way that will make everything hurt later.

Outside, the rain makes the streetlights bloom with a kaleidoscopic shine. The pack of cachers spills onto the sidewalk and splits, some jogging, some walking aggressively casual. Erin tucks her chin into her collar and finds the pace that pulls her ahead of the pack without looking like it needs to. Mark falls in on her left, half a step back, neither drafting nor leading.

"You're going," he says. "I thought the Yacolt cache might have spooked you."

"We're downtown, I'm sure it's safe enough. Besides, I'm just looking."

He nods. "Looking first is the same as going."

The group of geocachers cuts through an alley that smells like fryer oil and last night's beer. A cat watches from a dumpster lid without any sense of care. TrailWolf shoots past Erin and Mark, mouth open like an athlete running through tape. He jogs to the end of the alley and takes the street mid-block, refusing to slow for cross-traffic, sure of his rights to cross.

"FTF hound," Mark says to Erin with a shit-eating grin. His comment drips with disdain.

"Not likely, most hounds are trained," Erin replies, equally unkind.

The pin for Lamppost Lament sits in a parking lot, behind a strip of shops with cracked awnings and signs that have outlasted their owners. The lamppost in question leans a degree more than its neighbors, showing exhaustion from time and probable abuse. A car idles at the curb of the street, its driver half-lit by the glow of a device he studies with too much patience for someone waiting to leave.

Muggles, people who don't geocache, are thick here. Teenagers with skateboards grind curbs in the mostly empty lot, a couple carry a plant like a baby out of a store, and someone in scrubs is texting grief into their phone. The sudden mob of cachers goes feral-civilized, all of them suddenly practicing the ritual of pretending they've lost a contact lens or can't find their car, anything they think makes them look normal. Erin ties a shoe that's already tied. Mark studies a storefront reflection like he could buy what he needs. TrailWolf isn't playing along, he walks straight to the lamppost with a swagger so loud he figures it counts as camouflage.

He squats and lifts the skirt on the post's base. This type of cache is common and he's found enough, he doesn't even guess at where else it might be. He reveals and grabs a micro-sized container barely larger than a thimble, banded with a strip of orange tape. He holds it up, victorious and ridiculous. "First to find!" He twists the lid and unfurls the log with tweezers like he's pulling a splinter. His pen flicks, dropping initials that are a signature he'll deny is a brand.

Erin's lips press into something that would be a smile if she let it. She loves and hates these urban hides. They're lazy, but also perfect quick finds. Hiding in plain sight is the oldest trick in the book and sometimes, the best tactic. Mark shrugs off TrailWolf's brashness like he's ashamed to be amused. "I guess we let him crow," Mark says. "Roosters gotta announce the morning, or the morning thinks it's late."

"Do mornings think?" she asks, more to be contrary than for an answer.

He shrugs her off. "Mine do."

TrailWolf rolls the log up and places it back in the tiny tube, the orange tape catching briefly under his thumb, then hands the micro to the nearest pair of hands without making eye contact. The container starts its little pilgrimage through the group. People shake it near their ear for the paper rattle. Erin is the last to sign and she does so without her name taking up the width of the paper strip. SL / TFTC. TNLN. The shorthand feels like breathing into a paper bag.

She bends down to replace the container and someone behind her says, "Good hide," to the owner who is not present. They never are when you want to be polite and always are when you're swearing.

Jessa and Colt stage their own discovery five feet away with a spare film can they pretend is the cache. Colt gasps in a way no human has ever gasped unironically. Jessa's gum goes still for the shot, then she resumes. Erin shakes her head with a chuckle, recognizing the one good quality the couple have. Even though they act like they're big-league, they've always done a good job of not posting spoilers in their videos.

She kneels to replace the cache and that's when she notices the angle. The lamppost base points nothing but down, a metal skirt with no opinions. The micro itself, though, when she places it back in the lip, her fingers tell her the magnet wants north, which feels like nonsense. Magnets don't care about north when there's steel this close. She resets it anyway, turning the skirt seam until it aligns with the post's base, mindful to line the metal frame with the line of built-up dirt. She isn't simply replacing the base, she's trying to hide the fact this piece ever moved. It'ss an old habit she picked up that keeps her world from fraying. Mark watches the small and intentional care but says nothing.

TrailWolf pockets his FTF glow and turns it into a speech no one ordered. "See, you gotta keep your alerts tight," he says. "Publication windows are a tell. If you know the reviewers, you know the times they like to drop." He makes eye contact with Erin long enough to file her reaction. "Some of us are on a first-name basis."

"Some of us read the map," Mark says, mildly annoyed.

TrailWolf grins. "Some of us do both."

Still standing a few feet to the side of the group, Colt's voice competes with the sound of rain. "Don't forget to like and subscribe," he tells an audience who may or may not even be paying attention. Jessa's gum pops and she looks at Erin again with that quick, human glance that means I see you, then she looks away before the glance lingers.

Phones come out and the cachers log their finds, some hurrying to be second to find. A chorus of tiny audible dings marks the ritual. Erin types less than she thinks and more than she wants. *Signed Log/Thanks For The Cache. Fun urban. Good skirt.* Her thumb hovers, then she deletes 'Good skirt' because it sounds like she's flirting with a pole.

The group disperses the way flocks do, each bird remembering it was a separate animal all along. They know the way back to the coffee shop, where their event is still staged, waiting for their return, but each has their own path, their own buddies to share in tonight's micro-adventure.

Erin and Mark choose to take the alley back. They cross where TrailWolf barreled across the street, but without his reckless bravado on the return. The rain has shifted to mist, as is often the case in Vancouver, and the alley cat has decided to move on without a trace.

"TrailWolf knows reviewers," Mark says as though he's thinking about weather patterns.

"Or wants us to think he does." Erin sneers, then asks, "Why do you say that?"

"He was quick to find that cache. Do you believe it was a coincidence?"

"I believe in patterns we miss until they step on our foot." She glances up at him. "But it wasn't some luck, he just didn't care if Muggles saw him go for it while the rest of us did. If anything, he's just irresponsible."

Mark silently concedes with a nod and the two finish the short walk back in silence. They are the first back to the café and the barista nods, uncaringly at their entrance. On the community table, a trackable coin has vanished and someone has left a kid's meal toy with a cracked arm in its place. "Trade down, not up, I guess," she states with bitterness.

The small anger makes Erin want to set the world on fire in a way that surprises her. She blinks it into something she can carry, but Mark doesn't pay the table any mind and instead, finds the coffee he left on a table.

Her phone buzzes with a new alert which is not a publish. A moderator has commented on Hidden Hollow. She reads it with a tense frown, her alerts are coming in later than they should. *Listing archived at owner's request.*

Then, a moment later: *Owner account disabled.*

A third ping hits her phone she didn't expect, this one colder than the others. *Photo attachments removed for violating media guidelines.*

She feels that notification in her molars and glances at Mark. He looks up from his own phone, mouth open with a hint of awe. He sees her without watching her, then his eyes lock onto hers. "You still have the shot," he asks, quietly in the empty coffee shop. "The one you took at the cache site?"

She nods hesitantly, recalling he was standing nearby when she told dispatch what she had found.

"Back it up twice."

She already has, but she does again, copying the photo into a new folder on her phone, pausing for a moment as the haunted eyes of the girl stare at her, almost pleading. The image exists in three places now, which is almost the same as comfort and nothing like it.

GhostLogger hovers near the door, the red headlamp he always wears is unlit. He is humming a low, unrecognizable tune as he holds the door for other geocachers who are filing back into the coffee shop. He scrolls his phone when the alert hits his notifications as well. When it does, his eyes cut to Erin's and away. "I was at the park," he says to no one, to everyone. "Not that park. Another." He looks at his shoes like they might answer. "Found a thing before it was published once," he adds, and flushes as if he has confessed to a crime. "On accident."

"How," TrailWolf says from the event table, pouncing without the appearance of movement.

"Luck, I suppose," GhostLogger says, suddenly aware his story sounds suspect the longer he talks. "But it had something in the cache that I didn't feel should have been included, something that would have flagged it for deletion as well."

TrailWolf begins offering criticism and Mark, ignoring the interaction, walks to the community table where Erin still stands and picks up a trackable shaped like a tin fish. He reads the mission card and sets it down in the same spot, maintaining a small bit of order on the messy table.

"I gotta run," he says to Erin without looking at her directly. "I've got an early start."

"For what?"

"Land nav class. Still thinking about dropping it like a bad habit. Night classes aren't really my thing." He makes it sound like a joke with no punchline and no audience. He chooses to take his leave rather than entertaining any other conversation. The bell over the door announces his exit while Erin stares at the items on the table.

TrailWolf watches Mark leave and shifts his focus from GhostLogger to Erin. "He ever tell you why he bailed on Search And Rescue?" he says, casual as a breeze.

"No," Erin says. "And if you say you know, I'll bet you don't."

TrailWolf smiles into a reflection that isn't flattering. "Touchy."

"Just not a fan of gossip."

He shrugs. "You going to be at the park tomorrow?"

Erin sighs, looking from the table to him. "Which park?"

"I predict there will be a publish just before dawn, probably in West Vancouver." He winks like he won something. "It's a pattern if you pay attention."

Erin finds her coffee but doesn't drink it, she refuses to acknowledge TrailWolf directly. Beyond him, rain makes a quiet theater of the window. In the glass, the reflection of her face and the room and the street outside layer into one image that refuses to decide what picture to paint. "It's too late for this cryptic shit, I think I'm just going to go home."

He shrugs at her detachment but doesn't linger. Instead, he finds a new target for his smugness and approaches Jessa and Colt.

When she finally steps back into the damp, the night feels different, not because of the lamppost micro, and not because of the traded out trinket while no one was around, but because the game inside the game has started taking dangerous form. She's felt this before and she knows when a person plays a game long enough, the game starts playing back.

Halfway to her car she stops. Across the street, under a tree that has learned to grow around its restraints, a shape is present, a little too patient in the weather. Her hand finds her jacket pocket and quick-thinking fingers constrict around a small canister of pepper spray.

She watches the shape long enough to recognize a trash bin with a stack of soaking wet newspapers and a drenched alley cat huddling at its base. She curses the trick of light and laughs at her paranoia while damning her nerves.

She is nearly to her car when, through the whisper of misty rain, the coffee shop bell jingles. The door opens and closes. A voice calls her name. She pretends to not hear and climbs into her car. Before the person can cut through traffic to reach her, Erin manages to merge into light traffic and makes her escape.

Chapter 3: Needs Maintenance

Detective Mara Vance picks a table in the diner by the back door where she can see both exits and the reflection in the windows. She sets a legal pad next to napkin-wrapped silverware. The cloves come out of her pocket and are tossed next to the table. She stares at the small dark carton, the habit she'd promised her mother she'd quit and hasn't. She orders a coffee, sets a photograph of Erin on the table in front of her, and watches as headlights make their way into the diner.

Vance checks her phone more than once. She has a short fuse for a lack of punctuation, and the waiting is burning into her evening. Time ticks down to just over a minute before her target walks through the door, scouting the room blindly. Vance matches the girl with the picture, then waves her over.

Erin barely has time to settle into the booth before Vance begins. "Start clean," she says. "Explain the other morning, how you got there, what you touched. Paint me a real vivid picture."

The woman's bluntness causes Erin to pause. "You're the detective that called me?"

"Obviously." Mara taps the photo with her pen, clicking it with each strike. "I'm Detective Vance. I was assigned the follow-up for your little woodsy adventure. Now, can we get to it?"

Erin scans the rest of the diner, expecting hidden cops like a sting in a movie. "Okay, um, a new cache was published that morning, and I wanted to be the first to find it, so I drove out there before work."

"I'm sorry, the cash was published? What does that mean, are we talking about money laundering?"

"Not cash like money, cache like a container. It's a GPS game. Players hide caches anywhere in the world and then log where they placed it, then other players go to find where the cache is hidden, based on the GPS coordinates posted online."

Vance takes notes, her face is stone. Erin glances to the notepad and catches the words, *silly game*. Erin watches the detective rest her hand on the two words, purses her lips and continues, "Anyway, I got to the hiding spot, and after a few minutes, I found the ammo can."

Without looking up from her notes, the detective asks, "Ammo can? Like an actual ammunition container?"

Erin nods. "Cachers use empty ammo cans to place their hides because they're pretty weather resistant."

The detective makes a sound of acknowledgment. "Okay, so what did you see? What did you touch?"

"I mean, I opened the lid and picked around inside," Erin says. "I signed the log. I held the photo long enough to realize what I was looking at, then I put everything back exactly where it was."

"Was anybody with you?"

"No." Erin watches Vance write. When the detective pauses and looks up, she adds, "Later, Mark showed up. After I was getting back to the trailhead."

"The wilderness guy." Her gaze peers through Erin.

"Yeah, search and rescue. Well, former search and rescue."

Vance writes with focused determination, letting the shapes of the letters help her not say what she's thinking. She glances up once, calibrating Erin's face against the weather outside. "Tell me what you think you saw in that photograph."

"I'm not sure, but it didn't sit right." Erin keeps her voice flat, the way someone talks to a skittish animal. "The girl seemed distressed. More than someone taking a picture without permission, but like she was forced to have it taken. It didn't feel like a prank. If it is, it's a mean one."

"All good pranks are mean," Vance says. "That's why they work." She taps her pen against the pad, clicking it again. Her phone buzzes on the table and she takes a moment to glance at the text. "I just got notice from the office. Maybe this will make more sense to you. Our team says they flagged the listing with the website. The listing has been archived." She watches Erin for signs of recognition.

"That explains the commotion at our meetup earlier," Erin says. Vance gives her a blank stare so she elaborates, "Sometimes, the cache community has get-togethers where we can share stories and experiences. It's supposed to be a fun way to make friends and keep the game exciting."

"And did you share your fun and exciting story?"

The sandpaper of Vance's words tightens Erin's skin. "No, I didn't really talk to anyone. I felt this was something better kept to myself."

The waitress comes to the table and tops off Vance's coffee then looks at Erin. "Did you want to order, hun?"

She shakes her head and the waitress filters to the next table.

"I see," Vance states, bringing attention back to the interview. "The log. There are a couple of what I would assume are nicknames. You get to the site before or after these other cartoon characters?"

"I didn't realize anyone else got that cache."

"Okay." She pauses while watching Erin, examining her. "And at your little meeting, did anyone mention it? Was there any talk about the photo?"

"No. Are you sure others were there?"

"What I know is there was a little logbook with four signatures, each with the same date. I'm guessing yours was at the top of the list. If you were first, that would make you TrailSister." Vance lets the words crawl from her mouth as she watches Erin. She lets the silence hang and, just as Erin is about to explain, she continues,

"Next is LostMarker."

"Mark signed it?"

Vance continues as though she didn't hear. "Next is TrailWolf, and finally, there's the name Jackalope."

"I thought Mark left without looking for it." Erin picks at the edge of the menu. "That bastard, he said he wouldn't touch it."

"Priorities," Vance says, neutral. "What about the other names?"

"I didn't see anyone else. I don't even know of a Jackalope. I was alone in the forest that morning."

Vance writes *forest*, then scratches it out like the word is trying to be poetic and she won't allow it. She looks back at her earlier notes taken before the meeting, then underlines time: 05:14. "Cache culture likes early mornings," she says, noncommittal.

"We like patterns," Erin says. "So do people who want to profile others."

Vance looks up at that, long enough to file the comment. "You should teach," she says.

"I do."

"Right." She closes the pad. "Generally, I don't profile using only nicknames unless I'm investigating gang activity. Do you have contact information with real names for your little gang of tree huggers?"

Erin recoils at the sharpness of the detective's comment. She answers through tight teeth, "I already gave Mark's information. I only know TrailWolf by his handle, and like I already said, I've never met a Jackalope."

"Naturally." Detective Vance tucks her pen into her pocket. "We'll process what we have. If you think of anything else, call me." She slides a business card across the table that Erin stares at but doesn't touch. "One more thing. Don't go back."

"I won't," Erin says, meaning it, even as she imagines returning to see it again in the daylight.

Vance studies her, measuring whether that was a lie or a prediction. "Stay reachable." She pulls a clove cigarette from the pack before gathering the rest of her things. The clove moves in her fingers but she doesn't light it. She drops cash on the table and leaves.

Erin sits in silence, rerunning the interaction over in her head, stewing in the treatment she just received and the frustration that she didn't stand up for herself better. She damns herself for buckling under the presence of an authority figure before she storms out of the diner.

Outside, rain stutters, unsure if it should pour or mist. Erin drives by the meetup, looking for signs of familiarity. The coffee shop returns to the casual hum of a business. The event has wrapped up and only remnants that it ever happened remain. GhostLogger has vanished in the way quiet men do, silently blending into the background until nothing remains. Jessa and Colt remain, rehearsing a reaction in the window's reflection before giving up, probably because the light isn't flattering. Half a block down the street, TrailWolf paces by his car with his phone to his ear and his grin aimed at whatever voice confirms his myth. Mark is gone, but she knew he would be, he was gone before she was. She doesn't stop. She considers stopping at a liquor store but decides to go straight home.

Her apartment has the temporary smell of heat kicking on after months of silence, filling her nostrils with burning dust and old air. She toes her boots off before she enters, then she picks them up and carries them inside. She walks to her caching corkboard and looks at the mud in her treads. Two different colors spatter the sole, one is the park, the other is from her driveway. She scrapes it into the trash.

The board waits patiently. She scribbles on the note pinned for Hidden Hollow, labeling it as archived. She sets another pinned note for Lamppost Lament and writes *logged*, adding it into the myriads of other pins and notes that show where she's been. She stares at the board for a moment before silently conceding she might be tilting more toward weird than normal.

She looks at the Hidden Hollow pin again. The word *archive* causes her to pull out her phone and stare at the notification of the moderator killing the photo attachment. A small anger flares inside, not just from the shutdown of the cache, or the way the detective treated her, but because the notification felt like someone was trying to erase what Erin saw in the Polaroid.

She opens the photo she took of the Polaroid. Faces aren't maps until they are, and she tries to map this one. The smiling woman's hair is pulled back tight, with a flyaway strand catching the light. The background is unspecific on purpose, showing only plywood, a seam, a bruise of shadow in the top left that could be a rafter. There is nothing else in the picture, no calendar or poster. No manufacturer's label on the Polaroid itself the internet could track. Whoever staged it understands how investigation works and how to starve it.

She flips to the second photo, the one she took of the Polaroid's back. The GPS coordinates sit there in pen, written in a steady hand that doesn't match the chaos of the image. She types them into her map. They don't lead to Hidden Hollow or the parking lot, not even close. These numbers point toward the trails near Moulton Falls, where spring runoff hides its own noise. Erin closes her eyes and lets the coordinates live under her tongue like a pill.

She copies the numbers onto a sticky note and presses the paper against the edge of the board. She writes one word she hates herself a little for writing. *Body.* She hopes she's wrong, but the knot in her stomach doesn't listen.

She sits cross-legged on the floor and lets the room go quiet enough to hear her upstairs neighbor's sink and the drip that happens when they forget to turn the handle that last quarter inch. She tells herself not to go, but she finds her keys.

The drive to the Polaroid's coordinates is quiet, but loud enough for her brain to yell at her for making foolish decisions. By the time she pulls into the turnout, her thoughts have gone quiet as her headlights capture the memories of her childhood on the bank of the East Fork Lewis River. Summer kids belong to a different species than raincoats in October.

The water wears a different face at night. It mesmerizes the forest with a silvery sheen, and the alders at the bank lean over it like mourners too exhausted to stand upright. Yellow tape runs between two trunks on the far side of the lot as it flaps in the gentle wind. Erin is surprised to see the tape at first, then annoyed at herself for being surprised. The police are trained for this, and she isn't the only one capable of reading numbers.

A cruiser idles a few parking stalls away and a young uniform with the posture of someone still teaching his bones what to do with authority lifts a hand. "Trail's closed."

"I know," Erin says. "I called it in."

He looks at her from under the bill of his hat. "Detective said to keep folks back."

"She told me to stay reachable," Erin says. "I'm here." She hates how the sentence sounds like a teenager's logic.

He hesitates when confronted. "Don't cross the tape," he says, finding a way to make it sound like a courtesy.

Erin stands where the gravel gives way to wet soil and looks downstream. Around the bend is the sandbar where kids build dams to control their world. Upstream is the deep hole where someone's cousin swears there are fish big enough to take a finger. Here, between, the river is making a decision that is about to be a consequence.

A second car pulls in. Vance steps out and the clove smell arrives a moment later. She takes in Erin's presence, the caution tape, the river, and the cedar duff. "You couldn't not," she says, neither pleased nor surprised.

"I didn't touch anything. I just got here," Erin says.

"Good." Vance looks past her to the shore. "We've got a body downstream." She says body like it is a Tuesday. "If this is your first, keep your eyes up."

"It isn't," Erin says before she has time to remember. The tape reminds her of Danny who will be nineteen forever. His face surfaces from her memory, blue as the river that wanted to keep him, but compromised. Erin keeps a safe distance from Vance and the officer, watching headlights illuminate the road. Another vehicle arrives, this time, an ambulance.

EMTs gather their gear and a stretcher, then move toward the water, never once making eye contact with Erin. They move slow at the water's edge. The river makes itself loud to cover what people don't.

They stop down the bank. Vance turns to Erin, takes a drag from her clove, and points to the unwelcome visitor. "You stay outside the tape line, don't touch anything, and stay out of our way." She heads to the paramedics. Erin follows at a distance, in the way a crow might follow a person just close enough to watch but far enough to make an escape.

As she makes her way through the damp grass, just off the trail, she catches sight of what the paramedics have huddled around. The body is still and the legs are submerged in the shallow water. Detective Mara gives the approval they seek to move it, and they drag it fully onto the bank.

Erin's memory tries to shine through the moment. She doesn't look for the face. She looks at the hands. She looks at the hair. She looks at the way the shape was made smaller by being carried. She notices this was once a woman, but she can't stop expecting Danny's cold eyes staring back at her, vacantly watching her like he did that day.

Vance steps back to Erin and watches her memorizing the scene. "This the girl in the photograph?"

Erin fights every screaming warning in her head and lets her eyes land on the waxy gray face, greenish veins tracing up the neck and across the cheeks. She doesn't dare look higher. "Yes."

Detective Vance walks closer to Erin, softly reaching for her shoulder. She pauses when Erin flinches but continues gently until she makes contact.

"Ms. Caldwell, there was a reason I told you to stay away from this. I hope you understand now. But you being here was a great help, your quick identification will expedite processing this case." She guides Erin back toward the cars.

"I don't know why I came back, I don't know what I was expecting…but it wasn't that."

"Normally, I would end up reading someone like you the riot act. You did exactly what I told you not to." Vance feels the woman shiver under her palm. Her hand stays steady on Erin's shoulder, an anchor more than a comfort. "I don't know what we are looking at here and I don't know if it's connected to this silly game you and your friends play, but this has just escalated from a missing person case to a probable homicide."

Erin's steps are slow, her feet weigh a thousand pounds. "I understand."

"I don't think you do." She stops Erin short of her car and faces her with intention. "Because right now, you're likely the only person who's touched what might be evidence in a homicide. That makes you both a witness and a liability."

She exhales through her nose, the sound more frustration than breath. "Someone made it a point to take the picture, then put it in that box after she went missing. Not just any box, but one that is supposed to be hidden from most people, still begging to be found.

That's not coincidence, Erin, that's deliberate."

Vance looks back toward the stretch of river flashing through the trees. "So no, I don't think you understand. You didn't just find a cache. You found what someone wanted found."

Erin nods. The yellow tape snaps in the wind, and the change of air brings the smell that rewires a person's idea of acceptance. She breathes through her mouth to avoid the stench of decay and immediately tastes cedar, iron, and something rotten.

Vance points to Erin's car. "Now, go home. Take a long shower or a shot, whatever is going to help you wash tonight off."

Erin nods and shuffles toward her car. Vance calls to her as she opens the door. "Next time I tell you not to be somewhere, don't make me wonder if you're part of it." She lets the words sit there, quiet but heavy. "Right now, you're a witness. Don't test that."

Erin gets in, closes the door, and sits until her breath fogs the glass. The river keeps speaking past the cracked window as if repeating itself will make anyone listen more closely.

Back home in her Cascade Park apartment, the board waits, but she doesn't place any pins, instead, she sits on the floor cross-legged and stares at the picture in her phone. In the photo, the girl was alive, but the longer Erin stares, the more the green veins impose on what she sees.

She thinks about earlier in the night, when the magnet at Lamppost Lament wanted north when it shouldn't. She thinks about publish windows and men who brag about knowing reviewers and shy ones who find caches before they're published. She thinks about a figure in ferns who leaves no footprints you can see.

Then she kills the lights, lies down on the rug with her jacket as a pillow, and listens until the upstairs sink drips itself to sleep.

Chapter 4: Quick Find

The news never says Erin's name, only *local woman finds body near Yacolt,* but every time she scrolls the comments, she finds herself in the spaces between words: *she, woman, hiker.*

Days come and go in a haze. Erin avoids the woods the way people avoid mirrors after funerals. She buries her thoughts in classrooms and coffee mugs, in grading papers until the red ink looks like rust. Sometimes, mid-lecture, she swears she hears her phone vibrate in the desk drawer, phantom buzzes of expectation or familiarity. In those moments, she knows the ghost of the game is calling her back.

In her apartment, the corkboard hangs quietly against the wall. Pins, notes, and thread are ignored. She keeps telling herself she'll take it all down, maybe tonight, maybe after one more day that doesn't ache, but every night she finds a reason not to.

The evenings feel empty without the hum of GPS alerts, without the thrill of caching. Her trinket sack sits neglected under her pinboard, waiting to be taken out. The phone is too quiet since she muted notifications from her caching app, its blank screen is a digital space of loneliness that used to be alive with adventure.

At work, students turn in essays on erosion and ecosystems. She circles words like *flow* and *pattern* without thinking, her pen hesitating on each one, waiting for a pulse that's lost its rhythm. By Wednesday, she's in front of a whiteboard, pretending to care about sediment layers. The projector hums louder than the class. She draws a river delta with a blue marker that smells like solvent and the innocence of childhood.

"Erosion," she says. "The way water reshapes what it touches."

Half the students are tuned in, half don't even hear her words. That's the normal ratio.

A boy in the second row raises his hand. "Is that like when a river moves rocks downstream?"

"Exactly." She caps the marker. "It carries the pieces somewhere new."

He grins. "My dad took me to Moulton Falls bridge last weekend. It had a rock that looked like a heart." The room blurs for a second. The word *Moulton* lands in her stomach.

"That's… cool," she manages. "Just be careful near rivers. They change fast." The boy nods, obviously unconcerned by her warning.

When the bell rings, she erases the board. Blue smears across her palm, the same color as cold water, the same hue as Danny's memory. She scrubs harder than she needs to, until the board shines.

On the drive home, she takes the long route that skirts the forest. She tells herself it's because of construction, though the roads aren't any worse than it ever is in Vancouver. Each bend brings the wood line closer, the cedar is dark against a gray sky. She keeps her eyes on the white lines and pretends not to see the turnoff to the falls.

At home, after the heater kicks on, she pours a drink and sits cross-legged on the couch, staring at the corkboard. The quiet of the apartment moves around her with accusing presence.

She doesn't mean to keep thinking about her brother Danny, but memory, like water, finds the cracks, and seeing the dead girl at the river brings the flood back in. She recalls that day years ago with him at the creek, boots in hand, daring the current, full of laughter. His reflection breaks apart when he jumps in, followed by the sound of nothing the instant after. She tells herself caching was never about him; it's about puzzles, the chase, the pattern.

Her phone buzzes on the kitchen counter where she left it to create distance. The sound punches through the quiet. She ignores it at first, telling herself it could be work or spam, but a part of her hopes it is the app she swore she muted. She feels the corkboard watching her, so she walks defiantly to the device and turns it over, hiding the face. She wants to believe she can stop, but she also knows the quiet won't let her.

Moments later, her phone vibrates again while she's at the kitchen sink, rinsing out a mug. Her hands twitch for it, and that small lie she's been telling herself all night exhales between thought and action.

She turns the phone over, examining the lit face. The notification banner reads: *PNW Cachers Group – 36 new messages.*

She stares at it, anticipation and guilt churning in her stomach, then she swipes to clear. Another ping follows. Then another.

She sighs and opens the thread. The scroll is a mess of usernames and panic.

TrailWolf: "So, who's the sicko leaving photos in cans?"

MuggleEater: "This hobby's gonna get banned if people keep making it creepy."

MudMagnet: "Heard the girl who found that first one's been questioned twice."

CedarScout: "Probably some influencer stunt."

GeoMom73: "OMG. Please tell me you reported it."

TrailWolf: "I put it back and logged it Needs Maintenance. Not my circus."

Erin scrolls faster, jaw tight. MudMagnet's comment feels like it sticks out more boldly on the phone. Underneath his comment, someone has replied and posted a screenshot of the archived Hidden Hollow listing, showing her log activity. Her handle is blurred, but not enough.

MapNerd: "You can still see her username in the preview. Should we DM her?"

Erin's heart leaps and she closes the app before she can stop herself, half expecting the other users of the group to be watching her through the phone screen. For a while she just stands at the counter, her phone facedown, and the room humming with silence. Outside, a siren wails in the distance. Her nerves track the sound, somehow expecting the noise would grow louder, anticipating a police visit. The emergency is further away and the sirens fade.

When the next notification comes, she can tell by the length of the buzz that it isn't the group chat. She flips it over and the screen reads: *Mark Leland.* For a full heartbeat she considers not answering, but the idea of a friendly voice pulls at her, so she does.

"Hey." Her voice sounds like someone else's.

"Took you long enough," he says. His background is all road noise and wind. "Didn't think you'd ghost the whole damn map. Where have you been?"

"I haven't been in the mood."

He hums low, pretending not to worry. "You okay?"

"I'm fine." She presses her thumb to the kitchen window, leaving a fog print. "I just needed a break."

"Well, the game misses you. By *the game* I mean me, and by *me* I mean…" he stops himself with a murmur she can't make out. "Look, you hear what people are saying?"

"I'm trying not to."

"Hard not to when it's everywhere. Someone found a photo in a cache at Hazel Dell Community Park, on one of the far trails."

Her throat tightens. "Another one?"

"I don't know if it's the same thing. I'm sure it's just a troll, trying to copycat what's in the news to cure boredom." He exhales hard. "Anyway, people are talking. Forums, group chats, all that. Half of them think it's your fault and half think you're cursed."

"Cool. I haven't even been active since the caching meetup, how is it my fault?"

"Yeah. Cachers, man. They never met a rumor they didn't want to log."

Erin rubs her temple. "So, what, you called to update me on my PR crisis?"

"No," he says, softer now. "I called to get you out of your funk. There's a new park hide a couple miles from town. It's simple, urban, and we can log it in broad daylight. You can hate it in person."

She damns herself for liking his humor. "I don't know, Mark."

"You need to get back on the horse."

"I wasn't on a horse. It was a body." Her comment throws a blanket of silence on the call and the line crackles with distance.

"Yeah," he finally says. "That's kind of my point. You keep hiding from what happened and that's all it's gonna be."

She shuffles into the living room and slumps into the couch, staring at the looming corkboard. "You already there?"

"Naw, I figured I'd give you a head start."

"Why?"

"So you can beat me to it. A little First to Find between friends. Keeps the world normal. I mean, I'm sure it's already been found by now, but you could beat me to it."

Erin wants to tell him there's no such thing as normal anymore. Instead, she says, "Text me the coordinates."

"You got it. And hey…"

"What?"

"Don't overthink this one. Looks like it's just a simple micro, probably a bison tube." He hangs up before she can change her mind.

The phone stays in her hand, warm against her skin. The notification from Mark pings a moment later: *Cache coordinates.* For a while she just stares at the numbers as they blur into shapes. Then she walks over and touches the edge of the corkboard as she picks up her trinket bag.

The drive to Orchards Highlands Park takes longer than she

wants, not because of traffic, but because the hesitation in her foot refuses to encourage the gas pedal. Erin parks two spaces from Mark's truck and sits for a moment, watching him through the windshield. He's leaned against the driver's side door, one hand in his pocket, the other navigating an active phone screen. She kills the engine and steps out. The lot outside the park smells like cut grass and the sky is the typical Pacific Northwest shade of tin.

"You came," he says, smiling as though he's not sure if it's allowed.

"The traffic was heavy." She refuses to look at him through her lie.

"Mm-hmm." He gestures toward the footpath that loops the small city park. "Half-mile walk that way. Easy terrain. No dead bodies this time, promise."

She hates that he makes the joke. "You're hilarious."

The park is too bright for November. Sunlight cuts through damp air like a trick of the atmosphere, promising warmth but never delivering.

Children shriek at the playground, the sound bouncing off wet slides and metal swing chains. A birthday balloon bumps against its string, its reflection bending in a puddle, making the illusion of a warped eye. A golden retriever shakes water onto a bench where an older man laughs, even after the dog moves on. Erin waits for the danger on the edge of normalcy.

She keeps her hands in her jacket pockets, fingers wrapped around her pepper spray, trailing a few steps behind Mark. The path glitters with gravel and shattered bottle glass, both catching the same light. It all looks clean and sterile, though it shouldn't.

The smell of mulch and charcoal from a nearby grill collides with the memory of river silt, bringing the cracks of memories, but not of Danny, of the girl at the riverbank. She breathes through her mouth, trying to avoid the scent of damp earth, but the act reminds her of the taste of rot on the wind just nights before.

Mark stops ahead, scanning lamppost bases, trying to be as inconspicuous as possible but failing miserably. He's whistling off-key and tuneless. It makes her want to scream. "Feels good to be normal again," he says.

She nods, though it feels anything but. A jogger passes, earbuds in, and oblivious. Somewhere behind them, a sound like a camera shutter clicks just once, crisp and real. She glances back but only catches a man tossing breadcrumbs to pigeons. Her stomach knots.

Erin refuses to check her app, denies the urge to check proximity. She tries to find the cache without digital assistance and focuses on a nearby lamppost, putting sharp eyes on the skirt's dull sheen. She tells herself the spot is too convenient, too obvious, but she checks anyway. The steel is cold against her fingertips, but the cover is still tightly fastened. The sound of children laughing over and over, like a recording loop, itches at the edge of her periphery.

They continue walking, gravel crunching underfoot. The park is alive with neighborhood ordinariness; parents keeping a close eye on their kids at the playground, a couple jogging past with matching water bottles, the smell of barbecue still floating on the wind. It should feel safe, but it doesn't.

"So," he says, "forums are losing their minds."

"Yeah." Erin is yet to meet his face, instead, she maintains his location by the position of his boots.

"Someone found another Polaroid today. Not a person this time, though. Empty chair in a field. Kinda artsy, kinda creepy. Listing got archived an hour after it was found."

She glances at him, finally catching the stubble of his chin. "Archived by who?"

"I have no idea. The post vanished before anyone could verify."

Her stomach shifts. "You think it's connected?"

"I think people want it to be. It makes for better gossip."

They follow the curve of the path until it dead-ends at a line of leaning lampposts along the parking lot's far edge. Mark checks his phone. "Should be right here. Difficulty one-point-five. Cache description says *bright ideas under dull skies.*"

Erin crouches beside the third lamppost. The skirt wiggles when she lifts it, revealing the magnetic key holder tucked inside the base. She thumbs the lid off, thankful for the rough strip of tape someone added for grip.

"Huh. I guess it wasn't a bison Tube after all." Mark crouches beside her while she works the lid. The smell of rain off his leather jacket is sharp and earthy.

"You ever get tired of it?" she asks, meaning the mud, the bugs, the constant almost-getting-lost.

He shrugs. "Not the finding. The aftermath." He glances around at the families on the path and the jogger looping back toward the lot. "People think search and rescue work's about heroics. It's mostly waiting, hoping you're not finding what you think you're about to."

She stares at him, not expecting the depth of his response, but not wanting to diminish what he just poured onto her. "Is that why you quit?"

"Partly." He wipes his hands on his jeans. "You spend enough time pulling kids out of the water, you start wondering what keeps pulling them in." He ponders for a moment. "Guess we're all looking for something."

"You think that's what I'm doing?"

He doesn't answer right away. "You're looking for something you already lost." He stands and stretches like he just set down something heavy. "Which means you're human."

She watches him walk toward the next lamppost with the casual ease of someone who's done hard things in life. His comment makes her think about Danny, about the day the search ended, and the river didn't give him back. Then she shakes it off and pulls out the small sealable baggie. Her hands shake, but only a little. She steadies herself by clutching the container. Inside the bag is a folded log strip which is damp but legible.

"Typical," she mutters, pulling the log out.

"Beautifully boring," Mark says.

She unfolds the paper and scans the names. *TrailWolf. CachinMaven. MuggleEater.* And a new one, scribbled in small, neat letters: *Jackalope.*

She frowns, thinking about her conversation with the detective last night. "You ever heard of that handle?"

Mark shakes his head. "Nope. Sounds like a kid's alias."

Erin doesn't sign right away. The paper feels heavier than it should, edges darkened by moisture or handling. "Probably nothing," she says, but the word doesn't land right.

"Probably," Mark echoes, giving her space.

She signs *TrailSister* and hands it over to Mark, who also signs. He refolds the log and slips it back into the baggie Erin is holding. The pressure of his existence in her fingers makes her body go rigid.

They lock eyes and he softens the moment with a smile. Erin feels the heat in her cheeks and pulls away, sliding the log back into the container and replacing it under the skirt. The magnet clicks against the lamppost base, small but sharp, causing her to become acutely aware that someone could be listening if they wanted to. Her hands find her pockets before she even knows what she's doing.

Mark stretches, cracking his neck. "See? Easy. No corpses, no cops, no existential dread."

She gestures in agreement, but the motion feels mechanical. Something pulls at her peripheral vision, the sense of a shape watching from the street. Across the road, traffic moves slow through the drizzle. A delivery van idles by the curb, wipers squeaking a rhythm that doesn't match the rain. She can't see the driver through the glare on the glass.

There's a flash in that moment, maybe the reflection of light off a mirror, maybe a phone camera. It is gone as quick as it came and Erin struggles to locate the origin.

"Everything good?" Mark asks.

"Yeah," she says too fast. "Just thought I saw…" She stops herself. The words *someone* and *something* weigh the same and she doesn't want to choose. When she looks again, the van's brake lights glow, then fade into the line of cars turning at the corner.

Mark starts walking toward the path. "You coming?"

"Yeah," she says again, quieter. She gives the lamppost one last glance. A distorted version of her reflection blurs in the damp steel. It is stretched thin, doubled by light. For a second it looks like two faces, but she blinks and it's just her again.

"See, that helped, right?"

"I'm still working on it." She jogs to catch up. "Seeing that body shook me more than I expected."

"Baby steps." He grins, casually strolling along the path. "You want to grab some coffee?"

"No, I'm good." She catches up to him and matches pace. "Look, I appreciate what you did today, but I'm still not ready."

He shrugs and they walk back to their vehicles in silence, exchanging a brief farewell.

That night, the apartment feels more confined. The corkboard is waiting for her attention, the pins catching light like tiny compass points. She tells herself it's only temporary, that she's just organizing, not diving back in. She adds the cache to her board with a single note beside it: *Nothing strange. Just off.*

Her jacket is still damp with rain and she hangs it over the chair to dry before scrolling through her phone, looking for anything that isn't the game. She flicks between headlines, recipes, an email from her mother she's not ready to respond to. The silence between taps makes the apartment feel hollow.

Eventually, compulsion takes root and she opens the geocache app, cursing that habit wins. Her thumb hovers over the map, the empty grid glowing blue.

"It's just a name," she whispers. "Just a game." She repeats it until it almost sounds true. She finds the cache Mark dragged her to and logs it, immediately closing the app afterward.

The heater clicks on and upstairs, the neighbor's faucet begins its nightly drip. The rest of her world settles in for sleep, she sets her phone down and tries to join it.

CHAPTER 5: Archived Cache

The morning is gray, and the sky doesn't look cloudy so much as tired. Vance pulls into the parking lot of Hazel Dell Community Park, she doesn't fit her cruiser into the parking lines because every cruiser already on scene is crooked. The whole little lot is slanted like the scene itself is trying to shrug her off.

Two deputies linger beyond the playground, one keeps glancing toward the bushes where the cache was found. Vance makes short work of the distance and steps under the tape, gloving hands on her approach, allowing no wasted movement. She goes straight to the picnic shelter where the evidence tarp waits.

The cache container sits in the center, a clear plastic tube with dried leaves stuck to the sides. It reminds her of the bomb threat called in from Heritage High School a few years back and the memory of the ticking tube re-electrifies her veins. She hates that reaction.

A deputy crosses the distance to Vance, speaking low. "The couple who put the container out here are Daniel and Marissa Holt. They got some kind of automated alert on their phone last night, something about their box needing attention. They came to check it first thing this morning."

Vance nods once. "They're the ones who found the picture?"

"Yeah. Called it in right away. Patrol already took their statement and sent them downtown for a full interview."

The deputy returns to the perimeter and Vance turns back to the scene. She is so busy studying the construction of the tube, expecting wires, that she barely notices the CSU tech lifting an evidence bag. Inside is a Polaroid. "This was inside."

Vance doesn't respond, but she pulls her attention from the canister and leans in. The woman in the Polaroid is smiling. Too wide, too stiff, as though the corners of her mouth are being pulled by invisible fingers. Light is coming from above and behind the woman, and rope marks trace faint shadows along the top of her shoulders.

This is the Hidden Hollow victim all over again with a different face. This photo feels worse though, cleaner while capturing more pain, if that was such a thing. Vance breathes out through her nose, neither from shock nor disgust, but with a huff of recognition. "Second young woman in under a week. It could be unconnected, but we should flag it."

She doesn't focus on the front of the Polaroid for long. It's the back she's thinking about, something she didn't check soon enough at Hidden Hollow. A mistake she's not going to repeat. She nods to the tech. "Flip it."

He turns it gently, gloved fingers careful as if the plastic might smear the gloss finish. The back is blank at first glance, smudged with a muddy fingerprint streak likely from whoever handled it before deputies arrived.

She's disheartened to find what she expects. Not a note like one would write on the back of a family photo, but coordinates, sharp and precise. Written in the bottom corner in small print, with a tight, deliberate hand that doesn't waver: *N 45° 38.422' W 122° 40.095'*

Vance's jaw goes tight before she speaks, creating a small pause where her mind rearranges a scene faster than anyone else can see. "Shit."

The CSU tech frowns. "Is that part of the game?"

Vance says, "No, not like this." She takes a digital tablet from another deputy without asking, loads a map and enters the numbers. A pin blinks up on the screen, but not in the park, not even close. It's across I-5, past the strip malls, deep inside the industrial cluster. The area is full of warehouses, auto shops, and big windowless buildings no one looks at twice.

A long breath slides into Vance's chest, pressing hard against her ribs. "The photo placement wasn't an accident, and this isn't the dump site." She finally looks up from her tablet to the man she snatched it from and declares, "The numbers are the corridor and whatever's waiting at the end of that corridor, someone wanted a finder to see."

She taps the screen once with her thumb, pulling up the address before handing the tablet back. She looks back at the tech and points at the contents of the tarp. "Bag it, we're moving."

The route leads a police procession across the freeway and down a poorly maintained frontage road that smells like oil. Most of the businesses haven't opened yet. A welding shop flickers with early lights, a storage facility hums, but everything else looks shuttered or dead.

The convoy slows along a stretch of cracked asphalt, engines coughing mist into the cold air. Deputies step out before the tires stop rolling, boots crunching over gravel and bottle glass. Vance's passenger, Detective Tenner, angles his tablet toward a row of squat cinderblock warehouses. "Thirty-seven's down there," he says. "Walking gate's half-open. Looks fresh."

The chain-link gate is crooked, and the padlock has been snapped from the inside. Someone walked out, not in. Vance ducks under the metal throat of the bent fence, the asphalt crackling under her boots. The building looms ahead, a squat cinderblock rectangle tagged with old graffiti and a broken window like a punched-out eye.

She's walked into places like this before, meth labs, squatter dens, abandoned workspaces where something terrible clung to the building's history. This one is different, it's organized.

The front door is cracked open. Officers flank Vance and she pulls her service pistol for the first time in two years, then carefully pushes through. Inside, the light from the doorway cuts through the dark just enough to show the scene set in the large, empty room. A metal tripod tipped on its side, a coil of rope half unspooled, a loop of fishing line hanging from a nail, gently swaying, skid marks on concrete where someone dragged something heavy, a smear of something wiped clean too quickly, a shoe scuff beneath the window, facing inward. A deputy steps carefully toward the tripod.

"Don't touch it," Vance barks. "This is a crime scene, not a fucking treasure hunt." She scans the room, her eyes adjusting to the dim light. Something's off. It's too clean, too deliberate. She grips hard on her pistol, using the weight of the gun to center her thoughts.

The lighting makes sense to her now, the angle of the shadows in the photograph. This is where he posed her.

"Captain, I think I've got something," a uniform calls out, his voice echoing in the empty space. He's crouched near a stack of old crates, pointing at a small, almost invisible arrow scratched into the concrete.

"Follow it," Vance orders, her voice tight. "But be careful. This could be a trap."

The arrow leads him to a stack of pallets, behind which a piece of bright orange survey tape flutters slightly in the draft. Vance's heart pounds while surveying the room as she realizes this is more than just a crime scene, more than a body in a river. She sees the pattern, finding the victim has turned into the killer's own game.

"Captain, there's more tape here," the officer calls out, his voice tinged with a mix of excitement and dread.

"Keep going," Vance urges, her mind racing and her feet catching her up to the officer. "He's leading us somewhere."

They follow the tape to a broken window at the room's corner, where a small, painted rock sits on the sill. The rock is marked with a cryptic symbol, a rabbit with antlers. "The hell is that?" the detective whispers, more to herself than to her team.

At the wall adjacent to the window, half-hidden by a stack of old tires, is a small, concealed door. The door is secured with a simple padlock, but it's unlocked. "Captain, there's a door here," the officer says, his voice barely above a whisper.

"Careful," Vance warns, her mind flashing back to the container at the park, then to the high school sweep years before. "Check for a switch."

The uniform runs his flashlight along the seems. "Looks clear."

She pulls the padlock from its loops. "This wasn't to stop someone from coming in, it was meant to keep something from getting out."

She pulls the door open and motions to the others. They step into the hidden room, the beams from their flashlights cut through the darkness, revealing a scene that makes Vance's stomach churn.

A body hangs from the ceiling, suspended no more than two feet off the ground by fishing line and a pulley system. The bound girl is posed to look like she's sitting on a chair, with a fake caching logbook propped on her lap. The clear line bites into her flesh, pinching skin in some places and nearly cut to the bone in other spots. The victim's eyes are wide open, staring at nothing, a perpetual look of surprise frozen on her face. She hovers over a dark sticky pool.

This is the woman from the Polaroid, and she has been here long enough that the pool on the ground is almost completely congealed, suggesting to Vance that she has been hanging here for at least a day.

"Shit," Vance breathes, her voice barely audible. "Don't touch anything. Call forensics."

Vance approaches the body cautiously, her eyes scanning every detail. Rhythmic droplet patterns suggest she swung before she stilled, telling the detective that the victim was still alive when the suspension began. On the logbook in the victim's lap, she sees a message, written in tight, deliberate handwriting: *Congrats on the*

FTF!

"What does it say, Captain?" an officer asks, his voice trembling slightly as he moves closer.

Vance replies, her mind already racing a thousand directions. "He's congratulating us on the first to find, which suggests there's more to come."

Vance steps back, taking a deep breath to steady herself. She knows without question this just quit being a coincidence. "We need to process this scene," she says, her voice firm. "Every inch of it."

The killer didn't stumble into this place, it was chosen and used like a studio between takes. Vance walks the perimeter slowly, mind working the space, creating a mental blueprint of both the building and the kill. This isn't frantic, it isn't improvisation. This is someone rehearsing, refining. She stops by a nail with one end of fishing line. She examines a single, meticulous knot, and mutters softly, "He measures things."

She realizes, in that hollow warehouse silence, that she can't read the signs the way a cacher could. She needs someone who understands cache placement logic, stealth patterns, and why someone would use a public game to hide a private ritual.

Vance steps back out into the cold industrial air, the warehouse door settling behind her with a hollow metallic groan. Police radios crackle in the distance. Somewhere further down the lot, a truck starts up, the engine rattling like loose bones. Vance motions the nearest officer and points in the direction of the noise with two intent fingers.

She walks to her car, phone already out, flipping through her notes from the *Hidden Hollow* incident. Erin Caldwell's number sits halfway down the page, highlighted in yellow. Vance hesitates for the first time this morning. Just one breath. Then she hits call.

Erin is nestled into her couch with a warm mug of coffee, already doom-scrolling the Hazel Dell chatter in her caching forum.

Her browsing is interrupted by a pop-up notification, an incoming call from an unknown caller. She debates sending it to voicemail, but a pressure of dread expands in her chest. She answers, "Hello?"

There's a half-second of silence before the detective replies, feeling the cold space between professionalism and need. "Ms. Caldwell, it's Detective Vance."

Erin straightens instinctively, heartbeat kicking up like she's been caught doing something she shouldn't. "Is this about the… incident? At Hidden Hollow?"

"No, not that one, but it is a related matter."

The word lands heavy on Erin, *related*. "So, the Hazel Dell rumors are true."

Vance keeps her tone brisk and businesslike, with no warmth to soften the blow. "I'm looking at a cache log with several usernames in common and yours among them. We found another photo, similar to the one you discovered."

"Detective, I made that find over a year ago, I had nothing to do with this."

"That's not why I called." Vance pauses or mutes, then she returns to the conversation. "Ms. Caldwell, I need information that I don't think the department could provide quick enough. I don't understand this little game you play, but I do know it has a community and I need to see certain things through the eyes of a community member."

"Oh." Erin sits in the request, silenced for a moment. "Okay?"

Vance responds to her unspoken question, "I'm not deputizing you or anything, I simply need help identifying which of these handles are active and which are dead."

Erin swallows, throat suddenly tight. "Dead?"

"Dead accounts or inactive profiles. People who used to play this game but don't anymore. I'm trying to clear up some muddy timelines."

Erin rubs her temple with two fingers. "Right. Okay. I mean, I know the scene. I can look up who's legit. The first thing I would do when I want to know who has been at the cache most recent is to also check the dates of the signatures. Unless the logbook is full, that should be easy to see, but I know that cache has been active for years so, if the logbook hasn't been changed out, people would find any open spot to sign, like on the back side, a margin, next to a short signature."

"We have a team on that now."

Erin pulls her laptop from the coffee table to her knees and loads the caching website. "Could you tell me the name of the cache? I will look online and try to see what I can find."

Vance is silent again, then chuckles. "You people and your silly games. This cache is called Parkside Peekaboo." Vance's voice dips just slightly, not softer, but less guarded, knowing she's asking a civilian for something she shouldn't need. "I'd appreciate anything you can find."

Erin presses, "Detective, what exactly happened at Hazel Dell?"

Vance doesn't answer, not directly. Not immediately. "Without divulging, we found some connective tissue to the cache you called in."

Erin's pulse climbs. "So it *was* another Polaroid."

A sharp inhale from Vance, not confirmation, not denial, just a tell. "Ms. Caldwell, I'm telling you this because it's relevant."

Erin's mouth dries from the heat of her breath. "You think it's the same person."

"I think whoever did this is planning to do it again, and they understand your community better than I do." Her response is truth, simple and bare. "One more thing. Both victims so far have been young women. We can't ignore that. You can't ignore that."

Erin looks around her apartment half expecting something in the shadows to shift when she whispers, "I can help. Just… tell me what you found.”

Vance pauses long enough that Erin feels the weight of whatever she's not saying. “I'll follow up when I have more. In the meantime, if you see anything strange in the logs, call me.”

The call ends and leaves a kind of hollow pressure in Erin's apartment, and she feels the silence leaning toward her. She sets her phone down but doesn't actually let go of it. Her fingers hover over the screen while she realizes she was just handed something sharp.

She turns to the laptop, refreshing the open caching site without thinking, and locates Parkside Peekaboo. The drop pin is gray, signifying it has been disabled. According to the timestamp, it has been like this over a month. This cache was dead before Hidden Hollow even published. There's no reason this cache should be seeing activity now.

She scrolls the activity and notices a gap in activity shortly after she found it last year, then a surge of finds in the last three weeks. Odd activity for an inactive cache, but nothing strange in the logged visits until TrailWolf leaves a comment about a photograph.

She switches browser tabs and checks the discussion thread, the big messy one where everyone talks over each other about anything half-interesting. It's already buzzing:

CacheMeIfUCan: “Did you guys see cops at Hazel Dell this morning?”

GeoMom73: “Someone said there was blood in the restroom.”

CedarScout: “Looks like mods nuked half the comments.”

CachinMaven: “I heard it was a homeless guy.”

MuggleEater: “I heard it was connected to that weird forest cache.”

TrailTempest: “This is how rumors start.”

None of it is reliable, but all of it is troubling. Erin scrolls deeper. Her thumb slides across her touchpad with the kind of speed that comes from fear disguised as curiosity. Then she sees a username she doesn't recognize. *CryptidQueen.*

The profile picture is a black-and-white sketch of antlers wrapped in ferns. The tone of her comment is off, not frantic like everyone else, just quiet and cold. "Some coordinates aren't meant to be followed. They lead where the mapmaker wants to see the mark they put on the world."

It's the kind of comment that blends in if you're not paying attention; poetic, creepy, almost performative. Right now, it hooks under Erin's skin. She writes the username on a pad of paper.

She clicks on the name and the profile opens. CryptidQueen has a ridiculous amount of hides. Puzzle caches, multi-stage folklore trails, old event logs. She even has a blog link named *Myths Underfoot.*

One recently posted addition catches her eye: *"Urban legends don't fade. They migrate. Some of them into coordinates."*

A shiver crawls up Erin's spine. She goes back to the forum and refreshes the Hazel Dell thread. Someone has posted a blurry photo of the police taped crime scene across town, before the comments have been shut off. She scrolls through again and realizes comments that were there minutes ago are gone. She refreshes the page to find more have vanished. Someone is controlling the narrative. Vance may have police instincts, but Erin knows this ecosystem, and what she's seeing isn't normal cleanup or trolling activity. It's purposeful curation.

Her phone buzzes with a new publish notification: *Where the Path Broke*

Published: *5:14 a.m.*

Cache Owner: *OverlookLaneCrew*

Reviewed by: *Surveyor*

Erin stares at the screen until her eyes sting. She whispers without meaning to, "You want me to follow you." In response to only herself, she acknowledges, truly knows, that she will.

Erin sets her phone down on the table, but her body doesn't settle. There's a tight, static edge under her skin now. She adjusts her laptop with the heel of her hand, the screen warming her face in the dark of the apartment. She opens a text document and types without thinking: *Hidden Hollow, Polaroid, Parkside Peekaboo.*

It's frantic but feels less like panic and more like need. She opens the caching map and scrolls through nearby hides, disables filters, pulls up the list of archived caches. Most people don't bother with those, they're considered graveyards, dead listings, or clutter by most cachers. Erin knows dead things aren't always irrelevant.

She goes back to the Hazel Dell Polaroid comments on the forum. Someone had posted coordinates before the mods flagged the comment, "This isn't listed as a multi, why the second set of coords?"

She clicks the blog link on CryptidQueen's profile and reads a line about folklore mapping: "The earliest cartographers hid their fears in place names. Markers so the brave would know where not to walk."

Something in that line cracks her all the way open, fear and fascination fighting in her chest. She navigates to her text document and types CryptidQueen's handle, then edits: *Hidden Hollow, Polaroid, body at second site. Hazel Dell, Polaroid, second coordinates. Cacher group, deleted logs. Old archived caches with strange references. Cache owner OverlookLaneCrew.*

Her phone buzzes with evidence the forums are lighting up again:

GeoMom73: "Did you see the new one?"

ScoutPNW: "Where the Path Broke?"

FernFinder: "That title gives me the creeps. Is caching even safe right now?"

BirchAndStone: "Anyone going for it?"

MossRunner: "It published first thing this morning, why didn't

I get the notification until now?"

She slams the laptop shut realizing if she doesn't get some air, she's going to drown in this. But she's already written the new cache's name in her notebook and underlined it twice. She can hear her own heartbeat, fast, sharp, and hungry. Erin isn't following the killer, not physically, but mentally she's already in his map.

The apartment feels too small now, too warm. The air is thick with the heat of electronics and the metallic hum of her own nerves. Erin paces once across the room, her sock catching on a warped board in the floor.

When she turns back toward her couch, her eyes go straight to the notebook, the messy cluster of names, arrows, and timestamps. She stares at the beginnings of connections she isn't ready to say out loud. She sits again, not consciously. Her body just folds into the seat.

She opens the cache app on her phone and searches for *Where the Path Broke*. The listing is ordinary, it feels too ordinary, almost like it is trying too hard to be invisible. It lists as a traditional cache with average difficulty and terrain, which doesn't seem to match the geography on the map. The cache feels like it was posted by an amateur hider, but it was reviewed by Surveyor who usually catches these sorts of things.

Erin navigates through the cache details, looking for the thing that gives her an unsettled feeling, but nothing leaps out. She flips to her notebook, then back to the app. She tells herself she's imagining it, reading too much into the weight that shifts inside her, still her eyes linger on the new cache.

It can't be nothing, but she can't see anything. She feels a pull low in her body, the same tug she felt when Vance said "related." The same tug she felt when she clicked on CryptidQueen's profile. The same tug she felt when she zoomed in deep on that first Polaroid.

Maybe she's just jumpy from the *Hidden Hollow* murder, but maybe not. She whispers what she already knows is a lie, "I'm just going to look. That's all."

She's already up, grabbing her jacket, checking her GPS batteries, and tying her hair up so it won't whip into her eyes when the wind kicks up. Erin is already halfway out the door before she registers she's moving, that's when the detective's words hit her like a truck, "Both victims so far have been young women."

She checks her pocket for the pepper spray canister and feels it, but not the comfort it normally gives. Her eyes dart for something more, anything. Erin spins back to the entry table and yanks open the drawer. Inside, next to a tube of chapstick, a stack of papers, and some loose change is a trail knife, Danny's knife. the one she kept after he died.

Chapter 6: Coordinates Updated

The police lights throw cold shapes across the asphalt of the industrial yard while Vance stands just outside the crime scene's doorway, scribbling in her notebook. She's been here almost an hour, and the scene hasn't stopped shifting under her feet. Techs uncover partial details she wishes they'd found sooner. Beat cops haul in new statements from employees of nearby buildings and witnesses at the park where the cache was discovered. The evidence pile is thickening in ways that make her teeth clench. She's tired of looking at the photograph and she's tired of pretending this isn't connected.

The victim's body has been moved out, but the weight of it remains, the dragged pattern on the concrete, the lone sneaker half caught under a rusted trash bin, the faint smear against the cinderblock wall. The whole place feels planned in a quiet, awful way.

She breathes out slowly, knowing it is time to start pulling the threads, and signals Tenner over with two fingers. "Let's run it from the top," she says. "Tell me everything we know right now."

She falls in beside him as he starts reviewing, stepping under the tape and back into the heart of the scene, boots whispering over the cold concrete. CSU has already cleared the main angles for her, evidence markers blooming across the ground, small plastic yellow flowers no one would ever choose to plant.

She crouches near the drag pattern. It's faint and almost lazy in the way it curves, showing no sign of panic or struggle. The killer moved the victim with the calm routine of someone hauling a duffel bag across a gym floor with no sense of urgency. That quiet confidence is what bothers Vance most.

A tech gestures her over to a cinderblock wall and Tenner pauses his recital long enough to let the tech describe what he found. The man in the white jumpsuit points to a collection of dark spots. Vance studies the smear there, recognizing each is a patch of blood, subtle darkening but not from a braced hand. The texture doesn't fit the pattern of a palm, it shows more like the faint compression of knuckles. Two or three clusters in a line, striped with void, and jagged against the surface.

Tenner hovers over her shoulder. "Someone punching a wall?"

"Yeah, but I don't think it's a loss of control," Vance mutters. "Something about it looks purposeful, intentional." She scribbles the spotted pattern in her notepad and turns to the tech. "See if you can pull traces off this wall, maybe find some skin."

The two continue their walk. Near the restroom door, under a marker, a second photograph sits in its evidence sleeve along with various bagged items. She forces herself to look at it again. The victim lies on her back, eyes half-open, chin tilted slightly, listening to something only the dead ever hear. The photograph is framed with too much care. The shot is centered with no evidence of shake. She looks at the tripod in the center of the room.

Vance frowns at the angle. That's what's been gnawing at her, beyond the brutality, there's something about the composition. The killer didn't document the body, it was captured with a specificity she can't quite see.

She sweeps her gaze outward, retracing the drag line, the discarded shoe, a single smudge of blood leading out the back door toward the fence, and the faint imprint of a boot toe pointed inward, not outward. She stands, rubbing at the bridge of her nose with her knuckle. This wasn't staged for shock value, there's a story here, a message. It's the first moment she feels it in her gut instead of her head, this killer knows the terrain.

A shadow falls across her shoulder before the voice comes.

"Detective?"

Vance turns, finding Morales, one of the CSU techs, is holding a tablet in both hands like he's afraid it might bite him. He's young enough to still look shaken in the cold light but experienced enough to know when something matters. She gestures him closer. "What do you have?"

Morales angles the screen toward her, showing a side-by-side image of the Polaroid from Hidden Hollow on the left and the Hazel Dell Polaroid on the right. It has the same framing, same color distortion on the right edge, and the same faint shadow in the lower corner which could be a branch or maybe a coat sleeve.

Morales points at each picture. "Detective, these were taken at the same place."

Vance doesn't blink. The industrial hum around her drops into a low, uneasy quiet, like the whole place is listening. She studies the comparison longer than she should, not because she needs to, the match is obvious. She's buying herself a few extra seconds before she opens the door this discovery has just unlocked. "Neither of those photos were taken here."

Morales adds, voice smaller now, "There's something else. There are what look like tripod marks. We found three impressions near the north fence. Same spacing as Hidden Hollow."

Vance's jaw works once, a tiny shift. "Tripod?"

Morales nods. "Yes, ma'am. Or something functioning like one. Three-leg spread, stable, shallow pressure. He was staging at each location."

Her attention shifts to the downed tripod in the center of the room, to the rubber feet. They are clean, no mud, no dirt. As thankful as she is for the CSU, the frustration of getting puzzle pieces late sticks in her teeth. If she knew about the second tripod, she might have framed this scene differently. That's the punch, the thing that hits her low, right in the instinct. She stands and pushes away the tablet, then looks back at the wall, the drag line, the Polaroid sealed in plastic. Both Polaroids were taken at the same place, but not here. Whoever did this, they've done it before, and they're not finished. There has to be a Polaroid from this place still, and from the woods outside Yacolt.

A CSU photographer waves her over with a gloved hand. "Detective? We found something under the body."

There's no dramatics in his voice, which means it's either nothing or something he hasn't let himself interpret yet. Vance follows him to the kill spot and steps beside him while he kneels. He angles just enough so she can see the tiny plastic bag as he pulls it from the pool of blood. Inside is a folded scrap of paper, not large enough for a note, not shaped like trash. She nods for him to open it.

He slides it out carefully with tweezers, unfolding it like it's a pressed flower. A string of code stares back at her. *45.630310, -122.679112.* It is written in blocky, almost childish print. A strange calmness radiates from it, like whoever wrote it didn't feel fear or pressure. They had the time to choose their moment.

Morales mutters from behind her, "What is that supposed to mean?"

Vance doesn't answer, she knows it has the shape of a taunt. The arrogance feels familiar, but she refuses to give it the dignity of certainty. She takes the scrap of paper from the tech and holds it up to the light and turns the paper over. The back side is blank.

The quiet around her stretches thin and tight. She looks back at the evidence markers, the scuffed dirt, the Polaroid angled like a grim little trophy. It clicks together for her, this isn't a signature. It's a game mechanic.

"Bag it, tag it, and get it catalogued. Get the tech team on these coordinates and let's finish up here." She already hates the certainty she feels rocking her chest as she makes her way outside.

One of the uniforms is questioning a city worker a few yards from the front door. The man's arms are folded tight and his fluorescent vest is half-zipped against the cold. He keeps glancing toward the restroom, then away again fast, like the act of looking is a violation. Vance approaches with the steady, practiced calm of someone who's talked to hundreds of rattled strangers. She flashes her badge lightly, just enough to ground him.

"You're sanitation?" she asks, establishing the baseline.

He nods hard. "Facilities. Waste run and unlocks. I was on the south route earlier."

She waits silently. No need to pressure or rush. She lets him fill the silence.

"I, uh, heard the chatter on my radio when I was heading to the main lot. Our dispatch was talking about it, asked me if I saw anything. So, figured I should come back. There was something I saw earlier, before any of you were here."

His throat bobbles on the swallow, and he rubs at his jaw, eyes squinting toward the lot.

"It was early, not dark anymore, but not full light yet. I came in through the south entrance and saw a car leaving the employee lot. Didn't think much of it at the time. People park here sometimes to sleep or, you know…"

"Describe the car."

He hesitates, guilt bleeding into his expression like he thinks he's failed the test. "I didn't get the plate. I'm sorry."

"I'm not asking for the plate yet," Vance says, softer. "Just the car."

He nods gratefully. "Silver. Or, something light. A hatchback, maybe. Sort of boxy."

"Model?"

"If I had to guess? Subaru. Or maybe a RAV4? Something like that."

Vance files it away. A hundred Pacific Northwesterners drive that exact silhouette. "Did you see the driver?"

"No, our headlights made a glare on the windshield. I didn't think much of it in the moment."

"Understandable. Did you hear anything?"

"Just the way they left. They took off faster than you'd expect for this hour. That's when I thought it was odd, when they can burn out louder than the truck engine, that usually means something's going on."

She watches his eyes as he speaks, the way they flick down and left, he is calling for memory, not invention. "Did you touch anything at the scene?"

"God, no. Our trucks do all the lifting and the back gate was already open."

"Good. One more question. You keep looking at the restroom door, are you hoping it's open?"

He nods, his cheeks burning. His voice cracks. "Yeah. We haven't stopped in a bit." This time, he doesn't just look down, he turns away.

"You did the right thing," she says. "Go ahead. It's already been cleared. When you're done, if you could wait in your truck, someone will get your official statement."

He tries not to rush when he leaves. The officer escorts the man toward the building, the garbage man's shoulders are tight and his head hangs down as he follows. Alone again, Vance looks toward the empty lot and the direction the car sped out. It points northeast, toward the city proper and thousands of possibilities. It's a dead-end lead.

The form of it though, the generic description, the anonymity of the car, the familiar shape hikers and cachers use, creates a wedge in her mind. This wasn't random traffic, it was someone who knew how to blend, how to disappear into the ordinary.

Tenner waves her over from the north edge of the lot. He's

crouched in the gravel with a CSU tech, both of them angled over something in the dirt like amateur archaeologists. Vance steps behind them, letting her eyes adjust to the shallow patterns. Partial footprints, just two, stamped in mud or blood.

The CSU tech taps the ground near the toe with a gloved finger. "Based on the waffle grid we can see here, looks like a hiking boot."

Vance studies the pattern. The tread isn't crisp enough to give brand or model, and the spacing tells her only that the wearer had an average gait. Nothing irregular. Nothing that screams unique.

"Male or female?" she asks.

Ryan, the tech, answers analytically, "Stride says probably male. But small enough it could go either way."

Perfect ambiguity. Exactly the kind she hates. Tenner points to the fence across the lot. "Could have gone to the edge of the property or this might be where the car was parked."

She traces the path with her eyes, imagining someone stepping lightly, not wanting to disturb too much, not wanting to be seen. "Anyone make visual that would suggest the perp left on foot?"

"Negative."

She straightens, dusting grit from her gloves. These fresh prints don't tell enough of a story, yet. She tries to not feed the uncomfortable sense that something is already in motion out there, something she's now too late to catch. "Make sure these are documented. Get scrapings from the tire marks at the exit. Both need analyzed." Either possibility is a problem.

Vance returns to her car to get out of the cold, the door thunking shut and muting the chaos outside. She pulls her laptop closer on its swivel base at the dashboard and opens the geocache app the techs installed a few days ago, waiting for it to load. The laptop is old, making it slow and clunky, evidence of the department's budget. When the page loads, it is too cheerful for what she's using it for. A little compass animation spins. Someone thought that was cute.

Finally, the latest activity page pops up, and a cascade of drop pins populates the map all around her location, friendly in a way that feels wildly insincere for the crime scene sitting fifty feet away.

She scrolls through the Hazel Dell caches. The handles are a mix of goofy, juvenile, outdoorsy, and smug. At first glance, they mean nothing. At second glance, they mean too much.

TrailWolf. This name is everywhere. Condescending notes about "rookie mistakes" on caches he finds. Seems heavy with self-appointed authority. She flags him mentally: not as a suspect, but as a personality she'll probably hate.

GhostLogger. This name is also frequent, though not as much. Writes thoughtful entries and seems seasoned. Someone who might know the community well.

CedarScout. Another frequent handle that seems tied to the area, short responses and neutral presenting.

CryptidQueen. Not common in this area, but not absent. The queen's posts read as equal parts informative and dismissive. A bit of snark and condescension in her finds.

MapNerd. This user seems argumentative and corrective. A little too present in recent log posts. Maybe a new player.

MudMagnet. This user has an innocuous, cheerful log style. They only stand out because they've hit a number of caches in this area in the last couple of days.

The logs aren't giving legal names, but they are giving behavior, the very thing she knows how to analyze better than anyone. She mutters under her breath, "Who the hell are you people?"

This little digital world is bigger than she expected, and she can already feel she's missing something fundamental. She closes the browser tab and rubs her forehead with the back of her glove. There are answers hiding with the users, she knows that.

Vance taps her laptop's touchscreen twice, then three times, then harder than she needs to. The caching platform keeps looping her back to the same sanitized log page, all bright colors and cheery UI elements. She needs identities, real names. Addresses, IP logs, something.

She clicks a user profile but gets nothing valuable. She tries the link for a log but is given notice that she needs to be a member for access, then is redirected to a generic support form. Her jaw tightens. She pulls her phone out and calls IT at the precinct.

Harris picks up, voice already weary. "Vance. What's up?"

"I need identity data tied to a list of handles on this stupid game site, and I need it before this crime scene gets cold." She hears keyboard tapping.

"Yeah, that's not something we can just pull."

"Meaning?"

"Meaning the user info is stored on external servers. Overseas, in some cases. They don't hand out identities voluntarily."

"We have a homicide," Vance says, pushing the word harder than she means to. "Two, actually. That should qualify."

Harris sighs. "We need a formal request through their corporate. Or a warrant. Or a liaison contact who can escalate. You know this. The fastest route is the regional reviewer."

Vance frowns. "Reviewer?"

"Yeah. Every cache submission goes through a reviewer in that area. They approve everything. They have limited backend access, communication channels, that kind of thing. They might be able to steer you."

She drums her fingers on the steering wheel. "So, I need a reviewer name?" She clicks on the cache for the Hazel Dell park and scrolls the data. The name sits in the air like a dropped pin. *Surveyor*. Another damn nickname. Just another mask. "I've got Surveyor."

"You got a real name for this Surveyor?" Harris asks.

Vance laughs under her breath at the absurdity of digital anonymity woven into a homicide investigation. "No. That's the problem. All I've got is the handle." Vance doesn't like that answer any more than she likes depending on anonymous gatekeepers or the idea that someone with backend access may also be the one approving the caches connected to staged killings. "Find me anything. Whatever you can pull."

"On it, but Detective, don't expect miracles."

"I don't." She ends the call but keeps staring at the phone. *Surveyor*. A name that gives nothing except a role, not even a person. It feels like the kind of name someone uses when they want the world to look at their work, not them.

Outside her windshield, the industrial yard shifts in the cold breeze, making metal groan, causing tape to flutter, and gently wobbling evidence markers. Someone is building something in her jurisdiction, a pattern she can't read yet in a game she's not welcome to play.

Vance keeps the laptop open long after the call ends. The cursor blinks, its patient little heartbeat tapping against her nerves. She scrolls through the Hazel Dell logs again, then flips tabs to the file she hasn't wanted to look at since yesterday: *Hidden Hollow*.

The two windows, side by side now, two crime scenes that should have nothing to do with each other. Different terrain, different victims, different staging styles, different times of day, and different levels of violence. And yet, there is enough connective tissue to be sure.

Her pen taps against the notebook. This isn't random. Something about it speaks to timing, not just opportunity. Through all the differences, the structure remains the same. Someone is testing variables, figuring out what works best. The killer is building toward something. The idea hits her chest in a cold, heavy way. This isn't a spree, it's a progression, and she's been trailing further behind from the start. She murmurs, "What the hell are you trying to show me?"

She's not dealing with someone who kills for impulse. She's dealing with someone who kills with intention. Someone who understands terrain and timing. Someone using a game as the framework, but for what?

A CSU tech jogs toward Vance from the far edge of the perimeter, breath fogging in the cold. He knocks on her window and, when she rolls down her window, he doesn't wait. "Detective, we found a fresh set."

"Dammit. When is this scene going to stop producing?" She climbs out of her car and follows him past the concrete, past the restroom building, past the tape that flutters against the brambles. The path here is narrow, dirt pressed down by shoes, framed by blackberry vines and winter-dead underbrush.

The impressions are obvious once she sees them. The tracks are light, moving with purpose but not confidence, and avoiding rocks out of habit. She tries to determine if she's looking at a runner, a morning walker, or a cacher.

She crouches beside the first clear print, brushing a finger along the edge of the indentation. The soil is still crisp and the edges sharp. The moisture is yet to settle, suggesting these prints are maybe ten to fifteen minutes old.

No way the killer took this route. This track belongs to someone who passed after. Someone who moved through while the killer was long gone… or hiding close. She stands slowly. "Do they lead anywhere?"

"They head into the greenbelt," the tech says. "Trail splits after fifty yards. Could be a jogger, it just doesn't make sense they would dip so close to the yard."

Vance scans the direction the prints go. A faint path disappears into shadows beyond the break in the chain-link fence, up to a narrow line of trees. She imagines how many people could have walked it, which grows into the wonder of how easily a killer, a witness, or civilian could step into a crime scene without realizing what they're standing in. "Anyone see someone leaving the area?"

"Nothing so far."

She nods. Based on the two partials at the back door of the crime scene, the prints are too small to be the killer's. They are too light-footed, but too fresh to ignore. She stares at them a few seconds longer, something tugging at her. Someone was out here at dawn. Someone didn't call it in. Someone was close enough to the scene to be a problem.

Her mind builds a profile before she straightens. "Get casts if the soil will take it. Mark the direction of travel, and if we haven't gotten someone on camera duty by now, I'll be pretty pissed."

The tech nods and retreats. Vance lingers for a moment longer, alone with the breaths of wind slipping through the trees. Someone walked away from this scene. Vance is halfway back to her car when her radio pops to life with static breath followed by a too-tense dispatcher voice. "Detective Vance, Code Seven on your channel. Repeat, we have a flagged alert from your request queue."

Vance presses the mic. "Go ahead."

"The coordinates your team reported mark the Sheriff's Office."

Her pulse tightens into a racing constriction, the pain her doctor said she needed to pay attention to. "Come again?"

"Those coordinates are the exact block of the HQ."

She comes to a full, clean halt and the quiet in the industrial lot seems to fold in on itself. CSU Ryan murmurs somewhere behind her, but she doesn't hear what he says. Everything else holds still.

"Copy," she says. "Notify Command but do it quietly. I'm on my way."

She moves, fast but controlled, calling across the lot, "Tenner. With me."

He jogs over, reading the tension in her face but not the

meaning. He doesn't ask as they climb in. Vance gives the industrial greenbelt one last look, taking in the scuffed earth, the smeared foliage, the footprints leading nowhere. She doesn't know whose they are or what they saw, but she feels the dread in her lungs yelling a warning she's too late to hear properly. There are too many players in this game and one of them is already closer than she wants to believe.

Chapter 7: Swag

Erin arrives at the parking lot she pinned earlier. The gravel turnout barely fits two cars, and hers looks questionable sitting next to a vacant SUV crouched under the trees. Fog presses low over the road, thick enough to dull the shapes of the forest floor beyond the lot, but thin enough to let it breathe in slow, calm swirls.

Erin kills the engine and the sudden quiet makes her shoulders bunch. She notices the tension and realizes this is the first time she hasn't felt safe in the woods in over a decade. Danny's knife sits in her pack on the passenger seat, the shape of it hidden but present through the canvas. She pulls the strap over her shoulder and feels the hilt shift inside, providing a small anchor back to her wilderness safety.

She locks her car and moves, stopping where the gravel meets grass and pine needles. The trail sign there is damp when she touches it, no different than most of the Pacific Northwest. A posted warning about slick terrain has frayed around the corners where weather has handled it over time. She stares at the laminated printout and feels an uneasy twist in her stomach, some confirmation that says this isn't a game anymore, even if it looks like one.

The forest beyond the first bend is swallowed in a pale gray morning hush. There are no birds talking and the spot is too far away from Highway 14 to hear distant traffic. Erin is alone with the wet hush of branches shifting beneath the weight of moisture, something she has always found peace with before today.

She swallows once and checks her phone. There are no new messages, which should comfort her, but today it doesn't. She tells herself to quit stalling and start moving. She pulls Danny's knife from her sack and tucks it into her belt, finding his encouragement with its presence.

The trail narrows faster than she expected. Moisture beads on the blackberry vines, the weight pulling the thorns down until they bow across the path like they're warning strangers from passing. Erin maneuvers around them with each stretch and ducks under a sagging branch, feeling a bead of cold water kiss the back of her neck.

As she ventures further into the woods, the fog pools in layers, thickening at her knees, but thinner by the time it reaches her waist. The smell of wet cedar and damp soil hangs thicker than the fog. She moves lightly, testing each step. Each time, her foot lands soft on the muddied duff. There's no crunch or echo, no sound to prove she's here except her own breathing, which feels steadier than her racing heart.

Halfway across the old wooden footbridge, she pauses. The creek below usually chatters even in the low flow of a restless little ribbon, but this morning it isn't. It just gives the faint whisper of water slipping under the boards, gentle and quiet, muffled by the mist. Erin presses her hand to the railing, feeling the light sheen of moss against her palm, slick and cold. She stops for a moment, waiting for the woods to give her a sound, a sign, anything to track. It doesn't, so she forces her feet forward. Her fingers brush the shape of the knife on her hip. She doesn't draw it, beyond her own paranoia, she has no reason to. Just knowing it's there helps the tightness in her nerves loosen a fraction.

The trail ahead curves around a fallen cedar, its roots pulled up in the shape of a blackened ribcage. Erin navigates through the roots, careful not to snag on the gnarled tangle or slip on the wet bark. The muted echo of a soft scrape, followed by the shifting of rocks on the ridge above her. She freezes and her breath stops in her throat. The fog holds perfectly still, waiting with her, and nothing else moves.

The hairs on her arms rise slow and certain.

She swallows hard, clearing her choke, and tells herself it was a squirrel, then keeps walking. She paces just steady enough to pretend she believes herself, just steady enough to pass for someone who didn't hear a thing.

The trail bends again, this time around a stand of alder, before widening into a clearing that shouldn't exist this deep in the woods. She glances over her shoulder, reminding her fear that some cache owners love pushing seekers deeper into the woods, away from everything familiar. Erin usually welcomes the challenge, but today it feels overbearing.

She slows as she enters the space. The fog thins just enough as it spreads into the clearing to reveal a concrete slab half-swallowed by moss, the remnant of what might have been a picnic area decades ago. A rusted trash barrel leans on its side in the undergrowth, exposed metal showing through flaked paint.

Broken glass glitters across the concrete. There's no reason for it to be here and no explanation other than vandals or kids. Still, the forest reclaims the mess that humans left behind. She steps carefully, heel sliding on a shard buried under wet leaves. The wet haze creeps low over the slab, making the abandoned rest stop feel like a stage after an audience has gone home. Empty, but not forgotten.

Near the tree line, an old culvert pipe juts from the hillside, half buried, and dark inside. The drip of water echoes from its throat in an irregular pattern, each fall tapping metal with a slow, uncertain rhythm. Erin rubs her arms through her jacket, chasing a chill that wasn't brought on by cold air. Her phone buzzes once and the GPS arrow freezes, then angles toward the culvert. She hesitates but follows the drift. Her boots crunch softly over the glass, but the sound is swallowed fast by moss and the fog.

The coordinates pull her toward a cedar stump sprawled beside the concrete retaining wall. Rot has eaten half of it and its hollowed heart looks deep enough to hold secrets. She kneels, brushing aside damp needles and dislodging a chunk of wood that didn't originally belong to the tree. Her fingers find a familiar plastic edge in the blackness. A foot long, weathered lock-n-lock, speckled with mud and pine duff.

She lifts the container out and rests it on her knee. The latch cracks when she opens it, the sound is alarmingly loud in the quiet. Inside, she finds a logbook curled from moisture, a tiny plastic compass someone dropped years ago, a rusted trackable tag, and a sealed gallon-sized Ziploc nestled at the bottom.

The Ziploc is out of place, it isn't weathered, not clouded by time like everything else in the container. Its edges are crisp, the seal is pressed tight, and the plastic still carries a faint factory shine. Erin picks it up gently. The contents inside shift, not heavy, but rigid. There are two shapes, one flat and one angular.

She opens the bag with slow, careful fingers and slides out the first object, a Polaroid. It's a picture of a man, his face caught between fear and confusion, eyes widened like he's listening to something, or someone, just out of frame. The fog behind him curls in the same soft whorls that surround her now. Her pulse drops into a cold, steady thud. Erin recognizes him. This is the cacher MudMagnet.

She doesn't breathe until she feels the second object against her palm. A long shard of mirror wrapped in a scrap of cloth that's damp at one corner. The fabric is soaked with a faint blotch of blood. The mirror shard is cracked down the center, splitting her reflection into two slivers that don't line up. The base of the shard is wrapped in orange flagging tape, creating a makeshift handle.

A pressure inside her chest folds and she realizes she is holding someone else's secret. She looks back at the stump, at the ruined rest stop half-swallowed by fog, at the dark mouth of the culvert. None of it feels abandoned now.

The mirror shard trembles faintly between her fingers, not from movement, but from the way her pulse hits her skin. Erin shoves the mirror fragment back into the bag and closes the Ziploc, then seals it tight with hands that look steadier than they feel. The clearing has changed, not visibly and not in any way she can point at, but it has shifted.

The fog dips lower now, dragged down by air that suddenly feels heavier and thicker. The glass on the concrete slab catches a dim thread of light and scatters it in dull, broken glints, causing tiny reflections to blink and die. Erin straightens, the pack strap sliding across her shoulder with a whisper, and her hand dropping to the comfort of Danny's knife. She listens to the forest, but hears nothing, not birds or critters, even the dripping from the culvert seems to pause. In that silence, there's another sound of accidental movement that reaches her ear from above the culvert. She snaps her head toward the hillside.

The fog is thick enough to hide everything except the suggestion of movement she can't prove she heard. Her skin prickles, heat rising despite the cold, and she steps back from the stump, her gaze sweeping the tree line. A fir branch trembles where the rest stand still. She tells herself it's wind, even though the air is dead still. Her chest tightens in recognition. She is not alone. Her breath shrinks shallow and she presses her thumb to the strap holding the hilt of Danny's knife, but she doesn't draw it. The gesture is enough to keep her knees from buckling.

She scans the hill again, slower this time. Still, nothing moves, but the feeling wraps around her like wire. Someone is watching. Erin shifts, eyes locked on the ridge. She's certain she hears it this time, another tiny sound, maybe a shift of stone, barely audible through the fog. She whispers to herself, "Don't look scared."

A voice breaks the quiet behind her. Not from the ridge, not from the trees, but close. "Erin?"

Her whole body jerks. The mirror shard bites her palm through the Ziploc before she remembers to unclench her fist and the cache tumbles off her lap onto the ground. She spins on her heel in time to see Mark step out of the trees. His jacket is damp, his hair pushed back where he combed his fingers through it. He's breathing too fast for a slow approach. She slips it into her jacket, quick and instinctive, before she even realizes she's hiding it.

"What the hell, Mark," she says, voice thinner than she expected. "You scared me."

"Sorry. I've been calling." He lifts his phone, showing a dark screen. The gesture is quick and defensive.

She slides from the knife to her own phone and checks. "I don't have any missed calls."

"The signal's garbage out here, Erin. You know that." He's not wrong, but the response comes so easy, almost practiced. He steps closer, eyes flicking not to her face, but to the container at her feet, the spilled lock-n-lock. His gaze shifts to the wet stump, then the curtained tree line, lingering a fraction too long, which causes her eyes to follow.

"You didn't answer my texts either," she says, returning her attention to her own phone.

Mark shrugs, the kind of shrug that's meant to close a door, not open one. "Didn't see 'em. I drove over as soon as I could."

As soon as he could, his words pulse in her ears. He's here now though, at the exact moment she found the Polaroid, the exact moment she felt watched.

"You okay?" he asks. The question hits the right notes, but there's a delay in his voice that seems rehearsed.

She nods, though she isn't. "I found a photo."

Mark goes still with a pause that doesn't belong to fear as much as calculation. "Like the last one?"

She considers lying, but that feels wrong, so she nods and raises the photograph up. "It's MudMagnet,"

Mark's jaw sets and his eyes drop to the forest floor, staying longer than the news should require. When he finally looks up, his face is arranged with a concern smoothed into something manageable. "We should leave," he says softly. "This place doesn't feel right."

Erin glances at the ridge again. It is still heavy with fog, still hiding the source of the noises. "There's more." Her voice barely raises above a whisper.

Mark's shoulders stiffen. It's the smallest movement, but it's there. "What else?"

She doesn't show him the mirror shard. She doesn't know why, maybe because Mark's timing is too perfect. "There are coordinates on the back." She flips the picture over, showing numbers that don't point far, two hundred yards, maybe less. It's close enough to taste in the air, close enough that the forest feels complicit. "The picture leads to something else, just like Hidden Hollow."

Mark steps forward and leans in, careful not to touch the photo. His eyes flick across the numbers, then toward the hill behind her, almost as though he knows the direction without consulting his GPS. His swallow is audible. "Okay," he says. "I suppose we should at least check it out."

She wants to trust him, wants his presence to mean safety, but the air around them has become thick with unease. The forest hasn't relaxed and Mark's arrival didn't break the tension she already felt, it just changed its shape.

Erin tucks the photo into her jacket pocket and starts toward the tree line. Mark falls in beside her, a half-step behind, his footsteps soft but still present. The fog swirls around them, thinning in one direction and thickening in another, misleading her feet until any semblance of a worn trail disappears almost immediately. What's left is an animal path, little more than faint depressions in wet earth, a break in the blackberry canes, and the suggestion of forgotten movement through ferns. Erin pushes through and feels the cold mist kiss her cheeks, her wrists, and the back of her throat each time she breathes too deep. This is the one sensation she's thankful for, wetting her dry mouth.

Mark pauses and glances around. "You sure this is right?"

Erin lifts her phone. The arrow stutters, then settles a few degrees east. "Yeah, this way."

He nods but his movement is stiff and he keeps looking off in another direction, the same direction. They climb a narrow rise thick with cedar needles. Erin grips a mossed-over root to steady herself and when she looks back, Mark's face is tight with an expression she can't name. He catches her looking and refocuses quickly, flashing a smile that feels plastic.

At the top of the rise, the fog thins enough to reveal a narrow corridor between two ridges, a place where the forest floor dips in a shallow bowl. Erin stops at the lip and her pulse stutters once, hard enough to shake her breath loose. The coordinates match this exact spot, but there's nothing on the ridge. She knows she should feel relieved, but her chest feels tight with a pressure that has nothing to do with exertion.

"This is it," she says, though she already knows she doesn't want to go any farther.

Mark stands beside her, staring down into the fog-drowned hollow. He doesn't speak or move. The forest silence folds over them while they stare, just two people who shouldn't be here.

Erin steps down into the graveyard of trees fallen through the centuries, covered in damp soil and moss. The forest sinks under her feet and the fog thins just enough to show shapes instead of silhouettes. Erin's boots whisper through wet ferns, each step taking her farther from anything that feels like safety.

Halfway down, the smell hits, a coppery sting through the

earthen aroma. Mark follows behind her but stops. His hand clamps her shoulder sending ice to her veins, but she doesn't look back, torn between what might be behind her and transfixed on a shape just ahead.

The fog refuses to move deeper into the basin, seemingly held at bay by the presence of a man set against a thick tree trunk. Erin goes still as a stone and peers at him, her fingers coiled around the knife hilt. His back is propped against a cedar trunk at an angle that looks almost casual from a distance, but he isn't moving, not even the slight rise and fall of his chest. Erin cautiously moves close enough to see why he's holding so still.

His arms are bound with stripped roots, pulled tight against the bark until the skin is strained around them. His head hangs forward, chin touching his sternum, and his shirt has been sliced open down the center. The fabric isn't quite ripped, it looks cut with careful, almost delicate intention, but with a crude tool. Beneath the splayed shirt, the skin is carved with a pattern that doesn't belong to any wound she's ever seen, deep lines are dragged through the flesh in a language of malice. The shapes make no sense at first glance, but each one looks carved with a steadiness that makes her stomach clench.

One of his hiking boots is missing and the sock on that foot is soaked and dark with mud. The missing boot sits a few feet away. A new Polaroid rests on his thigh. Erin's knees nearly buckle.

The photo is angled facing outward, pointed at whoever finds him, at the direction Erin came, from the body's point-of-view. Mark swears softly behind her. Though her instincts are screaming at her not to, she sets a finger under the man's chin and lifts his heavy head. His face tells Erin what she dreads, this is MudMagnet. Erin recoils and his head drops effortlessly. She can't speak and she can't look away. Erin's hand finds her mouth, she feels her breath shaking through her fingers. He didn't just die here, he was displayed.

For a moment, everything inside Erin goes silent. Not the world, but the part of her that knows how to stand, how to breathe, how to think. She doesn't move until Mark does.

"Jesus…" he whispers, the word landing off-pitch, like he's trying to match a feeling instead of having it. He steps back, not away from danger, but away from her. His boot slips in the mud and he catches himself on a trunk without looking at her.

"We need to call someone," he says. There's a beat of hesitation before he pulls his phone out, like he had to remind himself of the steps humans take in moments like this. Erin nods, but the motion feels detached from her reality. Mark lifts the phone to his ear, then lowers it, then lifts it again, rapid and jittery.

He moves uphill for better signal, farther than he needs to and farther than someone would if they wanted to stay close to her. She hears but doesn't acknowledge his words. "Yeah, dispatch, we're at…" His voice trails with each step of distance. He turns slightly, shoulders angling away.

Erin watches him. Her chest tightens the same way it did when she sensed movement on the ridge. He's not looking at the body, he's not looking at her, he's looking off-trail, toward the thicker fog. What is he expecting?

Another small crack sounds from the ridge. Erin spins toward it, but Mark doesn't, he doesn't even flinch. Instead, he presses the phone harder against his ear and says too quietly, "Yeah. I hear you."

She can't tell if he means dispatch or someone else, which makes her stomach flip. A chill creeps down her spine. She backs a step toward the slope. Her voice is barely a whisper, "Someone's still out here…"

Mark doesn't respond, not until he ends the call. Then he turns around with a face presenting too quickly, too neatly. "They're sending units," he says.

This time, Erin doesn't believe the reassurance in his voice at all. She backs away from MudMagnet's body, not far, but just enough so the cuts aren't the entire world in front of her. The pattern etched into his skin, deliberate strokes dragged with an unhurried hand, stays burned behind her eyes. She can't look at the body anymore, but she can't look away.

She presses her hand to her own body and that's when she feels it, the weight in her jacket, the mirror shard. Her fingers drift beneath the jacket before she realizes she's doing it. The shard is cold under her palm and she freezes with a single, sickening thought flickering into her mind, "This cut him. This touched him. And now it's touching me."

Her stomach flips violently. She nearly pulls it out from instinct, from panic, and desperate need to get it away from her skin, but Mark steps down the embankment toward her, phone still in his hand, and the motion snaps her back to the bigger moment.

If she pulls it out now in front of him, in front of the body, what would Mark think? It would look like she brought it, like she had something to do with this. Would he think she carved him? Her pulse spikes hard enough that she sways.

She pulls her hand out and presses the jacket flat with her hand, wincing at the shape beneath the fabric. She wants to drop it, she wants to throw it into the ferns and let the forest bury it. She wants it gone, but she can't move, can't admit what's pressing against her ribs.

Mark reaches her, his breath is thin and quick. "Did you hear me? They're on their way," he says. His eyes dart between her and the ridge. He doesn't notice the hand on her abdomen.

Erin steps back a half inch, just enough to keep the shard between fabric and silence. The forest presses against the edges of her thoughts, muffling everything except the mirror shard which has become loud and sharp in her mind, warm from her body heat, dragging her focus back to the present.

Her mind begins to unravel in slow, spiraling circles. She could still drop it right now, slip it into the moss, nudge it under the ferns with her boot. Let the forest eat it. For one dizzy moment she even pictures it, the glass shard in the dirt, soft needles blanketing it, the rain sinking it deeper into the mud until no one could ever find it again.

Each fantasy is shattered with the knowledge that her fingers have already touched it, her palms have met the edges. Her prints will be all over it and if someone finds it later, it won't matter how it got there. It'll look like she brought it. She should have left it in the cache, but instead, she brought it right to the body. Her stomach lurches against the hard shard.

She imagines investigating the scene, then producing it like she found it, that would explain the prints. Her eyes land on Mark, realizing he hasn't looked away from her since the phone call. If she pulls it out, he will catch it and she doesn't trust what he'd think, what he'd say, or how he'd look at her afterward.

She looks at MudMagnet, mangled on the forest floor and another thought invades her reasoning. This could be what the killer wanted. She found the Hidden Hollow scene, what if the killer intended this for her? If she finds a way to plant the fragment of mirror at the body, is she undoing something he meant for her? If she keeps it, is she feeding into the game he's building?

She doesn't know the right move, only the wrong ones. Her pulse races until she feels lightheaded. She presses her hand over the pocket, not to hide the shard, but to keep herself from doing something irreversible. She'll have to turn it in to the cops when they arrive. What will they think when she pulls it from her jacket? They might arrest her, or worse, shoot her.

The sirens swell beyond the ferns. Branches crack under boots somewhere in the trees and voices start calling out. Mark raises an arm and shouts, "Down here!" His voice echoes off the bowl's edges.

Erin doesn't answer. She looks back at MudMagnet one last time, the staged body, the Polaroid trembling on his thigh, the cuts carved with a ritualistic calm she can feel in her bones. All she can think is that the killer wanted her to find this, and she brought a piece of him with her.

By the time the first deputy reaches them, Erin's hand is still pressed against her jacket, holding the secret, holding the guilt, holding the thing she cannot explain. She doesn't speak, doesn't look up. She just stands there, trembling as the forest exhales around her and her world fractures a little more.

Chapter 8: Watch For Muggles

The drive back to the station is slowed by commuter traffic, even with flashing police lights. Tenner keeps glued to the Mobile Data Terminal screen mounted between him and Vance, but the GPS marker it displays hasn't changed. It sits pinned to a block he knows by heart, at Harney and 12th, the Sheriff's Office. The exact center of their jurisdiction.

Someone had taken the time to write those coordinates, fold them, and place them beneath a dying woman. The killer wanted them to be found, but not just by anyone, by law enforcement.

Vance's jaw tightens as she swerves around a city bus. "Anything new? You sure the coordinates are right?" she asks.

Tenner taps the screen once with his knuckle, causing the route line to flicker before it restores itself. "Dead on. Whoever wrote it down, they're trying to kick a hornet's nest."

She anticipated that answer and hates that he said it out loud. Traffic thickens as they move off the industrial roads and into the downtown grid, through businesses yawning awake. A bakery's neon sign blinks on as they pass, and a city worker drags cones across a closed lane a block down. The world is greeting the morning with a casual numbness.

Vance's world is not numb, pins and needles shoot through her skin as she turns onto Harney. She skirts the tan brick bulk of the Sheriff's Office, monolithic and indifferent. She slows as they approach, watching a large white box truck exit the gates of the parking garage in the center of the building as they pull to the curb.

The coordinates don't lead to the front entrance. They lead to the service zone, the loading bay, the generators, the staff lot where patrol cars bleed in and out all day. The car stops across from the place no civilian should loiter, a place no one pays attention to, a place the killer has now touched.

Tenner shifts beside her, reading something in her silence. "Mara?"

"Turn off the lights," she says quietly.

Tenner nods and kills the overheads while the cruiser's engine cuts off at the curb, engine ticking softly as it cools. Vance feels the hush settle around them.

She checks the MDT Tenner has been monitoring the entire trip, scrutinizes the map pin at the intersection against what's visible out the windshield, then steps out of the car. A woman in a blazer enters the station through the staff entrance with a travel mug while a deputy crosses the covered lot on his phone, laughing at something unheard. Autumn has left leaves piled under a bench near the back steps.

Nothing looks wrong, but the coordinates on the screen say otherwise. She stands on the edge of the T-intersection, looking down each direction of potential traffic. The pin shows the middle of the intersection, but there's nothing noteworthy there, only bare asphalt. The killer wants her to see something here, but maybe it isn't on the street, just close.

Vance walks to the intersection for a clear view away from the curb and stop sign. She turns away from the Sheriff's Office and examines the large white storage buildings creating a corridor on 12th street, but there is nothing extraordinary. She turns back to face the most obvious landmark, the most audacious choice, the building of the department. She stares at the expansive brick building ahead of her.

Vance walks toward the loading bay. Tenner exits the vehicle and keeps pace at her side. She doesn't approach the garage opening directly, but with a slow, widening arc, letting angles shift, finding where perception changes. Her pulse stays steady, but her breath shallows with quiet and anticipation.

Tenner watches her, confused. "Vance, care to share your thoughts?"

She ignores him, focusing instead on what can be seen, pointing at the mounted cameras, noting where people are most active and what areas get ignored. She stops near the bollards and scans the drain grates with another accusing point of her finger. Tenner makes note.

Vance then focuses on the recessed doorway and maintenance lockboxes, approaching each of them cautiously, her steps ending mere feet away. Her eyes trace the cable conduits leaving the junction box, noticing they haven't been molested. Recognizing her killer wouldn't want to risk discovery, she mutters, "Tempting, but you know that's too close and you'd be seen."

She steps back to the curb and circles again. Tenner watches her watch the building, continuing his steady scrawl of notations. She heads to the white generator housing sitting in the shadow of the building, checking the cables first, then the access panels. There's no evidence of tampering here, either.

She circles it like prey until she reaches the shadow behind it, the narrow gap between the metal housing and the building's brick wall. This area is partially protected from street view, shielded from windows, and blocked from the security camera above the loading bay door, a perfect dead zone. It is also apparently a place where someone is storing empty pallets, despite regulations.

Vance stops. She shifts her stance left, then right, checking reflections and angles from rooftops. She counts the discarded pallets filed against the building and scans the ground for debris or trampled lawn, finding evidence that someone stepped into this gap recently. She looks at Tenner. "Get CSU," she says softly. "Now."

Tenner steps away to call CSU, his voice low, clipped, feeling unnerved but not yet sure why. Vance doesn't move, she just studies the narrow slit behind the generator housing, committing every angle to memory. The space is roughly five feet wide, enough room for a person to slip behind.

She crouches beside the pallet stack, her fingertips brushing the concrete. It's cold and gritty with silica dust, but nothing is disturbed on the surface, nothing has been scraped or dragged recently. The only things out of place are an old rusted washer bleeding rust onto the ashen concrete and a scattering of cigarette butts wadded up and decaying at the corner, something she'll have to address in a department meeting later.

Whoever came here placed something with care, but this time, it wasn't a body, not that she can see from her investigation. Tenner returns to her side. "CSU's scrambling. They'll be right out."

"Good." She doesn't look at him. "Take a step back."

Tenner knows the tone and moves. Vance lowers herself slowly, angling to avoid crunching loose debris, and peers between the slats of wood, then down the length of the cement pad that the generators hold down. That's where she sees it, a corner of metal, dark green, and too clean to belong to the detritus around it. She's sure it is a stashed ammo can.

Her pulse doesn't change, but a feeling inside her drops with a subtle, sinking certainty. She doesn't reach for it, she just memorizes the angle and stands, brushing grit from her palms.

Tenner sees her expression. "You got something?"

"It's there," she murmurs.

Two techs exit the man door just inside the garage gate scanning the side of the building until they find Vance and Tenner by the generator. Vance guides them with a tilt of her head. When they arrive on scene, with quick direction, they get to work. One tech performs a sweep, visually checking the top of the pallets and the upper slats, shining a light for wires, scanning for lines, and focusing on pallet bases for plates. The other tech begins scanning the perimeter of the generators, checking the mounting bolts in the process.

The first tech kneels, shining a low-intensity light behind the pallets. The beam catches the ammo can's side, illuminating the Army surplus stencil and weathered paint. "Position looks intentional," he says quietly.

Vance's nod is small and technical, devoid of emotions. She's profiling the hider, not the object.

The kneeling tech deploys a mirror wand, sliding it behind the pallets to check for triggering mechanisms. After verifying the clutter is clear, he turns to his partner. "Pallets first?"

She pulls a camera as a response and photographs the scene, capturing the cluttered clearance path, the generator and pallets, even the rusted washer Vance recognized earlier. While she is capturing the untouched scene, the other CSU marks the corner of each pallet with neon flags for a later analysis. Only then do they lift, not drag, each pallet, repeating the steps until the path is cleared.

Once access to the metal box has been fully uncovered, the tech threads a gloved hand into the gap, steady and slow, first measuring the can, then performing another tripwire investigation, and finally easing it forward without lifting it. He works it free inch by inch, pulls it from the manmade hole, and sets it down gently, waiting for his partner to photograph the evidence.

Tenner lets out a breath he's been holding. When the tech reaches for the lid, he asks, "Shouldn't we get the bomb squad?"

The tech stops mid-reach and looks at Vance. She shakes her head slightly. "That's not the goal of whoever left this here. They're killing individual people, not blowing up cop shops. There's something else in that can."

The techs look at each other, hesitating for a moment, then flip the latches with a precise click, and pries open the lid. One pulls his hand away and exhales, giving his partner the opportunity to photograph the contents. They both wait for the curse Tenner tried whispering into existence and are each quietly relieved at the silence.

Inside, an old analog camcorder is wrapped in clear plastic. The second tech takes one more photograph. Vance's lips go tight and she wishes in that moment it was a bomb.

The tech looks up. "You want us to turn it on?"

"No," Vance says, quiet and absolute. "Not out here."

She steps forward, snapping on gloves. The morning light catches the plastic exterior and throws a dull sheen across the lens. She extracts the camcorder from the can and rotates it in her hand, then hands it to the tech.

"Take it and dust it," she tells the techs. "Then clear a room with a projector."

Tenner starts to speak, but the look she gives him shuts it down before it leaves his mouth. The second tech takes the camera and the ammo box inside while her partner stands next to the pallets and radios for assistance.

Vance walks inside with Tenner mere steps behind. She stops long enough in the hallway to jot a few quick notes into her field log of the coordinates, container type, and placement, and the odd care taken to find a path to avoid station security systems. She points Tenner in the direction of their cubicles. "Get your notes in order, there's going to be a whole lot more."

She doesn't join him, opting to make her way to command for a brief update on the crime scene in Hazel Dell. She also discloses the other set of coordinates, providing enough information to alert them of the container outside and the potential connotations of a cat-and-mouse game with authorities. Her next stop is the conference room they've set aside. She enters the empty room and sits.

She hates waiting, it leaves too much room for the morning's victim to surface behind her eyes and for the killer's taunt to replay in her head. By the time CSU brings the camera in, her thoughts have settled into a low, steady thrum, preparing her for whatever comes next. The CSU tech plugs the camcorder into power and a video cable, ensures the projector is live, then leaves, closing the door behind her. Vance is alone in the conference room with the camcorder sitting in the center of the table. The plastic wrap has been removed, showing its buttons scuffed with age. She doesn't stall. She hits PLAY and the tape crackles to life with a hiss of static.

For a moment, there's only darkness. Then the frame lurches, stabilizes, and resolves into a concrete wall mottled with moisture. The camera shifts, framing on a man sitting on the floor. He is alive, but barely. His hands are bound behind him with something dark, maybe a cord, a wire, possibly a belt. She can't quite make out the restraint from the camera angle. His ankles are tied as well and there's blood on his cheek, which is smeared, not dripping. He's breathing fast and his shoulders are hitching.

The camera stays back far enough that the figure behind it is unseen. A voice speaks, but it is masked with a distortion modulator of some type, something that sounds cheap. The words are low and flat and the tone is so artificial its hum nearly drowns the words. "Look at him."

The bound man flinches at the statement and Vance's jaw tightens. The camera doesn't move closer, it just waits, as if expecting obedience from both its subject and its audience. The man tries to sit upright, his breath stutters from the attempt and his wide eyes focus on the person outside the frame. The voice continues. "This is what happens when a game has no rules."

Vance forces her breath to slow. The killer isn't talking to the victim, but to his audience, to her.

The captive whispers something the audio doesn't catch. He squeezes his eyes shut, shaking his head, as if pleading for sense more than mercy. A black nitrile gloved hand enters the frame, gripping a long shard of mirrored glass, long and cracked.

Vance inhales sharply, knowing this is going to be nothing more than torture porn disguised as justification. The camera angle never shifts enough to reveal the killer's body, just the hand and the tool. On screen, the victim panics and tries to speak again, but the words break into wet breaths. The killer's modulated voice interrupts, pointing the shard at him. "You leave evidence everywhere. Footprints. Logs. Photos. All of you. And you expect no one to notice?"

The captive shakes his head rapidly, a pathetic, instinctive denial. "Oh," the voice hums, "but she notices."

The bottom drops out of Vance's stomach. She. Not "they," not "you." She.

The gloved hand grips the man's jaw, forcing his face toward the lens and his eyes, wide with terror, lock onto the camera. "This one," the modulated voice says softly, "is not for them."

The shard lifts, angling toward the ribs. The captive convulses, teeth bared in a silent cry. The slice lands with a sickening tear, ripping through the fabric of the shirt and slicing flesh. The man screams, high and raw. Vance's fingernails dig into the table edge.

The camera watches the victim doubling over. It sees the point of mirror buried shallow, withdrawn, buried again. The stabbing isn't frenzied, the gloved hand is mindful, particular about the motions. The killer remains precise, rhythmic, and controlled, while the voice speaks over the screams. "You want motive. You want pathology. You want boxes on a form to dismiss what I see and do as deranged."

Another strike. "You want me to fit into a case file so you can shut it and claim justice has been served. You want to make me one of your solved cases." The gloved hand sets the shard down with a soft clink. "But I am not yours."

The killer steps backward, never entering frame and never

dropping the modulated voice. Then, calm as an electronic lullaby, the killer says, "She'll understand. Not you."

The camera remains steady for eight long seconds, letting the victim's gasps fill the audio, before clicking off, allowing silence to swallow everything. Vance stands motionless. For a long moment the only sound in the room is the faint hum of the fluorescent ballast in the ceiling and the soft settling of the camcorder's machinery cooling down. She realizes her hand is still on the table, gripping the edge so tightly the joints ache. She releases it slowly, flexing her fingers. The killer had spoken directly to the camera, to her. He's challenging her.

Vance pushes off the table and steps back, needing space. The overhead light flickers once, a harmless electrical quirk she's seen a thousand times, but today it feels like the building is trying to say something. She forces herself to analytically replay the tape in her mind, careful to force out emotions.

This was someone who planned the recording as carefully as the kill, who knows forensic limitations. This person thinks they can beat Vance in behavioral profiling. They were careful to avoid showing their body, didn't wear rings under their gloves, prepared the lighting to avoid casting a shadow. They want to play games, they want to be known, want fame at Vance's expense.

Vance rubs her temple with her thumb, pushing down a rising throb. She tries to stand straight, but she feels slightly off-center, like gravity has shifted an inch left. There is something in the one line that won't leave her, 'She'll understand.'

The words ring in her ears and she tries to shove them aside, tries to ground herself in the familiar mechanics of profiling and procedure, anything that feels like control, but her thoughts keep slipping, refusing to land where they should.

She thinks of Erin Caldwell, of the Hidden Hollow. The thought comes fast and unwelcome. Vance tries to shove it aside. It doesn't make sense; it shouldn't make sense. She hates that her mind went there. It was a reflex, her mind was overloaded by the video, that's all. Still, the thought clings, impossible to shake entirely.

She looks down at the camcorder. The device shows no triumph, no signature flourish or taunting decoration, it's just a tool, a delivery system. This wasn't a trophy; it was a chapter. The idea makes Vance's skin prickle.

This person isn't killing for release or notoriety, and these aren't killings for anger or compulsion. These murders are designed to shape a sequence, to write a story and the police, the geocaches, the victims, they are pieces on a board this person believes is already mapped.

A soft knock breaks the silence, followed by Tenner's voice filtering through the door. "Detective? Command heard about the camcorder and wants another update on your findings, whenever you're ready."

She doesn't answer right away. She glances at the camcorder again, its lens dull in the fluorescent light. When she finally speaks, her voice is steady. "Have CSU check with anyone who was outside this morning. Staff, deputies, deliveries, anyone. Pull the last hour of badge-entry logs and video feed from all cameras."

Tenner shifts, unsettled. "You hoping for eyewitnesses?"

Vance rests her hand on the back of the chair to steady the part of her that hasn't quite calmed, the part of her the doctors keep warning about. She unplugs the camcorder and places it back in the forensics bag. Her pulse is a cold, tight thread. "Maybe," she says. "Or maybe we catch someone who thinks they didn't get seen."

She reaches for the light switch and the room drops into shadow. "This person was close," she adds quietly. "Close enough to study us."

Vance opens the conference room door with the camcorder sealed for evidence. Tenner waits in the hallway, straight-backed, and hands clasped around his field journal. Before she can say anything more, her radio cracks to life. "Unit Nine-Three, priority call." The dispatcher's voice is fast but monotoned.

Tenner straightens immediately. Vance reaches under her jacket and lifts her shoulder mic. "Nine-Three, go."

"We've got a 911. Caller reports a deceased male. Outdoor location."

Her breath leaves in a cold, controlled exhale. "Caller's name?" she asks, already anticipating the answer.

"Mark Leland."

That wasn't the name she expected, but it's close. Tenner mutters something under his breath. Vance doesn't register his comment, her focus narrowing to a single point. "Location?" she says.

Dispatch reads off a mile marker on Washougal River Road and the detective's shoulders lock, the smallest tightening of muscles beneath her coat. "That's an hour out. Is the caller on scene?" she asks.

"Yes, Detective. He states he's not alone, with a female. Another geocacher?"

Vance closes her eyes for half a second, feeling the weight of knowing settle. "You have a name for the woman?" She hopes for one she's never heard.

"Erin Caldwell."

The world folds inward. Of course. She snaps back to motion. "Dispatch, do we have responding units en route?"

"Affirmative. Two deputies rolling in from Salmon Falls. ETA eight minutes."

"Tell them this may be connected to a Hazel Dell homicide. I want the scene secured, no one in or out until I arrive."

"Acknowledged."

The radio clicks silent and Vance turns to Tenner. "Gear up.

We're going right now."

He hesitates, eyes dropping toward the evidence bag in her hand with the camcorder. "Detective, do you think this is the same…"

She cuts him short, "Yes."

Tenner swallows and nods. Vance steps past him, walking fast toward the exit, her boots quiet against the tile. The hallway seems brighter now, the hum of fluorescents invade against the reality hammering inside her thoughts. She takes the evidence to CSU and drops it on the closest desk. "Run every analysis you can on this recording and do it now."

She leaves as abruptly as she entered. The techs get to work, and the video already comes to life again behind her. The building feels smaller while the killer's message echoes through its vents. She doesn't look back, hitting the exit door at a stride. Outside, the daylight is crisp and clear and the world looks clean, though it feels anything but. Vance climbs into the cruiser with Tenner sliding into the passenger seat. She starts the engine and guns onto Harney without waiting for traffic to clear.

As the siren kicks on, she realizes her hands are strangling the wheel and she forces them loose.

She'll understand, the killer said. The words scrape at her nerves as the siren rises. Whether the killer meant Vance or Erin, she isn't letting this psychopath get another inch.

Chapter 9: Under Review

The squad car door shuts with a weight that doesn't match the gentle click of its latch. Erin sits in the back of the squad car waiting for a verdict with her knees pulled close and her fingertips pressing into the fabric of her pants. The wilderness pull-off outside is all motion from deputies threading in and out of the forest's edge or stretching yellow tape from trunk to trunk. She catches an occasional murmur of radio as an official passes the car, but the whispers are indecipherable through the door. While she can't hear the words, she can read the shapes they make on the uniformed faces.

Mark is near another cruiser, talking fast and motioning erratically, almost defensive. His hands move in sharp little arcs, his posture tight, and his shoulders are turned slightly away from the deputy taking his statement. Something in him looks cornered, but Erin can't tell if it's guilt or terror or just the shock settling into his bones.

She presses her forehead lightly against the car window. It's a cold, steady relief, until her reflection stares back with wide eyes and blown-out pupils. She looks away from herself, down at the mud spattered across her sleeves, specifically a smear near her collar she didn't notice until now. There is one dark spot that isn't mud and it isn't hers, it's MudMagnet's. She recoils from the recognition and swallows the thoughts flooding her solitude.

A radio outside squawks again and two deputies jog past the car. One glances toward her, neither unkind nor suspicious, just trying to place her in the chaos. She can see in that moment, even from where she sits, the gears turning in him, wondering if she is a witness, victim, or suspect.

At the edge of the already crowded lot, another cruiser rolls in quiet and without lights. Detective Vance steps out, her expression is controlled but sharp, cutting the silent scene beyond the window. An officer intercepts her before she reaches the tape, speaking quickly, pointing toward the thick of the woods, then toward Mark, and finally at Erin.

Erin can't hear the words, she only sees Vance go still, her stare becoming long and measured. She watches the detective nod, then starts toward the clearing. Erin exhales so slowly it feels like her ribs might collapse inward and she drops her gaze to her trembling hands.

She keeps watching the world move from behind the squad car glass. Deputies search using flashlights, they talk into their radios. Mark's voice rises and then drops at the other squad car. After a moment, Vance comes back into view, getting closer with every step, her expression unreadable as she marches toward Erin.

She sits straighter, finding ground between bracing and hoping. She has no idea what Vance is going to say, no idea what Mark is telling them, and no idea what she is supposed to do. She only knows one thing with absolute certainty, whatever happened in those woods, it isn't done with her yet.

The gravel shifts under Vance's boots as she crosses the pullout, her movements sharp and purposeful, but not rushed. Erin watches her through the streaked window, pulse thudding in her ears. It feels strange, being contained like this. Not arrested, not detained, but shut in, both protected and managed. The door only opens from the outside and Erin hates that.

Vance reaches the cruiser and speaks with the deputy posted at the hood. Erin sees the deputy gesture vaguely toward her and speak. She doesn't catch everything, but the officer's deep voice vibrates through the window enough for Erin to catch that he's saying she gave a statement and that they put her in the car to keep her away from the body.

Vance's expression shifts, a subtle disapproval at the handling of the scene, but not at Erin. She steps around the door, lifting the handle, causing the latch to release with a thunk. Cold air slips in as Vance opens the door wide.

"Erin," she says, her tone is sharp and procedural. "You can step out."

Erin moves stiffly, her body seeming to forget its own instructions. As soon as her feet hit the ground, she realizes how exhausted her knees feel, how shaky the earth underneath her seems. Vance keeps a half-step distance, enough to give space, but close enough to catch her if her legs betray her.

"You did the right thing staying put," Vance says. "My officer didn't mean to make that feel punitive."

Erin almost laughs, not because Vance's statement was humorous, but because she doesn't know how else to react. "I know. I just." Her throat tightens around a swell of emotion she has to breathe through. "I didn't want to touch anything. Or move. I just didn't want to make anything worse."

Vance nods once, slow. "You didn't make anything worse." The kindness stings more than any accusation would've.

Vance studies her for a steady moment. Erin tries to hold herself still, but her hands won't cooperate, so she tucks them under her arms to hide the shaking, squeezing her shoulders together in hopes the huddle hides the shape of the shard in her jacket.

"You're not under suspicion," Vance says, reading the tension without Erin having to name it. "But you are part of this. And that means I'm not comfortable sending you home alone tonight."

Erin's pulse flutters, the words hitting her in layers of relief, fear, and confusion. "I have people," she manages. "I can go to my sister's. I have a few friends. I don't know. I'm not planning to be alone."

Vance looks toward where Mark is still talking to a deputy. A muscle in her jaw shifts, the smallest tell of a reaction she doesn't voice. "I won't tell you where to go," Vance says. "Just don't isolate, not tonight."

The implication lands heavily, but Erin holds it.

"And Erin…" Vance adds, lowering her voice, a soft edge of warning threading through it. "What you saw in there is going to hit in waves. You're going to feel steady one minute and wrecked the next. That's normal. None of this means you did anything wrong."

Erin nods, but her stomach twists, because the mirror fragment in her jacket reminds her that she has actually done something wrong. She wants to tell Vance, to give her the evidence, but she can't. Not here, not with Mark maybe watching. Not with every gun-toting deputy in a fifty-foot radius looking for who killed MudMagnet. Vance watches her for a moment longer and Erin feels seen in a way that's both comforting and unnerving. She isn't sure if the detective is reading her guilt or reading her trauma.

Behind them, Mark raises his voice again and Erin flinches at the sound. There's heat under the syllables. The deputy tries to calm him and Vance tracks the argument with her eyes, then returns to Erin. "I'm going to talk to him next," Vance says. "You don't need to stay for that."

Erin nods again, feeling the slightest bit of relief. She doesn't want to relive that moment in the woods, and she certainly doesn't want to hear it from the man who stood behind her the entire time.

"But if I need you," Vance adds, "I'll call."

There's a grimness in her tone and Erin can't tell if it is a promise or a warning, but she doesn't care to stick around to figure out which it is. She goes to her car and leaves as fast as she can without looking like she's fleeing from the crime scene, carefully navigating through the maze of official vehicles.

A short drive and a thousand frantic thoughts later, Erin finally gets into the sanctity of her apartment and shuts the door with her heel. She locks the knob and the deadbolt, and for the first time in ages, slides the chain lock into place. She doesn't bother turning on the lights. The dark feels safer, like she won't have to see anything she isn't ready for. Her pack sags off her shoulder and hits the floor with a muted thud. The shard is inside, wrapped and waiting.

She shoves her jacket off and drops it straight to the floor in the entryway, the fabric folding in on itself. Her shirt follows, then her pants, which are still damp with creek water. Her socks smear a line of mud across the hardwood as she kicks them off with toes that are still frigid and barely working. She gathers everything into a single pile near the wall, creating a tightly bunched heap of fabric and grit. She makes sure it isn't touching anything else, keeping it contained and controlled. She doesn't think about why, she just needs it all in one place.

She turns back to the pack, naked now but no more vulnerable. Her thoughts remind her of the truth of the contents, even when she looks away. She hesitates through pursed lips, then grabs the bag by a strap, shivering at the touch.

She forces herself toward the kitchen, turning the overhead light on with a hand that trembles. She reaches into the pack, pulls the cloth-wrapped shard out by its corners, and sets it on the counter. She doesn't open it, she just stares. The shape beneath the cloth is small for its significance. Erin keeps thinking it is impossible that something so ordinary could pull so much blood. Her stomach rolls and she spins toward the bathroom.

The tile is cold under her feet, then her knees when they land on either side of the toilet. She stares into the porcelain abyss, breathing deep, bringing in the nauseating tang of bleach water. The chemical scent is the last encouragement her stomach needs to revolt.

The release is a momentary reprieve, and she lingers just above the swill, until the pounding in her head settles. When it does, she stands and turns the shower on hot, stepping in before the water adjusts. The burn is a penance that hits her bare skin. It should hurt, but she's too numb, her nerves feel like they're turned off completely.

She breathes in the steam, giving her chest the chance to expand fully. The heat finally makes her skin itch. Her skin, covered in murder, in MudMagnet. The silence of his corpse is on her, crawling through the pores, deep into her. She yanks her faded blue loofah from the shower shelf and scrubs herself violently, attacking her shoulders, arms, under her nails, anywhere the memory of today has touched her.

When she finally turns the water off, the quiet envelops her harder than the spray. She sits on the edge of the tub, dripping, arms folded tight around her stomach, and breaks apart without a sound. She gives in to the shuddering collapse her body has been holding back since the woods. Her cheeks are wet long after the shower water dries on her skin.

There's a thud outside, maybe a car door, maybe a dumpster lid, she can't tell which. It makes her flinch so violently her shoulder hits the sliding shower door. Her heart thrums through the veins in her neck and she holds her breath to listen, but she's met with silence.

She stands too fast and catches herself on the sink, facing her reflection in the mirror. For a split second, it's not hers at all, it's MudMagnet, slack jaw, eyes blown wide, in the exact moment his body stopped being alive. Her jaw quivers until the image evaporates into her own reflection, paler than usual, pupils huge, and her hair plastered to her cheeks. "Stop," she whispers to the memory, to the whole world.

She hangs her towel with a still-shaky hand and walks back to the kitchen in slow, disjointed steps. The apartment is too bright, even without the lights on. The shard is still on the counter. She looks away, but it lingers in the corner of her vision, condemning her decision to keep it. She edges closer until her hands are braced on either side of the fragment on the counter and she forces herself to face the truth sitting between her and the police. The blood stares back, dark and dry. The phantom metallic smell hits her. She clamps her jaw shut and breathes through her nose until the new wave of nausea passes. She has the last thing that touched MudMagnet, the thing that showed him death, but what does she do with it? She damns herself again, knowing she should have turned it over immediately, she should have told Mark. Now it's too late. Giving it to Vance won't look like innocence, it'll look like she had a reason to hide a truth she doesn't know.

Her phone sits on the counter where she left it. She unlocks it, and the GPS app is still open. She never closed it in the woods, now it stares back at her in judgment. She pinches the screen, zooming the map out and stares at the pindrops she set to track. North is Hidden Hollow, west is Hazel Dell, and east is the pin she dropped last. The last cache MudMagnet will ever find. All three pins pointing away from Vancouver in different directions, all three ended someone's story.

She zooms back in on the last pin with shaky digits and the map blurs for a moment, or her eyes do. "Stop," She warns herself once more. With a deep inhale, she closes the app.

The apartment feels even smaller now and the walls are closing in, watching, listening. She turns the kitchen light on to chase the shadows away and the shard on the counter catches it. She backs away from the reflection, wrapping her arms around her torso, standing bare while the world keeps tilting.

Outside, a neighbor walks past, jingling their keys. Erin's whole body flinches at the sound and she sprints to the door to double-check her deadbolt. She rests a palm on the door and presses her forehead to the frame. She tells herself she has to keep moving or she'll stay frozen in this spot forever.

Miles east, under a dying Washougal sky, Detective Vance hasn't slowed either. She stands with the last deputy on scene as CSU packs up their cases, their van idling at the edge of the pullout. The air still carries the trace of wet leaves and murder, Vance can feel it settling on her skin, another layer of human depravity she'll carry forever. She flips open her notepad and reviews her own scrawling. She's collected quick, sharp notes, connected by lines and arrows. Everything here should be adding up, but it isn't. She doesn't know all the missing pieces, but she can tell where they are supposed to fit.

"Detective Vance." A CSU tech approaches, gloves still on, mask pulled down under his chin. He looks tense, but not rattled. He seems seasoned enough to know his way around death. "We finished initial analysis," he says. "The wound patterns are controlled and show minimal hesitation. The depth and angle are consistent with a smaller weapon."

"Smaller how?" Vance asks.

"The entry wounds are irregular. The edges are sharp, but not clean. This isn't a precision cutting tool, more like..."

"A shard of glass," Vance finishes for him.

The tech looks surprised she said it first. "Yeah, something like that."

Vance glances toward the taped-off clearing. The grass is flattened where an army of footprints has passed. Deputies are rolling tape back onto spools. Flashlights scout the ground one last time, catching flecks of moisture and nothing else.

"Did you recover the weapon?" she asks.

The tech's hesitation is almost imperceptible, but Vance is trained for these micro-tells. "No. Nothing in the immediate radius. The trails are clear and there are no prints leading away with blood transfer. If I were to guess, the perp took it from the scene."

"How about the container site, anything in the box, or around the stump? Did you check the drainpipe?"

"Nothing, ma'am. We bagged everything there, including the container."

Vance's jaw tightens. "Check the gear again. Evidence bags, pockets, field tables. Make sure no one accidentally packed something sharp."

"We already did." His tone stays respectful, but certain. "We didn't miss it."

Vance doesn't press any further, she knows this team doesn't miss things. Which means someone else has the shard she saw in the video back at the precinct. She turns toward the first deputies who responded, two younger officers standing near their cruiser. She calls them over with a wag of her fingers. "You two were first on the scene?"

"Yes, ma'am," the taller one says. "We arrived seven minutes after the call. Both witnesses were still within vicinity of the victim. The man approached us. The woman was about ten feet from the vic. We secured the immediate area."

"Did either of you observe anything near the body? I'm talking about a shard of mirror, about this long." She frames a near footlong gap with her index fingers.

Both shake their heads and the shorter deputy adds, "No, ma'am. Nothing like that, just the hikers and the body."

"Geocachers." Vance corrects them, but they don't seem to acknowledge the difference. She dismisses the officers and looks back toward the trees. Somewhere in this clearing, a murder happened with a weapon that wasn't left behind and wasn't overlooked, it just no longer exists.

Her phone buzzes with a message from Command, requesting another status update, which frustrates her. While she's aware this is the closest Vancouver has come to a potential serial killer since 1989, she hates feeling like she doesn't have room to work. She types a short response and pockets the phone.

Tenner appears at her side, rubbing his hands together to keep them warm. "CSU's about packed up. Do you want the perimeter extended, see if we can get anything else further out?"

"Yes. Thirty yards," Vance says. "I want the fallen logs searched too. Any place where something could be stashed. These people play hide-and-seek every day, we need to be better at their little game." Tenner nods, but the look he gives her says he already knows they won't find anything.

She stands still for a moment, letting the breeze settle around her. The fog has crept further into the forest, but the air has a damp heaviness that feels just as thick. Her eyes track the faint path Erin must have taken. Vance tries to navigate the stretch of earth where Erin found the body, looking for a spot where she might've stepped over the weapon without knowing. The search is slow, Vance is used to urban investigation, but still knows the patterns of people, regardless of terrain. She makes her way to the cache first, then the site where the body was found, checking the forest with an investigator's depth, but still finds nothing. She can't shake the itch that the weapon should be here.

On her way back to the lot, she doesn't stop searching. When she leaves the forest empty-handed, she finds Tenner. "We'll wrap here," she says. "Meet me back at the station after transport arrives."

Tenner jogs off to relay the order. Vance stays a moment longer, scanning the clearing, waiting for it to confess, but the woods are dead quiet. The scene that was left for them today came with an absence, a gap from a puzzle piece she can't find.

That piece is displayed on Erin's kitchen counter. She's been staring at it for over an hour but can't bring herself to move it again, can't seem to push it out of sight. It sits there, wrapped in cloth slightly darkened with a stain she knows but refuses to name. She turns the kitchen light off before walking to the bedroom, hoping the darkness will blunt the edge of the memory, but it doesn't.

Her bed is soft when she sinks into it, but too clean, untouched by what happened in the woods. She lies on her side with her knees drawn up and she pulls the blanket over her shoulder. Her body curls in on itself before her mind recognizes the motion. She tries to breathe, to let the mattress ground her, but every few seconds the air thins and her chest tightens, forcing her to start over.

A car passes outside and its headlights push a thin bar of white across her ceiling. Her breath catches, waiting for something to step through the wall, though nothing does. She exhales into her pillow and her ribs shake. She presses her palms against the mattress, grounding herself in the texture of the fabric.

She keeps telling herself to close her eyes, and each time, for a moment, it's just darkness. MudMagnet's face invades that darkness, his jaw slack, his eyes open but vacant, and lips just barely parted, like he's about to whisper something he never got to say.

Erin's eyes snap open. Her breath stumbles out in a sharp, broken exhale, and she rolls onto her back, staring at the ceiling hoping it can stop the image from slipping under her eyelids again. It doesn't help. The afterimage clings to her vision, burned into her retinas.

She presses the heel of her hand to her forehead. Her skin is hot and her pulse is loud. She tries again to close her eyes, but again, the same face, that last expression frozen in a memory she can't forget.

She flips onto her stomach, burying her face in the pillow, trying to force the world into silence, and stays like that until her breath evens out just enough to keep from shaking. The apartment settles around her. The refrigerator hums and a neighbor upstairs walks across the floor. These are her normal sounds, familiar and ordinary, but none of them calm her. All she sees is the body and the blood. Erin stares at the dark until her eyes ache. She won't sleep tonight, she already knows that. Every time her blink lingers, he's there. She can feel it in a place she shouldn't feel. The killer meant for her to carry this moment with her, pressed a message into her skin.

Today wasn't a find, it was a warning.

Chapter 10: Within Range

Erin wakes up, not remembering when she fell asleep. The light in her apartment is gray and thin, lazily washed over the furniture through the blinds. Her mouth is dry, her eyes are gritty, and her back screams with stiffness. At some point, she moved to the couch but doesn't recall what time it was. She does remember feeling like the bed sheets were trying to strangle her. Her phone is face down on the floor beside a crumpled blanket. Everything in her apartment feels contaminated with dark memories now and none of it belongs to her.

She sits up slowly with her palms braced against the cushion in case the room tries to tilt. The motion gives a dull sting up her left shoulder, reminding her of the place Mark steadied her yesterday, she instantly pulls away from the memory.

She drags her gaze to the kitchen counter, recognizing the shard is still there, wrapped in the same stained cloth. She hoped it would be gone, that the mirror was just a part of a bad dream. She should have thrown it away last night. She wanted to smash it into a million pieces, to get rid of it, but she didn't. She'd left it exactly where she set it, and it stayed the night. She looks away, her jaw tightening at the return of the sickening feeling, her tastebuds tingling with the onset of excess saliva.

Her phone buzzes once, making a tiny tremor against the floor. The sound ricochets through the apartment and Erin freezes. Another buzz tells her it is a notification tone, so she doesn't pick it up, she doesn't even touch it. She waits until the screen goes dark again before leaning forward and flipping it over with two fingers, afraid it will bite her.

Her lock screen blooms with a backlog of alerts that filled her phone in the night. The pulldown shows news updates, weather, a notification from her bank, two missed calls from her sister, a message from Mark she refuses to open. At the bottom is a notification from the app, a message request from another cacher, **TrailTempest**.

Her teeth set. It's probably nothing, people message about caches all the time. Still, her fingers curl inward, expecting the phone might threaten her. She isn't ready to answer more questions, so she doesn't open the message yet.

She pulls her knees to her chest and stares across the floor, retracing last night's steps where her boots tracked in last night's forest mud she never cleaned. It dried overnight and flaked into little crumbs. She sees the Washougal trail in those steps and her breath gives a thin stutter. Her reality feels distant, like she's looking at her life through a dirty window.

She finally stands, slow and careful, feeling yesterday's stress aching throughout her body. She pulls the blanket over her shoulders and walks to the kitchen for coffee, checking the shard without touching it, just to make sure it is real. The gleam from the window confirms it which makes everything more surreal.

Downtown, the digital forensics room is alive with activity under bright fluorescent bulbs. It is a tight room full of electronic equipment, half-empty coffee cups, chairs that haven't rolled properly in ages, and a bulletin board that hasn't been updated in three months.

Ryan sits crooked in his chair with one foot tucked under a knee as he scrolls through the Discord server used by the Vancouver geocache community. His hair is barely dry, telling his partner he rushed in before finishing his morning routine, and the way he keeps rubbing his eyes says he didn't sleep much, either.

Across the table, Shannon has three tabs open: a Facebook

group, one of the geocache websites, and a spreadsheet she started this morning to keep things straight. "Okay, the Facebook group has… Jesus. Two hundred new comments since last night. I can't tell what's rumor and what's people running their mouths."

Ryan laughs, "First day on the internet?" He scrolls back up on Discord, watching messages cascade in real time. Emojis flare and users tag each other faster than he can read. "This group is losing its mind. Someone posted a blurry picture of a deputy cruiser at the Washougal site, so now half of them think it's a manhunt and the other half think it's fake."

Shannon responds without turning from her monitors, "General consensus on Facebook is that the river is flooding."

"You got the boomer duty," Ryan fires back with a chuckle, "I've even got one user who thinks it's aliens." He snorts once, a short, cynical laugh.

A post pings to the top of his feed:

LunaCacher: Wasn't WTPB just posted???? Why is it archived already???

Three replies appear almost instantly.

GorgeHopper: Because something bad happened. Somebody got hurt. Probably another murder.

GarminOffGrid: Stop spreading fear, dude.

MapNerd: Let's stay calm, everyone. Archivals happen for safety reasons. We don't have all the facts yet.

Ryan mutters, "This MapNerd guy talks like he's in customer service."

Shannon agrees in her own disinterested way, "He does sound helpful, but Facebook loves him. They keep quoting him like he's the voice of reason."

"Discord is roasting him for popping into conversations instantly. Someone literally asked if he's a bot." Ryan right-clicks the username and pulls it up in a second tab but doesn't stray far from the active conversation. Another burst of pings slams the screen.

TrailTempest: It's fine. Probably just Oregon Trail drama again.

CacheSiren: DON'T post the coords in here ffs

HarborHawk: Dude someone said they saw police out there

RidgeRabbit: stop being a ghoul omg

The messages collide so quickly Ryan stops trying to read them in order. He turns to his partner, ignoring the chatter for a moment. "You ever think about trying this hobby? It seems kind of fun when it's not," He gestures to his screen. "whatever the hell this is."

"Nope." Shannon doesn't even entertain the notion. She fills out cells in her spreadsheet without slowing for the response.

Ryan tilts his head. "That was quick."

"I'm not hiking into the woods to find Tupperware because a stranger said so."

"I'm sure it's not all Tupperware." He turns back to the scrolling chat.

Shannon pushes her resistance. "I'm sure it's not all dead bodies either, doesn't mean I want to get lost in the woods."

Ryan opens his mouth, then shuts it again. He concedes and hops over to the MapNerd profile. "…yeah, okay. Fair point."

She scrolls through the Facebook feed and pauses. "Huh."

"What?"

"Facebook's staying pretty calm. They're just confused. Asking about weather closures, trail hazards, SAR activity. Lots of secondhand 'my cousin said.' But nothing concrete." She clicks again. "Except here. Look." She rotates her monitor.

A post from the **Vancouver Cache Crew** group sits at the top:

Surveyor (Reviewer): This listing has been archived for safety. Please avoid the area until further notice. We will post updates when appropriate. Thank you.

It has thirty likes and no arguments. "No fights, that's a first. The thread slowed to a crawl under the authority of that one note."

"Surveyor." Ryan rolls the name around in his mouth. "Is he some official guy?"

"Absofruitly, and apparently, the community trusts him. Every question quiets down after he posts." She flips to another tab she has opened. "See, it happened here about a week ago on another discussion." She takes a sip of lukewarm coffee and grimaces.

"Discord is the opposite. Every time someone mentions police, it explodes. Like, look, they're literally making memes now." He flips his screen around for her to see. Someone has posted a badly edited Bigfoot holding a gun and a GPS unit.

Shannon sighs. "God help us."

Ryan taps a few keys, saving screenshots to a folder. "Okay, so we've got one group freaking out, one group trying to rationalize, and one dude calming all of them down."

"I'm logging it as community reaction. It might be nothing."

"Yeah. I don't have anything solid yet, just chatter."

"Chatter can still matter." She doesn't mean anything dramatic, just staying within procedure. She types a quick summary for Vance:

Where the Path Broke geocache community reaction high. Speculation wide-ranging. No coordinates posted. Reviewer present and calming threads. No direct threats or concerning language. Activity concentrated in Discord and Facebook.

She hits SEND.

The screens at both their workstations continue to fill with movement and noise from social pings, emojis, nervous jokes, comforting lies, anxious questions. The internet is breathing in its crowded, chaotic rhythm.

Far from that noise, Erin is in her apartment with a different focus. She hasn't touched the shard in over an hour, but it still feels like the center of gravity in her home. Every movement she makes arcs toward it, even when she's trying not to think about it.

She perches on the stool at the edge of the counter, now draped in a sweatshirt. The room is quiet except for her breathing and the occasional groan of the building settling. She gives the shard a side-eye while lifting her phone twice without actually unlocking it, once out of habit, once out of dread.

The third time, she surrenders and the caching app lights up her screen, telling her she made a mistake. The bright, cheerful interface asks her what adventure she wants today. Her stomach knots. She doesn't want adventure, she wants yesterday back.

But a red notification dot sits on the profile tab. Not a public message, a direct one.

From **TrailTempest**. She knows she put it off as long as she could, so she opens it. The message is simple, *"Hey, quick Q! For your Hidden Hollow find. Did you ever figure out if the coords had been off by a bit? I know it's archived but I was thinking about checking it out later and wanted to be prepared."*

She stares at it and her skin prickles. The timing is bad, so bad. It is probably an innocent question, people ask each other about caches all the time. Coordinates drift and logs get confusing, but the message is a hook in her gut anyway. She backs out of the DM before she can overthink it, and clicks on another notification, one from the Facebook groups. This is her second mistake, which throws her straight into the archived listing for *Where the Path Broke*. The comments fill the screen:

GorgeHopper: "Is it safe?"

CacheSiren: "Rumor is someone got hurt near the trail??"

GarminOffGrid: "PLEASE don't spread this stuff, god."

MapNerd: "Let's be patient and let the reviewer update us."

TrailTempest: "Y'all dramatic as hell lol."

MudMagnet: TFTC! Cool hide!

Erin flinches and the words blur a little. She scrolls faster, choosing to not read the comments thoroughly, but snippets stick anyway. *...heard something happened...my kid was gonna do this one...someone saw police ...if anyone knows the finder please message me...this is why we need better safety ratings...*

That one about the finder hits Erin. That user means her. Her throat tightens and she swipes away the entire app before she starts shaking again and sets the phone face-down on the countertop, then presses her fingertips to her eyes until little sparks flare behind them.

She told herself she wasn't going to get dragged deeper. She told herself she wasn't going to look, but something ugly and urgent pushed her anyway, more than curiosity, but not quite obsession. The fear of being misunderstood, of being blamed, has taken a hold that she can't break.

Sitting still makes Erin feel like she's drowning, so she stands, then walks over and pulls her laptop out of the closet where she stashed it so she wouldn't have to stare at it. She takes the half-dead notebook to her bed and grabs the notepad and sharpie from her nightstand. She tells herself she's just organizing her thoughts, just making sense of things so she doesn't lose her mind. By the time she admits it's a lie, she's pulled up her old cache logs, replayed routes she's taken, and started scribbling questions on sticky notes. *HH- Why no weapon? Why that spot? WTPB- Why MudMagnet?*

Over a dozen notes and twice that many clicks on geocache drop pins later, she realizes she's standing in front of her corkboard, holding a pen steady as a compass needle. She stares at the wall a long time before the first sticky note goes up.

Vance walks through the precinct hallway with her jacket still half unbuttoned and hair damp from the Pacific Northwest mist. Her boots are still carrying the forest on the toes. The precinct hums with phones and keyboards, its usual late-morning rhythm, but it all feels pitched an octave lower than it should. She doesn't bother stopping at her desk, her destination is CSU.

Ryan and Shannon sit in the glass-walled intel room. They share a mess of coffee cups and half-eaten pastries between their workstations. Both look like they've been awake too long. Ryan glances up first. "Detective."

She steps inside. "What have you got on the geocache case?"

He gestures to Shannon's screen. "We've got community chatter all over. Facebook groups, Discord servers, subreddits, the smaller cache forums. People are talking."

Vance gives a dry, humorless snort. "Of course they are."

"Yeah, but not about the body," Shannon says quickly. "At least, not directly. They're trying not to break some community guidelines, but they're skirting them."

She scrolls through a feed filled with usernames Vance doesn't recognize from her own queries.

CacheDragon: "Anyone else feel like something weird is going on near Washougal? No drama, just vibes."

PathPicker: "Please stop hinting. If we need to know, the reviewers will say so."

TrailTempest: "People get lost all the time. Chill."

MapNerd: "Let's respect the reviewers and wait for official word."

GorgeHopper: "Actually, does anyone know if the listing was archived because of wildlife or...?"

CacheDragon: "Wildlife doesn't call 911."

Ryan winces. "They're getting close. They're going to tear into each other soon."

Vance crosses her arms. "And what does the cache platform's administrative team say?"

"That's the other thing." Shannon taps another window open. This one is an official email thread showing support tickets, timestamps, and reviewer notes. "We put in a formal request for reviewer contact earlier this morning. The main office finally responded.”

The email sits at the bottom:

Reviewer: SURVEYOR (primary for PNW region)

Status: Active

Contact: Available for law enforcement coordination

Ryan leans back in his chair. “They're cooperating. Sent us his secure contact info.”

Shannon adds, “He's been active on the forums, too. Looks like he's keeping people calm, clarifying guidelines and shutting down rumors before they turn into wildfire.”

Vance processes through a tight jaw, but she doesn't comment yet, which prompts Ryan to tilt his head toward another window. “We pulled the usernames from all the public logs on the three caches tied to the case. Lots of overlap, but nothing unusual, mostly locals and people who probably don't even know each other.”

“Only consistent name you'll see,” Shannon adds, “is the reviewer. He's the one who green lights anything in this region.” She points to a linked handle. “See here? Surveyor.”

Vance nods slowly. “So, he's the only person connected to every listing without being physically present at any crime scene.”

“Right,” Shannon says. “He's the gatekeeper, on the site and in some of the groups. He might've seen something pattern-wise before anyone else.”

She quietly watches their screens for a moment. She observes the handles, the chatter, the static of a community trying to learn information not meant for them. She thinks of the camcorder, the voice that wasn't talking to her. Her voice comes out level. “Set up a meeting. I want to talk to Surveyor. Today.”

Ryan nods and Shannon descends on her keyboard. As Vance steps out of the intel room, Ryan and Shannon glance at each other, they know better than to say anything while the detective could still be within earshot, but they agree with each other in silence.

Erin sits on the edge of her bed with her hand pressed against her eyes and a blanket wrapped around her shoulders, clinging to her sweater. She has turned the bedroom light off in hopes of finally getting some sleep, but the apartment is still too bright. She's holding her phone in her other hand, mostly from habit. The lock screen illuminates the ceiling.

In the kitchen, the shard sits where she left it. The small, dark shape on the counter waits, whispering Erin's name, whispering accusations. She can't see it from here, but she hears it through the wall.

She lies back slowly, tugging the blanket to her chin. Her breath tightens when she closes her eyes, not from fear of the dark, but from what the dark might hold behind it. Every time her eyelids close, she sees MudMagnet's eyes and the way they didn't move. His face didn't have a final expression, just the shell of a man she once knew, now vacant like her brother, Danny.

She opens her eyes again, sleep isn't coming, no matter how itchy her eyes get. Tomorrow morning feels like a lie. She rolls onto her side and stares at the faint line of light under the closed door from the hallway, the only proof the kitchen still exists. After a long moment, she whispers into the dark, a truth she can finally admit to herself, "I can't pretend this didn't happen."

She doesn't know she's made a decision yet, but there's conviction in her voice. She doesn't bother closing her eyes , not tonight.

Chapter 11: Log Pattern

The precinct is already more alive at seven than Vance prefers, telling her the morning shift is already in full swing. The building isn't loud or chaotic with any emergency, just active in a way that reminds her crime doesn't stop while she's off duty. She stands beside the window outside Major Crimes with a cooling paper cup in her hand, watching the sun smear itself over the glass of the adjacent buildings. This might be the only moment of peace before she gets involved with what's sitting on her desk.

When she gets there, she's right. CSU dropped the preliminary Washougal report thirty minutes ago and she can already tell the patterns don't match the Hazel Dell kill. The victim type and MO are different, the scenes don't even come close to matching, even the weapon doesn't line up. She wonders why the killer didn't use the mirror shard at the Hazel Dell murder but did in the video, entertaining the possibility of a worst-case scenario, a copycat.

Tenner approaches with the printouts she requested. He looks tired in a way she recognizes, the kind that comes from trying to sleep with violent images cooling behind the eyes. He's no rookie, but she doubts he has seen anything like this case.

"Morning," he says, his words as lifeless as his face.

"Morning." She doesn't look away from the report until she's finished the page.

He hands her the stack. "CSU triple checked the transport rig. There are no loose items, no torn bags, nothing misfiled. The weapon is still missing."

"I figured." She flips the first page. "They don't miss things."

Tenner shifts his weight. "It means whoever took it, did it before we ever arrived on scene."

"Or never left it behind." She sets the report down. "If that weapon has personal attachment, like a trophy, he's not dropping that in a ditch."

A moment passes where neither speaks, both giving consideration to possibilities. Tenner finally clears his throat and lifts another sheet. "Legal forwarded us the reviewer contact from the Cache platform's office of the regional moderator with the handle *Surveyor*. We have the greenlight to reach out."

She looks at the printout. The reviewer has a painfully boring email address, an apartment in the Heights, and a plain face, but one she hasn't met yet. "Timothy Christopher Hale." Vance almost smiles. "Poor bastard has three first names."

"Want me to set up the interview?" Tenner asks.

"No, I'll take care of that," she answers. "I do want a timeline, though. Get with techs and see how long he's been reviewing listings and how often he interacts with cache owners. I want a list of who he rejects and who he approves. Pull whatever frequency logs you can find."

Tenner nods and heads for the hall. "I'll shoot you the details."

Vance sets the papers down on her desk and takes a sip of her coffee, savoring the bitter purity of it, before pulling out her phone. She takes a moment to commit this Surveyor's number to her short-term, then replays the digits on her phone screen. The line rings twice before she gets an answer. She transitions to her public relations voice, communicating the reason for her call and arranging a physical meeting.

Later that day, Vance parks two blocks from the waterfront park. She wants the walk, using the distance to scope the environment and possibilities. She doesn't like walking into a meeting blind, this also gives the two undercover officers ample time to set their positions on either side of the large park, affording them the opportunity to observe.

She arrives at the pier and takes in the scene. The afternoon light slants warm across the river, glazing the cable-stayed pier in gold. Families drift between ice cream carts and restaurant patios. Couples lean against the railings and joggers pass in pairs. It's beautiful here, deliberately beautiful, and Vance feels an ache watching families play in the grass while she's walking into the unknown. This was not her choice, Surveyor picked this spot, but if she was to meet him soon, this was the best option.

She generally avoids meeting spots like this, it's incredibly public, sightlines are open, there are too many escape routes and plenty of large crowds. The density of civilians makes tactical decisions irresponsible. She reminds herself this is just a meeting, simple data collection from an interested party.

She steps onto the main plaza beneath the massive cables, scanning faces. No one stands out, and Vance doesn't lean on her profiler instincts here. She isn't hunting a predator, she's trying to match a name to a face.

Vance lingers on the boardwalk for over twenty minutes before she finally checks her watch. He's late and late doesn't look good. She taps her watch, irritated at the time wasted, wondering if he will even show. She scans the crowd again, pushing back the creeping frustration, reminding herself to also be professional.

Just over her shoulder, a low voice, polite and reserved, asks, "Are you the detective who called me?"

Vance spins to face a man, one hand discreetly moving to her sidearm. He is ordinary with light blond hair that's clipped short but not stylish, and thick brown glasses that seem a decade out of date. He holds a soft, almost apologetic posture, shoulders slightly rounded, weight balanced like someone who doesn't want to intrude on the space he stands in. He lifts his hands, almost shy, and keeps them raised just long enough for her to see it, then drops them to his sides. He steps back, giving her room, letting her observe every step. "Apologies, I didn't mean to startle you."

Vance doesn't release her tension, but she adjusts her posture to feel more welcoming. She keeps her tone neutral. "Mister Hale?"

"Yes, ma'am. Does that make you Detective Vance?" he says. His voice is gentle and almost warm, but something about it feels practiced.

"Yes," she answers. She immediately clocks his gray windbreaker, tan slacks, and unfashionable sneakers. Her tone adjusts from tactical alert to evaluation.

He smiles, faint and symmetrical, a gesture that feels carefully practiced. "Thank you for accommodating the location. I don't usually meet people in person about review work, but… well, these are unusual circumstances."

Vance studies him with curiosity, letting the silence linger just long enough to see what he does with it. He lowers his gaze, just briefly in a respectful, but almost deferential gesture. Something about him feels soft and almost grounding.

She gestures toward a nearby bench overlooking the river, still within the bustle of the public, but with enough personal space to avoid being overheard unless someone tried. Surveyor nods, grateful she's chosen somewhere so polite. He sits with his hands folded loosely in his lap and his posture attentive without being stiff.

She stays standing for a moment longer, scanning the area, then lowers herself onto the opposite edge of the bench, pulling out her notebook. "Thank you for meeting me," she says.

He smiles again sympathetically. "I wasn't sure what the appropriate protocol was. I've never had law enforcement reach out about a cache review before."

"I'd wager there's often not cause." Vance studies him openly. "Unfortunately, I'm on an investigation that has led me to this game and two caches seem to be approved by you."

"The murders, of course," he says with immediate concern. "I read about the Hazel Dell case. Now, the one near Washougal yesterday. Terrible." His brow furrows with concern, or something close to it. "If there's any information I can offer, I'm more than happy to assist."

Vance turns from him and watches the river for a moment, letting him sit with his own words. "Let's start simple," she says. "Tell me what you actually do. Reviewer duties, how much human contact is involved, what do you see?"

He brightens in a small, earnest way, glad to explain his niche. "Well, each region has one or two reviewers who look over cache submissions before they publish. We verify the coordinates, ensure no guidelines are violated, confirm the owner has permission if it's on private land. We don't…" he hesitates politely, "we don't physically visit the hides. That's a misconception."

She nods. "So, all remote."

"Yes. I see a location on the map, then I check surroundings, border lines, judge proximity to infrastructure. It's a reviewer's job to avoid landmines like railroad tracks or sensitive wildlife zones."

"And the geocachers themselves?" she asks. "How many do you know in person?"

"None," he says simply. "Reviewers stay anonymous. We don't attend events in our reviewer identity. We're supposed to be neutral." Then, with a soft laugh, he follows up, "Besides, people argue about container sizes enough online. I can't imagine doing that face-to-face."

Vance almost smiles, his boyish excitement for his hobby warms her for a moment. Before she allows herself to become too comfortable, she changes direction. "Back to the two caches," she says. "Hidden Hollow and Where the Path Broke were both approved by you. Anything unusual when you reviewed them?"

He thinks with a 'hmm', closing his eyes and tapping his chin.

"I handle maybe forty submissions a month. Those two didn't stand out. The coordinates were valid and the hides were well within guidelines. No red flags from the owners."

Vance leans forward, elbows resting lightly on her knees. "Do you remember the owners?"

"I don't recall, no," he admits with a hint of embarrassment. "I'm sorry. I can look them up, but I don't memorize them. We get a lot of outdoor hobbyists with playful handles. MapleMoth, BikeNGrab, CacheCannon. It's hard to keep them straight. This game is global with hundreds of thousands of players."

He gives a small, almost sheepish shrug. "It's a huge community. There's one cache in Antarctica, actually. Also, did you know one went to space on the ISS?" He offers a small smile, aware the information is unnecessary, but he can't quite help himself. "People forget how wide this hobby really runs."

She watches him fold his hands again. "You seem very calm," she says.

He blinks behind the glasses. "Should I not be?"

"There's a killer using your playground. You're the one thread that touches every cache." She keeps her voice neutral, but direct.

Surveyor absorbs her statement quietly. When he speaks, his voice is softer. "I know, and I want you to find whoever's doing this. If anything about my work can help you stop them, I'll give you whatever I can."

He sits with a composed stillness, the kind of posture Vance's father used to call "polite waiting." His hands stay folded loosely with fingertips touching but not tense. When a jogger passes behind them, he watches the man pass by, then looks back to her.

"Good," Vance says. "Then let's keep talking."

The boardwalk hums with life around them, carrying the sounds of children playing in the grass, dozens of pocket conversations, and the low murmur of river under the cables, but none of it really touches the bench. Vance shifts, making a small deliberate adjustment meant to see if he'll follow, but he doesn't.

She tries another set of questioning, "You spend a lot of time watching how people behave online. Submissions, complaints, reviews. Does anything about this killer's pattern strike you as familiar, maybe something you've seen in the community?"

His answer takes a moment. "I see tendencies," he admits. "Not necessarily dangerous ones, just human behavior. People like being seen, they like being clever. This game appeals to puzzle-solvers and storytellers. They want to control an experience for the finder."

His fingers tap against his knee, subtle and rhythmic, then stop. He continues. "Whoever is doing this? They're trying very hard to control the story."

Vance watches his unreadable expression. "Control how?"

Surveyor's gaze lifts to the river and he speaks softly. "A cache is a conversation. The owner speaks first by hiding it, then the finder speaks back by locating it. This is different, this person isn't waiting for the finder, they're guiding them. It's more of a lecture."

"Guiding who?" Vance asks.

He considers that. "Someone specific, maybe. Not the whole community." The river breeze lifts the corner of his jacket which he doesn't seem to notice. "This person isn't interested in being found by everyone, they're interested in being found by the right one."

Vance feels his observation deep into her own. Something in what he says comes dangerously close to the line she crossed last night. She asks, "And what makes you so sure they're trying to be found?"

Surveyor turns back to her, his glasses catching a strip of sunlight that hides his eyes for a heartbeat. "Because they're using the mechanics of the hobby," he says, "but not the culture of it. They're not playing a game. They're telling a story."

Vance studies him, her face calm. She lets her words match.

"So, what's the story?"

He tilts his head. "That's what you're trying to find out, isn't it?"

His question lands between them like a shared secret neither person intended to tell, then the spell breaks as a cyclist speeds past, nearly colliding into a stroller, but banks hard and flips in the grass. The mother pushing the stroller chastises the bicyclist while a man rushes to check on him.

Surveyor adjusts his glasses, settling back into harmless neutrality. "I'm sorry," he says quietly. "I suppose that wasn't very helpful, I understand this is serious and people have died."

Vance nods once, showing restraint. "You're being helpful enough." She leans back slightly, letting the breeze cut between them. She's done with warm-up questions.

"Let's talk specifics," she says. "We've got three caches connected to ongoing investigations, two were reviewed by you."

Surveyor nods without hesitation. "That's correct."

"Walk me through your review process. Exactly how does it work on your end?"

He clears his throat, preparing himself. "I receive submissions through the platform. Owners include coordinates, a description, container type, and a general summary of the hide. My job is to make sure the listing meets guidelines. Like I said, proximity rules, safety concerns, permission requirements if applicable. I check the coordinates, the map location, any flagged issues. If it meets standards, I publish. If it doesn't, I message the owner."

"And you never visit the sites yourself?"

"Again, no," he says gently. "Reviewers rely on the honor system, community feedback, and the guidelines. It's not feasible to personally inspect every hide in a region. Some reviewers handle thousands of submissions a year."

Vance processes the answer, quietly annoyed her original

assumption was wrong, which never feels good in her field. She shifts. "It seems there is a lot of work in being a reviewer. Is this a full-time job? What kind of hours do you put into this?"

Surveyor considers her questions, a faint smile tugging at his lips. "It can feel that way at times, but it's all for love of the game, all volunteer work. I try to streamline my workload, so I'll go through my reviewer log first thing in the morning, go about my day, then review again just before bed. I'm a morning person, so I finish by eight o'clock each night."

"I see," Vance adds to her notes, then she asks, "So, on the day you reviewed Hidden Hollow and Where the Path Broke, did anything strike you as odd, not just the caches, but in the community?"

He shakes his head. "Nothing particular, maybe handles I didn't recognize. But that's common. New people join the game all the time."

"Did any of them seem coordinated? Similar writing style, similar submission habits?"

"Not in a way that raised suspicion," he answers. "But after your call this morning, I did recheck the cache data. I didn't see anything strange about the hides themselves, but I did notice something about the logs."

Vance's gaze sharpens. "Go on."

"Before the caches were found, they had more watchers than I expected. Not viral numbers, just unusually high. Sometimes people follow new listings out of curiosity, but this felt, I don't know, coordinated."

She raises a brow. "Coordinated how?"

"Two usernames popped up across multiple pages," he says. "Not suspicious by itself, they weren't the first-to-find types, but they added the caches to their watchlists. That caught my eye because it's early engagement for new hides."

"Usernames?" Vance asks.

"JessaLou87 and ColtTracks," he says apologetically. "Local players, I think. The only reason I found it odd is that I know they have a shared handle, YourCacheCrush."

She scrawls the cacher handles in her notebook, then clicks the pen absently while staring at the mostly clean sheet. "You wouldn't happen to have anything else, something out of the ordinary that might have slipped your mind?"

He shakes his head solemnly.

She shifts again, leaning slightly closer. "Alright," she says. "Last thing for now. Is there anything, anything at all, you think I should be looking for? Not as a reviewer looking at online data, but as someone who sees this game at your level. Something about the way this person is behaving that the police might miss?"

Surveyor thinks. Then he offers, "You're looking at the bodies and caches," he says mindfully. "That's logical, but if this person is using the hobby as their own game..." His eyes return to the river. "You should look at what they're not hiding."

She frowns. "Meaning?"

"These caches aren't hard," he says. "They're not meant to be a challenge, they're meant to be found. Which means the real puzzle is elsewhere."

Vance absorbs that. She clicks her pen rapidly, not because he might be right, but because she's been so wrapped up in the quirkiness of this game that she didn't think about it sooner.

He rises from the bench with the same gentle composure he arrived with. "I don't want to take up more of your time," he says. "But if anything else comes up, you have my email." Then he pauses and adds, "And I'm sorry you're dealing with something like this. Really."

He walks away with the gait of a man who has never been looked at twice in a crowd. She watches him long enough to note his posture as he weaves through joggers, the slight inward curve of his shoulders, the way he steps aside reflexively when a family moves past him. He doesn't look back at the detective, not once. She waits until Surveyor is fully merged back into the bustling weekend activity before she moves.

She taps her mic twice, a silent signal to the undercover officers posted at opposite ends of the promenade. One responds immediately, "North end clear. He's leaving on foot toward Grant."

"Copy." She keeps her voice flat.

She starts walking toward the edge of the boardwalk where the river churns against the boulders at the shore. Sunlight glances off the water in trembling shards.

Everything about this meeting should have been simple. He answered questions politely. He provided data, context, cooperation. He didn't hide anything she could catch, but he didn't actually give her anything either. She didn't have anything new, no name, no real leads. She's tired of feeling like she's three steps behind a killer and she hates that she can't find an angle to catch up.

She stares at her notepad, reliving the interview in her head. She fills the nearly empty page now she has relative privacy: *Meeting w/ REVIEWER. Composed, reserved. Avoids elaboration but not evasive. Provides answers, not insight. Comment: "Look at what he's not hiding," interpret? Check: submission timestamps, any linked patterns reviewer didn't see.*

She hesitates, then adds: *Face easy to lose in crowd. Keep photo?*

She pockets the pad and exhales. Riggs, one of the undercover officers approaches from the left, quiet and reliable. He keeps a respectful distance. "You good, Detective?"

"I'm fine." She doesn't look at him.

He glances toward the path Surveyor took. "You want us to shadow him?"

"No," she says. "Let him go, this was just an interview."

He doesn't give any argument.

Vance remains there after he leaves, staring out at the water. The afternoon wind has turned colder, lifting strands of her hair and snapping them across her cheek. She tucks them behind her ear and forces her mind to reassemble the case threads, cataloguing the weapons, caches, video, victims, sequence, and now a reviewer who fits nowhere and everywhere at once.

She closes her eyes enough to reset her focus. The killer has been putting story beats in front of them, giving structure to chaos. If she starts following the wrong through-line, even for another half day, she knows it will widen the gap.

She pushes away from the railing, deciding it is time to gather the team and regroup. She walks back toward the street, her steps brisk, boots striking the wood in controlled punctuation. By the time she reaches her car, the sense of neutrality she felt from the meeting with this Surveyor has sharpened from the comment she cannot unhear, *"Look at what he's not hiding."*

Chapter 12: Cache Chatter

Erin kicks off her boots and shrugs out of her jacket. The apartment is usually her peace after work, today it is anything but. Every shadow stretches further, closing the space between her and the dread reminders of the caches that have been haunting her.

The shard waits on the kitchen counter where she left it, wrapped just like it was when she left it this morning. It's been sitting there for two days, a silent guilt curled in place. She's walked past it so many times, sometimes staring at it until her eyes burned, sometimes pretending she didn't see it at all.

Two nights she's lived with it. One night she almost brought it to the police. Last night she almost drove it across the I-205 bridge and sent it to the bottom of the Columbia River. Tonight, she's too exhausted to do almost anything. She presses her thumb to the inside of her wrist, checking her pulse and grounding herself. Then she pulls a chair out, legs scraping across the tile, and sits down slowly. Her hands hover over the cloth. Underneath lies a long sliver of mirror, triangular, thick enough to kill with, and thin enough to vanish in a bag. Someone wanted her to find it.

She unwraps it and the exposed shard catches the lamp in one sharp line. Her reflection fractures across the surface, an eye is stretched, her mouth is bent, and her face splits into unfamiliar angles. She doesn't look at the Erin before all this, or the Erin after, she sees both stitched together in transition. She reaches out, touches the very edge with her fingertip and the cold flashes up her skin like static. She pulls back. "Alright," she murmurs. "Enough hiding."

She picks up the shard with the cloth and holds it with defiance. The weight isn't much, but it feels like it's leaning into her palm, accepting her challenge.

If she gives it to Vance, it disappears, getting bagged, labeled, and swallowed by the chain of custody. Another thing she'll never see again. Danny's absence all over again. If she keeps it, maybe it will be the compass on the map the killer laid out.

A knot in her spine loosens and she looks toward the sagging bookshelf across the room which is stuffed with years of weather-beaten notebooks and topography maps. The analog debris of her caching life before all of this, stacked without ceremony. Tonight is the night she stops being afraid and starts understanding.

She carries the shard with her to the bookshelf, held gently but with a grip of distrust. She pulls her first logbook out from the bottom row. The spiral is bent, the cover swollen from rain it never fully recovered from. Danny's handwriting is still inside the front cover in faint pencil, uneven from writing while walking. *Find what everyone else misses.*

Danny showed her this game. It was his world before it was hers, he loved the puzzles, the hikes, the quiet wins tucked into tree hollows and lamppost skirts. She'd moved out by then, old enough to build her own life away from their parents, but Danny stayed. He always stayed. He was three years younger and somehow still the one trying to protect their mother from the weather inside that house. The memory isn't warm, it's a family scar.

She sets the book down and pulls out two more, then another. Soon the coffee table fills with the quiet thump of lived years opening themselves back up. She sits on the couch, sets the mirror on the table, draws the lamp closer, and opens the top logbook. Ink feathers where water once soaked the pages. Her younger handwriting fills the pages, smaller, quicker, and hopeful. She flips through instinctively, her thumb pausing at half-forgotten notes. *Published early? Hint phrasing weird. Reviewer edit? Someone beat me by minutes… again.*

She never connected anything back then. Never thought she needed to. She reaches for her phone and loads the app, a curious gesture while she revisits these books. The listing for Hidden Hollow opens first. She scrolls until she hits the timestamp. 5:14 a.m.

Her gaze lifts to the corkboard on the wall, locating a single sticky note with those same numbers scribbled from days earlier, seeing where her superstition had whispered to write it down and she'd listened.

She checks *Where the Path Broke*. The publication timestamp is also 5:14 a.m. and her chest tightens. She opens the cache owner profile. **OverlookLaneCrew.** The account is over ten years old, with only three hides total, all in the same blur of weeks that everything has been going sideways. It isn't enough to mean anything, but hard to ignore. She writes the name down beside the timestamps.

Her fingers hover over a map for a moment before she drags it close and unfolds it over the table. Using the latitude-longitude grid along the map's edges, Erin pinpoints Hidden Hollow, Parkside Peekaboo, and Where the Path Broke. She grabs a pencil and darkens three points, then draws light strokes between them, faint enough she can erase them without leaving dents. There isn't a pattern here, just a triangle on the outskirts of the city with little more than geocaches to correlate.

She drops the writing stick which bumps a notepad enough to shift the piece of broken mirror. The shard catches the light on the table, its fractured edge sending a small flash across the map. Her jaw tightens. "Not now," she scolds. "I'm trying to think." She flips the shard face-down under the fabric, muffling its shine and muting a noise only she can hear.

Erin reaches for another logbook, already feeling the shift. It's not obsession yet, just the beginning of reclamation.

Erin has three logbooks open now, pages fanned across the table. The shard sits wrapped beside them, waiting for her attention.

She forgets it is there and is scribbling cache owners and publication times onto a scrap of paper. Her phone buzzes sharply against the wood, snapping through her concentration, and causing her to recoil from the table. The number is unknown, but the area code shows it is local. She answers. "Yeah?"

The line is silent except for a signal click, then, "Ms. Caldwell? This is Detective Mara Vance."

The detective's voice straightens Erin's spine. "It's late."

"Tell me about it," Vance responds with her own dry, pragmatic exhaustion. "Listen, I didn't catch you at a bad time, did I?"

Erin's eyes dart over the open logs and scrawled notes, toward the shard. "Depends on what you're calling about."

"Just thought I'd check in. I wanted to see if you had anything else to talk about after Washougal." Papers shuffle on the other end. "You left the scene pretty fast. I wanted to make sure you weren't sitting on anything you forgot to mention."

Vance's statement shouldn't sting, but it does. Erin slides a notebook over the shard, expecting Vance to see it through the connection, then immediately feels dumb for her action. "I told you everything," she says.

"Uh-huh." Vance's tone is neutral, but there's weight behind it, a subtle pressure that suggests Vance knows more than she's letting on. "You just seemed a little shaken, more than I expected you to be."

Suspecting Vance actually did see her hide the shard, Erin bristles, "Maybe because I almost tripped over a dead body."

Vance takes a moment before responding. "Fair point." She sighs. There's something real in it, something that almost softens the edge of the conversation. "I'm not calling to hassle you, just making sure you're safe, and to be sure you're not out there doing anything risky. These caches are getting unpredictable."

Erin's heart thuds once, hard. She forces her voice flat. "I'm safe, I'm home."

"Good." The detective pauses. "Mark Leland okay?"

The question comes from left field. "Why are you asking about Mark?"

"Well, he bolted out of there too, and he didn't respond when we called him for a follow-up." Her tone stays conversational, but Erin feels the needle under it. "I figured maybe you two checked in with each other."

Erin's pulse thrums and she can feel the heat in her cheeks. "No," she says. "We haven't talked."

Vance makes a small sound. Erin can't tell if it is evaluation or judgment. The detective continues, "He didn't seem entirely steady at the scene. Just do me a favor…" She pauses once more, "keep some space until we sort out which witnesses we need to circle back to."

Vance's statement carries the sound of concern, but there's a sinister trace to it. Erin's fingers tighten around the phone. "Is he in trouble?"

"Not right now, hopefully not at all." Vance's voice softens, but not in a comforting way, more like she's stepping carefully. "Look, Caldwell, you're close to this, emotionally speaking. Just be careful who you lean on."

Erin swallows, the dryness scraping her throat. "Thank you, Detective, I think. Is that all?"

"For now." Another round of rustling paper clutters the line. "Erin. This sort of thing can burn a person out, don't let it. Try to get some sleep." Vance disconnects the call before Erin can ask whether that was concern or a warning.

The phone goes dark in her hand, and Erin stares at her reflection on the black screen. She feels the smallest crack open in her trust. The quiet of the apartment presses in harder now, and the air shifts, building pressure. She sets the phone down with more force than she intends. Why did Vance bring up Mark? Erin rubs her hand across her forehead. "I don't have time for this." She tries to shrug off the call, but the cryptic check-in has already slipped into her bloodstream.

She turns back to the table. The map lies open where she left it, and the logbooks are all fanned out, waiting to be seen. The shard is still catching the lamp with a sharp glint, the reflection watching her. She exhales hard. "Shut up," she mutters at it, then presses her palm over it until the reflection is gone and the noise in her head diminishes by degrees. The act settles her enough to draw the map closer, letting an edge cover the condemning mirror.

One by one, she goes back to the logbooks she'd abandoned when the phone rang, grabbing the pencil on instinct, tapping it once against the table. She reviews the faint lines she'd sketched earlier, connecting Hidden Hollow, Lamppost Lament, and Where the Path Broke.

Vance's voice threads through her thoughts. *Be careful who you lean on. He didn't seem steady at the scene. Just keep some space until we sort out which witnesses we need to circle back to.* Erin fights the feeling rising in her chest. Mark didn't look steady at the scene, that part's true. He'd been distracted in a way she hasn't seen in him before. He kept checking his phone. He kept glancing down the trail. He kept looking away every time she tried to meet his eyes.

She pushes the thoughts away. She needs focus, not to spiral into baseless suspicion. She finds Hazel Dell's Parkside Peekaboo cache site and examines the logs. She then traces a faint boundary line around the OverlookLaneCrew hides, carefully comparing the data. There isn't enough to justify it, but something is there, it has to be. She can feel it crawling under her skin.

She checks the timestamp for Hidden Hollow again. 5:14 a.m. That same shows as the publication date for Where the Path Broke, and somewhere else, but where? She reaches out and presses her fingertip to time, just to feel something solid.

The room is unnervingly quiet. She can hear the hum of the refrigerator, the distant traffic beyond her window, the subtle tap of rain beginning to pepper the glass. She listens to a world that should feel ordinary but somehow doesn't. Erin drags the county map closer, leaning in and her breath warms her lip slightly as she exhales hard through her nose. Lamppost Lament.

She pulls up the page for the urban cache and finds it, the third 5:14 timestamp. This is the one that pushed through phones the evening of the cache meetup, the one people couldn't understand why the notification was over twelve hours late.

Three caches with one name echoing through her head. The cache owner is OverlookLaneCrew, same owner for both body caches. It isn't proof, and Overlook isn't quite a suspect, but it is a first thread. She tightens her grip on the pencil, ready to follow it wherever it leads.

Her phone buzzes again, but only once, suggesting it is just a meaningless notification that isn't actual contact. The sound still makes her jump. She steadies herself. "Jesus," she whispers, under her breath.

Her heart takes a long, uneven moment to settle, telling her this is the moment she should stop, turn the light off, and walk away. She knows she needs to rest for the night, but she doesn't. She leans over the map one more time, the pencil tip hovering over the faint lines she's drawn, her breath steadying as she realizes this thing has its hooks in her now.

Erin is buried in the logbooks when her phone buzzes again, this time with the distinct, longer vibration of an incoming call. For a heartbeat she thinks it's Vance again. When she looks at the screen, the name makes her cringe in a different way: **Mark Leland.**

She hesitates long enough for the call to almost time out before she answers. "Hey," she says, her voice barely louder than a whisper.

"Erin?" Mark's voice is rough, he sounds tired. He clears his throat. "You okay?"

He catches her off guard with the strange question, but only for a moment. Everything tonight is strange. "I'm fine."

"You don't sound fine."

"Mark, I've said three words." A brittle silence settles between them. Erin runs her thumb along the side of the phone, listening to the faint pattern in Mark's breathing.

"I should've checked in sooner," he says quietly. "After everything in Washougal."

"You ran out pretty fast," she says before thinking.

"You left first," he says with a quick defense, then adds quietly. "But yeah, I guess I did. That was a lot. I'm sorry if you felt like I bailed on you."

She doesn't trust that phrasing, or maybe she doesn't trust herself hearing it. She keeps her tone steady. "I'm not worried about it. Like you said, I left first."

There's another pause between them. "So, you're really okay?"

She looks at the table, the map with circled caches, the pile of old notebooks, the shard wrapped and facedown, sleeping under cloth. Her hand trembles slightly as she examines her mess. "I'm trying to be," she says.

Mark gives a soft exhale on the other end, and Erin can't tell if he is relieved or frustrated. "I've been replaying the other day in my head nonstop. The way you froze and the way I didn't. I didn't step in the way I should have."

"You're fine." She lies.

"Not really. I should have been better," he says, voice flattening. "I should have been there for you."

She swallows her emotions. "Mark, I can't do this right now. I'm trying to focus."

"On what?" he asks, his voice teetering between concern and

interest. Her mind flashes to Vance's voice: *He didn't seem steady at the scene. Keep some space.* Erin's tone sharpens before she can soften it. "Just things. Okay?"

He goes quiet again, then he speaks softly, "You're shutting me out."

She closes her eyes, trying to squeeze the hurt away. "I'm not," she says, but she hears the lie twist slightly in the words.

Mark sighs. "If you need space, then take it. I'm not trying to push you. I just didn't want you going through this alone."

She catches herself staring at the timestamps, the username OverlookLaneCrew, and the shard. The weight of everything on her table is crushing her, confiding in Mark might alleviate some of the pressure. Sharing this burden with someone, anyone, would have to be better than carrying it completely alone.

Vance's warnings tug against her harder and her chest locks tight. She can't, not yet, maybe not at all. "Thanks for calling," she says gently, trying to soften the edges she sharpened earlier. "Really. I'll check in later."

"Yeah," he says, his words stretch in a way that tells her he doesn't want to let them escape his lips. "Okay. Just be careful, Erin."

There's something in the way he says her name, sounds like the ache of worry or guilt, she can't tell anymore. She knows the longer they talk, the chance of her cracking grows. "Goodnight, Mark."

"Goodnight." He says, but his steady breathing tells her he isn't going to hang up, so she ends the call. She sets the phone face-down on the table, staring at the faint tremor in her hand. She can't tell if she's pushing him away because she doesn't trust him or because trusting anyone right now feels dangerous.

The weight of her conversations with both Mark and Vance has thickened the air. Erin presses both hands to the table, grounding herself. She's not ready to talk to either of them, not while she's tangled in something she doesn't understand.

Her eyes drift back to her notes, to the three caches, three identical timestamps. She pulls her phone closer, navigating to the app, her thumb hovering over the OverlookLaneCrew profile. She doesn't have enough yet, certainly nothing she could say out loud without sounding unhinged, but she can watch.

Erin taps the star icon next to the name and the watchlist confirmation pops up on her screen. She scrolls into her notification settings and switches every option to instant alerts: new logs, new hides, messages, forum posts, everything.

There's a slight comfort at how decisive the gesture feels. This isn't police business. This isn't Mark-and-Erin business. This isn't therapy "closure." This is a course she's charting for herself. "Alright," she whispers, mostly to steady her hands. "Let's see what you do next, LaneCrew."

She sets the phone down, screen up, the glow casting a thin line of light across her forearm. She doesn't fool herself into thinking she's in control. Erin knows what she feels isn't control, it's momentum. She returns to the map. It no longer looks like an impersonal grid of places she's already walked, now it feels more like she's reclaiming her world, or at least beginning to. Her fingers hover over the shard. She presses down gently. "Not now," she murmurs, letting the tension loosen just enough for her to breathe.

Erin turns off the lamp, plunging the room into a soft, bluish dark. Without the warm pool of light, the apartment finally feels larger, emptier, as if the walls have stepped back to watch her.

Her phone glows faintly from the table, the screen still open to OverlookLaneCrew's barren profile. She picks it up, hesitating only a second before carrying it to the bedroom. She sets it on the nightstand with the screen facing her, propped in its cradle.

The bed dips under her as she lowers onto the mattress. Her muscles ache with the kind of tightness that only fear and adrenaline produce. Her mind keeps replaying the day she found MudMagnet, the broken clearing, her interactions with both Vance and Mark, the shard.

The rain continues to tap softly against the window. The rhythm is one of the things she loves about the Pacific Northwest, the patter of the drops against the window usually lulls her. Tonight though, she lies stiff on her back, staring at the faint glow bleeding across the ceiling from her phone. Her breathing slows, but her thoughts don't.

She watches the doorway, half expecting someone to step through it, the same fear she's carried for two nights. Nothing moves and nothing changes. The world stays still in an ominous, waiting way. In time, her eyelids grow heavy and she rolls onto her side, facing the phone.

Just as she slips past the threshold of consciousness, the phone gives a soft, single buzz, a background noise she wouldn't notice on any other night. It shocks her awake for a heartbeat and she stares at the spam email notification on her lock screen. Just a momentary vibration in a world full of distractions.

She gives out a shaky, exhausted sound, and finally lets herself sink into the cool pillow. Erin's body finally releases, letting her mind slip under, not peacefully, but enough for the world to fade.

Chapter 13: Reviewer Note

Erin's phone vibrates before the alarm has a chance to ring. The sound is small, but the vibration rattles the cradle on the nightstand, cutting through her half-sleep haze. Her body moves on reflex, she's already reaching to check the screen. She looks bleary-eyed at the notification lighting up the room. **5:14 a.m.** The time hits her first, then the notification beneath it. **New cache published: The Look Back.**

The title burns into her eyes with a strange, familiar weight. She pushes herself upright, blanket falling to her lap, leaving her breath on the mattress behind. For one suspended second, she thinks she might have read it wrong or that she's still asleep and dreaming, but it's real. She opens the app and checks the cache details. The listing floods her screen, showing a traditional cache with a low difficulty and coordinates pinned east of Lucia Falls in a tight cluster of switchbacks. It is an OverlookLaneCrew cache, reviewed by Surveyor.

Nothing about the page looks dangerous, but neither did the other OverlookLaneCrew caches. She sits on the edge of the bed, phone glowing in her palm. Last night, she'd sworn she was done hiding from shadows, but the time stamp is here in the light, almost challenging her conviction.

Erin stands without thinking, tugging yesterday's jeans off the chair by her bed and grabbing a thermal over her tank top. Her head is still groggy, but her body moves, knowing the direction she needs to follow before she changes her mind. She moves through the apartment on bare feet, the living room is still dark, so she uses the light of her phone to guide her. She doesn't text Mark, and doesn't call Vance. After she grabs her pack, she finds Danny's knife and slips it into her waistband.

She shoves her boots on and grabs her keys, stepping out into the predawn world that is still asleep. The door quietly clicks shut behind her. The Look Back cache waits and she needs to hurry if she stands a chance at being the first to find it.

The roads are empty at this hour, washed in the faint gray-blue that comes before sunrise. Erin drives without music, without news, just the hum of the engine and the sharp awareness gnawing at her gut. Every few minutes she glances at the clock on the dash, seeing how much time has passed since the timestamp on the listing. 5:14 a.m., same as Hidden Hollow, same as Lamppost Lament, and same as Where the Path Broke. It is too precise to be chance, especially from one cache owner.

The wipers squeak across the windshield, smearing the misting rain. She passes a coffee stand and slows, debating a drive-by, but knows she doesn't have time. Her hands tighten and relax on the steering wheel, creating an unconscious rhythm, trying to shake something out of her bones or wake her senses.

The forest thickens as she leaves the last stretch of city lights behind. Pines blur past the windows, while dark shapes shoulder in close, towering silhouettes she knows by heart and once felt comfort in, but now no longer trust. She keeps replaying last night in her mind, reading the caches and logs, hearing Vance's warning and Mark's voice on the phone. She reflects on the imposing presence of the shard and the way it takes up all the space in a room. Erin breathes through her teeth, reminding herself that chasing this is a terrible idea, her idea.

She takes the Lucia Falls turnoff, and the pavement narrows into winding asphalt flanked by thick underbrush. Fog rolls in low waves over the road. She glances at the live map on her phone and sees the coordinates are close now, just over a mile but still two miles from the Falls parking area. This cache is near the park, but not in it, which tells her she will be hitting a trail. She slows, scanning the shoulder, hoping to see an empty pullout. The only one she finds already has two vehicles sitting angled toward the trees with condensation beading on their windshields.

Two vehicles aren't exactly danger, but they are a roadblock of her new private obsession within the public game. If this cache does have a Polaroid or a body, someone else finding it would complicate things, it would drag more innocent people into danger.

She recognizes GhostLogger's old Subaru. Next to it is a lifted Tacoma she doesn't recognize with a bright sticker on the bumper that reads **CacheHawk** and a cartoon hawk perched on a GPS unit. The back window of the truck sports a trackable decal, a graphic with a code underneath for other players to log. She considers logging it from habit but knows now is not the time.

Erin parks off to the side and kills the engine, listening to it tick as it cools. She steps out into the cold morning air and pulls her hood up both to keep the air out, and to hide from eyes in the woods. She's not alone on this hunt and that makes her skin crawl. Strangely not from fear of the killer, but because there is at least one innocent cacher out here and she needs them to get out of her way. At the very least, they need to follow her lead without realizing it.

Pine and wet earth mingle with the fog and linger in the air. One of the car doors opens up. GhostLogger steps out, stretching his back like he's been hunched in that Subaru for years. He waves at Erin with friendly recognition. The Tacoma's driver hops out after, a woman in her late thirties with a ponytail through a trucker hat. Erin stares at the other cachers with a furrow of confusion, First-to-Find runners usually don't wait around for others.

The woman lifts a hand in greeting. "Morning!"

Erin forces a thin, polite nod. "Hey."

GhostLogger squints at her. "Didn't expect company at this

hour."

"Didn't you, GhostLogger?" She cocks her head. "You know the FTF waits for no one."

They laugh lightly and the new girl's face lightens up. "Oh good, you're both cachers. I was worried I'd have to wait for Muggles to start their morning jog before I hit that find."

GhostLogger grins at the girl, obviously trying to be charming through his sallow, weathered face. "Young lady, do I look like a jogger to you?"

She chuckles with a shrug. "No, I guess not."

Erin steps past them, moving toward the trailhead. She doesn't have the caffeine reserves for small talk today. Besides, The Look Back is somewhere in these trees, and she needs to get to it first.

"Okay, then." CacheHawk huffs as Erin moves. "I guess she's the focused type."

GhostLogger leans in toward her, dropping his voice to a conspiratorial murmur. "Well, I mean, wouldn't you be? She's the one the whole board's been buzzing about. She's been through some rough stuff."

CacheHawk's eyes widen. "Rough like what, a bear?"

"Nah, nah," he says, eager to sound informed but clearly out of his depth. "More like, you know, those bodies." He adjusts the straps on his daypack.

CacheHawk exclaims in a shocked whisper as she double-checks her phone, stylus tapping against the screen with focus. "Oh. Oh shit. That's her?"

Erin notes all of it without showing it. The slow creep of realizing the rumor mill of the community has already pulled her in gives Erin an itch that makes her wish she had stopped for coffee. She hits the trailhead, recognizing the other two are overprepared and too relaxed. Her senses won't let her down and now she knows she also can't let her guard down.

CacheHawk jogs the growing distance between GhostLogger and Erin. She grins as she falls into step beside Erin. "So, you're hoping to be the first to find?"

Erin gives a noncommittal nod. "Just trying to get there before it crowds."

GhostLogger snorts behind them, laboring to catch up. "Crowds? It's us, the diehards and the insomniacs."

CacheHawk laughs. "Speak for yourself. I slept great."

Erin doesn't respond. She's already calculating the switchbacks, the likely hide points, and the terrain rating. The coordinates sit near a bend with a narrow runoff, the kind of spot she would expect a container tucked between roots or under a stone shelf. It will likely be easy, but easy only matters if the game is still the game, if her theory is wrong. The trail narrows, forcing them into a single file. Erin takes the lead without asking, picking up speed in hopes of being the first set of eyes on anything unwanted.

GhostLogger calls from the rear, "In a hurry there, TrailSister?"

"Just cold," she lies.

CacheHawk chuckles. "Sure, cold. Not competitive at all."

Erin doesn't bother to fake a laugh.

Every sound feels amplified, from the distant rhythm of trickling water to the rhythmic crunch of three sets of footsteps. The morning feels off and the growing suspicion that her prediction is about to be revealed tugs her tension tight. There's going to be another picture, another shattered life at the end of this trail, and she won't be the only witness to the finding. She hopes she's wrong, that maybe it's just her nerves. She hopes she's wrong, for the sake of the old-timer who, despite his awkwardness, is too nice to become a victim, and for the cacher she's never seen, never met, who is too peppy for a caching excursion at six in the morning.

GhostLogger huffs. "You always move this fast?"

Erin shrugs without turning. "Depends on who's behind me."

"Fair point." His tone is light but curious. "Still feels like you're running us into the ground."

CacheHawk laughs again. "Let her go. I wanna see the face she makes if the cache isn't even here."

Erin's jaw tightens, she doesn't want their banter or their company. She doesn't want them anywhere near this cache. She's not ready to carry the burden of responsibility if something happens to them, even the slightly irritating CacheHawk.

The path steepens, curving along a ridge that overlooks a drop into thick brush. The GPS arrow pulses toward the right and the distance shrinks in rapid jumps: 80 feet, 60, 40, 25. Erin speeds up, almost jogging now.

"Jesus," CacheHawk breathes. "Okay, maybe listen to the man and slow down."

Erin stops at the edge of a clearing. The coordinates land her at a tall cedar tree with a scarred trunk and a wide burl at its base. GhostLogger whistles low behind her. "Classic hide," he says. "It's gotta be tucked into the base somewhere."

CacheHawk is already crouching, hands brushing through the loose moss. "Anything under the roots?"

Erin doesn't answer. She's scanning the tree, the ground, the branches overhead. The placement feels too easy, excessively staged. She turns away from the tree and scans the rest of their surroundings while GhostLogger and CacheHawk crawl around on all fours. There has to be something else.

Ten feet off the trail is where she sees it, a small wooden plaque taped to a freshly planted pine stake, barely three feet high and nearly camouflaged by transplanted moss. Erin approaches cautiously, surveying her surroundings for any other unwanted visitors. A jackalope silhouette is burned into the surface of the plaque. In its center, a neat, crisp QR code.

CacheHawk watches Erin walk away from the trees before

spotting the sign. She straightens, brushes dirt from her knees, and follows. "Huh. Weird hide."

GhostLogger rolls his eyes. "Damn, I was sure it would have been here. I was planning on snaking the FTF."

Erin stares at the etched jackalope, but she doesn't scan it. CacheHawk waits a moment out of respect, but when Erin doesn't move, she scans it. Her phone begins to load a website, then freezes. She shakes it, expecting that to help. "Bad reception out here." Finally, it loads the page. She stares at it without saying a word. She's keyed in so long that Erin's skin prickles. "Is this the cache?" Erin asks.

CacheHawk looks up at her with a startled gaze and apology etched into her eyes. "Uh, TrailSister?"

Erin steps closer, angling to see the screen. "What is it?"

CacheHawk turns the screen toward her and Erin sees her own face. The website loads a scanned image of a grainy Polaroid which captured her and Mark when they found the Orchards Highland Park cache the other day. It was taken the moment she found that easy cache while Mark was laughing beside her. Below this image is another shot of her brushing hair out of her eyes. Then a third of her walking away down a path, the Hidden Hollow path.

"That's weird, right?" CacheHawk asks as she scrolls to another image of Erin's car, focusing on her license plate. Still another of her profile from behind, taken through trees.

The last photo loads and it is a shot of Erin stepping out of her car and looking over her shoulder. This photo was taken just this morning, CacheHawk's truck can be seen in the background.

A message appears beneath the final picture: **WRONG PLACE, ERIN. KEEP UP.** Erin's stomach drops.

"What does that mean?" CacheHawk asks, then sees Erin trembling. "Why are you all over this website?"

Erin doesn't have time to respond. Her phone erupts in

vibration, issuing notification after notification after notification. GhostLogger's phone buzzes too, as does CacheHawk's, creating a pulsing wave of electronic vibration rumbling through the ferns. Erin unlocks her screen.

People are screaming in group chats. The caching forums are exploding. Social media is flooding with links about a new cache. A video is going viral and the flood of notifications hits so fast her phone can't keep up. Erin scrolls without thinking, thumb jittering over the screen as messages stack in rapid succession.

what is happening in this video

is this a prank??

someone call 911??

this isn't funny

they're not alone

does anyone else see that behind them??

Omg are they live RIGHT NOW?

GhostLogger mutters a low curse, scrolling on his own screen. CacheHawk's brow knits, the color draining from her face. "This looks really bad, what is happening?"

Erin barely hears them over the pulse roaring in her ears. The morning air thickens until each breath feels like it has to push through molasses.

GhostLogger glances at her. "Are you seeing this?"

She's staring at her own screen, the video thumbnail now accompanies every alert, a still frame of a trail in bright daylight. Jessa's face is partially in frame and Colt is beside her. Erin taps the link. The video begins but buffers while the cellular signal stutters through the trees.

CacheHawk whispers, "I think the internet's already a few minutes ahead of us. Everyone's freaking out."

"Of course they are," Erin says barely more than a whisper. "The reception is garbage out here." Notifications take very little bandwidth, but a video is too much to load this far out. She's not seeing what everyone else is screaming about on the forums.

Finally, the stream stutters to life. Jessa is laughing while Colt teases her. The chat is flooding with heart emojis and dumb jokes. There's always a playful innocence with these two. Just a couple doing what they always do, filming their next find for their channel.

GhostLogger shifts beside her. "Why's it daylight? The sun's not even fully up yet."

CacheHawk shakes her head slowly, dread settling in. "This wasn't filmed today. Someone just uploaded it a few minutes ago."

The feed glitches and the audio drops out. For a moment, a burst of pixelated snow takes over the video. Jessa's laugh cuts mid-breath and Colt's voice distorts, then snaps back in on a higher pitch as the audio catches up. The camera shakes as if something bumped Jessa from behind. The stream jumps forward violently, catching up to the part everyone else has already seen. The chat has stopped sending hearts. It scrolls now in jagged, frantic blocks:

WHAT IS THAT
BEHIND YOU
TURN AROUND TURN AROUND TURN AROUND
this isn't staged
someone help them

Erin clutches the phone tighter as a shape moves in the background, not fully visible. The audio distorts again and through the lagging warble, there's a rustle of branches, then a grunt that isn't theirs.

GhostLogger's breath stutters beside her. "Shit… oh shit."

CacheHawk covers her mouth, eyes wide, frozen.

The camera lurches and Jessa's scream tears through the speakers. The camera hits the ground hard, the video skidding sideways. The sky, the branches, a blur of Colt's shoe, all spinning before a shadow collapses into view, then nothing. The stream fractures into a blur of color and static, then goes black. A dead silence hums from the phone.

GhostLogger stares at his screen still trying to process what he saw. He wipes a hand over his mouth. "We… we should call someone."

CacheHawk whispers, "No… no…" like her denial might undo the video.

Erin feels everything drop out from under her. All she can do is watch helplessly as the killer's real cache unfolds miles away and hours ago. She lowers her phone slowly, numbed to the world around her which has grown muted and distant. A soft breeze moves through the trees, brushing the back of her neck and the quiet around her sharpens her focus. She turns around and scans the dark shapes at the forest edge, expecting to find someone standing there.

Her mind keeps replaying the last hour, the minute the notification woke her, her rush out the door, showing up to two cachers strangely waiting in the lot instead of racing for a FTF, the QR Jackalope, the video. The photos of her. That's when the thought slams into her hard enough to make her step backward, snapping together with brutal clarity.

The killer brought her here and knew she would come. This cache wasn't for the community, it was for Erin. This was a perfect diversion, a trap. For the first time in this entire nightmare, she understands something with perfect, horrifying clarity: This wasn't a hunt. This was choreography, and she followed every step exactly the way the killer wanted. Her chest tightens and her breathing shallows.

"TrailSister," CacheHawk says, cautiously approaching her with raised hands. "Are you alright?"

Erin realizes she can't stay here. She backs away from CacheHawk and GhostLogger, her boots crunching through pine needles. "I need to go," she says, voice stripped down to bone. She doesn't look at them and doesn't offer an explanation.

When she reaches the trail, she turns to the direction of her car and walks quickly without looking back. She doesn't listen when CacheHawk calls her name and she doesn't acknowledge the phone buzzing over and over in her pocket.

All she can hear is that last scream, the one that cut off mid-plea. All she can feel is the cold imprint of the Polaroids on that website. Whatever the killer started, she's already in it deeper than she ever meant to be. As the trail curves and the forest swallows her, Erin realizes she isn't chasing a killer, never was. The killer is leading her.

Chapter 14: Out Of Bounds

Ryan leans over the evidence table, clicking through the last transfer of photos from the 'Where the Path Broke' murder scene, when a notification blinks across the corner of his screen.

Perfect View (Jessa & Colt) Livestream active.

He frowns. "What the hell…?"

Across the bay, Shannon swivels in her chair. "What?"

Ryan taps the notification to load the video, his brow tightening. "This is weird. It's tagged as live." He points at the video's time length. "But this is a prerecorded video. It looks like a full upload."

"Full upload?" Shannon asks.

"Yeah." He exhales sharply. "Like they streamed their live on one platform and recorded it for a later upload."

Shannon wheels closer, peering over his shoulder. "Why's it just dropping at six in the morning?"

"No idea, but it's trending stupid fast." Ryan points to the flood of comments rolling in under the video. "And people have started watching in droves."

Shannon's gaze sharpens. "So, this is the first time the forum is seeing this video?"

"Looks like it."

Ryan downloads the video from the link, then clicks the play button.

The video opens on a burst of sunlight so bright the lens flares into soft gold. The camera shakes once, in a way that suggests someone is tapping the equipment to make sure it's recording, before it settles into a smoother frame.

"Okay, okay, I think it's on," Jessa says off-screen, her voice full of that effortless cheer she always has in the couple's videos. She steps into view. Her hair is pulled back in a messy ponytail that somehow looks perfect anyway. She grins, leaning close to the lens for a second before backing up to center herself.

Behind her, the clearing glows with late-afternoon color, capturing a slant of light through fir branches. "Hey, friends!" she chirps. "It's Jess and…"

"The ultimate cache hound, Colt," he finishes, popping into frame behind her with two granola bars between his teeth. He frees one and dramatically hands it to Jessa. "Wilderness feast, babe."

She snorts. "You said these were protein bars."

"There's probably protein in it."

The chat in the corner of the screen floods with emojis of hearts, fire icons, and inside jokes from longtime fans.

colt u goofy

omg I love them

perfect day for a hike!

where is this??

Jessa turns, letting the camera pan over the ridge rising behind them. The trees are lush and their shadows are long. "Okay," she says, "today's cache is supposed to have an insane view. Like end-of-summer postcard vibes. So, if we get murdered out here, at least the backdrop is cute."

Colt groans. "Babe. Don't say murdered."

"It's a joke," she laughs, nudging him with her hip. "Relax."

The camera catches the moment just right, her laugh, his smile, the flirtatious press of their shoulders. Behind them, something shifts in the trees, a tiny movement barely visible, giving a flutter of shadow where nothing should move. The camera autofocuses on their faces again, glossing right over it.

Colt lifts the GPS in his hand. "Alright, looks like we're what, point-oh-two miles from the target?"

"'Perfect View,'" Jessa mimics the cache name in a dramatic announcer voice. "Let's go earn it."

They start walking, the camera bobbing with each step, and the woods swallow their laughter. The camera jostles as Jessa adjusts her grip, framing the trail ahead. Sunlight flickers through the canopy, slipping over her shoulders in warm, rippling stripes.

"Okay," she says, breath puffing more from excitement than exertion, "GPS says we're close but the signal's being a brat."

"That's the woods," Colt calls from a few steps ahead. "Not everything is Wi-Fi, Jess."

"Oh no," she gasps in fake horror. "Nature. Disgusting."

The chat explodes with laughing emojis.

girl no ur doing great

LOL the way she said nature. I'm ded. watch her fall again

colt protect jess!!

this place is BEAUTIFUL omg

Jessa pans the camera left, giving viewers a sweep of the slope dropping away into densely packed evergreens. A faint stream trickles below, soft and steady.

"You guys hear that?" she asks. "Soundtrack provided by Mother Earth."

Colt snorts. "You mean mosquito hell."

"Babe. Stop ruining my ambiance."

He turns back toward her with a grin and pauses. "The camera loves you," he says, tossing her a wink.

"Everybody loves me." She laughs and keeps walking. Something cracks faintly behind them. The mic doesn't catch enough detail to isolate it and the forest swallows the noise before it becomes anything more than background texture. Jessa keeps talking to the camera, oblivious of the sound. "So apparently this cache owner's whole thing is, like, scenic hides? Every cache is a 'viewpoint' or whatever."

Colt hums. "Makes sense. Place is gorgeous."

"It really is," she admits. "Like, if I were gonna get murdered…"

"Jessa," Colt groans.

"Kidding! Oh my god."

"You say that too much."

"It's a brand!"

Another wave of laughing emojis scrolls up the screen, despite Colt's obvious look of frustration.

The trail narrows between two leaning firs. Colt steps through first, ducking a low branch. When Jessa follows, she swings the camera around just in time for the lens to catch a shape, maybe, or a trick of distance, standing deeper in the trees. The autofocus locks onto the moving branch, blurring the background into a smear of green and shadow.

"We're almost there," he says, lifting the GPS. "Point-oh-one left."

She lifts the camera so her face fills the frame again, her cheeks are flushed and her eyes are bright. "You guys ready?" she asks, and more hearts flood the feed.

yessss goo

can't wait to see the view!!

this cache looks amazing

colt stop bullying her

omg i'm scared tho the woods r creepy

The trail ahead bends out of sight and neither of them notice the way the forest has gone still. Around the bend, the trail widens, spilling them into a clearing carved out between old cedars. Sunlight pours across the open space in thick, warm sheets with a golden-hour glow these influencers are notorious for filming.

"Oh my *god*," Jessa breathes, pivoting the camera to catch the horizon. "Look at this."

The view opens over a drop, revealing a crest of rolling green hills and an expansive lake below. A river bending far below feeds into the lake. She pans up to the sky bruised with late-afternoon purples. As she pans, a massive mountain with a flattened peak in the distance takes center stage. "OMG you guys! You can actually see Mount St. Helens from here. This is so pretty!"

Chat members detonate.

THIS IS GORGEOUS

Wowwwwwwwww

perfect view fr

postcard level omg

i want to go here holy crap

Colt whistles. "Alright, the cache owner wasn't lying."

For a moment, everything feels right, authentic, and perfectly pretty. Jessa settles onto a small boulder with the distant mountain in the background, accidentally making it look like a carefully staged photo pose. She opens her water bottle, talking between swallows. "Okay friends, point goes to the cache owner. This is wild."

Colt walks past her, scanning the edges of the clearing. "The container's gotta be around here. Probably tucked under a rock pile or something." He moves out of the frame, the feed catching only the sound of his boots crunching over loose rock.

Jessa leans back, sweeping her free hand across the scenery. "Tell me this doesn't look like a desktop background."

The chat agrees with a flood of heart reactions. She laughs at the reactions, bright and real. For a strange instant, the world seems to pause for her joy. Then the camera mic picks up a hint of noise beyond Colt's steps. Jessa doesn't hear it, but the camera does, and the chat does.

um did yall hear that?

what was that noise

someone else is there??

girl turn around

colt where u at??

Jessa adjusts her grip on the camera again, oblivious to the panic blooming in the feed. She continues walking, humming under her breath. Another crack is heard in the distance and this time, Jessa looks. "Colt, did you hear something?"

Colt's voice calls from off-screen. "Probably a deer."

"Or a bear," she says, nervously grinning.

"Jessa!" The viewers don't see his sour face but hear it in the tone of his voice.

"Kidding!" She winks playfully at the camera. The camera moves with her as she brushes dirt from her jeans. She pans toward the wood line, maybe for the view, maybe so their audience can try getting a look at what she missed. Sunlight slants between trunks, carving long shadows across the ground, but Colt never comes into frame. "Colt?" she calls.

"Back here," he answers. His voice is normal, calm, and focused on the hunt. "Jess, I found something weird."

Jessa perks up. "Ooh, spooky weird or cache weird?"

"You'll see."

She laughs nervously and the chat floods again.

no stop why would u go look

girl pls don't

this is how horror movies start

Jessa snorts, shaking her head. "Colt, you're freaking out the chat." There's a brief hesitation in her step before she heads toward him. She walks past the camera's earlier angle and the trees behind her rustle again, heavier this time. The autofocus clings stubbornly to Jessa's face as she moves, blurring whatever lurks deeper in the shadows into nothing more than color and motion.

"Babe," Colt calls, "Hurry and look at this."

"I'm coming." The camera swings toward him crouching near

the base of a cedar, one hand braced against the trunk, the other reaching toward something half-buried in the duff. The camera dips as Jessa approaches, breath quickening from the quick pace. "What is it?" she asks.

Colt doesn't answer right away. He shakes his head. "Not the cache."

Jessa angles the camera down. At first, it just looks like a scuff of disturbed earth, then the lens focuses on a small patch of moss that has been torn away, exposing the lighter, raw soil beneath. The ground around it is scarred by something dragging or twisting. Jessa frowns. "Was it an animal?"

"Maybe," Colt murmurs, though his voice carries a note that doesn't sound convinced. He brushes pine needles aside with two fingers. "Cachers aren't supposed to bury their hides. Could be a deer digging?"

The chat reacts instantly.

that's not a deer dig

nope nope nope

pls leave

that's so sus

Jessa zooms closer, the camera swaying slightly as she crouches beside him. "It looks fresh."

"Yeah." Colt rests his hand on his thigh, steadying himself. "Like within a day or two."

Jessa glances toward the thick of trees. "You think someone camped out here?"

"There would be more evidence of camping." He forces a chuckle. "Maybe someone buried a time capsule."

"Babe." She nudges him with her knee.

"What? People do weird stuff in the woods all the time." His words are light, but his tone carries a hint of concern.

The camera catches the way his eyes study the trees around the couple. A breeze slips through the clearing. Something shifts deeper in the brush, just enough movement to raise the tiny hairs on the back of Jessa's neck. She stiffens. "Did you…?"

"Yeah," Colt murmurs. He stands slowly, brushing dirt from his palms. "Probably just an animal."

"In the middle of the day?"

"Well, yeah. Maybe." This is the second time he doesn't sound convincing.

Chat explodes again.

NOPE GET OUT

listen to us…run

colt pls take her home

Jessa puts a hand on his shoulder. "Babe, maybe we should just look for the cache."

Colt nods and lifts the GPS. "Cache should be close. Like, right around here."

Jessa gives a shaky laugh. "Okay, the forest is being a creeper, but we're not bailing. Come on." She straightens and starts forward again, the camera bobbing again with each of her steps.

Behind them, a subtle shift rustles the forest. It barely registers in the audio. Jessa keeps talking, trying to fill the silence. "Okay guys, I swear this is the part where the killer jumps out in the movie," she jokes.

Colt groans. "Jess seriously, can you not."

She doesn't finish her sentence. The camera swings as Colt stops abruptly. She nearly collides into him, not expecting the sudden halt. "There," he whispers. "The cache."

A dozen steps ahead of the couple is a small rock cairn, neatly stacked, sitting just a few feet from the edge of the overlook. It is too neat to be naturally occurring. Jessa exhales softly. "Oh, that's…" She can't find the word. Neither can he. "Seems like a weird place for rock balancing."

The chat floods in warning, panic, and fascination. Colt approaches the little rock cairn, stepping slow in a way that doesn't match his usual "charge ahead" bravado. Jessa follows, the camera raised, trying to keep everything in frame.

"That's it, right?" she murmurs. "That has to be it."

"Yeah," Colt says. His voice is quiet now, stripped of his earlier playfulness. "It can't be coincidence this is out here. If it isn't the cache, it has to be a clue."

The chat streams with frantic commentary.

don't touch it

SOMETHING IS WRONG

that's not normal

pls leave

I hate this I hate this

COLT STOP

His fingers hovering over the top stone and he hesitates briefly, then flashes a smile at the camera before plucking it from the stack. Under the top rock lies a folded piece of paper. There's nothing else, no container, no trinkets, just the note. Colt frowns. "Where's the…?"

"Maybe it'll lead us to the cache?" Jessa offers weakly.

The paper flutters in the gentle wind but doesn't blow away. He takes the paper, careful to not knock over the remaining rocks.

Jessa angles the camera closer. "Well, open it," she says, trying hard to sound more excited than nervous.

"Yeah," Colt murmurs. "Yeah, okay." He unfolds the paper.

The camera tries to autofocus on the ink marking the paper between his jittery fingers. After a second, the words come into view. They're handwritten, sharp and neat. **LOOK BACK**

Jessa breathes a half-laugh. "Oh wow, spooky clue moment. Very creative."

Colt doesn't laugh, he glances at the camera, then reads it again.

Jessa shifts beside him, her voice going quieter. "Colt… what does that mean?"

He looks up at the camera. "I think it means…"

is this a prank??

someone call 911??

this isn't funny

they're not alone

does anyone else see that behind them??

A rustle behind them stops his sentence. It isn't the delicate flutter of an animal or wind. The sound is heavy, intentional, and close. The camera captures Colt looking from the camera to the distance behind. Jessa whips the camera around instinctively. The lens blurs on a dark shape, then clears, catching the tall cedar trunks of the forest in soft focus, sharply contrasted against deep shadows, but no movement.

The chat detonates.

WHAT IS THAT

BEHIND YOU

TURN AROUND TURN AROUND TURN AROUND

this isn't staged

someone help them

Jessa whispers, "Colt…?"

He doesn't answer. He's jumped ahead of Jessa, his motion a blur in the video. The camera doesn't follow him, it shakes as Jessa's fear takes over and her focus turns from influencer to survival.

"Babe?" she screams. The camera trembles in her hand, capturing her leg, the balanced stones, and arcs of the ground around her.

Colt finally says, very quietly, "Jess, run!"

The feed jitters, then glitches. Audio warps around a single, heavy footfall, then the camera swings fast. The video catches a blur of trees, the sky, and then the shadow of motion, but nothing clear.

The autofocus panics and everything fractures. Before the frame stabilizes, a noise hits the camera hard, the sudden impact of metal on bone. Whatever made impact is jarring and the screen briefly explodes into static. In the absence of video, there is a scream, raw and ragged, torn from the gut. The wail is primal and final.

The camera drops, knocking the visuals back into existence, and the video tumbles across the dirt. Rocks and earth are interrupted by flashes of sky, a branch, and a brief glimpse of two bodies, before it settles sideways, capturing only the edge of the overlook and a sliver of forest floor.

The feed blinks once, then freezes on a final frame. The image is a crooked, sideways still, capturing dirt, a wedge of sky, and the edge of the overlook with Mount St. Helens blurred in the background. The foreground is half filled with Jessa's eye wide open but unfocused, framed in streaming blood. She isn't moving. The sound cuts to a flat, empty hush. The blood stops flowing and for several long seconds, nothing moves.

The chat blows up.

WHAT JUST HAPPENED

did they fall??

SOMEONE CALL 911 RIGHT NOW

THIS ISN'T FAKE

WHERE ARE THEY

OH MY GOD OH MY GOD

this isn't a fucking skit

mods?? help??

why is the stream still up??

WHY IS NO ONE CUTTING THE FEED

The frozen frame is interrupted by a bird soaring in the distance, then it cuts to black. The feed doesn't end. The sound of Colt's voice screaming Jessa's name and begging for mercy fills the space left by the lack of motion.

Viewers begin arguing in the feed.

it's a prank. it HAS to be.

no it's not, did u HEAR that

that was a real scream

someone screen record this

i can't breathe

oh god someone do something

Hundreds of messages flood upward, and the chat scroll becomes a frantic blur, unreadable except for the occasional word that sticks out, screaming in text form:

HELP.

CALL.

RUN.

DEAD.

The viewer count spikes violently and then stutters, as though people are joining faster than the platform can track. A banner flashes across the corner of the stream: **Playback unavailable. Please try again later.** Then the screen snaps to black and stays that way.

For a long moment, neither Shannon nor Ryan speaks. The quiet inside the tech bay is immense under the overhead fluorescents. The last frozen frame of sky and dirt lingers in Ryan's mind, creating an afterimage burned through his eyelids.

Shannon exhales first, a long, uneven breath to cushion the fall of her stomach dropping out from under her. "Jesus Christ," she whispers.

Ryan's jaw flexes once. His hand is still resting on the mouse, frozen in position. "That wasn't staged," he says quietly.

Shannon shakes her head. "No, and that scream." She stops herself, pressing her fingers to her mouth, and looks away. "I didn't expect to start the day with a snuff film."

Ryan clicks furiously, checking properties, metadata, website timestamps, then drags a hand over his face. "It looks like this was filmed yesterday. Why post it this morning?" He swallows hard. "Someone wanted this to go up now."

Shannon steps back from the monitor, grabbing her phone. "We need to tell Vance."

Shannon taps Vance's contact, her eyes barely registering it while she keeps staring at the dead screen of the video. Her voice is small, stripped down. "Ryan, those kids were alive yesterday."

He doesn't answer. The video window flickers once, an auto-reload, and settles into a still thumbnail of Jessa's bright smile. Shannon flinches and Ryan clicks the window closed.

Chapter 15: Did Not Find

Detective Vance is fifteen minutes from the station when the screen of her phone lights up. She answers and is met by CSU Chesshir's voice. "Detective, we discovered a new possible homicide location this morning. It looks like another geocache out by Yale Lake, south and east from Saddle Dam."

The news snaps her out of her mindless commute. "Text me the details." She hits her lights and flips a U-turn at the next intersection. The south side of Yale is still within county limits, which means the new site is still within her jurisdiction.

It takes forty-five minutes of highways before she leaves paved road for gravel backroads. In that time, dispatch has already patched her into DNR, looping in forestry units, and flagging EMS to stage at the main access point. Deputies have rolled out from the north county substation. She flies by the first checkpoint as officers wave her up the way and she cuts the sirens before the cruiser rounds the last bend of the ruddy dirt road. Vance prefers it that way, letting the dead keep their quiet.

Two patrol SUVs sit crooked along the shoulder, their lights flashing amber in the thin morning fog, a warning for anyone else stupid enough to wander this early. A deputy stands near the trailhead, his arms are folded tight and his breath clouding in the cold. Vance steps out of the cruiser. The air here is sharper. She pulls her jacket tight.

"Detective." The deputy nods once.

"You find the scene yet?" she asks.

He gestures down a narrow footpath, barely more than a deer trail cut between ferns and brush. "Maybe a quarter mile in. We located it but didn't touch anything."

Vance moves past him onto the trail. The forest closes around her immediately with towering firs and thick moss, and her feet sink into the soft mulch of decades of needles underfoot. The deputy falls in behind her, adding his own steps to the forest floor. The air is cold enough that her breath nearly shatters the moment it leaves her mouth.

A single bird calls somewhere far off. "Northern Flicker," the deputy says behind her in a soft voice, stating the fact, trying to steady the air. She doesn't acknowledge his wilderness lore.

The path curves once and narrows, then opens into a flatter patch. Vance's boots stop sinking as she steps into the clearing, landing on firmer ground. She stops at the view, not of the dense clouds that have covered most of St. Helens, but on the ridge where the body of a woman lay exposed to the elements, just beyond the clearing. The soil here is darker and gouged with the marks of a struggle. Not enough to map the entire fight, but enough to tell her it was fast, violent, and desperate.

Vance skirts the tracks, stepping over potential evidence, making her way to the body. The deputy comes up beside her. He points to a small card on the body's hip. "License says the victim is Jessa Whitlow, twenty-six, from Longview."

Vance says nothing but recognizes the name. She steps closer, examining the girl. The influencer's brightness, her oversized smile and ring-light sparkle, all of it has been stripped away, leaving only the body she died in.

Jessa Whitlow lies on her right side with one arm flung forward like she reached for something she never made it to. Her clothes are torn in places that don't match the terrain, not the typical pattern for being snagged on branches. The rips indicate she was pulled or wrenched, showing signs of deliberate violence. Her hair is stained dark and has leaves stuck in it with bits of moss clinging to the strands. Her face is turned toward the lake, and her skin is washed pale against the forest floor. There's enough spatter on the ferns to tell Vance that Jessa died upright, and that whatever struck her, struck hard. She uses her pen and lifts tufts of Jessa's hair, finding a blunt-edge impact to the skull. The angle is low, coming from behind her left ear. Other secondary injuries are visible along her body, defensive wounds along the forearm, abrasions on the palms from falling, a small tear along the knuckles where she likely hit something, maybe the attacker, maybe the ground.

Vance steps forward slowly, breathing once through her nose, then again through her mouth. She leans closer, scanning the scalp wound. It's clean, not in the sense of neat, nothing about this is neat, but in the sense that the blow wasn't messy or wild. The strike was controlled. Someone struck her once and knew it would be enough.

Vance angles around the head to the victim's face. The girl's eyes are missing, and a number of abrasions pock her skin. "Did this son of a bitch take her eyes?"

"No, ma'am." He steps forward and points at the tiny lacerations. "These are peck marks. These smaller points, that looks like the Steller's Jay beak patterns. The larger ones are likely crows, which would explain the eyes."

She looks up at him, stunned, finally recognizing his wildlife skill. "Remind me to call you when I'm chasing Big Bird."

The deputy chuckles softly, but stops abruptly. His face wrinkles, trying to determine whether she just complimented or insulted him.

A torn camera bag lies near Jessa's hand. The strap is snapped and the canvas is torn. She looks at the dirt under Jessa's nails, finding them heavily compacted and forest-rich under the manicured nails. A scan of the scene around the victim tells her there isn't another body, her partner Colt is nowhere to be seen.

What she does see is a line of disturbed moss leading into the trees on the far side of the small clearing. She moves toward it and before she can reach the new trail mouth, her eyes land on a shape half-hidden in shadow just inside the brush. She inches forward to find a broken camera tripod, one leg bent and the hinge split. A smear of blood on the handle catches the morning light, highlighting a clump of Jessa's blond hair. That's the weapon.

Before she can process more, a rustle behind her makes her palm drop instinctively toward her holster. It's only the deputy at the tape line, talking to the radio crackling at his shoulder. She grabs his attention and points at the camera stand until he acknowledges.

Vance looks back at Jessa from this angle. The girl's backpack lies a few feet away, its zipper half open, showing a flash of teal fabric, maybe her windbreaker. Something metallic glints faintly, the edge of a portable ring-light collapsed into itself, still packed away and never used on this ledge.

Vance exhales slowly. This wasn't staged, not like Hidden Hollow, not like the Washougal body. This is opportunistic, fast and efficient. This feels less premeditated.

"Jesus, kid," she murmurs, walking back to Jessa.

From a distance behind her, a vehicle door slams. Moments later, gravel crunches and two sets of footsteps break through the underbrush, lighter and quicker than patrol. Vance doesn't turn until she hears Shannon's voice behind her, low and steady. "Detective, we're on scene."

Shannon stops a few feet from Vance. Her breathing's controlled, but her eyes are carrying something she didn't want to say over the radio. "Detective," she says quietly. "We need to talk to you before we start the grid."

Ryan lags a half-step behind her, carrying an equipment case that looks heavy in his tired arms. He gives Vance a nod that tries to be confident but doesn't quite make it. Vance steps back from the body so CSU can approach. Shannon doesn't flinch at the sight, but

Ryan does. Vance files it away, acknowledging he's good with screens but still needs field experience.

"What have you got, Chesshir?" she asks.

Ryan clears his throat, but Shannon shoots him a look that stops him cold. "It's about the video," Shannon says. Vance waits and Shannon continues, lowering her voice almost conspiratorially. "It wasn't live and whoever posted it, actually uploaded it this morning."

Ryan sets the case on the ground and fumbles with the latch, trying to steady his shaking fingers. "The recording timestamp was yesterday afternoon."

Vance doesn't react. "Where did it originate?"

Shannon glances at Ryan, and for a moment, he looks like he might lie or soften something, but he stays silent with a gentle shake of his head. Shannon answers without looking up. "Colt Rowan's phone."

Ryan adds quickly, "Not from the phone directly, though. The phone's been dead for hours. The upload came through a linked account, a scheduled publish. It's clean, with no traceable user signature except the device ID."

"So, the video was uploaded from Colt's phone," Vance finishes it aloud, not asking, confirming.

Shannon nods once. "Yes." She steps back, scanning the scene, then begins sorting through items in the case Ryan has prepared. She hands Ryan the camera, which he promptly prepares for use. While he does, she slides on a pair of neoprene gloves.

Vance lets the news settle over the clearing. The implications are ugly. Colt hadn't been a strong suspect before this morning, but his odds keep increasing. She watches the two techs set up, Chesshir placing markers and Maddox following behind, lining up shots.

While the team sets up the scene, Vance walks to the deputy. "Deputy, I need you to get me everything you can on a Colt Rowan.

He is connected with the vic. They are all over social media, so it shouldn't be tough to track down."

She turns back to the scene, Ryan is taking shots of the body and Shannon has crouched beside the rock cairn, carefully unstacking and investigating each rock. Vance pulls out her notepad and writes, trying to track each puzzle piece and determine which fits this picture.

Shannon lifts the last rock in the stack to reveal a small envelope. She stops immediately, and calls, "Ryan, I need shots."

Ryan rushes to the rockpile and aims, firing shots from different angles before Shannon nods with satisfaction. Vance steps closer, watching Shannon carefully examine the find. She turns the envelope over to reveal both sides are blank, so she opens it. Inside is a folded piece of paper and a Polaroid.

Shannon holds it steady, she already knows this part matters more than any trace. The Polaroid shows Erin in the back of the cruiser at Washougal, her face half-lit by the blue light glow of police lights, staring through the window, seemingly unaware someone was watching. Vance doesn't react outwardly, but a chill threads deep inside her, thinking about how they got so close to Erin without being noticed.

Ryan looks away, suddenly uncomfortable. "Oh shit, that angle looks like they were close. Whoever did this is getting bold."

Vance doesn't look at him, but Ryan feels her disapproval. "Or stupid."

Shannon adds quietly, "And the note's stamped. It looks like one of those rabbits with antlers. What do you call them?"

"A jackalope." Vance exhales slowly. "Read it."

Shannon unfolds the paper carefully, eyes scanning the short message before she passes it to Vance. The handwriting of the single line is neat and controlled. "She looks away when you talk."

Ryan shudders, fidgeting with the camera. Shannon refuses to move, waiting for her superior. Vance keeps her face unreadable, though the heat crawling up her spine is unmistakable. The killer wasn't just watching Erin, the killer was watching the whole scene.

Vance hands her the slip and says flatly, "File it."

Shannon folds the paper and slips it back in the envelope, then closes the flap. She hands it to Ryan who is already waiting with an evidence bag. "I noticed coming in that there's more drag patterns along the edge of the woods. We'll follow them out, but Detective?" She hesitates slightly. "It looks like Colt's not here."

"I know." Vance nods once. "Find where he went."

"On it." Shannon rises, signaling Ryan to start the grid sweep. She wipes her gloves against her pants out of habit, even though nothing touched her. Her eyes track outward, scanning the edge of the forest, the rocks, the faint glimmer of the lake through a break in the branches.

Ryan clicks another photo of the dismantled cairn, then lowers the camera slightly and scans the perimeter. "There's… um. No obvious direction he left from." He's not wrong, there are marks, but nothing that resolves into anything that looks like a clear exit path.

As they move, Vance looks back at Jessa Whitlow's still form and the lake flashing silver behind her from the sunrise. Something ugly settles heavy in her gut. Erin was never the only target, and Colt Rowan isn't missing, one way or another, he's part of the next message.

Shannon walks a slow circle around the perimeter. "Nothing consistent," she murmurs. "Some scuffs here." She crouches and touches a shallow disturbance near a root system. "It could be from the deputy when he came to confirm, or Jessa, if she was running."

Vance steps beside her. The marks don't form a line, they simply make noise at a crime scene. Footprints, disturbed needles, a patch of dirt that looks muddled enough, it could be from someone turning sharply or tripping. There's nothing that tells a story, nothing that has direction or intent. It isn't helpful, but she knows it also isn't random.

"Whatever happened," Shannon says, "it wasn't prolonged."

Ryan nods. "Or it didn't happen here."

Vance studies him for half a second. Ryan looks nervous saying it, but he's right. Shannon glances up, her brows tight. "Detective," she says, "there's no blood trail and no clear secondary struggle zone. If Colt was attacked here, we'd have something, anything."

"We don't," Vance says.

Ryan shifts. "Which could mean he wasn't attacked at all."

Shannon looks sharply at him, but she doesn't immediately disagree. "Or he ran," she counters. "Or chased the attacker."

"Or he was chased." Ryan follows up. "We don't have enough evidence."

"No," Vance agrees. "We don't."

The recognition hangs thick in the cold air before Vance returns to her prior vantage point of the scene. Shannon moves a little farther into the brush, pushing aside a fern with her wrist. "There's movement here," she says. "But it's one set, and heavy. Hard to tell if it's someone moving fast or carrying something light."

Ryan frowns. "How so?"

Shannon straightens. "The prints are sunken a little deeper than ours, but the heel never touches. It doesn't quite look like a sprint and the kick-off isn't pronounced."

Vance steps forward, following the shallow disturbance between tree trunks. It goes ten feet, then vanishes entirely into untouched ground. She considers Chesshir's theory and adds her own without a word, that this looks more like a false lead.

Ryan leaves the gear and follows. "Why stop here?" he asks.

Vance doesn't answer. She just crouches, her fingertips trace close to the dirt without touching.

Shannon joins Vance and Ryan, scanning the area again.

"Detective, this whole scene feels wrong."

"Define wrong," Vance says.

Feeling the unspoken test in Vance's words, she chooses her own carefully. "Deliberate without being useful."

Vance doesn't express agreement. After a moment, she looks at the CSU team and says, "Keep looking. This isn't the whole picture."

Ryan lifts his camera again but hesitates before clicking. "Detective, what if Colt left on his own?"

Shannon turns to him. "Why would he leave her behind?"

Ryan shrugs helplessly. "Maybe he didn't. Maybe he couldn't get back."

"Why didn't he report it, then?"

Vance stands and dusts off her knees. "Maybe he came back and didn't want us to know."

That shuts both CSU techs up. She looks over the clearing again at the scattered disturbances, the inconsistent footprints, the silence that has so many explanations and yet, none that provide answers. "Widen the search in each direction," Vance orders. "Mark everything that looks like movement, but don't draw conclusions. Right now, the scene is lying to us."

Shannon nods sharply. "Yes, ma'am."

Ryan swallows and follows her into the brush.

Vance remains alone at the shallow cutoff in the earth. If Colt ran, there should be a reason. If Colt is dead, there should be evidence. If Colt didn't kill her, he should've reported it. If he did, he had reason to leave her here. Every possibility leads in a different direction, but none are solid.

Shannon's voice breaks through the brush to Vance's right. "Detective, I've got something."

Vance turns toward Shannon standing near a patch of sword fern where the ground dips slightly. Something glints at the base of the fern, half-buried in damp needles. Ryan is already pointing his camera, muttering as he tries to get the autofocus to behave in low morning light.

Shannon waits for him to photograph, then crouches and lifts the object carefully with a gloved fingertip. It is a keyring with a leather tag and a single key, the head coated in a black rubberized grip.

Vance steps closer. "What might it go to?"

"No idea," Shannon says. "A house key or a storage unit?" She pauses. "It isn't shaped like a car key." She holds the key up to the gray morning light. There's a faint smear on the metal.

Vance extends a hand. "Let me see."

Shannon passes it over. The moment Vance turns the key, she notices a small stamp at the edge of the grip, barely pressed into the rubber, the outline of antlers.

"Shit," Ryan whispers. "Do you think it was dropped or left on purpose?"

Shannon nods grimly. "If it was intentional, why a key? What does it open?"

Vance rolls the key between her fingers, her mind already turning. "If it's here, at Jessa's scene, it's not random. Our unsub isn't messy, everything is orchestrated." She studies the antlers. "This was meant to be found."

Ryan frowns. "Like a next step?"

"Or a next location," Shannon adds.

Vance pockets the key in an evidence sleeve and seals it herself. "Keep combing," she says. "If this was left for us, it can't be the only thing. This is a piece to a bigger puzzle."

Shannon pushes deeper into the brush with Ryan following behind. Vance walks toward the narrowing ridge, scanning every angle, every indentation, every place where someone could've placed something with intention. Then she sees it, a rock deliberately centered on a fallen log far from the active scene. She approaches and the rock shifts easily under her glove. Beneath it lies a folded page from a map booklet with fresh fold creases. There are no moisture warps and no aging. It's a topography map of the county, but only one area is circled, a ridge to the south. There's another overlook, not far from here, but inaccessible from here without looping back to the main road.

Vance calls the techs to her. Ryan jogs up, breathing heavier than he should for field work. "You have something?" Shannon is a handful of steps behind.

"It's another coordinate," Vance says. "We are being led again."

"But why leave it here?" Ryan rubs his forehead, exasperated. "Why split the scene?"

Shannon answers before the detective. "Because splitting forces us to investigate. Someone wants us running."

Vance stares at the circle on the map, it's not wide, and it is precise to the contour lines. This isn't a kill site, it is a waypoint, she is sure of it. She gives Ryan room to document, then folds the map and tucks it into an envelope.

"Then, it looks like we run," she says, waving the deputy over. "Stay put, the coroner should be here shortly. Chesshir, Maddox, you're with me. We're hitting that second ridge."

Ryan hesitates, his eyes falling to the body behind them, then to the forest ahead. "Detective, do you think we're being watched?"

"We need to assume we are always being watched," Vance says, already walking. Shannon falls in beside her with Ryan lingering only a heartbeat before following.

They leave the scene of Jessa's tragic ending. For now, Colt Rowan is neither alive nor dead and, until Vance opens Schrodinger's box, she'll never know if he is a victim or a suspect. Ahead of them, the ridge waits.

Chapter 16: Needs Owner Attention

The trail spits Erin out, done with her as much as she is with it. She stumbles the last few yards to her car with heavy boots and lungs still tight from the scream she's holding in. The forest behind her feels wound-up, the trees are more tense than usual and even the dew seems afraid to fall. The sky hasn't brightened much, and the early gray light makes the world look thin and unfinished.

Her car sits alongside CacheHawk and GhostLogger's vehicles in the small gravel turnout. They are still the only cachers onsite, at least, that's how it looks at first. She slows, finally having the space to catch her breath. The adrenaline in her blood is turning sour, giving her that trembling drain that comes after terror.

She checks her pockets for her keys, her fingers barely closing around them. Her hand is shaking so hard it feels like it isn't hers. Now that she's in the clearing, her phone starts buzzing relentlessly with notifications she refuses to check.

The gravel crunches under her as she moves toward the driver-side door and fumbles with the key fob twice before the lock clicks open. Her breath fogs the air in a thin, twitchy ribbon. She wants to cry but she can't, the part of her that would break is numb. She just needs to be home.

Her hand closes on the door handle and she freezes as her eyes are drawn to an almost nonexistent reflection in her window. There's someone standing across the road at the edge of the trees. Erin tries not to look directly and instead, pretends to fumble with her keys while side-eyeing the shape. There's definitely a man, half-shadowed by a cluster of cedar trunks, hands in his pockets, with a loose posture, watching her with pointed attention. She slides her hand into her jacket and grips the pepper spray, knowing today is the day she'll have to use it. She takes her other hand off of her keys and slides it onto Danny's knife before facing the man full chested, ready to fight.

She sees TrailWolf, but he's not in a hurry to find the cache. Erin glances up and down the road, there's no car in sight. He isn't waiting to cross the road, he's just standing in the cold, staring. Erin's pulse strikes into her throat hard enough that she has to swallow the pain. He doesn't move or even wave, he just watches her like she's the one who's out of place.

For a second the whole morning tilts. She's still processing the video, the screams, the QR code, the taunt, the feeling of being steered like livestock. Now, the sight of him alone on the road, in the dawn, with no vehicle in sight, is nearly enough to break her. Erin's fingers tighten around the canister with a bone-deep alertness her body didn't ask her permission for.

TrailWolf finally shifts his weight, his first step kicking a rock into the road, giving warning that he is coming. He doesn't flinch at the sight of her stance and his eyes track the placement of her hands. If anything, he looks faintly amused. He crosses slowly, watching the woman frozen at her car.

"You look shook, TrailSister." He's not as loud as when he's trying to sound clever and overshoots into asshole territory. His voice barely registers in the quiet morning.

Erin doesn't move, but she plants her left foot deeper into the gravel. "What are you doing out here?" she asks, trying to keep her voice level but failing.

He lifts his shoulders with a lazy half-shrug. "Looking for a cache. Isn't that what we're all doing?" He gestures vaguely toward the trail she just escaped from. "Looks like you beat me to it."

She doesn't follow his gesture, she refuses to let him out of her sight, even for a fraction of a second. There's something off about him, he's too casual for the moment with an eerie stillness behind his eyes. He hasn't removed his hands from his pockets, almost mirroring Erin.

"Where did you park?" she asks.

He smirks slightly and nods to the left. "At the other trailhead."

"No," she says sharper. "There weren't any other turnoffs, I was looking on the way in."

"Turnouts aren't the only place a cacher can park," he fires back. "Come on, TrailSister, this isn't your first forest."

She hates that she can't argue with that, hates that he's right, hates that she can't tell if he's being defensive or evasive.

His gaze drops briefly to the pocket where she's holding her pepper spray. "You planning to pull a gun out of that little pocket, or what?"

She doesn't answer, but her fingers feel the spray's trigger, debating on letting him find out she's not bluffing.

His smirk fades. "Relax. I'm not the one you should be worried about."

The comment slams into her. The way he says it is smooth but carries an ominous knowing. "Why are you here?" she asks.

TrailWolf's expression shifts a millimeter toward annoyance. "Same as you, like I said. Notification lit up, cache was posted, and here I am."

"So, instead of going straight from your car to the cache, you walked down the road," she snaps.

He tilts his head, eyes narrowing. "We all take different paths."

Erin glances again down the gravel road, scanning the bend, behind the cedars. She doesn't see a car, doesn't hear an engine. "You telling me you walked a mile instead of pulling over with the rest of us?" she asks, her tone raising more than she wants.

"Maybe," he says, but the word lands like bait.

Her pulse ticks higher as her chest tightens and her brain starts spiraling. TrailWolf studies her face for a moment longer than feels polite. "You okay?" he asks, but it's not concern. It's curiosity wearing a mask.

"You shouldn't be here," she says. "Not today."

He huffs a single laugh. "Why? Because you say so?"

She catches her tone and tries to talk herself down. "Because it's not safe."

"Safe?" He steps closer, just enough to make her spine lock. "Sweetheart, safety isn't part of this game. It never was, you should know that."

She flinches at the word sweetheart. It's not flirtatious, he's mocking her. Dismissive in a way that confirms he has zero idea how deeply she's unraveling, or worse, that's what he wants. TrailWolf's gaze moves toward the trailhead behind her. "So what happened up there?" he asks. "You ran out like the trees were on fire."

Erin's throat clamps. She doesn't answer, and he seems to enjoy the softness of the wound he's pressed. "You know," he says quietly, "people talk. About you."

Her skin numbs. "What does that mean?"

TrailWolf doesn't answer. He just watches her, his expression unreadable and hands still buried in his pockets. In this moment, this single beat, Erin realizes she can't tell if he's trying to intimidate her or warn her.

A branch snaps at the trail's mouth behind her. Erin jerks, her pepper spray clenched tight. TrailWolf doesn't move, but his eyes snap to her pocket, waiting.

Footsteps and voices scramble down the trail. GhostLogger bursts out first, breathing hard, a sheen of sweat across his forehead. He freezes when he sees Erin squared off against TrailWolf, her jacket shifted just enough to suggest a blade or something equally as dangerous.

"Whoa, hey!" GhostLogger lifts both hands defensively. "Hey,

TrailWolf, you're too late."

CacheHawk steps out behind him, winded but bright-eyed, still buzzing with the adrenaline of the FTF and the chase they didn't win. "Jesus, TrailSister, you scared the hell out of…" She stops dead when she registers the scene. Her eyes dart between Erin's hands and TrailWolf's impassive look. "Is everything okay?" CacheHawk asks cautiously.

TrailWolf doesn't help the situation. "Depends on who you ask," he says.

Erin nearly stutters. "You two shouldn't be here," she manages. "You need to leave, now."

GhostLogger frowns, lowering his hands but not relaxing. "Why, and what the hell was up with that find? You bolted fast. Why was your picture…"

"Don't," Erin snaps, sharper than she intends. "Don't bring up that cache."

CacheHawk bristles at her tone. "We're just asking."

Erin ignores her, eyes pinned to TrailWolf. "Why are you here?"

GhostLogger answers before he can. "Same reason we are. For the cache."

TrailWolf smirks but stays quiet.

"And you believe that?" Erin demands.

GhostLogger's brows knit. "Yeah? Why wouldn't I?"

"Because he wasn't on the trail," she fires back. "He came from nowhere. No car, no gear."

GhostLogger shifts uncomfortably. "TrailWolf bushwhacks. Everybody knows that."

Erin shakes her head. "No. No, he came up the road and was just standing there, waiting. Tell me where his car is."

TrailWolf's jaw flexes. "You done?"

"Fuck you," Erin snaps. "Something's not right about you and everyone here is pretending not to see it."

CacheHawk folds her arms. "What the hell, chick. You need to calm down."

Those are the wrong words and the wrong tone. Erin's adrenaline spikes viciously. "Calm down? People are dying. Somebody just…" She can't finish it. Her voice cracks hard enough to scare her. "You saw the damn video!"

"Hey, it's okay." GhostLogger softens in a pitying way she can't stand. "TrailSister, let's just take it down a notch. I'm sure we can make some sense of things. Jessa and Colt are probably just staging something crazy for views."

"Oh my god," Erin mutters, stepping back. "Of course. Of course nobody gets how fucked this is."

"We didn't say that," CacheHawk interjects, defensively quick.

"You don't have to," Erin says, looking at each of them. "Your faces say everything."

TrailWolf finally speaks, slow and cutting. "First, you think the killer is out to get you, now you think everyone's out to get you."

Erin whips her glare toward him. "Sounds like something the killer would say."

He shrugs again, but doesn't deny it.

GhostLogger steps between them. "Okay, enough. Nobody's accusing anybody of anything. We're all concerned about what's happening, all right? Let's just stop and think."

"Think?" Erin lets out a brittle laugh. "You want to think? How about the fact that someone lured us up here on purpose?"

CacheHawk's expression shifts into guilt, fear, and denial, all blurring together. "We weren't lured anywhere, TrailSister. We all chased that FTF."

"Is that what he did?" Erin releases her pepper spray and gestures sharply toward TrailWolf, her fingers still coiled around the hilt of Danny's knife. "He just happened to show up without a car? Without even pretending to look for the cache?"

TrailWolf's lip curls. "Take a breath. You're being paranoid."

"You bet your ass I am."

GhostLogger tries again. "TrailSister."

"No," she says. "I'm done." She doesn't look at any of them now, not their confused faces, not their fear, and certainly not their judgment. Instead, she turns to her car, the only safe thing in the clearing. As she moves toward the door, her phone buzzes in her pocket, loud and insistent. She flinches like it's a gunshot.

TrailWolf watches her reaction with irritating amusement while CacheHawk shifts uncomfortably. Erin swallows a tremor. She doesn't answer the phone, she just mutters, "I've gotta go. I need out of here." She climbs into the car and slams the door hard enough that all three of them jump outside. The sound rings through the turnoff, sharp in the cold morning air. She sits there, breath fogging the windshield, hands shaking so badly she has to grip the steering wheel just to feel anchored.

Her phone is still buzzing, three vibrations in a row, someone is calling her. She forces herself to look at the screen. The screen reads, **Detective**. Her stomach twists, of course it's Vance. Naturally, she would be calling now, reminding her the world didn't stop spinning just because Erin broke apart.

Outside the windshield, she sees GhostLogger trying to talk to TrailWolf, with animated hand gestures that don't get through. TrailWolf stands completely still, face unreadable, as if Erin's meltdown didn't register as anything more significant than weather.

CacheHawk leans against her truck with a slump, her arms are folded and she's chewing the inside of her cheek as though she's reconsidering her life choices. Erin's phone vibrates again, the word detective still glowing. She answers the call.

"Erin?" Vance's voice is wired. She doesn't offer a greeting or a formality, just the rush of a detective already in the middle of something terrible. "I need you to listen."

Erin opens her mouth, but nothing comes out.

"It's important," Vance presses. "Where are you?"

Erin looks at the trailhead, the lot, and the three cachers still lingering in a loose formation, holding court. "I'm in my car near Lucia Falls. A new cache was published this morning, The Look Back," she whispers.

A sharp inhale crackles through the speaker. "Erin. Stay in your car. Do you hear me?"

Her fingers clench around the phone. "Why? What's going on?"

She's met with silence, just long enough to make her teeth itch, then Vance answers, "There's been another murder."

Erin's chest caves inward, air thinning. "Jessa…"

"Look, just stay in your car," Vance repeats. "Send me your coordinates, I'll send deputies to your location. You are not safe there."

Erin flinches so hard she nearly drops the phone. "What? Why? What do you mean I'm not…"

"Lock your doors."

Erin reaches with trembling hands and hits the button. All four locks thunk in unison. Each cacher outside pauses to look at her. "Detective, what's happening?" She steals a glance at TrailWolf. "Do you know who it is?"

"I'll explain soon. Just stay put and send me your damn coordinates." She ends the call.

While she's staring at the screen, her phone buzzes again with another incoming call, this time it's Mark. She lets it go to voicemail. She does what Vance says, her fingers moving fast, switching apps, copying coordinates, then switching again to text the detective.

She looks at TrailWolf through the windshield. He's not looking at her anymore. He's staring into the trees, into the forest she just ran from moments ago. Erin squeezes her eyes shut for a moment, swallowing a sob she doesn't have time for. When she opens them, she sees GhostLogger following TrailWolf's gaze, then stiffen. She looks toward the trail and sees something shift in the trees. Erin pulls Danny's knife and she whispers through a stuck breath, "Please… not again."

Mark's name flashes a second time on her phone, but she still doesn't answer. She wants nothing more than to throw the car into gear and burn rubber, but the detective warned her to stay put. She turns the engine over and pumps the heater. The air takes time to warm, but when it does, she presses her fingers against the vents.

Mark tries a third time and again, she refuses to accept him. She watches his name disappear, then glances at CacheHawk, the unknown player. Finally, her eyes settle on TrailWolf, the smug bastard still scanning the trees.

Mark tries again, but this time, with a text. Each missed connection lands with a vibration against Erin's leg, sharp against the silence rising outside. She doesn't read it, she can't. The car becomes a pressure cooker and she cracks the window to let out the buildup. The cold air slips in, cooling her skin.

Her eyes stay locked on the tree line, on the same patch of shadow TrailWolf won't look away from. GhostLogger takes half a step in front of him, squinting into the woods, trying to see what TrailWolf sees. "What is it?" Erin hears him ask through the cracked window.

TrailWolf doesn't move. "Shhh."

"Don't shush me, man, what is…" A sharp sound cuts him off. It isn't loud, but it's not natural. CacheHawk stiffens and Erin's entire body goes cold from the inside out. GhostLogger mutters, "What the hell?"

CacheHawk takes one step closer to her car, her face draining. "Is someone out there?"

TrailWolf's jaw works, that same unreadable expression

flickering across his features. "They were."

Erin's breath stops, and she asks out the slit in her window. "Were?"

He finally looks at her. His eyes are flat, steady, and unsettlingly calm. "Whatever made that noise, it's gone now."

Erin grips Danny's knife so tightly her fingers ache. "Gone where?"

TrailWolf's gaze shifts back toward the trees, then up the access road, then to her car. "Hard to say."

GhostLogger's voice cracks a little. "Should we call someone?"

Erin lets out an exhausted noise. "Good call," she says bitterly. "You should."

Her phone buzzes again with another text, this time from Vance: **Deputies almost on site. Do not leave. Do not speak to anyone until they arrive.**

Erin looks at the message, then back at the three faces outside her car, one frightened, one confused, and one unreadable. Her fingers hover over her screen, but she doesn't interact. Instead, she goes for the window button, sealing herself into the car again. TrailWolf watches her through the glass. He doesn't step closer but doesn't look offended. He just tilts his head slightly, studying her through reflection and shadow. GhostLogger shifts beside him and CacheHawk says something Erin can't hear. She is back on trial.

All three turn their heads as something along the edge of the forest catches their attention. Erin inhales and braces herself as she turns her attention. Headlights appear at the far end of the road, one pair, then another. They are Sheriff's units, and they move fast. GhostLogger exhales as relief visibly washes over him. Erin doesn't hear him but can make out the words plain as day. "Oh, thank God."

CacheHawk sags a little with relief, but TrailWolf doesn't move. He watches the lights, looks down at the phone in Erin's lap, and then back at the lights again. Only when the first cruiser nears the turnout does he finally take his hands out of his pockets. He lifts one palm toward her car, but not to wave. He leans to the window and says loud enough for her to hear through the barrier, "You were right, today isn't safe."

Then, calm as fog, he turns and walks toward the woods. He makes the edge of the clearing before the first car slides to a stop. Erin's heart slams hard.

"TrailWolf!" GhostLogger calls out, startled. "Man, where are you going?" He's gone before the question finishes.

The cruisers screech to a stop and deputies fan out through the vehicles. Erin sits in the driver's seat, knuckles white on the knife, staring at the darkness TrailWolf disappeared into. For the first time since this nightmare began, a truth settles cold and sharp inside her. Someone is moving pieces faster than anyone can follow and she isn't just behind, she's being played.

Chapter 17: Night Cache

Vance disconnects the call with Erin Caldwell. The drive to the south shore of Yale Lake is longer than she expects, slowed by guessing which access road will be a dead end and which will take her to the GPS coordinates found at the murder site. The forest road snakes and Vance shreds gravel under her tires as she drifts through the switchbacks, her vision obscured by the fog creeping between the trees and clinging to the road.

Shannon rides shotgun with her tablet balanced on her knees. Ryan is in the back seat, clutching the equipment case to keep it from being launched at every turn. Shannon tilts the screen toward Vance. "The coordinates are lining up with the circle on the map."

Vance keeps her eyes on the road. "I don't know what we're walking into, so I'll need you both to be ready."

Ryan mutters, "So we're following breadcrumbs now. Love that for us."

Without taking her eyes off the road, Vance fires back, "That's exactly what detective work is."

They bounce over a rut deep enough to scrape bottom and the trees close in, forming a tunnel of dripping branches and compacted earth. The deeper they go, the more overbearing the woods feel. Shannon double taps the tablet screen, zooming in. "A hundred meters. There's a turnout coming up."

Vance takes the sharp turn onto a rut-filled dirt lane. She slows only when the brush breaks into a narrow pull-off sitting on the ridge above the lake with barely enough room for one vehicle next to the drop-off. The water below stretches out beyond the trees, dark and opaque, creating a mirror of the clouded sky. There are no other cars, just the emptiness of the forest swallowing morning light. Vance kills the engine and scans the area.

Ryan steps out of the car, gripping the forensics case, and his boots sink into a thin film of mud. "Jesus, this place is dead."

Shannon follows Ryan's lead and scans the shoreline. "It matches the radius, but there should be something, right? What do you think we're looking for? We weren't led out here for nothing."

Ryan shrugs, genuinely stumped. "I don't know, but you get the camera now." She begrudgingly takes the case he hands her.

After surveying the area, Vance is the last one out. She walks straight off the dirt road and crouches at a trail of snapped ferns, her fingertips brushing the torn stems. They're not fresh enough to be from this morning and not wide enough for a body.

"Detective," Shannon approaches quietly behind her, adjusting the camera strap. "That path keeps going. I can see up ahead where moss has been scraped off. It looks like someone walked this line more than once."

Vance agrees with a grunt and begins down the path. The forest grows denser the farther they go, a narrow choke point of cedar trunks and sword ferns funneling them down a natural corridor. The birds seem muted here, their chirps compressed into nervous ticks. Vance keeps her hand near her holster as she moves. Whoever did this is long gone, but the intention still hangs in the air.

"This way," she calls softly. She's several paces ahead, already kneeling to study a patch of disturbed soil. The woman's eyes are sharp, even with how little sleep she's gotten. "This trail is fresh. Some of this breakage isn't from a natural walking path. Our perp wanted us to find this."

Shannon steps beside her, looking past the disturbed earth and there it is. At first, it looks like a natural shadow in the trees, a dark slash between two moss-eaten stumps, then her eyes adjust and she realizes it's man-made. She taps Ryan and points, it's barely a structure, a shell of what it could have been. The roofline sags in the middle, boards tilting inward from time and the elements crushing in on them. The door is slightly ajar, wedged by a root curled up from the ground. There's a red U.S. Forest Service stencil on the siding, faded to an exhausted pink.

Ryan swallows audibly. "Oh hell no." He sets the case at his feet and pulls out three sets of shoe covers, and passes out a new set of gloves. After he has gloved up, he pulls a monitor from the case.

Shannon absentmindedly takes what he hands her but doesn't move. She's staring at the shack, already cataloging whatever nightmare sits inside. Vance pulls on the shoe covers and steps forward, hand brushing back a low hanging branch. She carefully maneuvers the narrow footpath leading to the door with her hand loosely brushing her pistol's grip.

"Detective…" Ryan says again, softer this time. "This looks like, I mean, someone lived here."

"Not lived," Vance murmurs. "Squatted, but not recently." She points to the overgrowth of grass at the threshold. She steps closer until she can touch the door and peers through the crack, witnessing a covering of trampled needles, a scatter of bird skeletons, the broken shell of what might've been a lantern, and a rusted chain tangled in weeds.

Shannon lifts her camera. "Do you want CSU to clear it?"

"No," Vance says without hesitation. "I'll go first."

She won't send her people into something she was meant to see herself. She rests her palm on the warped door. The wood is cold, damp, and swollen from years of rain. It takes more effort than she expects to push it open.

Inside is musty and dark. The smell hits heavy with rot and mildew, then the second wave hits, a sickening smell that she can only imagine as blood baked into old timber. Ryan covers his mouth with his sleeve. Shannon doesn't flinch and instead, steadies the camera. Vance steps across the threshold and the temperature seems to drop ten degrees.

The door drags over the floorboards with a wet groan, leaving wood dust from grinding against the floor. Vance pulls a flashlight that cuts a narrow wedge through the dark, which tries to swallow the light. Dust and spores swirl in lazy spirals. Under her boots, the floorboards groan, not so much from her weight as from carrying the burden of memory.

Detective Vance steps over the old root, cautious to check behind the door. Shannon steps just far enough inside to aim the camera. The red autofocus beam trembles on the far wall.

"Holy…" Ryan whispers over her shoulder, then clamps his mouth shut.

The beam lands on the left side of the room, where a long workbench struggles under the weight of time, holding smashed ammo cans and Tupperware amidst carcasses of forest animals in varying stages of decay and geocache trackables twisted until their chains have snapped and their codes have been mostly scratched clean. Altoids tins litter the ground, crushed like they've been stomped repeatedly. Scraps of small paper sheets are scattered through the debris. On the far end of the bench, a row of small animal skulls, raccoon, rabbit, squirrel, are drilled through and threaded on wire, making some sort of death necklace.

"The hell is all of that?" Shannon asks, completely perplexed.

Vance points her light against the wall. "Looks like stolen and destroyed geocaches," she murmurs. "Years worth, by the look of it."

Some containers have dates written on them in Sharpie, while some have angry scratch marks instead. Some are arranged with meticulous care, as if part of a private taxonomy. Vance lets her light linger on the graveyard of containers and corpses. Ryan asks, "Is this some sort of trophy room?"

"At first glance, I could see how it looks that way," she says. "but it's not on display. There's something more going on here."

"Preparation?" Ryan tries. "Maybe where the killer puts new caches together?"

"No," Vance says, her voice stays flat. "Just the opposite, those containers are destroyed. That's private rage."

Above the cache graveyard, a cluster of old sun-bleached toys hang from fishing line, swaying slightly in the air current that was created when this room was disturbed. Their shadows jitter across the wall behind them, creating a play of forgotten tragedy and lost memories.

Not finding answers, the detective flashes her light to the right wall, finding a collection of maps tacked to the aged boards, dozens of them, layered haphazardly. Some are stitched together with duct tape while others are pinned with nails. Several lines have been drawn and erased so many times the wrinkled paper is rubbed thin. That's where she will find answers.

She moves a step, then lowers her light to ensure a solid walking path and sees something that freezes her mid-step. A pile of old hiking boots sits in a collapsed heap, with sizes ranging from adult men's to tiny children's. Some are mud-caked and some are chewed at the toe or heel. One has a name written on the sole in faded marker, but the name is smeared beyond reading.

"Chesshir, shoot these." She hits Shannon in the midsection with her light, then points back to the boots. "Maddox, when she's done, take them outside and try to pair them. Pull whatever information you can."

She doesn't wait for acknowledgment before continuing to the maps while flashes of light strobe from the photos Shannon takes. Vance's inquisitive gaze slowly crawls the wall. Some of the maps have childlike handwriting in pale crayon, labeling simple landmarks. *river turn, big hill, secret tree, home*. Circles are scrawled in marker and warnings litter void space. ***Not safe, stopped here, gone too long, FIND HIM***. Erratic pencil scratching lays X marks and question marks throughout the county. The scrawling in long dried blood is where Vance's attention focuses. ***Find him! Try again, go to Where the Path Broke, FIND HIM, TRY AGAIN, TRY AGAIN!***

The rafters come alive with the racket of a panicked bird, sending clouds of settled decay into the air from the creature's territorial wings. Vance grips her pistol and shines the light upward through old flags and dangling sheetrock. The flash spooks the crow from its nest, and it drops from its perch, flapping frantically before finding its way out the front door, nearly clipping Ryan's head on the way out.

There's a shape standing behind the door Vance didn't clock on entry. She curses herself and shines her light, finding a coat rack covered with bulk. The outermost layer is a child's windbreaker, once bright red, now brown with age and wear, twisted at the collar around the hanger's grasp.

Below the rack is a cluster of bones intentionally arranged. They're all small animals, cleaned, organized, and set in a pattern of spirals and lines. In the center is a mound of dog tags and more trinkets, each with a label or laminated card. On each card is a code constructed from a combination of numbers and letters.

Ryan steps back into the shack to collect the last of the boots when he glances at what the flashlight is illuminating. A grunt escapes him, half disgusted and half fearful. "This sicko is escalating."

"No," Shannon murmurs, still standing in front of the remaining boot pile. "More like remembering."

Vance doesn't acknowledge either theory. Instead, she turns her light into the room, the single support beam for the room is covered in blunt force gouges and Polaroid photographs. Each small memento is outlined by long, splitting gashes, creating crowns of splinters on imprisoned memories.

Shannon whispers, "He practiced."

"Practiced what?" Ryan asks, but Vance already knows. The shape of the gouges matches the wound in Jessa's skull.

She steps closer, examining each moment of time silhouetted by the picture frame. Random people, none looking at the camera, most of them are outdoors. Adults, children, men, women, the pictures didn't discriminate, and they didn't offer any privacy. Some were playing ball, swimming, lovers lost in each other, but most were hikers.

"Maddox, when you're done with the shoes," she says, pointing at the post with her light, "these will take investigative priority."

She continues into the den, stepping around a toppled crate, the floor thick with trampled debris, and finds the bathroom door half-rotted, hanging open just enough to show a mirror shattered inward, a large section of the breakage missing. The sink is filled with leaves and rust-colored water, but not nearly as dark as the brackish cesspool in the tub. A child's toothbrush balances on the rim, the bristles chewed flat. Beneath the stained sink is a dead rat floating in a bucket under the dripline. The toilet looks thoroughly abused and Vance is unsure whether the streaking over the outside is feces or blood, either way, it is thick and cracking. Graffiti is sprayed onto the walls in half-readable script: **"COME HOME COME HOME COME HOME"**

Vance backs out. When she calls this site in, she'll request Clark County Fire's hazmat team.

Shannon sweeps her camera upward again, capturing everything, when she accidentally angles her lamp into the back corner of the room. That's when claustrophobia slams full force. There's a cot shoved up against the wall with blankets balled tight, a pillowcase stained dark at the center, a candle burned down to its last wax, and a stack of notebooks opened and left mid-sentence, pages warped from moisture.

Vance and Shannon both approach. The top notebook lies open, its pages covered in childish handwriting, then crossed out and replaced with angry adult handwriting. Whole paragraphs are smothered under black ink. Names are scratched out, trails are circled, and one number is repeated until the paper is smashed thin. **5/14**

Ryan follows up and speaks in a whisper now. "This whole room feels like we are watching someone deteriorate in real time."

Vance doesn't answer, she's staring at the far wall. The one hidden behind the tarp that hasn't been pulled back yet. Something is there, a shape draped under the canvas cover, stiff with age and grime. Whatever's beneath it is large and intentionally concealed, and Vance knows it is the reason they were brought here. She realizes they are not in a murder site, they're in a private museum of a broken person's childhood. "You two, grab the corners," she instructs quietly. "I'll lift it over." Her hand returns to her holster.

Shannon nods. Ryan swallows and squares his shoulders. The darkness leans in closer, listening. Vance edges toward the tarp with a sense she hasn't felt at a crime scene in years. It is colder than fear and more intimate than revulsion. Shannon and Ryan grab each corner of the tarp, gingerly pulling it up and loose. Vance peels it back slow and careful, mindful of anything fragile waiting underneath.

Beneath the tarp is an uneven, hand-built table, scorched at the edges like someone kept burning it to just feel something. On the table itself is a shrine to a child. The objects arranged on it don't sit in cast-aside clutter, they are placed with intentional pattern, symmetrical in a way that sharply contrasts with the rest of the room. This is the centerpiece, the heart. In the middle of many cherished relics is a plastic jackalope piggy bank, cracked down the ear and missing patches of fabricated fur which should coat the thing entirely. It is a simple, childish thing, the kind bought in cheap gift shops or backwoods gas stations. It is perched atop a small stack of crayon-drawn maps, some laminated, others weathered and aged.

Shannon steps closer. "Detective, these are the same markings from the wall, the same handwriting."

Vance gently lifts one that shows a scrawled forest, rendered in bright crayon, a river that curves wide, a hill labeled "THE BIG ONE," and near the bottom, a stick figure with spiky hair labeled **EVAN.** Vance lowers the map before her voice can betray anything she's feeling.

A bundle of trackables lies in front of the maps, not damaged or twisted like the ones on the workbench. These are arranged neatly, almost reverently, their chains polished, their cache code touched up to prevent fading. Someone used unfulfilled promises to care for these tiny objects.

Ryan breathes out, voice shaky. "This isn't a kill room. This is…"

"A memorial," Shannon finishes with a tone as empty as the inside of the shack, but too soft for the violence soaked into the walls.

Vance's flashlight catches reflection from glass inside a wooden, handmade photo frame which sits propped at the back of the altar. Inside it is a Polaroid photograph of a boy, maybe eight or nine, holding a hiking stick taller than he is. He's missing one of his front teeth and his shirt is stained with dirt. He's grinning like the world has never hurt him. She murmurs, "To him."

It's the items around the frame that hollow out the air. Arranged neatly are a small blue inhaler, a pair of children's binoculars with a missing lens, a preserved caching badge that reads "Junior Explorer," a trail medal with the ribbon torn in half, and a tiny hiking boot. Just one, with the toe chewed through and laces missing. Every object is placed with care, grief, and ownership.

Shannon's flashlight tilts upward, catching something strung above the altar, a piece of notebook paper, yellowed at the edges, taped and re-taped so many times the corners have formed permanent curls. It holds just two sentences, carved in heavy, shaking handwriting that cuts into the paper as though the writer pressed with a knife instead of a pen. **"I'm sorry I left you. I love you, little brother."** A silence follows that no one wants to break and even the shack seems to hold still.

Ryan stares at the words, trying to reconcile them with the skulls and the photograph covered practice beam and the kill site up the ridge. "Detective…" he says quietly. "This person is grieving."

"Grief is private," Vance replies, her eyes tracking the meticulously placed mementos. "It stays in the gut, but this? This is public. Even if no one was ever meant to see it, they're mourning. They've turned their life into a perpetual funeral, and they're forcing the whole world to attend the service."

Shannon looks at the altar again, her eyes softening under Vance's explanation. "The perp is hurting and wants someone to understand. That's why we were brought here."

Vance feels the truth land heavy. "Maybe," she says metered, "but sympathy doesn't excuse violence and it has no place when determining justice."

At the base of the altar, Shannon points to a folded slip of paper. This note doesn't carry the burden of age the rest of the shack does, it is white and crisp. Vance picks it up and unfolds it to find a jackalope stamped in ink so dark it bleeds through the back of the page. Below it is a single line, thin and sharp, **"Do you see him now?"**

Vance's fingers tighten against the note. She doesn't address the room, doesn't acknowledge the killer, doesn't allow words even to herself. Shannon and Ryan wait, still as the rest of the shack. Vance finally breathes one sentence with determination, "Bag everything."

The three of them fall into a grim rhythm after Vance's order. Ryan moves methodically, laying down evidence markers, afraid to breathe on the scattered memories. Shannon snaps photos in near silence, each camera click is a violation in the cramped dark. The shack absorbs every movement, swallowing sound rather than echoing it.

Vance turns from the shrine and begins a slow, deliberate sweep of the rest of the room. The deeper she goes, the thicker the air feels. A second doorway sits half-collapsed along the back wall near the bathroom. The frame bows inward, swollen from rain and warped from heat. Vance tests the door with her foot, and it gives way with a groan so human it sends a jolt up her spine.

She angles her flashlight into the room. The beam catches another scatter of bones on the floor first, an unidentifiable creature that's been dead long enough its fur has become mulch. Above it, strings of sinew cling to a nail hammered into a ceiling beam, long dried and pulled thin. This isn't a hunter's skinning hook, someone hung something here to practice.

Shannon steps through the rotted door and stands beside the detective with her camera raised. "Jesus…"

Vance lifts her hand and stops her. She points at busted floorboards in front of them. "Photograph from the threshold. No one crosses until we know what's stable."

Ryan adjusts his view from the doorframe to get a glimpse of the new room. Something drips further inside and the corners he can see are mounded with pellets of old insulation and rodent scat.

Vance's light moves up the wall, finding more childlike drawings, but not like Evan's. These are adult hands trying to mimic a child, dragging crayon lines and smudging marker strokes, in an attempt to recapture something lost. Pages are pinned with rusted nails, curling outward. Some are just trails, some are maps, and some show two stick figures, one big and one small. The pictures always show the figures near the same ridge.

One picture is different. It is a charcoal smear with frantic pressure marks. The big stick figure is bent over and the small one is lying down. Shannon inhales sharply. "Detective…"

Vance nods but doesn't comment. Her throat has gone tight in a way she refuses to name. There's more. A stack of spiral notebooks bound together with twine sits beneath a broken chair just inside the doorway. She nudges it with her boot. The front cover is torn clean off. The first page is a block of handwriting, jagged, looping, repetitive phrases filling every inch of the paper. It reads, *"He didn't look. He didn't come back. He didn't look back. He didn't look."* Beneath it is another line, *"The wolf is on the trail now, and it's time to hunt."*

Vance shines her light on the stack. "I want this thoroughly examined," she mutters.

Ryan hesitates, voice small. "Detective… I've got something else."

She turns. He's standing beside the far wall back in the main room, pointing not at the paintings, not at the maps, but at something embedded in the wood. Her flashlight follows his gesture to a carving of a handprint. It's child-sized, etched into old rot and age-softened timber. Scarring on the wood leading from the fingers makes the print look like it is smeared into an upward drag.

Below it, shallow scratches mark through the wood grain. **EVAN** is carved over and over, until the lines grow shallow and thick, suggesting the blade dulled. Vance stares at the handprint until her vision blurs at the edges.

"This is trauma." Her voice is low, not for them, for herself. "This whole place is trauma."

A branch snaps outside and all three officials freeze. There's another crack, closer this time. The sound isn't a twig under an animal, it's heavy and intentional. Every instinct in the shack's air flips from dread to threat. Vance is already moving silent and controlled, her weapon half-drawn. She motions for Shannon and Ryan to stay behind her, and they fall in without question, both knowing they don't have field experience for confrontation.

For a single suspended moment, Vance is certain someone is standing just beyond the wall, watching, listening, waiting for them to understand. Then the forest settles with a long exhale of shifting branches.

Ryan whispers, "Were we followed?"

"No," Vance says, though she's no longer sure. Her voice firms. "That doesn't mean we aren't alone."

The shack seems to close around them again, less a structure now and more of a confessional sealed in dirt and rot. The forest never fully settles after that sound and, even when nothing else moves, the tension hangs thin and stretched, humming between the trees. Vance keeps her weapon out for several seconds before holstering it again, though her hand never strays far.

"Let's finish this," she says quietly.

Shannon and Ryan both nod, shaken but focused, as they move with new urgency. Every camera flash feels like a beacon for attention, illuminating the fragments of a life cracked open and left here to fossilize in grief and rage.

Shannon finishes photographing the carved wall. Ryan finishes bagging the photos on the beam, then moves to the notebooks, the maps, the inhaler, the crayon drawings. The jackalope piggy bank goes into its own evidence container, padded and sealed from contact with the world outside this shack.

Vance turns toward the small back room one last time. A shape keeps tugging at her peripheral vision. Tucked into the shadows behind the broken chair is a metal ammo can geocachers use for outdoor hides. Except this one is different, almost reverent, cleaned ritualistically.

She kneels and pulls it toward her. The hinge squeals when she opens it, loud in the suffocating quiet. Inside is a single object, a child's hiking shoe, small, mud-stained, and weather-softened. The twin to the one sitting on the shrine table, but this one is in worse condition. The leather is cracked and the heel is aggressively worn down. The lace eyelets are warped like they were pulled hard by a small pair of shaking hands trying to find a freedom lost. Vance's breath stills in her chest.

The shoe sits atop several items packed with precision. Among them is a folded Polaroid and a well-used logbook. She doesn't touch the Polaroid right away, going for the logbook instead. Inside are the signatures of all players who visited the once active cache. It's old and beaten. In block print, the cover is stamped: **THE BIG ONE.** Underneath, scratched in frantic pen, someone added: **CACHE #0278.**

The ink is faded and the laminate is peeling. The face is chewed by time. She flips it open with gloved fingers. Every page is smeared with rain or dirt, signatures stacked in messy layers of ink and smeared thumbprints. Near the back, one entry stops her cold, written in confident, careless handwriting: **TrailWolf – 5/14 – TFTC**

Her stomach tightens, but not because TrailWolf signed it. Under his signature is a stamp, crooked and deep, pressed hard enough to dent the paper beneath it, and the ink of a jackalope symbol has bled through the page. Vance calls out softly, "Chesshir, Maddox."

They come closer and Ryan's face drains white. "Oh damn," he whispers. "That shoe is the match…"

Vance sets the logbook aside and finally opens the Polaroid. The photo isn't a child this time. It's a teenage boy, fourteen maybe, with longer hair and broader shoulders, but his face still carries the same soft features from the shrine photos. He's standing in front of a different forest overlook, squinting against sunlight, smiling a little, an unknowing ghost of a life that never happened.

Shannon steps forward. "Detective, that's…"

"I know," Vance cuts in.

On the back of the Polaroid, written in small, tight pen strokes, is one line, **You finally made it, little brother.**

Vance closes her eyes for a slow, controlled breath. Shannon presses her knuckles to her mouth. Ryan looks like someone punched the air out of him.

"This cache…" he says hoarsely. "Detective. Was this the brother's cache, the one he never reached?"

"No," Vance says quietly, her voice steady but not cold. "He reached it. Just, not in his lifetime."

Their shared silence falls over the cabin's dust. The shack, the maps, the broken practice beam, all of it rearranges itself in Vance's mind. A boy died out here and a sibling carried the grief for years. A killer was born in that grief, and every breadcrumb since has been for one person.

Shannon finally manages, "Detective… is this what the unsub wanted us to see?"

"No," Vance says. "It wasn't meant for us." Her gaze drops to the photograph of the boy again. This wasn't a taunt left for law enforcement, it was a eulogy.

She stands, sliding the Polaroid into an evidence sleeve. "That's enough here, collect what you have," she orders quietly.

Shannon nods and Ryan exhales with a force that shakes his body. Vance takes one last look at the shoe sitting in the ammo can, the reminder that a child never made it home. The game isn't about caching anymore, it never was. The three of them collect their evidence and haul it from the cabin.

"Detective," he says quietly. "What do we tell the captain?"

Vance looks back at the sagging structure, the shadows yawning inside it, the life built from grief and the violence kneaded into the walls. "We tell her," Vance says, voice flat and certain, "we just found the beginning of everything."

This is about loss, obsession, punishment, and the long, straight line between them. The forest feels somber, silently mourning the revealed secrets. "For now, we're done here," she says.

She turns toward the vehicle. The lake beyond glints silver, indifferent and ancient. The truth burns her sternum, they aren't done, not even close.

Chapter 18: Cold Coordinates

Erin slams the apartment door closed behind her and leans against it, jamming the deadbolt in place with the same force the world has jammed her. Her body is vibrating with leftover adrenaline and her skin still carries the cold of the forest that has seeped inside her. When she finally moves, her boots leave a faint sprinkle of trail mud on the floor. She stares at it, breathlessly cursing the tiny, meaningless pieces of the morning that won't stop following her.

Every time she blinks, she sees TrailWolf's smug face in the parking lot, and the way he analyzed everything, watching, knowing, or pretending he did. She curses him too.

The shard is still where she left it on the living room coffee table. She hasn't had time to touch it today, not that she wants to, but she can feel it judging her as she passes by on her way to the kitchen island. She drops her keys on the counter, and they clatter loudly in the still apartment. She squeezes her eyes shut. The sound shouldn't rattle her, but it does, everything is rattling her.

Her phone buzzes on the counter, reminding her of the cascade of notifications which flooded in while she was driving home. She flips it over, face-down, trying to shut that last thread of the outside world out. The silence afterward feels staged to lure her into a false sense of security.

She walks toward the living room and stops at the big corkboard she started back when it was all just fun coordinates and hidden containers, back before she got wrapped into crime scenes, before her life was invaded and continuously violated. She stares at the board, at the pins on the map, at her handwriting on notes posted to herself. None of it looks like investigation today, it looks like unhealthy obsession. She feels like a conspiracy theorist trying to prove lizard people are real. The activity covers most of the board now, spilling off, and reaching along the wall. What used to be a neat grid of her favorite finds has mutated into something frantic. She's added layers of post-its slanted and overlapping, circled locations, and jammed pins deep into the cork. The only thing she's missing is the red string. She whispers, barely audible, "Why me?"

She's not lost in self-pity, just feeling the raw truth that she has been targeted and doesn't know the rules anymore. She pulls a bright red pin from the top corner of the map and presses it into the board with more force than needed, immediately recognizing the irony of her unconscious color choice. She pulls out previously placed red pins, replacing them with other colors, any other colors, then replaces the marked caches where bodies were found to match this morning's cache, The Look Back. The line of red pins is starting to form a pattern she doesn't understand yet, a shape she keeps almost recognizing before it slips away.

Her eyes drift over everything she's pinned, starting with Hidden Hollow and the secondary pin for the body, then moving to Where the Path Broke in Washougal, and now today's The Look Back. Each of the caches that stabbed Erin with trauma. Her attention shifts to the softer pain, Parkside Peekaboo, the one lighting up the forums that she didn't have to experience. The last one she stares at is the red pin in Lamppost Lament, the most innocent cache with the dead pin. She knows a life wasn't lost for that microcache, but the twelve-hour timestamp glitch still hasn't sat right with her.

Her eyes dart between pins and notes. The number of times the word 'body' is now present when, two simple weeks ago, it didn't exist on this board makes her shudder. She studies the notes she has been tracking and each one reads subtly more sinister than the one before.

She steps closer, one hand braced against the wall, the other smoothing the edges of the clutter. She knows the action won't help her see the shape, but it does soothe her own agitation. "Okay," she murmurs. "Okay. What am I missing?"

Her eyes jump from note to note, thread to thread, and cache to cache. Each one is a breadcrumb, but each breadcrumb is a lie, she can feel it. The board is incomplete, and she can't tell what terrifies her more, the idea that she seems to be the center of it all or that she wants to see where the story leads.

Her gaze lands on the new Lucia Falls pin again. She reflects on CacheHawk, a new player who was so eagerly present, watching the way TrailWolf spoke with his silence, and how GhostLogger vouched for him. None of it fit. She slaps a post-it note on this morning's cache and writes, **"TrailWolf - WHY HIM?"** She pulls the pin out and restabs it, tacking the note against the cork.

The board doesn't give her any more answers, which causes her to pace without realizing she's moving. This morning wasn't normal fear, it was feral. It raised something primal inside her that learned how to recognize danger from angles she didn't know existed.

Her phone buzzes again with yet another alert, another echo of Jessa's last scream. She's not ready for the world, so she ignores it. The board is louder and her brain starts turning in circles so fast it feels like she could burn through the wall.

The pattern is her, she can feel it, the real message, if she could just breathe. Her fingers tremble as she touches the Washougal pin. "Come on," she whispers. "Show me."

A soft, deliberate knock hits the door and Erin's entire body goes rigid. Her eyes leap from the corkboard to the coffee table. The shard is still there, fully exposed. It may as well be under a spotlight. The knock comes again. It's professional, but not impatient.

"Shit," Erin breathes, barely audible. She moves fast with instinct born from guilt. Her fingers close around the shard and she flinches as it bites into her flesh, nearly drawing blood. Where does she put it? Her gaze ricochets around the apartment. The bookshelf is too obvious. The coffee table is a crime scene investigation. The kitchen counters are bare. Her pulse thunders so hard she can feel her fingertips throbbing.

The knock comes a third time, firmer. "Erin? It's Detective Vance."

Her chest caves inward as she drops to her knees and shoves the shard deep under her couch. Dust coats her palms on her withdrawal. Erin stands too fast and her balance wavers for a second. She wipes her hands on her jeans, trying and failing to slow her breathing before rushing to the door. She barely has the presence of mind to flip the deadbolt. When she opens the door, Vance fills the frame in a dark jacket and stone expression.

Erin forces a smile and asks, "Aren't you supposed to say, 'police, open up' or something?"

Vance ignores Erin's statement. "You alright?" she asks, cataloguing her short breath, tense expression, and the way her pupils are dilated.

Erin nods quickly. "Yeah. I… I'm fine."

Vance doesn't buy it. She looks inside, waiting for an invitation. "You mind?"

Erin looks behind her at the couch, then back to the detective. Without saying a word, she steps to the side and motions her in.

Vance visually sweeps the apartment, clocking the corkboard and the scattered coffee table notes, her gaze lingering half a second longer in those places, making Erin feel exposed. "You've been busy."

Erin closes the door and stares at the board. "Trying to make sense of it."

Vance shakes her head. "I would rather you leave the investigation to the officials, but I'm not really surprised." She turns to Erin, full of earnestness. "Look Caldwell we need to talk."

Erin's blood electrifies and she wonders in the space of a heartbeat if Vance somehow knows about the shard, if Vance suspects tampering. Her brain grabs for anything defensible in case this is the moment everything collapses. She focuses on every muscle in her body to not react.

Vance moves to the couch and lingers near the stacks of notes, spending a moment to read what's on top. Her attention then locks on Erin's face. "You alone?"

Erin glances at the hallway to her bedroom, then the front door, dumbfounded by the question. "I was."

Vance stares at Erin, watching her chest heave. "Did I come at a bad time?" Her eyes drift toward the bedroom door.

"No." Erin walks toward the kitchen, keeping her distance from the couch. "What do we need to talk about?"

The detective looks at the corkboard again. She's seen crime maps, obsession walls, and survivor boards. Erin's is all three. "You didn't hear the news yet," Vance says quietly.

Erin's stomach pulls tight at the memory of this morning's video. "No," she lies. "I… I ignored my phone."

"That's probably for the best." Vance folds her arms. Erin hasn't known this woman long, but she's never seen her look like she's choosing her wording this carefully. "There's been another incident."

Erin's heart cracks sideways and she braces for the impact of hearing what she already witnessed. Without thinking, she mutters, "Jessa."

Vance's eyebrows lift a fraction. That tell says everything to the detective. Erin hit the right answer, she already knows. "Yes, that was quite the guess," Vance says, pausing, but when Erin doesn't fill the void, she continues. "We confirmed the identity early this morning."

Erin looks away. She already knew the truth the second that

Jessa's scream tore through her phone outside Lucia Falls, but when Vance says it out loud, the reality settles.

"She was found on the south end of Yale Lake," Vance continues. "Her fiancé, Colt Rowan, is unaccounted for."

Erin feels the sickening sensation of puzzle pieces shifting again, rearranging themselves into a pattern that still refuses to make a picture. Vance watches her reaction closely, and Erin feels the weight of scrutiny under her skin like heat.

"You knew them?" Vance asks.

"Not really, no. Only casually." Erin scrubs a palm across her mouth. "As much as everyone else did. They were big in the caching scene because of their social media presence, but they didn't really connect with people unless they thought it would get them viewers."

"Were they big enough to be targeted? Did they piss anyone off?"

"I don't know." Erin answers, already speculating that they were chosen because they were visible, predictable, and easy to track. "Maybe."

Vance steps closer, lowering her voice. "Erin, I'm going to ask you something, and I need the truth."

Erin stiffens and Vance's stern gaze holds her steady. "Does the name 'Jackalope' mean anything to you?"

Erin tenses before she can stop herself, as the outline of the antlered rabbit stamped around the QR code at Lucia Falls flashes behind her eyes. She jerks and her fingers twitch toward her pocket for pepper spray she isn't holding. She wants to run, to grab the shard she hid under her couch, but her hands stay at her sides. She shakes her head once, sharp. She swallows hard. "I've seen the name online, in logs. You mentioned it once, I think."

Vance tilts her head, assessing the complete shift in Erin's body. "That's all?" She presses. "Nothing else? No encounters? No messages?"

Erin forces her voice steady. "No. Detective, I swear, I haven't met anyone using that name."

Vance studies her for a long moment, then gives a slow, disbelieving nod. "This person is escalating. Whatever this is about, whatever they want…" She looks at the corkboard, "All the evidence says it's circling you."

Erin's blood goes cold. Vance doesn't mean it as blame, she's giving a warning, but Erin feels like it's an indictment, a truth she hasn't been brave enough to name. She looks away in silence.

Vance rubs her brow. "Look, I'm not here to accuse you. I came to make sure you're alive, and to tell you the news before it goes public."

Erin waits, keeping her expression still only by sheer will. "Wait, why tell me if you don't want me trying to figure this thing out?"

"There was something at the latest scene," Vance says. "Something that may imply you're a target, the target."

Erin's knees almost give and she braces herself on the counter. "What… What does that mean?" she asks quietly.

"It means you're in danger," Vance says. "I need you to stay inside today. Don't go out chasing geocaches. Don't go anywhere alone."

Erin stares at the board. "I'm trying to stop him."

"That's my job," Vance says sternly. Her next statement isn't unkind, just honest. "If you keep chasing this, I'll have to bring you in for interfering with an investigation. Or I'll bury you in protective custody, so you don't end up dead next."

Erin flinches at the realization and the granite expression on the detective's face. "Whatever message this person is trying to send," Vance warns, "don't help."

She waits for Erin to acknowledge, but no words come, her throat won't form them. She nods instead, which is enough to satisfy the detective.

Vance steps toward the door and rests her hand on the knob. She stares at it and then at Erin. She opens the door and, before she leaves, she turns to Erin one final time. "Erin. You need to stop chasing this, it will not end well for you."

Erin doesn't answer, she just waits, skin growing flushed with guilt. Vance leaves and the door clicks shut, leaving Erin alone in her apartment, pulse pounding, skin humming, staring at the corkboard. The silence that settles afterward is pressurized with a vacuum forming around the edges of her thoughts. She stands there for several seconds, staring at the deadbolt like it's supposed to protect her, like it could.

Her phone buzzes again on the counter, an echo from the world outside trying to claw its way back in, but she ignores it. She walks slowly, stiffly, until she reaches the couch, but she doesn't sit. She braces both hands on the back of it and lowers her head, trying to hold herself together under the weight of everything in her life falling down on top of her.

Vance's words loop through her in mismatched fragments. *You're in danger. Escalating. Circling you. Stop chasing.* Each one hits a different bruise, and she squeezes her eyes shut. The floor feels like it's falling out from beneath her. Her nails dig crescents into the fabric of the couch for stability and she whispers, "I'm not the one chasing." Her voice breaks on the last word.

She pulls back from the couch and paces, sharp and restless. Everything Vance said worms through her body, not because the detective is wrong, but because the killer is ahead of all of them and Erin can feel the stakes rising in ways she isn't ready for.

She stops in front of the corkboard again and really looks at it. Vance saw obsession, saw danger, but Erin sees something else. She sees movement, intention, a message trying to speak. She drags her fingertips across the map in a shaky line, touching each pin with

OverlookLaneCrew's name on it. Her eyes dart from notes pressed against pins, pins pressed into coordinates, and coordinates pressed against the question of her own sanity. "What am I missing?" she whispers again.

She traces the outline of Yale Lake where Jessa was found. There's no pin, it isn't a cache she has found, and she questions if she has the right to mark it. Her pulse climbs. Erin pulls a red pin from the bundle and sticks it in the lake, near the south shore.

Then she sees it, an absence in the map, a pocket of space on the board that draws her attention more than all the caches pinned around it.

"No… no, I didn't…" Her voice cracks because she knows this feeling, this void in a pattern. She's been here before, when she was standing over Danny's belongings, trying to understand how something so close could slip through her fingers.

Her phone buzzes again. She doesn't acknowledge it. Vance told her to stop chasing, but the killer has been chasing her long before any of them knew.

Erin reaches up with a trembling breath and grips the edge of the corkboard, bracing for an impact only she sees coming. A burn inside her, quiet and stubborn and furious, starts to rise in her chest. She shakes her head. "I can't stop," she whispers. "I won't."

She looks toward the couch, not to retrieve the shard, but because she feels its presence like a second heartbeat. The killer's touch, the intent.

The board waits in front of her and the room hums. Her phone buzzes a third time, matching the pounding in her ears. Erin stares at the one gap in the pins that scares her more than anything she's already marked, the place where the next cache has to be waiting.

Her phone buzzes again. This time she can't ignore the persistence, not because she wants to know, she doesn't, but because she knows whoever it is, won't stop until she finally answers. She walks toward the counter and lets her frustration flip the phone over. Of course, it's Mark. She hesitates, her thumb hovering over the screen. For a moment she thinks she should ignore him, let him stay wherever he is, let the distance between them harden enough to create a boundary instead of a wound.

"You're too damn persistent," she groans before opening the four consecutive texts: *Hey. Erin. TrailSister. You home?*

Her jaw clamps together. The question is simple, but his timing after Vance's warning hits a nerve. Or maybe she's just too raw to interpret anything neutrally. She types back: *Yeah.*

A few seconds pass before he responds: *Just checking in. How are you holding up?*

For a second, she hesitates. Someone asking how she is almost feels normal, a moment of kindness in a whirlwind of torment. The softness of it cuts through her frayed nerves, just a little. She types back before she can overthink it: *Detective was here. Just left. She told me about Jessa.*

Three dots pulse, stop, then pulse again before his response drops: *Shit. I'm sorry, Erin. That's… a lot.*

She exhales, leaning a hip against the counter. "A lot" doesn't touch it, but she doesn't have the energy to unravel the rest. She doesn't respond and a moment passes in silence.

He texts again: *Did she say why she came to you?*

The question lands oddly pointed, like he's trying very hard to make the concern sound casual. Erin stares at the screen. She thumbs a reply, clears it, and tries again: *She thinks I might be in danger.*

The typing bubble appears again almost instantly: *Do you want me to come by? Or call? Whatever you need.*

The immediacy of his response is comforting, but a little too eager. It shouldn't bother her, but it does. She wants comfort more than anything else in the world right now but staring at this morning's chat history and hearing Vance's words in the back of her mind ignites her distrust. She types: *I'm fine.*

The typing bubble appears instantly. It stops, then reappears. He stops again, then finally: *Erin, don't get involved in this anymore. Please. Let the police handle it.*

She stares at the message. They should feel protective, feel kind. Instead, heat crawls up her neck from anger, or shame, or the kind of fear that curdles into defiance. Maybe because Vance said the same thing, or maybe because the only people dying are the ones who thought someone else would take care of it. Her fingers shake. She types before she can stop herself: *Do you know something I don't?*

Mark doesn't respond. Her heartbeat ticks in the hollow of her throat. Then: *I just don't want you to get hurt. That's all.*

"That's all," she repeats under her breath, the words feel like static. She stares at the screen as another bubble appears.

His text comes through: *And TrailWolf didn't do anything. Don't go after him. Seriously. He's an asshole, but he's not this.*

Erin freezes. Her blood goes cold. She never told Mark about TrailWolf being in the parking lot or the confrontation. She whispers, "How do you know about TrailWolf?"

Her thumb hovers over the keyboard, but she doesn't type anything. This doesn't slow Mark down. The typing bubble appears again: *Look, just stay home today. Promise me?*

The phone feels like a burning ember in her hand. She drops it on the counter and stares at his words on the screen. A new question blooms, sharp and poisonous, What does Mark know?

Chapter 19: Signed Log

The online meltdown doesn't start with a scream, it starts with a screenshot. By midafternoon, the local geocache forums are a nest of tabs and red notification bubbles. Someone posts a blurry screen grab of the livestream, a freeze-frame of Jessa's face and her arm flung out. The caption reads: **YourCacheCrush missing after stream??**

The replies hit hard and fast.

PineNeedlePinCushion: Missing or just offline? Calm down.

CacheHawk: It cut off midstream. She screamed. That wasn't fake.

BenchMarker89: I watched it. Someone hit her. That didn't look staged.

OvercastDad: …are we sure this isn't clickbait? C'mon, guys.

Within ten minutes, someone drops the first rumor:

RiverRiddle: Friend in SAR says there was "an incident" out by Yale Lake. Not sure if it's them.

No one fully believes it, but everyone has to comment. Another thread pops up on a different board, this one already three pages deep by the time anyone sensible finds it. The subject is: **Local cache killer?**

CamasCrawler: Okay, listen. There was a body by Washougal the other day. Now this. Both connected to caches. No way that's random.

SignPostLegend: That Washougal thing was a hiker, not a cacher. Don't start.

CamasCrawler: You sure? I heard different. Heard a cacher found him.

GhostLogger: People die in the woods every year. Nature doesn't have safety rails.

CacheHawk: Dude, not the time.

TrailEtcher: You weren't there.

GhostLogger: Were you at Yale? Don't act like you know more than the rest of us.

Lurkers become participants while people who haven't logged a find in months show up to say they "always knew this would happen." A user changes their avatar to a clip art image of a monster with red eyes and the caption "FTF or die." They get banned and rejoin under another username.

By the time the first local news station posts an article titled, "Influencer Couple Missing After Forest Livestream," the caching world has already written six alternate versions of the story, and none of them are close to the truth.

Erin is huddled on her couch. She hasn't eaten, there's cold coffee on the table with a film on the surface and a dried brown ring on the wood. Her laptop glows on the cushion next to her, balanced on a throw pillow. She told herself she wouldn't look, but she's watching the fallout, waiting for someone to give anything of actual value.

She logs into the most active regional forum under her *TrailSister* handle and the home page slams her with unread threads. The top one is pinned by an admin, the title all caps: **PLEASE PAUSE GEOCACHE ACTIVITY IN CLARK COUNTY UNTIL FURTHER NOTICE**

The post beneath it is measured, and ends with the statement, *out of respect for an ongoing investigation* and *we encourage caution*. Erin reads every line twice. Nowhere does it say Jessa's name, or Colt's. Nowhere does it say *murder*.

The community fills in the blanks. She clicks a thread labeled: **Anyone know TrailSister IRL?** Her stomach knots. She shouldn't click it, but she does.

GeoMom73: Heard cops were at her place this morning.

LambertLurker: How do you know?

GeoMom73: Neighbor. Friend of a friend. Said squad car out front.

PineNeedlePinCushion: TrailSister's not a killer. Seriously. She's the one who runs the newbie meetups. She brings snacks.

TrailWolf: You think you know people, but you don't.

Erin's teeth grind together as she stares at his username and the casual poison of his comment. He didn't make an accusation, but he definitely planted a seed. Someone else piles on:

OverlookLaneCrew: Let's not witch-hunt, folks. We don't know the facts yet.

The hypocrisy of that doesn't even register to most of them. They just see another voice stepping in, a community veteran trying to calm the waters. Erin knows they're just covering their own ass, considering their caches are the ones in question.

CacheHawk: She ran. She was at a Jackalope cache and she ran. Not saying she's guilty but…

BenchMarker89: Wouldn't you?

CacheHawk: I was there and I didn't run. I wouldn't leave my friends.

The words hit harder than a physical blow, who the hell is CacheHawk to talk about friends? She's new to the scene. Erin pulls in a ragged breath, and her fingers descend on the keyboard. She could explain what was happening. She could type until the bones in her hands ache, and it wouldn't change the fact that she bolted from the QR Jackalope, that she's still alive and Jessa isn't, that the internet was there, and it saw what it wanted to see. Her cursor blinks in the reply box, but nothing comes.

She clicks away before she can read the next page, but the next thread is more of the same. This subject reads: **So is this all**

TrailWolf finally snapping or what?

    SwitchbackStan: Stop. He's abrasive but he's not a killer.

    MuddyBoots: Abrasive is one word. He used to run newbies off trails for "ruining the game."

    GhostLogger: That was years ago. He's mellowed out.

    CamasCrawler: Didn't someone say he was at Lucia Falls this morning?

    CacheHawk: He was. Ask Ghost.

As active as GhostLogger has been on the forums today, no reply appears. A minute passes, then five. His silence is its own answer. The rest of the community doesn't wait, they have their own input to provide.

    BenchMarker89: He logs everything. If he was there, we'll see the find soon.

    CamasCrawler: Unless it wasn't about the cache.

A new rumor enters the bloodstream.

    RidgeRabbit: Check this out. A friend DM'd me, someone using the name Jackalope signing caches around here for a while. Same rabbit logo as that QR code by Lucia Falls.

The thread explodes.

    OvercastDad: I've never seen that listed online. Not in digital logs, not in forums. Bring something real or don't bring anything at all.

    PineNeedlePinCushion: I've seen that stamp in a logbook at an old ammo can east of Yacolt. Didn't think much of it until now.

    CamasCrawler: What if he's been doing this longer than we know?

    TrailEtcher: "He"? Why not "she"?

    UrbanPuzzler: Yeah, probably some hiker-chick with a revenge complex.

    GeoMom73: Or maybe it's all staged and you're feeding into it like idiots.

The name crystallizes on the thread, a shape Erin has already felt breathing down her neck; *Jackalope*. Seeing it out in the open feels like standing naked in the middle of a highway. Her laptop fan whirs louder, straining to push air out through the pillow fabric. She realizes she's been leaning so close her eyes are dry and burning, so she forces herself to sit back. Her spine feels like wire.

She opens a private tab and searches the site logs for Jackalope. The results are empty, save a few recent mentions of the name. The community is sewing its own red string into Jackalope's veiled presence.

She clicks into another board, one she usually only uses for geocache trip planning. Today, it's a bonfire. One subject stands out:
DO NOT GO ALONE

OspreyNest: Until police make a statement, maybe we pause solo runs? Buddy up or don't go.

BenchMarker89: Seconded.

OvercastDad: This is overblown. I'm not halting my streak because two influencers pulled a stunt.

CryptidQueen: The forest remembers what the community forgets.

That one-line post sits there, full of cryptic gravity. The replies split instantly.

MuddyBoots: What does that even mean.

CamasCrawler: It means this has happened before.

UrbanPuzzler: Here we go, CQ pulling her crazy witch shit.

BenchMarker89: CQ, you talking about old missing persons or mythic creatures?

CryptidQueen doesn't respond in the forum, and her silence turns the sentence into prophecy fitting her handle. A new notification pops in the corner of Erin's screen. She sees her own handle tagged and feels her blood run cold. She clicks the new thread before she can talk herself out of it, recoiling at the subject:

TrailSister, you seeing this?

RidgeRabbit: @TrailSister you were at the last cache, right? Anything weird before the stream cut?

OvercastDad: Don't drag her into a public inquisition.

RidgeRabbit: She's the one the killer seems obsessed with. Look at the pattern. Bodies where she caches.

SwitchbackStan: Stop dude. That's not fair.

MouthyMuggleMagnet: It's a legit question.

Her lungs lock. She scrolls with hands shaking as more comments load.

UnderbrushKid: If I were her, I'd log off and lay low.

UrbanPuzzler: OR she's the one staging this for attention. Check her find count. She's everywhere.

CamasCrawler: Not cool.

OverlookLaneCrew: Everyone, please stop speculating about cachers. Focus on safety.

The cache owner with the body count is commenting again, neutral and reasonable. The response twists in her gut, surely, other people can see it is their caches getting all the attention. Erin's cursor hovers over the forum reply box again, desperate to tell her side of the story, but she doesn't want to defend herself to strangers who only know her trail name. She doesn't want to give Jackalope the satisfaction of watching her flail in public. Most of all, she doesn't want to sit here and breathe in other people's fear until it becomes her own. Her fingers choose her action.

TrailSister: I saw the stream same time everyone else did. I don't know what happened. I'm not involved in whatever this is.

She posts the comment before she can edit the softness out of it. The reply notifications flare so fast she doesn't even see the gap between them.

CamasCrawler: Thank you for saying something.

OvercastDad: So you *did* run.

FernFinder: Not cool to blame her for surviving.

UrbanPuzzler: Convenient she was "gone" when things got real.

TrailEtcher: You don't owe anyone an explanation, TS.

BenchMarker89: So, you weren't at the kill site this time, but there was a stream. Convenient.

The screen swims with responses and Erin squeezes her eyes shut for a second, but that only makes the memory of the Lucia Falls cache sharpen. She hears the gravel under her boots, shivers from the cold air, and sees TrailWolf standing across the lot with his hands in his pockets, watching. If she says his name here, the community will devour it, warp it, turn it into a narrative that doesn't match the truth. Worse, he sees. A new reply blinks into existence.

CacheHawk: I was with her at The Look Back cache. She's not lying, but she accused TrailWolf in the lot. Ask Ghost.

The choice is stolen from her. Now it's out there and she can't even take it back because it isn't her post.

UnderbrushKid: Whoa, for real?

OvercastDad: If TrailWolf was there too, how could they both be innocent? Anyone smell set-up?

UrbanPuzzler: If he's innocent, calling him out like that is messed up.

SwitchbackStan: Guys, enough.

The thread fractures into side arguments and accusations mutate with each refresh. In some versions, Erin called TrailWolf a murderer. In others, she "attacked" him. In others still, TrailWolf "saved her life." None of them are what actually happened, but all of them will be repeated as fact.

A private message icon pings. She clicks it and is instantly filled with regret. It is from CacheHawk: *You need to stop talking in the forum. Nothing you say is going to make them see you. They only see the story.*

Another line arrives before she can call CacheHawk out for her comment: *For real. Log off, TrailSister. Don't make this worse.*

Erin's fingers hover over the keys. Worse for who? She doesn't type it, but the question is already gnawing at her, punching a hole straight through her chest.

She tries one last corner of the internet, the small group chat that used to be for planning weekend runs and trading coordinates. It's a small group with only ten members, all core locals. The backlog is full of timestamps from earlier.

GhostLogger: Anyone know if Colt's ok?

ScoutPNW: Heard nothing.

GorgeHopper: I'm out. No more caches until we get some answers.

BirchAndStone: Drama. But yeah, maybe I'll stick to Sudoku for a bit.

The last message is an hour old. Nobody's said anything since. The silence is both a welcome reprieve and a creeping dread. Erin types slowly.

TrailSister: Is everyone okay?

She gets no response. The little "seen" indicators don't even light up. She waits five minutes, then ten. Finally, a single dot appears under her message, then vanishes. Someone opened the chat, saw her words, and backed out without answering. The isolation lands hard. A handful of names she expects to see aren't posting at all, and their silence rattles her more than the accusations.

She closes the laptop before she throws it. The apartment shrinks around her. The muffled sounds of her private life, the hum of the fridge, the faint traffic outside, they all feel distant and irrelevant. Her phone buzzes on the coffee table. She flinches, then reaches for it, full of apprehension. It's a new text, but not from Mark this time. The number is unlisted, a number she's never saved. It reads, "Don't let the mob confuse you. This isn't random. Myths don't start without intention. If you want to talk, I'm heading to Crave Grill off Fourth Plain for lunch."

She stares at the message, trying to read the tone or the intent. She hopes someone is watching the same pattern, that someone isn't screaming on the forums, or speculating, or panicking, but who knows the difference between noise and signal. Her first instinct is to text back, *Who are you,* but she's not sure she would trust the answer.

The list of suspects from the online forums churns in her head. TrailWolf, Colt, GhostLogger, Jackalope. She sets the phone down. If she answers, she tips her hand. If she ignores it entirely, she loses a thread she might need. If she goes there blindly, she's a target.

She looks back to the corkboard, at the absence she felt earlier, still humming with a faint pressure. Think like the hunter, she tells herself. Not the prey. Not anymore.

Crave Grill is public, busy at lunch. She could drive by and park, just see who shows, maybe look for a familiar car. She might see a familiar face. She might find an answer for why she's caught in this spiderweb.

For the first time, she understands something Vance didn't say out loud, the cops can't control this story. The community can't understand it. This is being written line by line, and it isn't going to stop until the message is delivered. She grabs her jacket and leaves her apartment, alone.

Chapter 20: Park And Grab

Vance hits the front door of the precinct at 8:30 according to the clock in the lobby, already feeling behind schedule with her entire day. She had hoped stopping by Erin's on the way in would have felt more useful, like she'd walk out with a cleaner direction, having something she could hand CSU for them to chase, but all she walked away with was the look of suspicion on Erin Caldwell's face. She can't follow the brittle mix of fear and adrenaline from when Erin said Jessa's name, or how she kept glancing at the coffee table full of amateur investigation. Even though there was something off, she recognized Erin was drowning in trauma, but that trauma wasn't actionable.

She signs past the front desk and moves through the humming bullpen. Phones are crying and printers spit out incident reports. Two employees are arguing about football near the door to Records and it grates against the thin film of sleep she had last night. She takes the stairs instead of the elevator, preferring the simple and mechanical climb so she doesn't have time to linger on words like "livestream" and "influencer."

When she reaches the Major Crimes Department, the whiteboard is worse than she left it last night. A new printout is taped to the corner, a still image from the video of Jessa mid-scream. The other side of the board now has a printout of both Jessa and Colt's DMV photos. There are more post-its with scrawled notes reciting cache log comments. She hates when other people work her case during off-hours.

Thankfully, her desk is still the same mess that she left last night. The open case files are fanned out like a hand of cards. Next to them is her legal pad with half a dozen thoughts scrawled across the page. Even yesterday's Styrofoam coffee cup, half-drunk with a dark ring inside, still sits uncomfortably close to the edge. She drops into the chair and rests there a second, letting the room move around her. She stares at the last three lines she wrote at the end of her shift yesterday on her notepad, the only things she wrote from her debrief with the sergeant:

"PR wants a statement by noon tomorrow…"

"…we don't classify as 'serial' yet…"

"…cachers are blowing up non-emergency again…"

She adjusts in the chair, her exhale hissing through her teeth, and rubbing her eyes with the heels of her hands. The room drones around her. Vance pulls her phone from her pocket. She sees the text from Shannon about lab queues first, then two unread emails from the captain and one from PR. What she doesn't find is a miracle.

Erin's apartment is still in her head. She plays back the way Erin opened the door with breath caught in her throat like she'd been doing something she didn't want seen, the jitter in her hands when Vance told her about Jessa, the way her whole body went rigid at the mention of Jackalope. Erin wasn't just scared, she was threaded tight with a dangerous certainty Vance couldn't deduce. The whole interaction has burrowed deep under the detective's skin.

She straightens in her chair and opens her notebook instead of her email. She works methodically through her lists of bodies, locations, timelines, and cache names. She reviews her shorthand of the game rules she understands and a longer list of the parts she doesn't. The coordinates she's recorded next to the cache names have stopped meaning places and have started looking like missile commands.

She stares at the page, tired of playing a morbid guessing game. She knows how to read a crime scene, how to read a witness. She does not know how to read the ecosystem this person is hunting in.

Vance flips back a few pages until she finds the line she wrote after a first meeting by the waterfront: *Surveyor. regional reviewer. Odd but informative. Community trusts him.*

The name sits there waiting on the page. She figures he sees every listing that goes live. He must know every cache, every event, every weird little description, the whole game passes over his desk first. Her gaze drifts to the board again, at marker lines tracing out from Hazel Dell to Yacolt, to Washougal, and to Yale Lake.

Vance taps the capped end of her pen against the paper. She could keep chasing half-informed theories through forum threads and cache pages, or she could ask the one person who actually knows how this machine is built and where the cracks are. She closes her notebook and pulls up a saved contact in her phone, the one CSU Maddox provided her the other day when they first mapped reviewer patterns across the county. **Surveyor (Reviewer, PNW Region)**

She thinks about the quiet way he spoke by the river, that apologetic softness in his voice, the way he made himself small even while explaining a system he clearly knew inside and out. If the killer is operating within these rules, she needs someone who helps moderate them. She presses call, expecting it to voicemail, but he answers on the second ring with the same soft tone she remembered from their last meeting. "Detective Vance. I figured you'd reach out."

Surveyor picks the meeting place, a small café on Fourth Plain with painted windows and mismatched tables, where retirees and grad students both frequent, creating a strangely functional, generational neutral ground. Vance arrives early and takes a seat where she can see the door and the parking lot, a choice made from two decades of experience. The waitress brings coffee. She doesn't normally drink coffee after noon, but today she feels the need to make an exception.

Surveyor walks in exactly one minute before their agreed time. He looks painfully ordinary, wearing almost the same clothes he wore on their first visit. He's dressed in a dark jacket, well-worn hiking boots, tan khakis, and the same round wire-rim glasses Vance recalls thinking are a few years out of style.

He spots her instantly and lifts a small, polite wave before approaching. "Detective Vance," he says with a mild smile. "It is an unexpected pleasure to visit with you again." His voice is soft but steady and carries a more familiar tone this time around.

She stands and they shake hands, the confidence in his grip is surprising. They sit and Surveyor places a small notebook on the table. He runs his hand over the cover once with his palm before folding his hands neatly. "You said you had questions about the review process."

Vance nods. "A lot of questions."

"Well," he says, delighted by the prospect, "I have a lot of answers."

With each prompt from the detective, he begins explaining the workflow. She learns how caches are submitted, how reviewers check for safety and proximity conflicts, that timestamps are methods of tracking caches and preventing duplicate caches within a tenth of a mile from one another, even how people sometimes try to cheat, and how those attempts usually fail. He speaks with a gentle precision and his answers are forthcoming, but also direct and with little personality.

"Reviewers see everything before the public does," he explains. "But only what's submitted. We don't see field edits. We don't see private exchanges, and we can't detect intent."

Throughout the conversation, two things strike Vance as slightly off. The first is that he remembers each cache she mentions, every single one, even Hazel Dell's Parkside Peekaboo from four years ago, which he didn't review. The second is that he seems to anticipate her questions, as though he's been rehearsing this conversation.

"What about user accounts?" Vance tries for something more direct, "Would a reviewer know who is hiding these caches, beyond their user name?"

He nods tightly. "Not specifically. We see their user name and can review their account. We are encouraged to do so, actually. This tells us how long they've been playing, how experienced they might be, and if they've hidden before, how they maintain their other caches." He pauses while she writes, giving her the opportunity to keep up. "The thing with account creation though, what I hear you asking, is that there is no requirement to input your legal name and address. You could input John Doe and that's the only way the system would know you."

Vance keeps notes while Surveyor sips his tea. "At the moment," he says, "your killer hasn't broken any review rules. They're clever, using the system exactly as designed."

It's the way he says clever with a quiet admiration rather than fear that makes something in Vance's head tilt. "Tell me about the username," Vance says. "Jackalope. Does that one mean anything to you?"

Surveyor gives a thoughtful hum, tilting his head almost mirroring hers. "I would assume there are dozens of jackalope-themed accounts in the geocache world. It's a whimsical creature that's half myth and half mascot. People might use it to lend mystery to their hides." His response seems perfectly reasonable, but his eyes slide slightly to the left when he says it. "Same could be said for Bigfoot, or Chupacabra."

"And the symbol?" she presses, ignoring his offering of other mythic creatures. "The one stamped in the logbooks?"

He smiles faintly with an edge of recognition. "Personal creativity. Cachers like branding. Some collect stamps and others collect patches. There's a whole subsect of the game where stamps are frequently used, it's called Letterboxing."

She was certain the stamp would have been a solid lead, but his response slams the door hard in her face, so she shifts gears. "What do you know about TrailWolf?"

Surveyor exhales softly, his eyes lifting as he searches his memory. "He's a passionate cacher, I suppose," he says. "He's competitive, some say he's too competitive. I've had to warn him about misleading coordinates before. He likes to post spoilers in his logs or hints that don't match the actual cache. He did it this week at a cache up near Lucia Falls. He creates drama, not by stirring the pot, but more with his behavior. All that said though, he's usually harmless."

He offers more with concern that sounds genuine. "He can also be abrasive, if your investigation concerns him, I would recommend using caution. The community tolerates him because he's talented, but temper and ego make a volatile mix." Vance writes in her notebook as he talks.

He continues before she's finished, "If I were you, Detective, I'd start with the disabled caches list. People still chase them sometimes because once we disable them, we expect the cache owners to go clear them, but they usually don't." In the margin, she jots 'disabled caches.'

Surveyor finishes his tea, folds his napkin with surprising precision, and places it beside his cup. "If there's anything else I can do," he says warmly, "please don't hesitate to ask."

For a moment, his expression drops to suggest old, buried grief wearing a polite smile. Vance notices and recognizes the weight behind the mask, it is the same weight of keeping long nights and putting in too much work, the same feeling she's had for a week now. "I appreciate the meeting and I won't take up any more of your time."

They stand and Surveyor extends his hand again. She shakes it. "A pleasure, Detective. Truly." He places cash under his cup, picks up his own notebook, and walks out the door.

Vance finishes her coffee, then pays the waitress. She steps out of the café and takes a deep breath, analyzing the parking lot. The traffic on Fourth Plain is steady, and the afternoon crowd is filtering in and out of small storefronts. It grinds against her memory of Jessa Whitlow on a slab at the morgue.

She crosses to her cruiser, but her mind hasn't left the table. Surveyor gave her everything she asked for with clear explanations, technical insight, names, dates, and reviewer procedures. Nothing in what he said was defensive, but something still scratches against her nerves. Even with the information he provided, she's not seeing how this Jackalope is hiding within the coordinates.

She sits in the driver's seat and flips open her notebook. Her handwriting from the meeting is controlled and cleaner than usual. She underlines several phrases: *Proximity rules, Timestamps hard-coded, TrailWolf- volatile, ego-driven.*

She stops on the name, TrailWolf. The way Surveyor said it was nearly the only time he showed emotion. The tone wasn't hostile or biased, but he said it with a practiced caution. Perhaps he was nudging her toward a direction that made sense without violating some reviewer code. She circles the name and frowns, closing the notebook, then starts the cruiser. There was a lot of information in what Surveyor said, but she can't help but feel there was more to be told in what he didn't say.

As she drives back toward the precinct, she replays the meeting detail by detail. He remembered every cache mentioned, including caches he never reviewed. He had no hesitation in those responses, he didn't even check his notebook.

She chases the thought deeper until she figures she's being paranoid. Experts don't need to check their notes. She doesn't flip through her pad when she needs to recite Miranda Rights, she doesn't consult a book to remember Penal Codes. She's tired and overloaded, she hasn't been able to pin down a solid answer on this case, she's probably just looking a gift horse in the mouth. The Surveyor is the only person who has given her straight answers since this case started.

By the time she parks at the precinct, she's dismissed it entirely. The department seems louder than usual this afternoon. A wave of chatter breaks around her desk before she gets to it. Two deputies are arguing about whether the livestream uploader had inside knowledge. A civilian waiting for a meeting is complaining the vending machine ate their money. A detective two desks over is grumbling about a drunken raccoon report. Vance tunes out the noise and passes her desk, walking straight to the whiteboard. Nothing has been added to it or changed since she saw it this morning. Everything matches what he told her.

Her phone vibrates with a new message from PR asking for a preliminary statement draft. She sees it but chooses to ignore it again. She finally commits to her desk and unlocks her computer, opening a new email window and starts typing instructions to CSU; *Compile all data for caches connected to victims. Cross-reference approval timestamps with login IP logs. Request reviewer audit logs for last sixty days.*

Her fingers rest on the keyboard. Reading the message back to herself, she recognizes it is too wide a net. She deletes the last line, trying to give the search parameters room to breathe while staying practical. Whatever itch Surveyor left under her skin doesn't present enough evidence to chase. What she does know is that she has four bodies, a missing person, a community in open panic, and a killer exhibiting escalation patterns, and all of these factors are somehow revolving around her main witness, Erin Caldwell, who is circling a breakdown.

Vance knows the case keeps moving whether she sleeps or not. She exhales slowly and pulls up Colt Rowan's last known GPS metadata. She taps her pen against the desk. "Alright, mister Rowan, let's see if you can tell me something I don't already know."

She types the coordinates into the map, and it zooms down from Clark County to a parking lot in a neighborhood not far from the Sheriff's department. The layout is familiar and the name of the business attached to the lot is even more so, a diner Vance goes to when she needs to forget the world, the same diner where she met Erin for the first time.

Vance pushes back from her desk, ready to head for the diner lot herself, but she thinks better of it and picks up her desk phone. "Dispatch, I need CSU and two units to the corner of 19th and Broadway," she says. "I need this to be a soft approach with no lights. I'm also going to need a scene canvass pertaining to the geocache investigations."

She's halfway to the building exit when the captain intercepts her with a stack of PR questions. She realizes she can't avoid the report, so she provides it verbally. The whole exchange costs her seven minutes she doesn't have.

When Vance arrives on scene, the lot is nearly empty, except for the sheriff vehicles taking up half of the eleven parking stalls. Most of the activity is near a low retaining wall made of red brick that's been patched and repatched over the years. Vance pulls in behind the CSU van, shielding her eyes from the reflection of the afternoon sun.

Ryan meets her halfway across the asphalt with latex gloves already protecting his hands. "Detective, we already started a grid," he says, then points to the two dumpsters near the alley. "The trash is pretty much empty. The waitress inside says it was picked up this morning."

"So then, what else do we have?" Vance asks, glancing at deputies slowly walking the lot with their heads craned low. She trusts they're searching for evidence and not just wasting tax dollars.

"While I was inside, I also asked about suspicious activity," he gestures toward the building. "She didn't recall anything."

Shannon steps out from behind the retaining wall, the camera hanging from her neck. "Detective, good, you're here. You'll want to see this."

Vance follows them toward the corner of the wall. The skirt around the lamppost is crooked by a hair, something no civilian would notice, but in their world, an uneven line is suspect. Ryan crouches and lifts the skirt two inches, revealing only wiring and dust. He lowers it again. "Nothing there."

"No, not that." Shannon taps the brick wall. "Right here, third brick from the base."

Vance kneels, feeling the ground press cold through her slacks. The brick looks exactly like the others, massed with time and weather, and the surrounding mortar is cracked, but when she presses two fingers along the bottom edge, the brick gives a millimeter.

"Maddox," she murmurs.

He joins her and slips a thin pry tool along the upper seam, shifting the brick outward. He works it further and reveals a notch on both the top and bottom, which he uses to pull it the rest of the way from the wall. The flat face of brick falls into his hand, revealing a hollow cubby in the wall. Impressed, he glances at Shannon. "That's clever."

Vance angles her flashlight into the gap. In the wall cavity is a container, a cache of sorts. Her nostrils flare at the absurdity. "Get me a glove," she says.

Ryan passes over a fresh pair and Vance slides them on, slow and precise. She reaches in and grips a container hidden inside, which pulls out cleanly. The small plastic box holds just two items, a cell phone and a laminated card.

Ryan sweeps the interior of the hole with his flashlight. "The rest of the hole is clear." He looks up at her.

Shannon steps closer, camera ready. "Detective, is that Colt's phone? Is this why we're here?"

"Likely," Vance says as she reaches in and lifts the phone, holding it by the edges. It has a black case and cracked corner. The screen is black and tapping the power doesn't bring up a lock screen. The battery is dead, but the device is intact. The card is stuck to the back of the phone with something tacky and shiny, pinkish and hardened at the edges. Gum, Vance hates gum.

She peels the card free and reads the bold printed line across the face: **THE WOLF IS ON THE TRAIL NOW AND IT'S TIME TO HUNT.**

"I want this phone processed immediately," Vance says. Her voice is steady, but the feeling crawling up the back of her neck isn't. "Run DNA on the gum."

Ryan takes the phone and stuck card from her, eyebrows pinched, he recites the phrase from the card and looks at the detective. "We saw this at the cabin."

Vance nods once, the empty container still in her gloved hand.

Shannon photographs the cavity, then whispers, "If this is the killer's, they weren't trying to get rid of evidence. It was saved for later."

"This is a trophy," Vance says quietly while looking at Ryan. She hands the container to Shannon. "Mark and document the rest of the scene. The Jackalope isn't just killing, they're curating a story."

Chapter 21: Took Nothing, Left Nothing

The palm trees at the parking lot's entry make the shopping center feel out of place, like it migrated north from California. Crave Grill sits in a squat little corner of the parking lot across from a crowded gym with glass walls. Erin parks where she can see the entrance, because she doesn't want to walk blindly into anything anymore, even lunch. She sits for a moment with both hands on the steering wheel, breathing slow, trying to maintain control. She's noticed *CryptidQueen's* log posts for years, admired the strange poetry she sometimes wrote into cache descriptions, and respects the quiet empathy she has shown newer players. She's not famous, but she's been a quirky community staple.

She doesn't just watch the restaurant, she checks for odd vehicles and for people who aren't leaving their cars. Inside, the lunch crowd is thin, but the layout of the place echoes enough that it still sounds busy. Erin notes the two exits and tries to examine faces through reflective surfaces. The woman behind the counter wipes laminated menus with an expression of terminal boredom.

CryptidQueen doesn't look like her profile picture, that photo was all misty forest, braids, and moonlight. The woman sitting in the corner of the small bar is wearing a hoodie with a faded band logo, chipped black nail polish, and a messy bun that lost its structural integrity hours ago. She has just taken the first bite of her lunch.

Erin stops mid-step, thrown by the image. She'd assumed CryptidQueen was a vegan who sipped herbal tea, or something more Pacific Northwest aligned. Instead, Erin watches her take a second unapologetic bite of the fattest burger Erin has ever seen. The woman wipes sauce from her chin with a napkin and glances up with soft eyes the color of wet moss.

"TrailSister?" CryptidQueen asks, smiling like they aren't living through a community meltdown after watching a woman die on camera yesterday.

"Yeah," Erin says. Her voice wavers once. "Erin. Hi."

Cryptid gestures to the empty chair across from her. "Have a seat. No offense, but you look like you haven't slept in days."

Erin takes the chair across from her. The moment feels strangely safe, but that could just be the illusion of fluorescent lighting and formica and the lunch crowd. Cryptid leans her elbows on the table. "I'm glad you came. Should I start with the obvious 'you're not crazy,' or do we work our way toward that?"

The comment almost makes Erin laugh. "I don't know why you reached out," Erin admits. "Or how you even got my number."

CryptidQueen shrugs and nudges a tater tot toward Erin in wordless offering. "Cacher circles aren't as big as people think, and when someone sends up smoke signals as obvious as yours, someone like me tends to notice."

Erin feels heat rise in her chest. "I wasn't sending smoke signals."

Cryptid gives her a long, knowing look. It is sympathetic and attentive in a way that makes Erin want to crawl out of her own skin or collapse into her lap, maybe both. "You were, though," she says gently. "But that's okay. You're not wrong to be scared."

Erin glances around the diner again. Everyone here looks normal, oblivious, unthreatened, making her whole world feel misaligned. She aches for something to help her forget the feeling of being watched, so she nods to CryptidQueen's meal. "That looks messy."

"Zombie burger." She grins maliciously. "This is the best burger anywhere. Lots of beef, bacon, ham, egg, and the best part is the habanero relish. You should definitely get one."

Erin smiles. "If I had an appetite."

"Fair." CryptidQueen sips her soda, then sets it down and swallows. "Tell me what you saw at Lucia Falls."

Erin freezes. "How do you know about The Falls?"

CryptidQueen's smile turns small. "Because the community is chewing you alive today. Half of them think you're the killer, the other half think you're bait, and a very loud handful believes this whole thing is some kind of cursed multi."

Erin looks down at her hands. They're trembling again. "And you?" she whispers. "What do you think?"

CryptidQueen studies her with an unnerving gentleness. "I think," she says, "you stumbled onto something dangerous wearing an older story, and the person behind it wants you to understand that story."

Erin's stomach drops. "Jackalope."

Cryptid nods once. She wipes her hands with her napkin, then folds it with careful precision, the motion suggests she's choosing her words before choosing her tone. "Interesting you mention that name," she murmurs through her food.

"I saw the symbol. It was at the cache with a QR code. It was basically a virtual cache, but it wasn't labelled as one."

CryptidQueen doesn't seem shocked. "Most people think of jackalopes as tourist-shop nonsense," she says, taking a sip of soda. "Postcards, T-shirts, cheap plastic coin banks, that whole 'Welcome to Wyoming, please buy something ridiculous' energy."

"I never even thought twice about them," Erin admits, "until recently. Now I can't stop." She almost smiles, but it dies as quickly as it came.

"But," CryptidQueen continues, "every region twists their myths. And geocache culture?" She shrugs. "We're basically folklore magnets, whether we want to admit it or not. It's no surprise though, as much time as we spend out in nature."

"Why a jackalope, though?"

CryptidQueen grins. "Well, here's the fun part. The jackalope didn't start as ancient lore or anything mystical. It was invented in the 1930s by a couple of Wyoming dudes who got bored, glued antelope horns on a dead rabbit, and accidentally created American folklore."

Erin blinks. "Seriously?"

"Seriously." Cryptid leans back in the booth. "That's the thing about myths though, once they're out there, they evolve. In some circles, a jackalope isn't just a cute bunny with antlers. It's a role, a symbol for people or things hiding in plain sight."

Erin's throat tightens. "Like caches."

"Like secrets," Cryptid corrects softly, her tone losing its playful humor. "Caches are just the medium our little subculture uses, but a jackalope? That's the trickster archetype. The thing everyone thinks they understand, until it grows horns."

Erin shifts, uneasy. "I don't think this is just flair. Whoever's using the symbol…"

"Is sending a message," CryptidQueen finishes, watching Erin more closely. "But maybe not to everyone."

Erin's breath snags. "Why would you say that?"

CryptidQueen pauses her reach for a tater tot, studying Erin for a long moment. "Because myths don't choose everyone," she says. "They choose their target."

Cryptid tilts her head with the focus of someone fitting a human being into a constellation she's been mapping quietly. "You looked hunted when you walked in," she says. "Which is understandable, most cachers are scared because of what's going on. You're different though, you might be scared, but you're trying to decode something."

Erin doesn't explain. She can't, not to someone she hardly knows.

CryptidQueen picks her tater and dips it. "Look, I don't know what you've been through. I haven't read every rumor and I don't want to. I texted because you sounded like someone who might need context instead of chaos."

She pops the bite into her mouth and then taps a finger thoughtfully against the rim of her glass. "You know jackalopes shed their antlers," she says. "In real cryptid lore, not the souvenir-shop stuff. They grow them new every season. The shedding, that's the important part. It's about transformation and rebirth. Leaving something behind to experience something new."

Erin frowns. "What does that have to do with the killings?"

CryptidQueen gives a soft shrug. "Maybe nothing, maybe everything. Whoever's behind this is using a symbol that's always meant change or loss. Something torn away and regrown. Prey becoming a predator."

The hairs on Erin's neck stand on end with the last word.

CryptidQueen continues. "People think monsters are born. But in most stories, they're made. By loss or betrayal, something that breaks a person's foundation."

Her gaze drops to Erin's hands. "Jackalopes show up in stories when the world wants to warn someone, or when someone needs to be understood." The air at the table thickens.

Erin whispers, "You think this person wants attention?"

"I think," CryptidQueen says, leaning in, "this person needs meaning, and meaning is dangerous when someone starts carving people into it."

The words conjuer an image which sends a chill trickling through Erin's body. She watches Cryptid take another bite of the massive burger, then asks, "Why do you think Jackalope chose now?"

CryptidQueen studies Erin while she chews, seeing the familiarity of a girl staring at the same kind of darkness. "I couldn't answer that, only Jackalope can," she says softly. "But I can tell you are the one chosen to see it."

Erin's fingers curl around her water glass. "You don't know that."

CryptidQueen gives a small, maddeningly calm smile. "I know obsession when I see it, and symbols don't escalate unless someone's feeding them energy." She motions vaguely toward Erin. "Or unless someone's feeding you energy."

Erin stiffens. "You think I'm encouraging this?"

"I think you're tangled in it," Cryptid replies. "And I think you're trying really hard not to look directly at whatever part of it scares you most."

Erin's pulse spikes at how accurate that sounds. CryptidQueen softens a little, leaning forward. "Look, people like us? We chase patterns, we can't help it. Myths grow teeth because someone keeps returning to them."

Erin swallows. "I didn't choose any of this."

CryptidQueen leans back in her chair, staring at what's left of her lunch. "No, but the Jackalope did." The sentence lands sharp in Erin's spine.

She doesn't push, she simply watches Erin's reaction with an unsettling patience, waiting to see whether she accepts or rejects the possibility.

Erin steadies her nerves. "Then let me ask you something."

CryptidQueen's eyes spark with intrigue. "Of course."

"What kind of person," Erin says carefully, "uses a jackalope as their calling card?"

CryptidQueen doesn't answer immediately. She looks out the window, thinking. When she speaks, her tone is precise. "Someone who wants the world to underestimate them." She lets the moment settle before speaking again. "Someone who thinks they're the only one who sees the truth. Someone who survived something they weren't supposed to."

Erin's stomach drops.

CryptidQueen finally meets her eyes again. "And whoever your Jackalope is? They've been building this myth for a while."

Erin feels sweat prickle at her palms. CryptidQueen isn't rambling. She isn't guessing.

CryptidQueen's gaze sharpens to a scalpel. "You know what else jackalopes symbolize?" she says, swirling the straw in her soda. "Adaptation. They change shape depending on who's telling the story." She lets that comment hang before quietly adding, "Kind of like your killer."

Erin's jaw tenses. "My killer?"

Cryptid reaches for her drink. "I mean the killer," she quickly corrects.

Erin watches the woman across from her play with the straw without drinking. "You said my killer," she says slowly. "Why would you say that?"

Cryptid doesn't blink. "Because you're the only one Jackalope is talking to."

"What does that mean?"

Cryptid leans forward, resting her elbows against the table, deciding how to capture the burger in front of her. "You're not the only one reading the pattern, Erin. After the last cache dropped, anyone paying attention can tell Jackalope is steering you."

Erin's stomach twists. "Everyone is talking about Jessa. How would you know the Lucia Falls cache is connected?"

Cryptid's eyes widen just enough to betray the mistake. "I didn't say…"

"You just did," Erin snaps, the whisper sharper than she intended. "How do you know that?"

Cryptid opens her mouth to respond as the waitress appears. "Doing okay over here?" she chirps, seemingly oblivious to the tension slicing the table in half. Erin jerks back in her seat. CryptidQueen leans away, her social mask sliding smoothly back into place. The waitress looks to Erin. "Need anything to eat, hon?"

Erin forces a breath. "No… I'm fine."

The waitress turns to CryptidQueen. "Another refill? Or dessert?"

Cryptid smiles at her. "Oh, no darling, thank you but that burger about did me in. Just the check when you get a chance, please and thank you."

While the women discuss payment, Erin's eyes drift involuntarily to the muted TV above the counter. A breaking news banner scrolls across the bottom: SEARCH CONTINUES FOR MISSING HIKER COLT ROWAN. AUTHORITIES INVESTIGATING POSSIBLE CONNECTIONS TO RECENT DISTURBANCE.

A grainy photo of Colt fills the screen and a second line beneath it flashes: IF FOUND, DO NOT APPROACH, CALL AUTHORITIES.

Erin feels her skin crawl and her phone buzzes on the table with a new text message from Mark. She's so fixated on his name, she doesn't catch CryptidQueen also noticing. He's texting midday, which means he's mid-shift. She doesn't understand why he's messaging her now. He asks: **Did that detective tell you everything? About this morning?**

By the time she returns her attention to CryptidQueen, the waitress is walking off, and her geocache companion is folding her straw wrapper as if nothing happened. CryptidQueen watches her with a quiet knowing. "See?" she says gently. "Stories change shape fast."

Erin doesn't answer. Her attention keeps pinging between the TV and her phone, between Colt's photo and Mark's text, between the warning banner and the memory of Vance's voice in her apartment a couple of hours ago. Every corner of her life suddenly feels like it's turning toward her at the same time.

CryptidQueen studies her without intruding. "You know him?" she asks softly, nodding toward the TV.

Erin swallows. "Everyone knew Colt and Jessa. They were… hard to miss." Her voice goes somber. "Now she's dead and he's missing."

Cryptid hums low in her throat, almost sympathetic. "Jackalopes don't hunt randomly. They pick targets with emotional gravity." She taps one finger lightly on the table. "People who leave a mark."

Erin's lips tighten. "What does that mean?"

Cryptid gives her a long, assessing look. "It means the killer isn't chasing fame, they're chasing meaning. Some people attract that kind of fixation without realizing they're doing it."

"I'm not attracting anything."

Cryptid lifts an eyebrow. "A livestreamed murder and your username was connected to it. You're the last person who gets to decide you're not in the narrative."

Erin feels the blood pull from her skin, hears her pulse thudding disjointedly in her ears. Before she can respond, her phone buzzes again and again, it's Mark. **Erin. Are you home? Please tell me you're okay.**

She grabs the phone but doesn't respond. She can't shake the feeling he's always texting at either just the wrong time or exactly the right time. Cryptid notices the tremor in Erin's hand. "You trust him?" Cryptid asks casually.

It's an innocent enough question except it isn't in the moment. Erin manages a quiet response through her constricted throat. "He's… a friend."

Cryptid's smile is small and almost kind with a hint of pity. "Friends can blindside you in ways enemies never could."

Erin flinches at the contrast between the woman's words and

expression, but CryptidQueen doesn't press further. She lifts her glass, takes a thoughtful sip, then sets it down with delicate care. "You know what I think?" she says, her voice dropping into quiet certainty. "Something's been chasing you longer than you realize."

Erin's voice goes thin. "Why would you think that?"

Cryptid shrugs one shoulder. "Patterns don't start with the loudest event, they start with the first anomaly." Her eyes drop to the patch of dried mud on the sleeve of Erin's jacket. "You've had an anomaly recently, haven't you?"

Erin's breath stutters as the memory of the shard under her couch floods her awareness. She looks down unable to answer. Cryptid leans back, giving space to the moment. "You don't have to tell me," she says. "But you should tell someone eventually. Preferably before your hunter decides to escalate."

Erin drops her hand beneath the table and curls it into a fist in her lap. The waitress returns with the check and Cryptid takes her credit card off of the receipt with a subtle grace that Erin barely notices. When the waitress leaves again, Cryptid stands. Erin blinks, she hadn't realized their conversation was over. Cryptid adjusts her jacket, then rests her fingertips lightly on the table, a gesture that feels strangely ceremonial.

"One more thing," she says. "Jackalopes aren't monsters. They're watchers, guardians, legends built on grief." She looks down at Erin with soft intent. "If someone is invoking that myth, they're not doing it to scare the community. They're begging for someone to hear their truth."

Erin whispers, "Me."

Cryptid gives a small, unreadable smile. "Maybe. Or maybe you're just the one finally listening." She turns to leave, then pauses, just long enough to add, "Be careful who you think you're safe with, TrailSister."

Erin wants to respond but the loss of words won't let her.

CryptidQueen fills the void. "And be even more careful who thinks they're safe with you." She walks out.

Erin sits frozen, watching her vanish through the door, the cold air from the parking lot drifting in for half a second before the door swings shut again. Her phone buzzes a third time from Mark: ***Erin. Answer me. Please.***

The text sends a chill rolling through her. She can't tell whether Mark is being protective, panicked, guilty, or something much, much worse. She's not ready to respond.

The café is nearly empty now, and Erin sits alone in the bar. For the first time since this nightmare began, she realizes she no longer knows who in her life is a threat and who is trying to save her. The doubt wells in her to a point of suffocation and she stands frantically, throwing money on the table, even though she only had water, and pushes through the door. The cold hits instantly, cooling the burn overwhelming her senses.

She expected daylight to clear her head, but instead the world outside feels sharper. She steps off the curb and hurries toward her car, but something forces her to stop. She is overloaded by the sudden flood of stimuli and realizes she forgot to ask how Cryptid knew about the last cache. The thread slipped right through her fingers.

Further down the lot, a compact car idles, windows dark from the afternoon glare. Erin can't see the driver, only the faint outline of someone's shoulder pressed to the window. She's not being paranoid, cachers spend half their lives noticing who's watching them dig around in bushes. Attention has a weight, and Erin knows when it's on her.

She checks her phone to seem inconspicuous, but it shows another new text from Mark: **Where are you?**

She pockets the device in frustration. When she looks up again, the car is still there and the silhouette hasn't moved. She walks toward her own car with deliberate calm, gripping her keys with sharp end between her fingers. Her shoulders are tense and every step is measured. When she unlocks the door and slides inside, she checks the mirror to see the darkened car hasn't budged, but the silhouette is gone.

She scans the side mirrors for activity, hoping for an innocent explanation, but she doesn't wait for one. She pulls out of the lot, and when she hits the first stoplight, her phone buzzes again. Mark just won't let up: **Erin, please talk to me.**

She powers the phone off and turns it face-down on the passenger seat. The light changes and she drives. The conversation with CryptidQueen worms into her skull. She forces her breathing to steady, but as she merges onto Fourth Plain, she can't shake the feeling that she didn't leave the café alone, something left with her.

Chapter 22: Bring Your Own Pen

Vance pushes through the double doors with a lukewarm paper cup in hand, half-filled with black coffee, the second serving of a broken pattern. The fluorescent lights in the precinct always feel harsher at night. The glow highlights every flaw, from the smudges on the glass to the shadowed hollows beneath tired eyes.

Half the lights in the Major Crimes Department are off to avoid the brutal illumination in the rest of the building. A detective from burglary sleeps sitting up with his head tipped back and mouth cracked open. Vance doesn't wake him, she both understands his need for a power nap and envies his ability to sneak one in.

Vance navigates to her desk, cursing herself for not just going home, but knowing she wouldn't be able to stop trying to piece her case together. Jessa Whitlow's autopsy report is waiting for her, printed, clipped, and placed dead center on her desk. Shannon left a sticky note on it that reads, *"You'll want to read page 3."*

Vance sits and opens it, knowing already she's going to hate what she finds. The clinical wording doesn't soften what she finds inside the folder. Her cause of death reads as *exsanguination due to sharp-force trauma* and the manner of wounds is listed as deliberate, obviously. The coroner listed them as controlled with no hesitation marks and no defensive wounds.

Vance closes her eyes. The detail, *no defensive wounds* feels blatant, even without reviewing the video stream. Jessa was fit and strong, her financial records show both an active gym membership and regular payments to a local judo school. She was a girl who knew how to resist, how to fight back, which means the killer didn't give her the chance. Before she can sit with that thought, the phone on her desk chirps: **PR NEEDS STATEMENT BY MORNING. DISPATCH SWAMPED W/ CACHER CALLS AGAIN. REPORT OF "SUSPICIOUS MAN IN WOODS" 13th TODAY.**

It's the same problem every time an investigation leaks into public consciousness, half the county thinks they're detectives, the other half thinks they're bait. She tosses the phone aside and flips to page three. *Strangulation marks inconsistent with panic or frenzy. Grip strength notable. Height estimation: approx. 5'9"–6'2".*

She closes the folder. Jessa didn't die on the video feed, she was stunned. Jackalope strangled her after.

The bullpen outside continues to drone in movement. Vance rubs her brow, exhausted but locked in, and murmurs, "Alright, Jessa. Show me what really happened to you."

She doesn't get two lines into her next case note before Shannon Chesshir approaches her desk, holding a manila envelope and a tablet. Her ponytail is damp like she showered at the lab sink instead of going home. Ryan loiters behind her, chewing the last of a vending-machine snack he definitely regretted buying.

"You two are still here," Vance says. "Tell me it's something good."

Shannon gives a humorless huff. "Define good."

She drops the envelope on Vance's desk, and taps her tablet awake. "Prelim DNA on that gum you found with Colt's phone."

Vance's spine straightens. "You got a match?"

"Yeah," Shannon says, flipping the tablet so Vance can see the confirmation line: **DNA MATCH: ROWAN, COLT. 99.87%**

Vance frowns. "How the hell do we have Colt's DNA on file?"

Ryan answers this time, shrugging. "His influencer account did one of those mail-in ancestry kits two years ago. Their dataset got subpoenaed during a separate case last fall. His profile was included in that batch."

Vance rubs her forehead. "Christ. Of course it was."

"It's tentative," Shannon adds. "We'll run a second test, but the initial result lines up."

Vance leans back. If Colt handled the gum, then he was at the diner, recently enough to leave trace. Which means the moment before his phone vanished, he wasn't running for his life or being dragged, he was standing still, long enough to chew, spit, maybe stash something.

"And what's this?" Vance opens the manila envelope. Inside are printouts of old cache logs tied to *The Big One,* the cache the team learned of from the cabin, ammo can marked #0278. The printout shows dozens of usernames she doesn't recognize, but one of them makes her pause, TrailWolf. He signed the logbook first with **"Old cache, new log. TFTC."**

Underneath it are three comments from other cachers.

"TrailWolf came back to 'FTF' a new logbook? Cool story bro"

"Ugh, found one of his cards in the container again. Guy needs a hobby."

"Those edgy wolf cards give me the creeps ngl."

Vance stills at the comment of a wolf card, just like the one they found this morning with Colt's phone. "Maddox, tell me again exactly what that card said, the one we found today."

Ryan recites without hesitation and without referring to a notepad, "The wolf is on the trail now and it's time to hunt." He doesn't ask why and Vance can tell by the way he gives Shannon a side-eye, that they came to the same conclusion before bringing her the evidence.

That phrase was in the shrine cabin, both etched onto Evan's lost logbook and carved into the floor. "The wolf on the trail." Vance groans. "Damn my eyes." She didn't make that connection until now. TrailWolf was caching in this area when the Evan boy disappeared.

"Shannon," Vance says quietly, tapping the log entry, "pull

every cache TrailWolf logged that year."

Shannon grabs her tablet and starts typing. "On it."

Ryan clears his throat, he's afraid to interrupt but does it anyway. "Detective? There's also this."

He slides over another printout, smartphone metadata recovered from Colt's device. The screen shows a timeline with two video files. One is the influencer livestream. The other is a corrupted clip with a timestamp thirty-two minutes after Jessa's estimated time of death.

"Video after the murder," she says.

"We can't open it yet," Ryan admits. "But it proves the phone wasn't destroyed at the scene. It was used after."

So, Colt wasn't just present, he was active. Vance exhales slowly. "Keep working the corruption. I need that timestamp authenticated, but more importantly, we need to see what's on that video."

As Ryan leaves, Vance glances at the red blinking voicemail light she ignored earlier. She presses play and a ranger's voice crackles from the speaker, "Detective Vance, this is Ranger Adams from the Mount St. Helens unit. We finished at that cabin you and your CSU team investigated. I remember working that case, the one where the boy died up there, thought you should know. I'd be happy to send my notes over if you think it would help your current case."

She hits 3 to save the message. "Chesshir."

Shannon doesn't look up from her tablet. "I just pulled what I could from the database."

Vance exhales once. "What do we need to know?"

Shannon steps closer, sharing the screen. "The report is for an accident involving a child, fourteen years old, who disappeared during a hike. Report actually mentions geocaches. Search and Rescue recovered the body two days later. Cause of death was ruled exposure, with contributing negligence but no criminal charges filed."

Vance's jaw tightens. "What about family?"

Shannon hesitates while she scrolls the data. "Report shows parent, still married. They weren't residents of Clark County. Names are there, but anything beyond next of kin is redacted pending jurisdictional request."

"Why?"

"Because the responding SAR unit also wasn't Clark County," Shannon says. "I'd guess with a different chain, there are different archive rules. Some of the supplemental reports are sealed unless we formally reopen."

Vance leans back in her chair. Of course they are. She studies Shannon's screen again. The report's location is a close match for the GPS coordinates of *The Big One*. This happened nearly five years ago. "Any indication the family pushed back?"

"They filed a complaint," Shannon says. "Against a cacher, but it was cleared, with no follow-up."

Vance nods slowly. Grief without justice has a way of fermenting. "I want the full file," she says. "Everything. SAR logs, responder names, original cache records. Put in the request."

Shannon's fingers are already moving across the screen. "It'll take time, I won't be able to put in the request until their records office is open tomorrow."

"I know. Until then, see if you can catch our department before they leave, see if they have anything at all."

Shannon acknowledges and quickly leaves the room. Vance relaxes in her chair, seeing the lines finally starting to connect, crookedly, but they're connecting nonetheless. She has a dead boy, a negligent cacher with a temper, and a calling card. TrailWolf is no longer background noise, he has become a viable suspect.

Vance reads Jessa's report five times, each pass making her hate the clean wording more. She needs to know if and how he connects to the dead influencer.

On Vance's sixth pass through Jessa's file, a tired clerk approaches her desk with a thin file in his hand. "You requested a missing persons archive," he says. "I pulled this using the information I received from Chesshir."

Vance thanks him, taking the file before dismissing him. The file is about as thin as she expected, she has seen a lot of tragic cases and most of them are barely a handful of pages. She leans forward in her chair and opens it.

MISSING PERSONS REPORT. JUVENILE MALE LOCATION OF INCIDENT: SOUTH SHORE, SOUTH YALE LAKE

She skims the report which reveals a family trip and a boy who was passionate about finding a geocache while the parents were fishing. The mother reported the boy missing hours later when he didn't return. There was a search that went well into the night and picked up the following day. It was reclassified after his body was located three days later by two volunteer Search and Rescue members, Mark Leland and Daniel Rourke.

At the bottom of that page is written a neat note in blue ink. *Follow-up interviews w/ witnesses indicate "TrailWolf" helped family pick route up ridge, offering a "shortcut."* The note doesn't prove motive or guilt, but it sharpens the narrative.

"Alright, TrailWolf," she mutters. "Step into the light."

She pulls a page from her legal pad and writes his handle in block letters at the top. Under it, in outline format, she makes a list. *Prior complaints? Known associates. Employment. Vehicle. Firearm registrations. Last verified location.*

She takes the note to the CSU room and places it in front of Shannon who looks up from her desk through eyes that are gritty but alert. "Chesshir," Vance says, "TrailWolf just graduated."

Shannon straightens. "To what?"

"He's now my main person of interest," Vance replies. "Run everything you can get without a warrant. If it smells dirty, we'll push more paper."

Shannon doesn't say anything, she just grabs the paper and goes to work on her computer. Vance returns to the Major Crimes Department and reviews the information posted under TrailWolf's handle on the corner of the scene board. For a moment she just stares at it, the name sitting there between Jessa's photo and Erin's profile. It isn't much of an answer, but it finally feels like the first target she can try hitting.

The door to Major Crimes opens and the shift lieutenant walks in with his jacket draped over his arms and his sleeves rolled up. He doesn't sit, which tells her everything she needs to know. He's going to dump bad news before going home for the night. "PR's losing control of this," he says without preamble. "We've got cachers flooding dispatch, influencers naming suspects on livestreams, and the county prosecutor wants to know why we don't have a face attached to this yet."

Vance doesn't rise to it. She taps the edge of the young boy's file once with her finger. "Because we're still verifying."

"That's not what they're hearing," he replies. "They're hearing hesitation, and hesitation reads like incompetence when people are scared."

She finally looks up at him. "You want a name?"

"I want direction," he says evenly. "If names keep getting mentioned online and we don't acknowledge them, the narrative gets written without us. Once that happens, we're chasing optics instead of evidence."

Vance leans back in her chair. Her spine aches and she points to TrailWolf on the board. "I have a solid lead on this one, but he's not clean," she says. "I'm not ready to call him a suspect yet, not publicly."

The lieutenant studies her for a moment, then nods once. "Fine, give me something I can defend."

"Then you need to give me twelve hours," Vance says, her words come out steadier than she feels. "I'll give you something in twelve hours."

He pauses, feeling the weight of her deadline. "Alright," he says finally. "Twelve. After that, I need solid movement." He steps back toward the hall, then stops. "And Vance?"

She looks up. "Yeah."

"Be careful who you let steer this," he says. His warning isn't friendly, but it isn't accusatory either. The door closes behind him, and the latch clicks soft but final.

Vance sits there for a moment, staring at the empty doorway. "Seems like the wrong people are already grabbing the wheel," she grumbles, pulling the TrailWolf notes closer to the center of her desk. The clock on the wall ticks louder now, acting as the Lieutenant's little reminder. Twelve hours won't be enough time, but it does give her slightly more room to work.

Vance studies the page again. TrailWolf's profile page sits there with facts stacked beneath it of dates, locations, complaints, and a phrase that keeps surfacing where it shouldn't. On paper, it's enough to make a case uncomfortable, enough to make a man nervous, but not enough to make it hold.

She knows the difference between probable and provable. She's lived inside that difference for most of her career. She sees the gap between the story she can see forming and the one she can defend in a room full of attorneys. She closes the file, dissatisfied with the amount of speculation she would need and the growing pressure of finding results. If she pushes now, he lawyers up, if she waits, the pattern keeps moving without her. Either way, the clock doesn't stop.

She needs something that doesn't rely on interpretation. Something that doesn't ask a jury to follow a thin trail of breadcrumbs through a hobby they won't understand. She just needs one clean anchor. Until she has that, he stays where he is. Close enough to feel the heat, but far enough to keep talking. She stands, shoulders tight, and heads back to the CSU Department.

"Chesshir," she says. "I need you to get the specific technical identifiers ready so I can draft an affidavit to subpoena the company that runs this game. I want the full subscriber jacket tonight. I'm not just talking about posts. I want edits, deletes, IP variance, burner overlap."

Shannon looks up. "You're pretty certain he's our guy, then?"

"I think," she says carefully, "he's the variable that breaks this case if it goes sideways."

"Understood." She spins in her chair and immediately begins pulling up files.

"Be sure to include a non-disclosure order for this. If the company's legal does anything to spook the suspect, this whole op is wasted." Vance isn't finished. "I'm going to need all of this for the DA's Office ASAP."

Shannon nods along to her words. "Heard."

Vance gives Shannon her final command. "I want you to set up a digital tail on TrailWolf. Keep it low profile and don't ping his servers, but if he sneezes, I want to know which direction he turned his head."

Vance looks at Ryan who is watching the two coordinate. "Maddox. I want that corrupted file cracked yesterday. If there's even a single frame intact, I want it. And I want to know where the phone was when it was recorded."

Ryan nods. "On it."

"And the diner," she adds. "Expand the canvass. We need to see foot traffic. Security cameras within two blocks. Anyone who lingered. Anyone who doubled back." She pauses, then lowers her voice. "Especially anyone who looks like they weren't there to eat."

Ryan's mouth tightens. "Yes, ma'am."

Vance steps back, surveying the room, watching the sparks from her controlled burn. She's narrowing the focus now, which means paperwork, oversight, and explaining herself to people who don't care about patterns or gut instinct. She's giving the Lieutenant what he wants, which is fine. If she's wrong, the case slows. If she's right, it gives everyone what they need. She knows surveillance doesn't catch killers, but pressure does.

She leaves CSU, moving next to Records. She finds the same clerk tidying up his desk before he leaves for the night. Her arrival brings a chest-dropping sigh to his lips. "I just turned off my computer."

"That's fine," she says with a face of stone. "First thing in the morning, you need to compile every geocache incident from the last five years, complete with escalations." She watches him make a note.

Vance doesn't go back to her desk. Instead, she takes the side stairs down to the main floor and pushes out the rear door of the precinct into the alley. The night is brisk, sharp enough to sting the inside of her nose.

She leans against the brick building and finally lets herself stop moving. The pack of cloves waits in the inside pocket of her jacket, dented slightly from her shift. She pulls one out and rolls it between her fingers for a moment before lighting it. The first drag burns sweet and acrid at the same time, grounding in a way coffee never is.

TrailWolf fits cleanly with his temper, the growing history, the phrase that has bubbled to the surface, and a body in the past that never resolved into consequence. He makes sense in a way she needs to hang the case, but not in a way she feels good about.

Nothing in this investigation has been clear, though. Vance exhales slowly, watching the smoke unravel. Jessa wasn't killed in a panic. The video wasn't made to document, it was made to position.

The cabin wasn't a hideout, it was a confession staged for discovery. Even the phone, tucked away in a secret hiding spot, felt less like disposal and more like a trophy, but for whom?

Then there's Erin Caldwell, the perpetual witness who absorbs information instead of hiding, and her dance with the unsub who keeps nudging her rather than silencing her. The cacher who sees patterns before Vance can justify them on paper, with her own personal corkboard mapping faster than the investigation.

Vance flicks ash and takes another drag. If the boy at Yacolt was the spark, he chooses how the fire burns and where it spreads, driving a pair of living hands to orchestrate this whole mess.

The clove burns down to the filter. Vance crushes it under her boot and straightens, squaring the weight of the case back into her shoulders. Erin can't be left alone in this current. Vance pulls out her phone and scrolls until she finds Erin's contact, letting it sit there on the screen. The detective doesn't call, she just stares at the name, attempting to watch the same direction the killer is watching.

Vance slips the phone back into her pocket and heads inside. The case isn't narrowing, it's choosing sides, and Vance needs to see all sides.

Chapter 23: As The Crow Flies

Erin has stripped the corkboard down to what still holds, removing tracked caches before Hidden Hollow and removing the speculative notes which haven't held ground. The half-formed theories, the emotional shorthand, the things she wrote when she was scared and needed to see movement even if it wasn't real, all of that is in the trash now, folded and refolded until the paper tore. What's left is quieter, less busy. Photos are aligned by location instead of chronology. Names and times are correlated to respective caches. The board looks less like a rat's nest now and more like a field kit.

She steps back, examines the board, then steps forward again and shifts one photo a fraction of an inch to the left. The need for it to line up surprises her, but she follows her instinct. She stares at the photo held on the board by an orange thumbtack, fixating on the bright plastic. Something about it feels familiar.

The mental itch won't leave so she goes to her laptop which is sitting open on the kitchen counter. Erin scrolls through her photo archive, past screenshots and trail selfies, until she finds the Hidden Hollow image again. She pulls up the image she took of the Polaroid. She doesn't look at the woman this time, instead she zooms in on the container behind the captured photo, past the metal edge of the dirt-smudged ammo can to the notebook inside. On the face of the logbook, almost lost to shadow, is a strip of orange tape. It is half peeled and pressed flat again.

Erin doesn't remember noticing it that day. She does remember the cold, the quiet, and the weight of the Polaroid in her hand. She remembers how signing the log felt necessary, almost moral. The tape didn't draw her attention that morning and it doesn't mean much now. Many cachers use duct tape as a sort of label, naming the cache or writing the original placement date, but this tape is blank.

She leans away from the laptop and exhales through her nose. She navigates to Jessa and Colt's streaming page, scrolling through their candy-coated relationship until she reaches the Lamppost Lament video and sees the micro in Colt's hand. The tape is there too, wrapped tight around the tube. In the frame, it looks like utility, but nothing else.

Both have the same orange tape. Both caches were hidden by OverlookLaneCrew. Her eyes shift to the coffee table. The mirror shard sits where she left it, still half-wrapped in a scrap of flannel. She hasn't removed it from the piece of mirror since she wrapped it when she got home from Washougal. She told herself wrapping it was practical, safe. She told herself not looking at it was the same thing as containing it.

She stands between the couch and table, leaning forward and pulling the shard close to her, then hesitates with her hands hovering over the fabric. There's a faint resistance in her chest, a quiet don't in her skull. Erin unfolds the cloth gingerly, inch by inch. It catches her reflection and fractures it, her face splitting in two down the crack. She barely registers that part anymore.

She pulls the last wrap of flannel from the base, exposing a wrap of orange flagging tape where it would bite into a hand. It is creased on one side and severed clean at the other. She stares at the makeshift handle, practical and deliberate, but quickly fashioned without ceremony.

She steps back hard, her heel smashing into the couch. She steadies herself by pressing her palms flat against the table, fingers splayed and eyes locked on the shard. The killer didn't just grab what was nearby, this shard was intentional and the preparation was premeditated.

The realization comes with a cold, steady certainty that settles in her core and refuses to move. Whatever story Jackalope is trying to tell isn't over, and she knows it involves her. Erin stares at the empty pinholes across the map of her geocache board, desperately trying to remember who she might have upset, whose First to Find she might have stolen.

Her phone buzzes on the counter. Almost in response, a knock hits her front door, three raps close together. Erin jumps upright, then hurriedly flips the flannel halfway back over the shard, not thinking, but trying to hide the evidence.

She goes to the door and opens it a crack, finding Mark on the other side, with one hand still raised, unsure if he should knock again. He looks tired in a familiar way. Relief spreads across his face when he sees her. "Hey," he says. "You didn't answer your phone."

"I didn't hear it," Erin says, only half remembering it buzzed.

He nods, accepting that without pushing. "Can I come in?" He smiles.

She hesitates, trying to recall how long ago her phone went off. She looks inside the apartment, then back to him.

"If now isn't a good time…"

"No, it's fine," she says and moves back, offering him entry. He steps inside and guides the door to click shut behind him, sealing the quiet back into place. He pauses just inside the apartment, tracking the room automatically. His eyes move along the corkboard and maps to the way things have been shifted. It's subtle, but it's different. "You reorganized," he says.

"Yeah." She realizes she's holding the handle of the entry table that contains Danny's knife, so she lets it go. "It was getting messy."

He hums, thoughtful, and shrugs out of his jacket, walks over and sets it on the back of the chair without looking. His familiarity and comfort with her space flares her irritation. Mark moves closer to the board, careful not to crowd it. "This looks…" He trails off, searching for the right word. "More focused."

She watches his reflection instead of his face, catching it fractured faintly in the glass of the framed picture of her and Danny next to the corkboard. "I needed it to make sense."

He nods at her response, looking from the board toward the coffee table as he's about to speak. Erin feels the shift before he sees it, and her shoulders draw instinctively inward. The flannel lies on the table, out in the open, and the fabric is bunched loosely with one corner flipped back just enough to expose a glimpse of mirror and orange tape. He keys in on it, his original comment never spoken. "Erin," he says, softly. "What's that?"

Mark doesn't investigate, he stands just inside the kitchen, realizing he's stumbled into something private and isn't sure if stepping forward would make it worse. His eyes stay affixed on the coffee table, on the edge of the flannel and the glint of mirror.

Erin freezes, feeling exposed in a way she can't quite describe. "It's not what you think," she says, immediately regretting it. The sentence comes out defensively and she hates that she's already planned an argument with him in her head.

Mark's eyebrows knit together with judgment. "I don't think anything," he says. "I just asked."

She moves toward the table, deliberately casual, and pulls the flannel the rest of the way over the shard. The motion is careful and almost reverent. "It's evidence," she says. The words feel strange in her mouth, heavier than they should. "From Washougal."

Mark nods slowly. He doesn't step closer. "From MudMagnet's body?"

"From the cache." Her response gets his attention.

He moves closer, stopping a few steps away. He leans just enough to see the outline beneath the cloth. "That's glass."

"A mirror," Erin says. "Or what's left of one."

A loaded silence stretches between them, building an uncomfortable tension while Mark's jaw tightens. He whistles through his teeth. "You brought it home," he says, more of a statement of fact than an accusation.

"I didn't know what else to do," she replies. "Vance had already left. And I…" She stops herself. She doesn't want to explain the rest, that she hid it from Mark, why she carried it. She doesn't want to say the part about how leaving it there felt like abandoning something unfinished.

Mark studies her for a moment instead of the shard. "You should've told me."

"I didn't want to make it real yet."

He winces, understanding what she didn't say. His gaze drifts back to the table, to the flannel. He reaches out, then stops himself, his hand hovering in the air above it before dropping back to his side. "Mind if I look?"

The question is gentle, respectful, but Erin hesitates, knowing there's a certainty that comes with her answer. She realizes that the moment he touches it, the shard won't just belong to her anymore. She gives an exhausted nod.

Mark lifts the corner of the cloth just enough to expose the edge of the shard. "That's…" He trails off, searching.

"Not random," Erin says quietly.

"No," he agrees. "It's not."

He straightens, stepping back as if the thing might reach for him. His expression has shifted from easy familiarity into something more guarded. She's seen that look on him before, when he's talked about searches, about debriefs. It's the face he makes when he's cataloging risk. "How many times have you touched this thing?" he asks.

Erin's chest tightens. "Enough."

Mark slowly shakes his head. "Then we need to talk about what that means."

She doesn't answer right away. The word 'we' lands heavy

between them, further complicating the mirror. She looks past him, at the corkboard, at the clean lines and careful order she'd just built. For the first time since he arrived, she feels a shift from relief to distance.

Mark stays near the table, arms folded now, and his gaze uncomfortably drifting anywhere but the shard. "You know that detective is going to ask questions," he says. "About all of this."

She nods, her eyes still on the board. "I know."

"Not the kind you can feign ignorance, either." He shifts his weight. "Real questions that will remove you from the witness pool and make you a suspect."

She shoots him a cursing look, then moves toward the corkboard without thinking, drawn by it. The maps are clean now, stripped down to terrain and coordinates. She studies them so she doesn't have to acknowledge his statement.

He exhales slowly, then adds, quieter, "She's going to be especially interested about why that thing is here."

She doesn't turn around. The clock on the wall ticks loudly, counting the seconds in the silences.

"Erin," he says, careful now. "I get why you took it, I do, but bringing it home… what are you thinking?"

"It was going to rain," she says. The answer is automatic, but she hears how weak a defense it is. "I already held onto it too long to seem incidental."

Mark nods, accepting the response but not the logic. "I'm not saying you meant to do anything wrong. I'm saying that if they decide you did, it won't matter what you meant."

She grips at her pants, her knuckles whitening against the crumpled fabric, and turns to him directly. "You think I obstructed justice."

"I think that's what it could look like," he says, mindful of the accusation. "I don't want you anywhere near something like that."

Silence stretches and the refrigerator kicks on. She turns back to the board, refusing to respond.

"Especially after Lucia Falls," he adds.

She turns back, her eyes burning with a feeling darker than surprise. "What?"

Mark hesitates, looking down slightly. "The parking area. With TrailWolf. You told me about it."

"Did I?"

"You mentioned it," he says carefully.

Her lips purse and she strains to recall. "I guess, maybe I did, I don't know anymore."

He nods. "Right, and I just mean, that's the kind of thing they'll stack. Small moments, suspicious behavior." He gestures vaguely toward the board. "They'll want it to line up."

Her gaze follows his gesture and settles back on the board. "I suppose you're right."

"When things get like this," Mark continues, filling the space because he can't help himself, "they stop caring about intention. They care about sequence, things like who touched what, and in what order."

Sequence. Erin scans the board absently, the maps, the pins, the clean notes she's used to track the chaos.

"The problem isn't the bodies themselves," he says. "It's the gaps around them."

She looks at him. "Gaps?"

"Yeah," he says. "Handoffs. Assumptions. Places where everyone thinks someone else has it covered." He waves his hand vaguely around the room. "That's where things get muddy."

She turns back to the board, looking again at how the pins don't form a line. She examines the pocket of empty space inside the pin cluster, the space she anticipates where Jackalope is going to strike next, and debates whether she should share her theory with Mark.

Mark is still talking, unaware. "There's always a gap, you know? In searches, it's never the hard terrain that gets you. It's those quiet stretches. They are the ones that come back to bite you, and if you get caught with this thing, you're going to get bit, really fucking hard."

Erin doesn't answer, but she hears his lecture. Her eyes trace the blank area again, the absence between Hazel Dell and Washougal, the quiet stretch north of Vancouver where nothing has happened yet, at least nothing that's been found. She checks the timestamps on each of her notes again. 5:14 every time. She doesn't need to say it out loud to feel it settle. Jackalope has a reason for scheduling every cache, but the board isn't telling her what that reason is.

"Erin?" Mark says gently. "You with me?"

She nods, but she doesn't look at him. She grabs a new sticky note and writes a single line, *sequence over motive.*

Mark watches her with deepening concern. "What's that?"

"Nothing," she says. "Just something I don't want to forget."

He hesitates, but lets it go, focusing instead on her concentration. "I don't love that look."

She sticks the note in the center of the storm. The space on the map doesn't feel empty anymore. "Mark, I just have a lot on my mind right now."

He hovers, feeling like there's something else he should say but can't find the shape of. Erin lets the silence stretch until it solves itself. Eventually he clears his throat, reaches for his jacket, and gives her a look that tries to be reassuring but falls just short of resignation. "Cool, well, when you want to share any of what's on your mind, call me," he says.

She nods and he makes his way to the door, closing it behind him. Erin stands alone in the apartment again. The quiet gives her a brief sense of relief. She sits at the couch and opens her laptop. She pulls up the local Facebook group and Discord threads she's skimmed a dozen times without really reading. She scrolls, watching timestamps. She sees Jessa's name appear again and again. She filters through both shock and speculation, examining threads that should spiral but don't. In a new browser window, she navigates to a conversation running on about the *Look Back* cache near Lucia Falls.

There is an early post from TrailTempest, not adding anything to the mass speculation, just reminding everyone to 'wait for facts.' Another comment, this one from MapNerd, explains how the caches might be getting misunderstood before commenting on how panic spreads faster than truth. People thank him and even quote him later in the thread.

Erin opens another tab. Looking at a thread discussing *Where the Path Broke*. It carries the same rhythm, though not the same words. She scrolls faster now, not reading every comment, just watching the patterns in how certain accounts appear right as conversations crest, making sure the conversation doesn't tip too far in a bad direction.

OverlookLaneCrew doesn't comment at all, anywhere, and that absence feels louder than any defamatory post. Erin leans back, rubbing her eyes, thinking of the word Mark used. Sequence. It seems to describe the online chatter in the way the comments go and how the soothsayers show up before anyone knows anything real.

She looks back to the corkboard and the sticky note in the empty space she can't stop seeing now, to the idea that whatever comes next almost has no choice but to manifest where she suspects.

Erin closes the laptop for the first time all night. The quiet of the apartment settles differently now, steadier. She picks up her phone and scrolls, muscle memory guiding her thumb until Vance's name sits centered on the screen. She stares at the name, feeling Mark's warning press in.

Sequence. What might it look like from the detective's perspective? She imagines the questions, the way intention would get flattened into procedure, and how quickly control would leave her hands once she started explaining. She's not ready to call Vance, so she sets the phone face down on the table, next to the shard, the flannel shifted just enough to remind her it exists.

This time, when she lifts the cloth, she doesn't flinch. She studies the mirror shard once more, the tape at the base, the crack running straight through her reflection. She doesn't try to interpret it, she doesn't need to. Whatever it means, it isn't going anywhere. She takes it to the kitchen and places it into a plastic bag, seals it carefully, then sets it inside a second bag. Erin leans against the counter and closes her eyes. What comes next has settled into place, quiet and inevitable.

She doesn't write it down, knowing secrets are better held in the body. She crosses the room and pulls a clean sheet she hasn't used in ages from the hall closet. It airs the scent of detergent and dust when she unfurls it, draping it over the corkboard and letting it fall where it wants to. The pins and photos vanish beneath the fabric, and the sharp geometry softens into suggestion. She needs the board out of sight, even if it's not out of mind. She just needs a night of silence, a night of rest.

She switches off the kitchen light, then the lamp by the couch. Erin stands in the dark for a moment, listening to her own breathing. She sets an alarm for the morning, earlier than usual, before retiring to her bedroom. She's not giving up, but she's obsessed as much as she can, and for tonight, that's enough.

Chapter 24: Watch List

The trailhead is already active when Vance arrives. Her headlights cut through the trees in a low arc, flashing white against metal posts and the brown park sign which lists rules nobody reads. TrailWolf's vehicle is angled crooked in the lot, taking up two spaces. He backed in when he parked, pointing toward the exit like he expects to leave in a hurry. A flashlight is propped on his back bumper, and a pack peeks out from inside the open trunk. He's mid-zip on his jacket when the lights wash over him.

TrailWolf squints, lifting a hand against the glare, then smiles like he's just been caught sneaking a cookie instead of being boxed in by two sheriff units. A ranger truck rolls up sideways to close the gap by the trunk. He realizes this isn't a random crowd, so he sits on his bumper.

Vance steps out of her vehicle slowly, closing the door behind her with a solid slam. Her boots crunch on frost-coated ground as she approaches. The morning air is sharp and heady with the scent of pine and wet earth that never dries this time of year. Tenner is already out on her right, his jacket is zipped to the neck, and he holds a clipboard tucked under his arm. He gives the lot a quick scan, then motions to the deputies fanning out behind the headlights.

"You know this lot fills up fast," TrailWolf says, nodding toward the sideways vehicles crowding empty spaces. "People are gonna want to park here."

She clocks everything about him without breaking stride. His trekking poles are already extended, and his GPS unit is attached to his pack on a carabiner clip, lit with coordinates. "TrailWolf," she declares.

He laughs once, surprised she's using his geocache handle. "Yeah," he replies. "That's me."

"Put your hands where I can see them."

He complies immediately, lifting his arms with a theatrical patience that's just shy of mockery. "This about that girl?" he asks casually. "Because I already told your people…"

"My people," Vance says with a hint of bitterness slipping through before she reins it back in. She says firmly, "Palms out."

He stops talking and looks at her properly for the first time, and recognition creeps across his face. "That's not what I was trying to say," he adds. "I meant the cops."

Deputies move in from behind the headlights, efficient and practiced. One of them grabs his wrist, bringing it behind his back, then grabs the other arm. TrailWolf doesn't resist, in fact he shifts his weight to make it easier, rolling his shoulders once to provide himself an inch of comfort and access for the official.

"This is a mistake," he says, conversational. "You got the wrong guy."

Vance watches his eyes while the cuffs are secured. She notes the way he scans the lot, the vehicles, and the trees beyond the beam of the headlights. He's not searching for escape, he's taking inventory of his situation. "Maybe," she says. "But you're coming with us anyway."

"You gonna read me my rights?" he asks, more curious than hostile, like he's quizzing her.

"Not yet," Vance says.

He huffs something close to a laugh, and wisps of fogged breath escape his lips. "Figures."

One of the deputies reaches for the pack leaning against the open trunk.

"Hey," TrailWolf says sharply. "That's mine."

The deputy pauses, glancing to Vance.

"We're gonna bag it," Tenner explains.

"You better." TrailWolf continues, already irritated. "Poles, GPS, everything. If my shit walks, I'll be filing a report before you finish your coffee."

Vance meets his eyes. "It'll be inventoried."

"Do it right," he says. "Because I know exactly what's in there."

Tenner's pen whirls along his clipboard. "Bag it here," he tells the deputy. "Photograph before transport."

As they guide him toward the cruiser, he looks back to the trailhead. The path disappears into darkness, patient and unmoved. "Shame," he mutters. "It's a good morning for it."

Vance doesn't ask what he means.

A deputy opens the rear door of the cruiser and TrailWolf pauses just long enough to look inside, assessing the space. He ducks his head and slides in without protest. The door shuts with a solid, final sound that recalibrates the cacher's morning. Vance watches the reflection ripple across the window as she opens her own door. Tenner is already settling into his seat, setting the clipboard on the dash long enough for him to buckle in.

TrailWolf settles in the back without slumping, his wrists are pinched between his back and the seat. He watches out the window as they move, tracking the trees thinning and regrouping beyond the glass, noticing the places where the road bends just enough to hide a turnout. He sees freedom pass him by and wonders how long it will last.

Vance watches him in the rearview mirror. Most people fill the silence once they realize they're secured in the backseat. They become animated with anger, find ways to bargain, or attest to every measure of innocence they can concoct. TrailWolf doesn't do any of it, he just waits until the tires hit pavement, and settles into a long drive. It isn't until they take the onramp to I-5 that he speaks his first words. "So, which part of this am I supposed to be scared by?"

Vance keeps her eyes on the road. "You can save it for the interview room."

He snorts. "Alright, tough cop doubling down." He shifts in his seat, adjusting so the cuffs quit biting into his back. "You mind telling me what this is about, or is mystery part of the process?"

Tenner says without looking back. "Considering you mentioned 'the girl'," he says, "I think you already have a pretty good idea what this is about." The response earns him a glance from his partner.

"This isn't how you handle a situation," TrailWolf says. "Not for a misunderstanding."

Vance merges onto the highway. "You think this is a misunderstanding?"

"You know, if this is about Lucia Falls, you're too late."

She steals a glance in her rearview. "Too late for what?" she asks.

"For smearing my name," TrailWolf says calmly. "That bitch has already done that."

She says nothing, but her grip tightens on the wheel. Tenner glances sideways at Vance, then back to the road.

TrailWolf continues. "Yeah, I was there. I'll tell you that now, save us all some time. I saw the cache, same as a hundred other caches on just as many mornings. Cache hunting doesn't run on a schedule you people understand."

Vance accelerates down the interstate. "You think we don't understand schedules?"

"I think you don't understand ours," he replies. "Different rules for different games." He glances at her through the mirror, searching for reaction, but she doesn't give one.

Tenner descends on his clipboard and his pen scratches against the paper.

"I didn't do anything to her," he adds, pushing his point and finally cracking in the way Vance expected him to. "I didn't even recognize her until I walked up to her. She spooked herself."

Vance doesn't challenge anything he offers, but she does file it away for later.

"And my car?" he continues. "Wasn't where she thought it was because I don't park like an idiot. Anyone worth a shit knows that bend cuts farther out and having too many cars there is asking for an accident." He leans back, satisfied he's just checked the box that proves him innocent.

"You're real quick to explain yourself," Tenner says.

"I'm orienting you," he corrects. "There's a difference."

The traffic is still light on the interstate ahead of them, but the increase of cars on the road suggests the morning rush hour is about to slow their travel. After a moment, TrailWolf tilts his head. "She pressing charges?"

Vance glances at him through the mirror again, but doesn't answer. His expression hasn't changed from mild annoyance. He catches the detective and smirks. "She's got a habit you know," he continues. "Makes herself the center of attention. Chases danger, then acts surprised when it bites." His smile thins. "You see it a lot in the game, the privileged ones think the world belongs to them and they throw their little fits when they don't get their way."

Tenner's jaw tightens and he looks back. "You done?" he asks.

"Let him talk," Vance tells Tenner without taking her eyes off the road.

"Look, all I'm saying is," TrailWolf continues. "When a victim isn't getting the attention she wants, she's going to flip the narrative."

The cruiser hums along the highway. "I'll tell that to the bodies in the morgue," Vance says flatter than the pavement.

The cruiser signals then drifts toward the exit ramp. Concrete replaces trees and buildings begin to stack into neighborhoods. TrailWolf watches the change without comment, he simply stares at his reflection ghosted in the glass. Vance navigates the streets to the station and slows inside the parking structure, letting the fluorescent lights replace the break of dawn. When they stop, a waiting deputy opens the rear door and TrailWolf steps out, careful with his footing, his cuffs guiding the shape of his movement. Tenner signs once on his clipboard and hands it to the deputy, passing TrailWolf from one set of hands to another.

The interview room is a blank canvas that smells like cleaner. The table is bolted down, and the walls are a dirty shade of beige. TrailWolf clocks all of this as he's led in. He is still mildly annoyed, but he sits when told. He doesn't ask for water or a lawyer.

An hour later, Vance enters and takes the chair across from him. Tenner remains standing for a moment, sets his clipboard down, then sits in the chair beside her. The door closes behind them with a muted thud, and the silence stretches as the detectives review notes.

He breaks the awkwardness first. "So, rooms. Do I get to pick mine?"

Vance doesn't respond. She flips open a thin folder, leaving a thicker one untouched. TrailWolf notices the choice as Tenner clicks on the recorder. "This interview is being recorded," he says evenly.

TrailWolf shrugs. "I figured."

Vance closes the folder and folds her hands on the table. "You know why you're here?"

He smiles wryly. "I've got theories."

"Of course you do," Vance says. "How about we start with the morning you confronted Erin Caldwell."

TrailWolf studies her for a moment, then leans forward, his forearms resting on the table and the cuffs clicking softly as they settle. "I went out early," he says. "Earlier than most people like, but that's kind of the point." He glances at the recorder, then back at her. "It's nice to get out before dawn. There aren't many cachers out while it's dark. Fewer idiots to get in the way."

Tenner picks up his clipboard and writes.

TrailWolf watches him for a moment. "I checked the app over coffee," he continues. "There were no new caches posted overnight. The map was dead as…" He watches Tenner's pen move again and stops himself. "Anyway, I grabbed my pack and headed out for a cache I hadn't found yet. They don't all have to be first to finds, it's just more fun when they are."

"Which trailhead?" Vance asks.

He answers without hesitation. "I wasn't on a trailhead. I parked under some powerline transformers, just past 302nd. There's a traditional cache just north of the road there."

"And Lucia Falls?" she asks.

"I didn't come from that direction. The cache wasn't live when I was headed that way, so I took the back route." he says. "I didn't see the new posting until I got to the cache I was hunting for, and I figured I could just cut down the way to get to the new listing faster, so I went for a hike. You know how it goes, timing matters."

Vance lets the words stack up, giving him a chance to build a clean timeline. "You see anyone," she asks, "who stood out?"

"In those backwoods?" he says immediately. "No. Who the hell you think's going to be wandering around back there in the dark?" He gives a chuckle. "Just me and Bigfoot."

Tenner stops writing for half a second, then resumes. Vance lets his snark sit without paying attention. "So, you were at the Lucia Falls cache."

"Yes, I did end up there," he says without hesitation. "Same as I said in the car."

"How about the cache in Hazel Dell the other day?" she asks.

His lips tighten. "That's not what we're talking about," TrailWolf says. "I don't know anything about Peekaboo."

Vance catches that he calls the cache by name, but she doesn't call him on it. She opens the smaller folder and slides a single photograph across the table, face down. The paper makes a soft swishing sound against the laminate. "Turn it over," she says.

He does and sees a crime scene photo of a fence line at early morning light, with wet grass pressed flat where someone moved through it. Just beyond the chain-link, half-caught in the mud, there's a familiar rectangle of laminated cardstock. TrailWolf stares at it. "Okay. So what?"

"What you're looking at is evidence of a murder scene associated with Parkside Peekaboo." She emphasizes the cache name before sliding a small, mud-stained business card in a forensics bag across the table. The plastic sleeve sticks faintly to the card. There is a single line on the face, bold, and impossible to miss. **THE WOLF IS ON THE TRAIL NOW AND IT'S TIME TO HUNT**

His jaw tightens with recognition. "That's not…" He stops himself and adjusts. "That's my calling card."

"Yes," Vance says. "It is."

He looks up at her now, his irritation sharpening into something more precise. "I leave them in logs to show I hit the cache. People collect that shit, you know that."

"Do they?" Tenner asks quietly.

TrailWolf's eyes dart to him with a cold glare. "Yes."

Vance turns the photo sideways and taps the edge. "This one wasn't in a log. It was found just beyond the fence, blocks away from Parkside Peekaboo, at the scene of a murder."

Silence presses in and TrailWolf leans back slightly, testing his space. His gaze shifts between the detectives. "So, someone grabbed one of my cards and dropped it there. That's your theory?"

"It's not a theory," Vance says. "It's evidence."

"Evidence of what?" he asks. "That I exist?"

She opens the folder again and slides out another page. "Fibers with the same material as your pack's straps were recovered from the scene."

"That's not unique," he says immediately.

"No," she agrees. "But it's consistent."

He exhales through his nose. "That's a fucking stretch."

"We're establishing presence," Vance says. "At a scene you said you weren't involved with."

"I said I didn't know about any incident there," he corrects. "Not the same thing."

Tenner makes a note while TrailWolf's gaze drops back to the photo. His thumb rubs once against the table edge with a small, unconscious movement. "Wait, you're not asking why it's there, you're trying to pin me to the scene of the crime."

"That's one possibility," Vance says. "Another is that you were actually there. Seems like both options could be a stretch, we just have to decide what direction we go."

Vance's framing gives him pause. For the first time since the trailhead, he fully comprehends this goes beyond his confrontation with Erin. "This isn't just about Lucia Falls, you brought me in because you're looking for a killer," he says slowly. "I'm going to give you some free advice. Be careful how you hunt, because you're putting together pieces that don't fit, and that's going to get people hurt."

The detectives share a quick glance. "We brought you in," Vance replies, "because you were tied to a death-adjacent scene by physical evidence. We don't want any more people to get hurt, so why don't you help us find the pieces that do fit."

He looks sharply at her. "Death-adjacent."

"Words matter," she says. "You're quick to remind us of that."

The silence that fills the room is thick, causing TrailWolf to straighten and recalibrate. "You know that card isn't a threat," he says carefully. "It's branding. A quirky piece for a fun game."

Vance meets his eyes. "Then you should be very interested in who uses it on your behalf."

For a long moment, TrailWolf says nothing, then he speaks with a quiet the detectives haven't heard from him, "You should talk to Surveyor."

Tenner's pen stills but Vance doesn't react. "Why?"

"Because he understands the system," TrailWolf says. "And because if someone's playing games with the cache community, he'll see it."

"You don't?" she asks.

He hesitates, reacting almost imperceptibly to Vance's jab. "I see a lot of things."

Vance closes the folder with a motion that feels final. "Then tell us what you see and which of those things matter," she says, certain her play on his ego will drive him to answers.

"Or…" TrailWolf leans forward in his chair, his confidence becomes deliberate and calculated. His words are metered and slow. "You two can do some actual police work instead of throwing darts and seeing what sticks."

Tenner stands and looks down at TrailWolf. "We're done for now," he says, walking toward the door.

TrailWolf watches Vance, waiting for her to play into his bluff. When she doesn't, his mouth tightens slightly. "Guess I'll see how this plays out."

"You will," Vance says, gathering her folders.

Tenner opens the door and gestures for the officer waiting outside. TrailWolf rises like he understands the protocol. As he's led out, he glances once over his shoulder and Vance watches his confidence morph into something closer to indignation, but he stays silent as the door closes behind him. Vance doesn't stand right away. She gathers the photograph and the calling card from the table. Tenner watches her tension as she collects the evidence. When she looks up, his eyes fall to his notes. "You good?" he asks.

"Yeah," she says in her flat tone, which tells him she isn't.

He knows not to push, so he redirects back to their suspect. "I think booking's going to stick. We can at least get him for obstruction and trespassing. DA's already primed."

"Good," Vance says. "That gives us time to do this right."

Tenner hesitates. "You don't sound relieved."

"I'm not paid to be relieved."

He gives her a look, but he doesn't go further. "Press is going to get what they want," he says instead. "A known troublemaker and physical evidence. It makes a clean narrative."

Vance closes the folder. The sound is final. "Clean," she repeats, the word feels foul on her tongue.

Tenner stands. "I'll walk him through intake."

"Inventory his gear personally," she says. "Every item. Every card."

"I will," he says as he leaves. Vance stays seated, staring at the beige wall where nothing ever sticks long enough to matter. On paper, it works. TrailWolf was at the edge of multiple scenes. His calling card turned up where it shouldn't have. He's arrogant enough to believe he's untouchable. It's an easy story to tell. She opens her notebook and writes one line beneath the blocks of print. *If this is the answer, why does it feel like a shortcut?*

Vance closes the notebook and stands. Down the hall, TrailWolf is being processed with his shoes off while his property is being logged and bagged.

The bullpen has become busy by the time Vance steps out of the interview wing. She moves through the department quietly, careful to avoid walking too close to anyone who might need her. When she reaches the Major Crimes Department, Vance shuts the door and leans back against it for a long moment. Before she draws any real attention, she pushes off the door and drops the file on her desk. On paper, the case seems solid enough and TrailWolf is a suspect who fits the narrative. She stares at the case log, knowing it isn't really enough. Booking him with this is the easy part, but the courts will let him go unless she has something undeniable.

TrailWolf mentioning the reviewer doesn't sit well with her, it hasn't since he said it. She pulls up her phone and scrolls to Surveyor's number. She taps call, and the line rings four times, then goes to voicemail. She ends the call without leaving a message. She looks back at the file. If this is the right suspect, she thinks, why does everything else feel untouched? TrailWolf becomes the answer everyone's been waiting for. Everyone except her.

Chapter 25: Premium Only

Erin sits in her car, sipping hot coffee in the dark before morning. The town of Battle Ground hasn't woken up yet, the strip mall is dark, the roads are clear, the birds haven't even begun their morning songs. The lot she's pulled into is an asphalt scar that disappears behind the grocery store on Main and 20th, next to brush that's grown wild where no one bothers to trim it, hiding Mill Creek. She killed the headlights ages ago but left the engine on for heat. Her dashboard says 5:10 a.m. and she's been sitting in the darkness for nearly an hour.

The map on her phone sits open on the passenger seat where her notebook normally rides. This morning, she doesn't need notes, she's only interested in locations within the absence. That absence is what brought her here, the pocket of nothing north of Vancouver, wide enough to be a signal.

She watches the sky pale by degrees. Just beyond the tall grass, she hears the first sign of morning as a toad calls out from deep in the marsh. She checks her phone for a notification, but there's nothing new. As the minutes tick slowly forward, the part of her that hopes she is wrong shrinks under the anticipation that she might be right.

She leans back in her seat and waits, not for a vehicle or a person in the shadows, but for the clock to show the minute. She doesn't believe Jackalope is going to be waving a flag or using a spotlight, she doesn't expect to see the rabbit with horns in this parking lot, she just wants to be close to the void in case a cache appears in this space and at this time. She wants to prove TrailWolf is the person behind the façade. Her phone buzzes, but she ignores it without bothering to look. The dash says it's only 5:12.

She thinks about Vance's voice, flat and careful, telling her to stop chasing this thing. She thinks about Mark's concern and the way he packaged it as reasoning. She lets those thoughts pass through without holding onto them. She assures herself this isn't impulse, she isn't hunting a killer, just verifying a pattern. She can do that safely and still help the police do this the right way while ignoring the questions she asks about why she didn't offer the theory to Vance and why she had to physically come this far out if she just wanted to know.

5:13. Her pulse picks up when the minute turns over. She resents that her anticipation feels like complicity. She refreshes the map page but nothing changes, so she holds her breath and counts the seconds with tense lips. The minute takes an eternity to arrive and once it does, she refreshes, but there's still nothing. Erin curses, wondering if she was wrong, quietly damning herself for wishing she was right. Her chest deflates, but as she reaches to refresh again, the phone buzzes, causing her to jolt, half expecting a shock.

The listing populates with a new cache. A traditional named **Under the Line**, Posted at 5:14 a.m. by OverlookLaneCrew, located north and west from Battle Ground, about five miles. The map says ten minutes, she knows she can make it in less.

Erin breathes slowly. There's no rush in her body and no spike of triumph, just a cold, steady click as theory aligns with reality. Before she can talk herself out of it, Erin puts the car in gear and drives.

Within minutes, she's out of town, putting blacktop and open fields in her rear-view. The back roads twist and dip while she navigates them with white knuckles, blowing through stop signs and hoping she doesn't drift too hard on gravel at the bends. When she descends on the map's pin, the turnoff doesn't announce itself.

Erin passes it once, then slows and eases back in reverse,

slowing to a stop at the concealed fork. She stares at the stretch of Storedah Pit Road, then at the map. The pin confirms what her gut is saying, that's the wrong road. A chain link fence and a shipping container turned office lay dormant to her left. The gate is shut, but beyond is a gravel road leading into a tunnel of overgrown branches, creating an archway of darkness. She scans the perimeter along the roadside until she spots the break in the fence and a sign half-swallowed by weeds. She pulls over on the shoulder and kills the engine.

The sky is dark and the world is still. There's no traffic yet, just the hum of distant power and the occasional bird call testing the day. The construction site sits quiet behind the fence, inert machinery forms hulking shapes without purpose. She opens the car door and steps out into the damp grass. She locks the car out of habit and pockets the keys. The map is no longer empty and the new pin feels like an invitation.

She checks the chained gate in case it is open, but it is indeed locked, and the padlock is rusted by weather, telling Erin this place has been ignored for a while. A sign bolted to the fence reads *AUTHORIZED PERSONNEL ONLY.* The words are sun-bleached and cracked. Someone has added a tag beneath it in black marker, a mess of lines and a crude piece of art. Next to it, in fresher ink, is the silhouette of a jackalope. The horned rabbit dares her, and she studies it, asking if she's ready for that dare.

She skirts the chain-link along the road, toward the edge of the site where the fencing bows inward, pressed by brush that's grown impatient with boundaries. With little effort, she scales the low point into the yard. The dirt access road beckons her, rutted and uneven, tire tracks hardened into place. It would be easy to drive if the gate were open.

She checks the app again. The distance ticks down as she walks the edge of the impacted dirt. In the corner of her screen, the signal bars on her phone dip once, then recover. The noise of babbling water calls out nearby.

Erin moves carefully under the archway of branches, watching the trunks and the dark spaces in-between. The growth above crowds her vision, shrinking her view and her determination all at once. She slides her hand into her pocket and finds comfort in the cold aerosol can of her pepper spray.

Roughly thirty feet in, the branches overhead retreat and the road leads her into the open. The dirt drive is clearer here, cutting a pale line up to a fence before banking and leading away from the construction site, deeper into the green.

At the far corner, the construction fence ends where the land drops into marsh and scrub, leaving only the old access road to continue into the green. Erin hesitates and looks over her shoulder. She's already trespassed, so she's beyond worry about walking into private property, but this fence is more than that, it stands as a sentinel into unwelcome territory.

With a breath of resolve, she moves into the clearing, still flirting with the edge of the road. The ground changes underfoot and she sinks more into damp reeds masquerading as solid ground. She steps onto the access road, opting for solid footing over concealment of tracks. The coordinates on her phone screen tighten with each step forward, and the woods flank off just enough to make the road feel less like forbidden infrastructure.

The access road narrows as it dips, and the gravel eventually gives way to packed dirt and slick patches where water has claimed the low ground. Erin moves carefully now, feeling the urgency from the drive bleeding off, realizing the proximity needs a more deliberate approach. The road ahead dips, which is the only real sign in the dark that the scenery has changed shape.

The tunnel announces itself with an absence of foliage. The dirt road doesn't end so much as it vanishes beneath a concrete mouth cut into the embankment, leading to an old drainage tunnel, now half-swallowed by time and neglect. Faded hazard striping clings to the edges of the opening, yellow and black ribbons dulled into something sickly. Water seeps down the concrete walls in thin lines.

Erin stops just short of the threshold. The sound changes here. The creek she's been hearing collapses into echoes and every drip is magnified, the sound of every movement carrying farther than it should. She pulls up her phone to open the flashlight only to find her reception bars have all disappeared.

She lets out a long exhale and steps inside. The temperature drops immediately. The air is thick with the odor of rust and the decay of old leaves. Her boots take turns splashing through shallow puddles and sinking into sludge. The beam of her light cuts a haze of illumination ahead of her, catching graffiti layered over itself along the walls.

Deeper into the tunnel, she sees another jackalope silhouette, sprayed in black, overlapping older tags. She grips the tube in her pocket tighter, trying to see beyond the light into the depths of the tunnel, but the emptiness seems to stretch into an eternity.

The coordinates pull her deeper, but the needle jumps erratically from the lack of reception. The tunnel ceiling lowers ahead, forcing her to duck beneath a run of old piping that snakes along the concrete like exposed veins. She crouches, careful not to snag her pack, and feels the damp through the knees of her jeans.

After she rounds a shallow bend, the tunnel opens slightly into a maintenance alcove built into the wall. The app radar counts down the feet as she maneuvers the darkness until it twitches on zero feet, leaving her standing ankle deep in chilled sludge, hoping her stillness will quiet the echoes. A rusted utility box sits high on the concrete wall, outlined in orange tape bright against the grime. She rolls her eyes. "Real subtle."

Erin slides her fingers on the seams between the box and the wall, feeling for a gap, a string, anything that can be pulled out of hiding. There's nothing but cold metal and moist concrete. She examines the utility box, the lock on the corroded handle has been popped out ages ago. She pulls it open and the inside is empty except a standard ammo can.

Erin hesitates, then pulls it out, settling the can on the driest spot she can find. The sludge underneath gives a little, sucking the base tight to the ground. She wraps the fingers of her free hand around the clasp but stops. The mirror shard flashes uninvited through her mind, evidence she hasn't turned over yet, sitting in her apartment. She thumbs at the phone still in her hand, smearing wet grime across the screen as she navigates to her call list. Both the ammo can and Vance's name wait for her to make a decision.

Erin knows she is in over her head, she knows this is a police matter and she has no business interfering. One call and this becomes a handoff, but then it turns into a version of events filtered through someone else's voice, someone else's priorities. One call and she's back where she started, waiting to be told what it means, waiting to know if she's still in danger.

The tunnel drips around her, patiently waiting for her decision. Erin lowers the phone without making the call. She wants the truth before it's framed for her, packaged neatly with enough details concealed that she will never feel resolution.

She flips the latch and inside is a logbook, clean and new, with a jackalope portrait stamped on the face. The black symbol on the red cardboard of the log's face glares at her, daring her to go further. Her skin prickles and she shoves it to the side with disgust. Underneath is a folded sheet of paper. She opens it carefully, finding another slip of paper, older and time-worn, torn in half. At the top of the newer page is handwriting, a single line that says, *You keep walking past the right story.*

Her breath catches, shallow and sharp. Erin's name doesn't

appear on the page, but this is meant for her, she sees it in the curves of the letters and the starkness of the straight lines. She stares at the words, forgetting the biting cold of the water soaking in her shoes. Finally, she turns over the torn fragment of older paper. She doesn't need the light to know what it is. The handwriting does that for her. The page is part of an old log entry, when caching was still a shared language for her instead of a coping mechanism. This sheet belongs to a cache far away, and on it among the other names is her brother Danny's signature, slanted slightly to the right. His words always leaned forward, impatient to get where they were going. Her fingers tremble as she lifts it into the light.

She stares at the sheet, her mind going back to the look on his face when he excitedly showed her how to find her first cache. The memory stings her eyes and she wipes angrily at them with the back of her hand. Taped inside the lid beyond the page, almost hidden behind the hinge, is a Polaroid. The captured image cores out her insides. It's her, standing at Hidden Hollow, the day this all began. The morning light barely washes the forest and her face is turned just enough that she isn't looking at the camera. She's holding the Polaroid from that cache in her hand, mid-movement and unaware. It was taken from a distance, but she feels herself in that moment even now. On the white border is a set of new coordinates. *45.807, -122.6177.* She taps them into her map and the pin falls nearby, easily within walking distance.

The echoes of water behind her manifest into the sound of footsteps. She snaps the lid shut and straightens fast, her phone's light skittering across the walls. Erin seals the cache and pushes it back into place. The tunnel answers with echoes of her scrambling, denying her the option to hide.

"Erin?" Her name carries down the concrete, freezing her in place. The footsteps grow louder, splashing through the shallow water she just crossed. The beam of another light crawls along the wall. Her hand flies to the pepper spray at her hip before her brain catches up. She turns, heart hammering, light fixed on the shape moving toward her through the tunnel.

"Erin." Her name is called again. The voice is distinct now without the reverberation of distance, it's Mark's. "Are you down here?"

He steps into her light with his jacket unzipped and breath fogging the air. His face mixes with a range of expressions, distorted further by the deep shadows cut across his skin from her phone's light. He stops short of her, and she stares, unable to reconcile him with the space.

"How did you…" she starts, then stops herself. He steps forward and she watches his feet, the way he navigates the uneven ground, like he knows where to step. Mark takes another step closer, and she instinctively takes one back, feeling the tunnel narrow around them. The distance between is measured and intentional.

"Are you out of your mind?" he says. "Do you have any idea how dangerous this is?"

She laughs once, sharp and breathless. "Funny," she says. "I was just thinking the same thing." The drip of water keeps time behind them.

"You shouldn't be here," he continues. "This place isn't safe. I've been calling you for…"

"How did you know where I was?" she asks, the question coming out quicker than she intends, but not nearly quick enough. The tunnel seems to wait for an answer with her.

Mark hesitates before jabbing a thumb over his shoulder. "I saw your car," he says. "Back at the road."

"That's not a good enough answer."

He shifts and his irritation flares. "You've been chasing this thing all over the county. It wasn't hard to guess you'd be here."

"Guess," she repeats, feeling the disdain of it leaving her lips.

She steps past him, trying to keep as much distance as she can from him while heading for the exit. He immediately follows and she can feel him trailing too close, so she speeds up.

His voice rises through the tunnel around them. "You can't keep doing this alone," he says. "You're not thinking straight."

She stops so abruptly he almost runs into her. "You don't get to say that," she says quietly. "Not when you keep showing up where you shouldn't."

His mouth opens, then closes. A mix of calculation and restraint flickers across his face. She sees it before he hides it. "Erin," he says, lowering his voice. "Let's just get out of here."

She studies him for an explanation, but the line has already shifted, and she knows it. She glances at the pin on her phone. She needs to get to the second coordinates, but without Mark. "Yeah, sure. I just need some air, this tunnel reeks."

They make their way out of the service tunnel and the fresh air immediately replaces the stench of stagnation. Erin breathes in hard before she continues walking, angling toward Storedah Pit Road without saying why. Mark doesn't speak, but he continues to match her pace.

She glances at her phone as she pushes through the tall weeds. The pin sits where she already knows it will, a green patch of land breaking the surface of a nearby pond that's big enough to register on the digital landscape. It is located on the other side of the road, but she figures it is close enough to reach.

He watches her check her phone a second time and knows the habit of a cacher on the hunt. "Where are you going?" he asks.

"Getting air," she says. "The tunnel stinks."

"That's not air, that's marsh," he says while squinting ahead. "You're not thinking about going out there, are you?"

She stops. "Out where, Mark?" she asks.

He nods across the road, toward the clump of trees gathered

near the waterline. "To the island."

Erin spins and really looks at him. His expression is neutral and concerned, far too casual considering the last five minutes. She turns to the direction of the coordinates. She can't see the island from here, which means he can't either. She doesn't answer him. Instead, she drops her phone to her hip and thumbs back to the address book where Vance's name still lingers. She slips her phone into her pocket and presses the call button without looking. The line connects while she begins walking again.

She jumps the roadside fence at the edge of the property, cutting through the grass onto the road, and immediately cuts across to the other shoulder. Erin keeps her pace, steadily counting her steps, aware Mark is just behind her.

"Erin. Come on." There's almost a plea in his voice. "Let's just go back toward the cars, I think we're trespassing."

She stops again and turns to face him. "You followed me into a construction site before sunrise. Don't pretend you care about boundaries now."

Frustration flashes with a scowl across his face. "I care about you not getting hurt."

"You care about being involved," she says. "Lucky for me, you always are." Her words drip with venom.

"That's not fair. Erin, I'm…"

Her laugh is quiet and sharp, cutting him off. "The hell do you know about fair?"

Erin starts walking again without waiting for a response. She angles through the field toward the trees lining the water. The island still isn't visible yet, but she memorized the map enough to know what side of the pond she needs to be at.

"You shouldn't be doing this," Mark says. "The detective told you…"

"Vance isn't here," Erin cuts in. "But you are, strangely

enough."

He slows a step, struck by her words, then closes the distance again. "You don't have to prove anything," he says. "Not to Jackalope, not to me, or anyone else."

Her jaw clenches. "Who?"

He doesn't speak.

She turns so fast he almost collides with her. "Say it again, Mark. Who?"

"You know…" He stops himself. "Whoever's playing these games."

"Games?" she asks, her eyes wide. "People are dead, Mark."

"I know that," he snaps, then reins it in. His voice drops into a weary octave. "I know."

She storms toward the pond and the waterline appears through the trees, a dark mirror broken by reeds and low fog. The small island sits just beyond, close enough to make the crossing feel possible, but far enough to be deliberately difficult. Erin's phone hums faintly in her pocket, still connected.

"Tell me how you keep showing up at the right time," she says, swinging her arms to improve her circulation. "In all the wrong places."

"Says the girl who has happened across more murder scenes in a month than most people do in a lifetime."

Her glare turns cold. "Deflection isn't an answer, Mark."

"I told you…"

"You told me you guessed," she says. "You guessed Washougal. You guessed the cops were at my place. You guessed a tunnel no one knows about unless they've been here before."

His eye squints and he opens his mouth, but doesn't say anything.

"That's a lot of good guesses," she says quietly. "I'd be playing the lottery if I were you."

He looks out across the water, then back to her. "You shouldn't go out there and you know it."

"Why's that, Mark?" she asks.

"Because it's dangerous."

"Because you know what's there."

The silence stretches thick as the fog creeping over the water. Somewhere in the trees, a startled bird breaks cover and takes flight. Mark steps closer. "Erin, listen to me. This doesn't end the way you think it does."

She meets his gaze and hears how cold and precise his words are. "You don't get to decide how my story ends."

She steps toward the water and he grabs her arm. Her breath catches at his violation of space while the water laps against the bank, patient, waiting. "Let go," she says sternly.

He doesn't. "I'm trying to help you."

"Don't fucking touch me." She jerks her arm from his grip and stands resolute, meeting his eyes. When his hands raise in submission, she turns back to the large pond and continues along the bank until she is where the island is closest. There's maybe thirty feet of water between her and the pin.

The bank slopes gently at first, and the mud gives way to slick stones hidden under a skin of dark water. Erin tests it with the toe of her boot, then another step. The water is colder than she expects, biting through denim, climbing fast enough to chill her spine. Behind her, Mark says her name again, but she doesn't look back.

The water tightens her calves as it climbs to her knees. She keeps moving and the water tugs at her with a slow insistence. Reeds whisper against her thighs, bending as she passes, snapping back into place behind her. Each step has to be chosen as the bottom drops unevenly, soft in some places, firm in others. Her phone is still warm in her jacket pocket, still connected.

"Erin," Mark calls again. "This isn't safe."

The island feels further than it looked from the bank, and smaller, revealing that it's not an island so much as a rise, little more than a stubborn knot of land refusing to sink like the rest. Alder and scrub crowd its edges, roots exposed where the water has gnawed at them. By now, the water climbs to her hips, pressing cold and firm into her muscles, stealing her momentum. She braces a hand against a half-submerged branch and hauls herself forward, boots sinking, then releasing.

"Don't," Mark says and she can hear him entering the water now, as well. His voice carries across the water. "Please," he says, but that word shouldn't come from him.

Erin reaches the edge of the rise and drags herself up, water pouring off her jeans, hands slick with mud. The ground here is firm and matted with dead grass and flattened reeds. She isn't the first person to reach this mound of dirt stranded in the pond. She reaches the flat of the island and the stench of bodily decay warns her what she's about to find.

Colt is laid out just past the trees, positioned with a care that feels personal. His wrists are bound by a cord that's wrapped clean and deliberate. His body has been turned toward the water, toward the path she took. He was meant to be found from this angle. The reeds around him are pressed down in arcs. Erin's knees threaten to fold. She plants her feet to fight the drop and braces herself on a tree trunk rough with lichen. The world sharpens and blurs at the same time as details rush in without order. She notices the way his jacket is pulled tight at the shoulders, the angle of his bloodied head, the missing teeth. She clutches at her phone through the jacket fabric, lifting the pocket entrance toward the sky. "Vance, I really hope you're there," she says. "If you're listening, come fast and bring help."

Water sloshes behind her as Mark steps up onto the rise, breathing hard. He stops short when he sees what she's looking at.

His silence stretches as he stares. "Jesus," he says finally.

Erin doesn't turn. Her voice is steady. "You knew."

"No," he says quickly. "I didn't."

She turns and looks at him. His eyes aren't on her, they're on the body, staring with recognition.

"You told me not to come out here," she says. "But you wouldn't say why."

He swallows. "Because I didn't want you to get hurt."

"Quit acting like this is your Search and Rescue training." Her words spill out in a near growl. "You didn't want me to see this."

He doesn't move or even bother to respond.

Erin lowers into a crouch, careful not to disturb the area. She catalogs every detail of the body, despite the nausea rising in her throat. The low angle brings her head closer to her phone, and she knows she needs to be the eyes Vance doesn't have without revealing the call. "Colt's dead."

Mark stammers a response. "What do we do?"

She looks up at him. "You're unbelievable, you know that?" She's surprisingly calm when she speaks. "How you keep knowing exactly where the bodies are, but you keep pretending you don't know what is going on."

Mark doesn't answer her, and she's not even sure he's listening. He looks past her shoulder, scanning the trees, the waterline, the reeds pressed flat by her path. He's not panicky, his focus is too calculating for that, which unnerves Erin.

"Don't move anything." His voice takes on a more decisive shape. "We need to…"

"No," she cuts in. The word is quiet, but it stops him. "You're not going to manipulate this."

He blinks, caught off-guard by her accusation. "Erin, we are standing over a body."

"A body?" Her voice grows louder. "That's not a body, Mark.

That's Colt. We know him!"

She rises carefully, backing away from Colt's body until she's standing again at the edge of the rise. The water catches a hint of shine as the morning finally commits to daylight.

Mark runs a hand through his hair and paces a few steps, then stops. Every mix of emotion that has played across his face this morning is suddenly concealed behind the solemn look he gives her. "Do you realize how stupid you are, coming out here alone?"

His immediate change of tone nearly pushes Erin into the water, but she stands resilient. "I didn't come alone, Mark. You followed me," she says.

"I was worried."

"You were tracking me," she corrects.

He freezes, just for a fraction of a second. "That's not…"

"Don't," she says. "Just don't."

Silence settles into tension and Erin feels certainty clicking into place. The same cold clarity she felt back in the parking lot when the cache posted exactly when it was supposed to. This wasn't a lure for anyone, it was a test. She looks past Mark now, across the water and field beyond, toward the road she walked in from. She mentally tracks her footsteps toward the tunnel and the cache still hidden behind a false maintenance panel against concrete. She looks back to Mark. "You didn't once ask me how I knew where to look," she says.

Mark's mouth tightens. "Because I didn't want to know."

"You're lying."

She can tell he's trying to maintain his composure. "We need to get back to the road so we can call the cops."

"I already did," she says.

He frowns, and his hands ball into fists. "What?"

She finally pulls the phone from her pocket and the screen is lit, showing a call that's still connected. She lifts it just enough for him to see the name at the top. **VANCE**.

"I made the call before I stepped into the water," Erin says. "They heard everything."

Mark's face drains of color, realizing he stepped onto ice he thought was solid.

She angles the phone toward the water, then toward the body and the flattened reeds around it. "You say you want me to stop chasing this thing, but you're always following a step behind me," she says. "You think I won't figure it out. You called me stupid." Her glare locks onto him. "But I'm the one who knows how to follow the trail, and when I find what's at the end, I won't be alone."

Chapter 26: Mystery Cache

Detective Mara Vance rubs her eyes before turning off the clock's alarm, cursing the arrival of morning and the sleepless night before it. The buzz of a phone rattles her nightstand. It isn't her personal cell, but the department-issued one sitting next to it.

She gives up on five more minutes of rest. "Vance," she answers without looking at the name on the screen. Her voice is dry and rough. There's a muffled sound of rubbing on the other end and a distant bird call is her only greeting. She immediately thinks of the park ranger the other day, and his knowledge of birds.

Vance looks at the screen and sees Erin's name. She swings her legs over the side of the bed and sits upright. The wood floor is cold on her feet. "Erin, are you there?"

The muffling sound diminishes and is replaced with other noises which are difficult to make out. One sound stands out, a crunching sound, footsteps on gravel. Vance closes her eyes for half a second, then opens them and stands. She keeps the line live and grabs her personal phone, dialing into the department. When that line connects, she gives her badge number and requests to be connected to Tech Services. "This is Detective Mara Vance, put a live trace on my department cell. I need the location of the caller, stat."

Vance doesn't wait for confirmation before she slips on yesterday's jeans and pulls a blouse from her closet. On Erin's call, she hears a voice that isn't Erin's, it's a man. "Erin, come on. Let's go back to the car, I think we're trespassing."

That's enough to tell her Erin didn't accidentally dial her. Vance grabs her keys, shoulder-checks the bedroom door on her way out, and aims for her boots at the front door. She confirms on her personal line that the trace is running, then directs the tech team to provide both her work cell and dispatch with updates and a location when they have it, then hangs up. Her next call is backup. "Tenner," she says as soon as the call is live, "I need you moving. We might have a situation."

Vance hits the driveway at a jog. The phone is still live in her hand, and Erin's call stays muted while on speaker as she unlocks the cruiser and slides in, already running through scenarios in her head. The engine turns over and she throws it into gear. Her personal phone buzzes against the console and she taps to answer, her eyes never leaving the road. "Go."

"Trace is narrowing," Tech says. "The signal is weak but narrowing. Looks like the caller is north of Battle Ground, near La Center. As long as they stay on the line, we will keep triangulating."

Vance hisses through her teeth. "Get me a rolling update every thirty seconds. Keep dispatch in the loop and flag this as active movement."

She flips the lights on but leaves the siren silent. It's still early enough, there's not enough traffic yet on the road to yell at, and sirens wake people or scatter them. On Erin's open line, a man's voice comes through, close, controlled, but trying to sound reasonable. "You shouldn't be doing this alone."

Vance's jaw tightens. She recognizes the tone of a man trying to direct Erin. The voice sounds like it belongs to Mark Leland. Another fragment catches Vance's attention, this time it's Erin's voice. Her voice is steady and pushed low. "Vance isn't here. You are." That hits Vance like a punch to the gut.

Her radio crackles, letting her know dispatch is already directing and that other units are closer than she is. Sheriff's patrol is coming in wide, pulling deputies from both Battle Ground and La Center. She keys the mic. "Any unit responding, be advised caller is a female and may be on foot near water. One potential suspect, male, in vicinity. Do not approach hot. I want eyes before contact."

She hangs up and calls Tenner again. This time he answers on the first ring. "I was just updated and am en route," he says.

"Good," Vance replies. "The caller is Erin Caldwell. She's not talking but she's keeping the line open. Mark Leland is with her, his involvement is unknown. If you get there first, I need you to think containment, not confrontation."

"Copy that," he says. After a pause, his tone changes, "Mara, this is the third time she's been in front of us like this. It isn't a coincidence anymore. If this goes sideways, we have to own that."

"I know," Vance says. "That's why we have to get there fast."

She hangs up and accelerates, opening up on the long, empty stretches of asphalt.

Within minutes, the city falls mostly behind, and fields fly by in gray-green smears as dawn threatens to show itself. She keeps one ear on the open call, listening to footsteps evolve into splashing. Mark speaks again, barely audible over the feedback. Vance only catches him say, "Erin. This isn't safe."

She glances at the clock on the dash, cursing that too much time has passed and not enough distance has been covered. Whatever situation Erin has found herself in, she's been in it too long.

Tech cuts back in on her radio. "We've got a tighter fix. Storedah Pit Road. Near a water feature. Units are less than five out."

"Good," Vance says. "Keep the trace live."

Storedah Pit Road doesn't ring a bell for Vance, so she pulls it up on her dash's map. It displays a dead-end road north of Battle Ground and east enough to pull lowland marshes into play. The long roads create limited access, which will also make slow approach for units that don't know where to look. Worse, the approach won't be concealable.

When Vance passes Battle Ground, Erin's line, muted but open, speaks to her directly, "Vance, if you're listening… bring help."

The cruiser tires burn with determination as Vance drops the pedal to the floor. Her focus narrows to the road and the growing certainty that she's about to arrive after the worst moment. She listens with sharpened intention, tuned into the voices that sound close to each other again. An argument is heating until it breaks with the sound of muffling again. Erin's voice comes clearer than Vance has heard the entire call, "Colt's dead."

The map shows Vance that she is over two miles out from the Storedah turnout when Erin's voice comes through the line undisrupted by muffles. Radio chatter overwhelms the cabin of her cruiser, louder than the live phone. Vance swears at the sound before killing the radio and all she hears of Erin is, "I won't be alone."

Barely slowing, Vance takes the turn onto Storedah, nearly sliding into the ditch. Red and blue lights from multiple vehicles cut through the marsh fog in staggered pulses, reflecting off standing water and low brush. Patrol units are already staged at the bend ahead with doors open. Two deputies move with careful efficiency through the field toward a pond. An EMT rig idles farther down, and responders are already at the back door, securing their gear.

Vance pulls in behind the units and kills her lights. She steps out and the damp air clings to her immediately. A deputy meets her up the road. "Detective Vance," he says, relief leaking through professionalism. "Caller was located on a small rise off the marsh. Female, conscious. The man was with her. There is also a body that needs to be secured."

"Anyone touch it?" Vance asks, moving toward the pond without slowing.

"No," he says. "We got them back to the bank. That's it."

Vance accepts the update and scans along the road. "Get your men and walk the perimeter of this property. Our unsub has a bad habit of being close enough to take pictures. Make sure there's no one else out here." She walks around her cruiser toward the field.

Crime scene tape flutters between alder trunks, already strung but not yet complete. A deputy stands watch at the waterline, his boots sunk past his ankles, scanning the trees like he expects something else to come walking out.

Erin sits on the ground a few yards back from the tape, wrapped in a blanket pulled straight from an EMT kit. Her jeans are dark to the hip with mud caked along the seams. Vance notices that she's not shaking. Her posture is rigid and her hands clenched around the fabric, with a stare locked on nothing but distance.

Mark stands several feet away, unrestrained, but not free either. He's got his hands on his hips and his pants are also soaked. He's pacing a short, contained line. One of the deputies watches him without staring, providing both professional distance and provisional trust. Vance analyzes it all in seconds.

She approaches Erin first. "Hey," she says quietly.

Erin looks up. Her eyes are bright, but focused. "You're late," she says without accusation.

"I know," Vance replies. She crouches in front of Erin, bringing herself level. "Are you hurt?"

Erin shakes her head. "Just cold."

Vance nods and stands, surveying the scene. Dust kicking up on the road signals another car has arrived. She watches a moment and Tenner approaches, taking inventory of the people in the field. She waves him down and jerks her head toward Mark. He follows her lead and changes his course to the man with the EMT.

"Mark," he says evenly when he gets within range. "Walk with me."

Mark hesitates just long enough to register the new player on the field, then nods. "Sure. I want to cooperate."

"Good," Tenner replies. "Then this'll be easy."

They move off down the road, away from the water, away from

Erin. Mark doesn't look back and Erin doesn't watch him go. Vance waits until they're out of earshot, then she turns back to Erin who looks smaller in the moment. Vance recognizes the vulnerability but doesn't soften for it. "Walk me through him," she says. Not what happened, but him.

She looks up at Vance. "What do you want to know?"

Vance crouches again so they're level. She keeps her voice even. "Did he touch you?"

"He grabbed my arm," Erin says.

"Did you tell him to stop?"

"Yes."

"Did he?"

"Yes."

Vance nods, filing it. "Did he threaten you?"

"No."

"Did he block you from leaving?"

"No."

"Did he try to move the body or touch anything?"

"No." Erin hesitates. "I wouldn't let him."

Vance studies Erin's face, looking for the cracks people don't realize they show. "Was he on site before you?"

"I don't know," Erin says without hesitation. "I can't prove that."

"How did he know where you were going?"

Erin pauses, choosing her words carefully. "He said he guessed."

Vance speaks again, this time her voice is lower, sharper. "You disobeyed a direct instruction."

Erin doesn't argue. "I followed the trail."

"That trail ends with bodies," Vance says. "And you've been standing one bad decision away from obstruction."

Erin finally looks at her fully. "If I hadn't come, someone else would have. Another cacher, maybe with kids."

"That's not your call."

"No," Erin agrees. "It's his."

Vance studies her for a long beat, then exhales. "Whose? Who is he?"

"TrailWolf." Erin stares at Vance with eyes wide in disbelief. "The killer."

"TrailWolf didn't do this." Vance rests a hand on Erin's knee.

"What?" Erin's brow furrows. "How can you say that? He's been hounding me for weeks. He was at Lucia Falls."

"Erin. He's in custody," Vance says. "Has been in a cell since yesterday morning. He didn't post this cache, he couldn't have."

The two stare at each other in the swaying weeds. Erin searches Vance's face for anything that tells her the detective is lying but finds only sympathetic sincerity. Erin stares at the detective with open-mouthed disbelief, recalibrating her assumptions in real time. "Then who…"

"We don't know yet," Vance says. "But whoever it is just forced our hand." She straightens and looks past Erin, back toward the island, the tape, and the body waiting to be pulled from the reeds. "And yours."

Vance notices that Tenner hasn't brought Mark back. The road is long enough that voices don't carry, but she can see them calmly walking. In the field, the deputies have done a good job creating lanes of space so EMTs can bring their gear and rescue board to the water. One paramedic breaks from the trio and moves in close to Erin, checking her vitals, wrapping her boots in plastic, and documenting without asking questions that might break her concentration. Erin answers when spoken to, but she doesn't volunteer anything beyond hard facts, which worries Vance more than if she had.

A uniform approaches with a clipboard. "Detective, medical can transport her for evaluation now."

"Not yet," Vance says.

The deputy pushes back cautiously. "She was in that water a while. The cold exposure…"

"I said not yet." Vance's eyebrow furrows. "She's a witness, and I need her statement while the events are still fresh. I'll sign off when I'm done."

The deputy nods and backs off, staying quiet while Vance turns back to Erin. "You're going to hate what I'm about to say."

Erin doesn't look at her. "I'm not sure that would be anything new."

"You're done hunting," Vance says, pretending to not hear her. "As of right now, you don't go near another cache tied to this case. You won't follow coordinates at all. You're done chasing caches as of now."

Erin snorts through her exhaustion. "You can't actually stop me."

"I absolutely can," Vance replies. "If you test me on that, I'll put you in holding faster than you can sign a log. I don't want to, but you keep inserting yourself into my investigation and it doesn't look good for either of us."

"I didn't insert myself," Erin says. "I was invited."

"That invitation keeps getting people killed."

Erin flinches at that, enough to show Vance she was heard. She continues while she has Erin's full attention. "You're not wrong about one thing. This path is being built for you, but that's exactly why you don't get to walk it anymore."

Erin watches the detective's attention follow a deputy walking the ridge on the far side of the road. "You think we're being watched."

"I do, yeah," Vance says. "Every time there's another murder, a picture of you at the crime scene shows up afterward." She gestures back toward the island. "That's the only reason you aren't on the shortlist of suspects."

The radios crackle again and this time Vance answers. "Vance."

Tenner's voice comes through, controlled and tight. "I'm with Mark."

"Talk to me."

"His story checks out so far. He arrived on scene so quick because he lives outside Battle Ground. Rents a place north, on Northwest 21st. He's got no priors that connect cleanly to our investigation. SAR background explains some of his behavior, but not all of it."

"Does he explain the tunnel?"

Tenner pauses. "Says he followed Erin."

"And?"

"That he saw coordinates go live for a new cache while he was making coffee and wanted a first to find."

Vance closes her eyes and pinches the bridge of her nose. "Log him as a material witness."

"I already am," Tenner says. "But Mara, something's not right with his story. I can't explain what exactly, it just feels like there's more, but there isn't enough to keep him. I have nothing actionable."

"I know," she replies. "This whole investigation feels off."

She looks back at Erin, whose gaze is fixed on the water again. "Tenner says his story lines up enough," Vance says. "Timeline isn't good, but it's not unreasonable. That means unless you're telling me he did something you haven't said yet…" She lets the sentence hang.

Erin pulls the blanket tighter around herself. "I'm not saying he's innocent."

"I didn't ask that," Vance replies. "I asked if you're giving me grounds to hold him."

The silence stretches. "No," Erin says finally.

Vance straightens. "Then we don't have him. Not today."

Erin swallows. "So, you're just going to let him walk?"

"I have no good reason to hold him," Vance says. "And you need to understand something." Her tone sharpens. "If he's involved, letting him walk is dangerous. If he's not, holding him makes *you* dangerous to the case."

Erin looks away.

"Which side of that you're on," Vance continues, "depends on what you're not telling me."

That gets Erin's attention. She looks back up but gives nothing.

Vance holds her gaze and waits, then nods once she realizes nothing is coming. Erin made her decision. Vance fills the silence, "Go with the paramedics." She helps Erin to her feet. "And Erin?"

"Yeah."

Vance steps closer. "You did the right thing calling me."

"I didn't have a choice," Erin says. "You would have found two bodies on the island."

Vance almost smiles at that. She straightens and looks out over the scene one more time, the tape, the water, the body being carefully claimed by process. "You know this doesn't end here," she says. "Not for the person doing this, and not for you, but the rules are there to be followed, and for you, they just changed."

Erin nods once, understanding what Vance didn't say. "I'll learn the rules."

Vance watches the vacancy in Erin's eyes show a gleam. "Then I'll make sure the next time," she says quietly, "you don't get to be first."

Erin meets her eyes, expression unreadable. "Then you better learn to keep up."

Chapter 27: Hidden In Plain Sight

Erin has tried to sleep since calling out of work but was finding herself drifting in and out without success. When she finally gives up and sits at the kitchen counter, the early afternoon light outside reminds her that she's not holding her life together as well as she should.

She checks her phone and finds the cache *Under the Line* is disabled. She refreshes the listing every few seconds, giving in to compulsion, but nothing changes. Erin studies it the way she studied maps as a kid, knowing there's something important in front of her, but not knowing how to read the information.

She opens the log field, knowing it will be blank, that the cache was marked disabled before anyone else could find it. Leaving a cache without a comment feels like a slap in her face, especially knowing she was there. She expects heat or adrenaline as she stares at the empty space. Instead, she finds clarity and a cold, deliberate calm about what she needs to do.

She writes, knowing the rules and choosing to step just outside them: *You didn't break me. I'm done playing your game. You chose the space. You chose the timing. You chose the markers. I see your pattern now and I'm done following it.*

She rereads it once to be sure there are no threats, no accusations, nothing a moderator could point to and call unhinged. It doesn't mention bodies and it doesn't name any players. She adds one more line, carefully placed at the end: *There won't be another.*

Erin posts the log and for a second, nothing happens, then the page refreshes and her words settle into place beneath the disabled notice, visible to anyone who looks. She knows how this works, most people will never see the comment, but the right person will.

She sets the phone down on the counter and exhales the tension from her chest. Her coffee pot beeps, letting her know the brew is finished. For the first time since this started, Erin feels like she's not reacting, she's acting.

She notices Mark's name lighting up her phone while she's pulling a mug from the cabinet. She lets it ring twice before answering. "Hey," she says, neutral, already pouring from the pot.

He doesn't speak immediately, and the lack of sound tells her he is checking his footing. "Hey," Mark replies. "I was… just checking in."

Checking in, she muses. Not about yesterday, not about the cache, not even about the log post she just made that she knows he's seen. Vaguely checking in so the other person leads the conversation. "I figured you might be," she says.

He gives another pause. He's being careful, and he damn well should. "How are you holding up?"

She chooses not to offer anything with substance. "I'm fine."

He exhales with almost exaggerated relief. "Good. That's good."

They sit in the quiet for a moment, the space between words stretching through the phone. Erin imagines him somewhere familiar, his truck, the gym locker room, a place where he feels oriented. She listens to his breathing, listens for some kind of noise in the background.

"You doing anything today?" he asks.

There it is, not what are you planning, just another vague probe. Erin wipes the counter where the coffee dripped. "Not really," she says. "Catching up."

"Yeah." He is eager to find his way in, she can hear it in his voice. "That makes sense."

Mark shifts tactics. "Listen, I've been thinking about yesterday," he says. "I don't want things to be weird between us."

Erin gives a dry smile. Weird, that's the word he chose, not 'bad'. Weird implies social friction, not bodies in water. "I don't either," she says, not really committing to the answer, but not putting in the energy to say what she feels.

"If you want," he continues, "we could grab coffee and just talk it out. We can go somewhere neutral, somewhere public."

He says it and Erin recognizes the suggestion immediately for what it is, he's attempting stabilization, something to slow her brain down and get her back into familiar rhythms where he can read her again. He offered somewhere public, though. He picked it without her prompting, that either shows he's worried or earns him a point for consideration. "Sure," she says in the same flat tone. "That might be good."

"Cool." Relief flickers through the phone before he reins it in. "There's a place on Fourth Plain I like. It's busy with big windows."

Erin almost laughs. He's learning or pretending to. "Works for me," she says. "Give me two hours."

"Yeah. Yeah, no rush." He pauses again. "Erin?"

"Yeah?"

"I'm glad you answered."

She doesn't respond to that. She ends the call instead and sets the phone down again. Instead of letting it go to sleep, she opens the cache page again. Her post is still there. Mark didn't mention it once, which tells her more than anything he could have said.

The coffee shop is already half-full when Erin arrives. Afternoon light slants in through tall front windows, catching dust and steam and the constant motion of people. There are no booths, just small round tables and the low hum of unknowing witnesses who aren't watching but are present enough to set Erin on edge. She orders, then finds an empty table near the window where she can see the street and the door without turning her head.

She notices CryptidQueen before she sits, wearing a different jacket, but sporting the same hairstyle. She carries the same posture, but instead of hovering over a burger, her laptop is open at the counter. She has one earbud in. They make brief eye contact but choose not to show acknowledgment.

Mark arrives three minutes late, which is out of character for him, she knows he likes to be early so he doesn't miss anything. He scans the room before he spots her. When he does, his shoulders ease just slightly. He holds up a finger, acknowledging her, as he steps up to place his order.

After grabbing his cup, he takes another glance around the shop, then approaches her table. "Hey," he says, sliding into the chair across from her. He doesn't offer a hug or provide any kind of touch. Good.

"Hey," she says, barely looking at him.

They talk about nothing at first, he starts with simple pleasantries like weather and sleep. She keeps her hands wrapped around her cup to anchor herself. Before the moment drifts too far into awkwardness, Mark breaks. "You scared the hell out of me yesterday."

She nods. "I know."

"You can't keep doing that," he continues. "Running ahead of everyone."

She lifts her cup, takes a slow sip, and sets it down carefully before answering. "That's funny."

He frowns. "Why?"

"Because it felt like you were right there with me."

The response is layered with deliberate snark. Erin watches his hands as she speaks. His thumb tightens against the rim of his cup enough to turn his knuckle white. "I was worried about you," he says.

"You keep saying that," she replies without commitment.

He studies her, trying to decide where this is going. "I don't want things to spiral."

"They already did," Erin says quietly.

A server passes by them and sets down a drink at the next table. Laughter breaks out three tables behind Mark. Life around them is continuing, oblivious that this table is balanced on a fault line. "You posted on that cache," he says at last.

The way he says it, not why did you, not what were you thinking. He simply acknowledges what she did. She can't tell if he sounds like a disappointed father or a judge.

"Yeah."

"That wasn't smart."

"No," Erin agrees. "But, it was intentional."

He leans back, eyes drifting once toward the window before returning to her. "You're poking someone who's already dangerous."

She tilts her head. "You sound sure of that."

"I'm saying you don't know who you're dealing with."

Erin holds his gaze. "I know exactly who I'm dealing with." Erin replies. Her voice doesn't rise, but her tone is just as harsh. "Someone who needs control. Someone who gets restless when the pattern breaks."

His jaw tightens. "This isn't a game."

"No," she agrees. "It's a hunt." The word fills the space at the table and he doesn't know how to respond. Around them, cups clink and the espresso machine screams as it works.

Mark shifts in his chair, discomfort breaking through his careful posture. "You don't need to do this yourself," he says. "You don't need to be the one pushing."

"I didn't volunteer," Erin replies. "I was pulled in."

"And now you're pushing back," he says carefully. "That's not a smart thing to do."

"You don't think so?"

"No," he says. "Because now you're visible."

"Good, because I'm not hiding anymore," Erin says. "I'm tired of being afraid of my own life."

He studies her. She's crossed a line he didn't expect. "Erin, visibility gets people hurt."

"So does silence."

He slowly shakes his head. "You should slow down, just let things settle."

"Things like this don't settle, Mark," Erin replies. "They keep claiming lives."

His face drops from stern to soft. "I don't want you getting hurt," he says.

"And I don't want you following me," Erin replies, her face still carved from stone. "I guess we don't always get what we want."

CryptidQueen shifts at the counter and Erin catches the movement in her peripheral. She takes a breath to calm herself, quickly nodding once.

Mark exhales, long and controlled. "Fine, if another cache drops, then call me first so I can meet you instead of following," he says carefully. "Just promise me you won't go alone."

She lifts her cup again and takes her time with the answer. "I won't even pretend to promise that."

His eyes sharpen and his chest rises.

"I will promise this, though." She sets the cup down, steady. "I'm not walking blind anymore."

He studies her, realizing he no longer understands her. The recognition makes him look away, out the window where a truck rolls through the parking lot with an orange safety vest tossed over the passenger seat. Mark tracks it while the driver hunts for an empty spot until he notices Erin watching him. He straightens and returns to their conversation. "Erin," he says, "I'm not trying to tell you what to do. I care about you, is all."

Erin traces the rim of her cup once with her thumb, watching the foam collapse, choosing to not acknowledge his statement. She isn't sure which emotion would come out in the coffee shop if she did.

Her silence causes him to shift in his seat, so he adds, "You don't know where this ends."

She looks up from her cup. "Neither do you."

He rolls his head back. "I've seen how these things go. People chase a thrill long enough and they can't quit, until it's too late."

The word hangs there in a way she can't immediately articulate. "A thrill?" Erin's nostrils flare. "You think I'm looking for a thrill, Mark?"

"Whoa, that's not what I meant," he says, backpedaling. "I'm just saying you've become compulsive about this situation."

She tilts her head. "Oh, this is a situation now?"

Mark blinks. "Seriously, Erin. Come on."

"Oh, I'm sorry," she says mildly. "I can't help myself, I'm just stupid."

His expression hardens, and he cranes his neck tight, issuing two loud pops. "That's bullshit, Erin. You know what I meant yesterday."

"I don't think I do," Erin's tone shows a hint of curiosity. "Maybe you can explain it to me but use small words so I'll understand."

"Don't play dumb." She watches his jaw tighten and the small muscle near his temple jump, which makes her grin. Mark shifts in his chair, and the metal foot scrapes loud against the tile. "You got out there fast. Don't tell me you aren't chasing this thing," he says.

Erin doesn't answer right away. She watches steam curl up from her cup. "Fast," she repeats the word like it's a question.

"Yeah," he says. "I mean, early. You didn't waste time."

She finally looks at him. "Neither did you."

He blinks. "What's that supposed to mean?"

"It means," Erin says evenly, "that you keep arriving right after I do. No matter where the cache is, no matter who might be closer."

He almost laughs. "That's what you're hung up on? We're cachers, we chase the same thing."

"Not the same way," she says.

He frowns. "What way is that?"

She leans back slightly, giving him space while tightening the moment. "When a cache goes live, I get there first, I've always found them before you. Sometimes, by days. When it's a body though, you're already nearby." She tilts her head. "You're never far away, not when it matters."

He starts to say something but stops. He glances out the window, past her shoulder at the busy parking lot. "That's coincidence."

"Maybe once," Erin says. "Not every time."

He shakes his head. "You're reading into patterns that don't…"

"Don't get decided by me?" she finishes calmly. "That's the thing. I didn't start noticing this until someone else made timing matter. Yesterday, you made that timing matter."

"Look," he says carefully, "you're exhausted. Yesterday was a lot."

"Yesterday wasn't the first time," she replies. Erin lifts her cup and takes a slow sip, giving him time to recover. She doesn't challenge him, instead she lets the moment pass as if it never happened while he sorts through the words she just threw. Behind Mark's right shoulder, CryptidQueen shifts in her chair, glancing up from her screen just long enough to measure Erin's stillness.

When Mark still doesn't say anything, Erin continues. "You know what bothers me?" Her voice is still level. "It's not that you show up, it's how you show up. You never really seem like you're searching for a cache, it's more like you're preparing for an outcome."

Mark stiffens. "I don't know what you want from me."

"I don't want anything from you, Mark." Her words come out in barbs. "I'm just paying attention now."

He studies her face and finds an emotion he didn't anticipate. "You're being paranoid. This is exactly why you should slow down."

"No," Erin corrects. "This is why I can't."

She lifts her cup again to buy herself a second. "If another cache drops," she says, almost casually, "I won't know if I'm being followed or tracked."

His eyes narrow. "That's not fair."

She meets his glare. "You're right. Fair would be if you weren't always conveniently there when something is majorly fucked up, like you're always on cue."

Mark folds his arms and leans back. He tries to reset his tension, to wash the burning from his face. "I'm trying to keep you safe."

"No you aren't," she says with a disturbing calm. "You're trying to be a white knight."

Mark hangs his head, realizing how she sees him. "I'm only trying to help," he continues with a softer tone, "I'm trying to protect you."

"I know." Erin sets her cup down carefully. "Everyone sees white knights for what they are, though. They're creepers and it's gross."

Across the room, CryptidQueen shifts, closing her laptop halfway, watching the two intently. Erin stands and grabs her pack. "I meant what I said," she adds, slinging her bag over her shoulder. "I'm not walking blind anymore, Mark. Quit following me."

Mark looks up at her, and there's something unsettled about his expression, something Erin can't quite determine. As she turns toward the door, she catches him watching the street again, hopefully hearing her this time.

Erin gets into her car, shuts the door, and rests her forehead briefly against the steering wheel. She doesn't leave the parking lot right away, she needs emotional recalibration. Her breathing evens out before she lifts her head and looks through the windshield. Mark is still inside the shop. She watches him through the glass, his reflection doubled against the street beyond. He pulls out his phone, and she expects hers will vibrate in a moment.

He stands and turns slightly away from the counter, like he's trying not to be seen making the call. That alone would mean nothing, it's how fast he makes it that doesn't sit right with her. Erin lowers herself in the seat just enough that her dash blocks the view of her face while keeping him in sight.

Her phone buzzes once in her hand. She expects to see Mark's name, but it is a text from CryptidQueen. *You good?*

Erin doesn't reply immediately. Inside, Mark is talking into his phone with a hand cupping the bottom. His shoulders rise, then settle as he nods, then speaks again.

CryptidQueen texts again. *He's on the phone. Sounds like he's updating someone. He sounds pissed.*

Erin's fingers tighten around her phone. Mark ends the call but doesn't pocket the device right away. He stands for a moment, staring at nothing. He finally turns and scans the room again. Erin watches CryptidQueen duck her head behind her laptop.

Mark steps outside and the late afternoon sunlight cuts across his face. He pauses on the sidewalk, eyes sweeping the lot. Erin keeps her gaze forward, trusting the cover of her dash.

He doesn't look at her car. Instead, his focus aims toward the far edge of the lot, where a delivery van is parked alone, crooked in two spaces. After a moment, he turns to his truck near the front of the building. He leaves in a hurry, pulling out without looking back, his tires spinning on pavement as he exits onto the street.

Erin finally responds to CryptidQueen. *Thanks for showing up, I didn't know who else I could call.*

She counts to ten, then pulls out in the direction opposite of

Mark. As she drives, her phone buzzes once more. It is CryptidQueen again. *Whatever that was, that wasn't about you being okay. It sounded more like damage control.*

Erin doesn't reply, she plans to do that when she gets home. Between the coffee shop and the first stoplight, she understands with cold certainty that the log worked, and whoever has been setting the pace just realized she's no longer following it.

Chapter 28: Trackable

Mara Vance doesn't trust quiet mornings anymore. Lately, there's something new moving underneath the surface, something she can't see yet. The bullpen is half awake with the motions of shift change and the aroma of brewing coffee. A couple deputies drift toward the break room with mugs in hand.

Major Crimes is still mostly empty, which gives Vance the opportunity to settle in without rushing. Her own coffee sits untouched beside her keyboard. She opens her inbox and sees last night's unread messages still holding their ground, but there are no updates. She sips at her coffee, savoring the burn on her tongue. Too often since this case began, she's had to endure lukewarm coffee or miss the chance to have any.

She barely sets her cup back down when a new email drops in. **RE: Partial release, Geocache data request (Legal).**

The body contains a secure link with a time-limited token and a warning about scope and privacy constraints. Vance looks at her coffee, thankful she at least got a sip, before leaning in and clicking through digital hoops, inputting her clearance data and loading the secure email. It is filled with downloadable attachments. The first page is a cover sheet written by someone who obviously never had to tell a mother her kid was dead, brimming with legalese.

She skips it and moves to the next page, finding rows and rows of timestamps, reviewer actions, listing edits, and log posts. It all looks like mundane data that would be more at home on Maddox's monitor. Vance has lived long enough inside investigations that she's learned dull facts are where the truth hides.

She opens the document into a new workspace, which affords

her more screen to view the multiple pages. At first, it looks normal. Reviewers rotate through postings. Edits correct fat-fingered coordinates, fix titles, correct ratings, tweak hints. She sees the usual churn of a public system. Then she slows down, stopping on single entries and recognizing sequences.

She starts grouping the critical caches up by incident. Hidden Hollow, Parkside Peekaboo, Where the Path Broke, The Perfect View where Jessa was murdered, Under the Line, each cache that brought bodies. She starts with what should be obvious, who approved what and when, how fast the listings were edited, and what changed.

Vance's fingers hover over the keyboard, then begin moving again, faster now. Not because she's excited, but because the shape is forming and she can feel it locking into place. She highlights the IDs attached to each critical cache. She writes down names, the role each user has, and cross-references them throughout the caches. Patterns begin to form. One cluster appears with disturbing frequency, the same small family of user IDs. Vance sits back and the chair creaks under her, loud in the quiet room.

Her phone buzzes on the desk with a text from the county attorney's office: *That's all we can release right now. More will require the proper warrant language we discussed.*

She stares at the message for a moment, then sets the phone down, choosing to stare at the monitor screen. There's a second layer here, she can feel it. She opens the access logs and looks for outliers. She scrutinizes edits at odd hours and review actions that don't match the declared schedule she remembers Surveyor explaining the last time they spoke.

He'd said something that stuck. Rules don't stop accidents, people do. She'd almost admired it, then. Now she scrolls until she finds a timestamp that makes her stop, it is a reviewer action logged after midnight by Surveyor. The cache owner's name isn't familiar, so she checks the location and sees it's adjacent to a known site. The cache isn't in her investigation, but it was approved the same night Surveyor claimed he'd been done approving for the night.

She pulls up her notes from their meeting and flips to the page where she'd jotted his timeline in the margin. Eight p.m. was when he said he made his last approval. Her eyebrow knots, maybe she wrote the wrong date. Maybe he shares duties with another reviewer using the same profile. She knows she's reaching, but she has to consider the possibilities.

Vance prints the open pages, then stands and crosses the bullpen toward the glass-walled office that holds the printer. The papers land warm in her hand. She stares at the print of the approval log which shows the midnight action, carrying it back to her desk. She picks up her personal phone and calls Shannon Chesshir.

Shannon answers, her greeting is short and alert. "Go ahead."

"Chesshir. It's Vance." She keeps her tone controlled. "Legal finally let go of the leash and I've got partial backend logs. There were some errors on the warrant request, so I don't have legal names, but I have enough to fit more pieces together."

Shannon's voice shifts. "Pieces how?"

"Same small group of cachers have been touching every cache that matters. I'm not just talking approvals. I'm seeing edits, cleanup, quick suppressions."

Shannon responds evenly. "That tracks with what Ryan and I were seeing from the outside. We just couldn't prove it without the backend."

"Now we can start," Vance says.

Shannon is silent a moment, then she says, "You want us in early?"

"Yes, like now," Vance responds. "I want you and Maddox pulling everything you can from these logs. You two are better suited at finding what doesn't belong in documents like this."

"Understood," Shannon says. "I'll call Ryan, and I can be there in thirty."

Vance ends the call and immediately composes a secure transfer to Ryan's email, adding Shannon to the chain. When she attaches the files, she hesitates on the final one, the midnight action, but adds it anyway. If she's wrong, she'll own it.

Dispatch rings her desk phone. She answers without looking at the caller ID. "Vance."

"Detective, Tech Services called down. They want to confirm you still need that preservation request active on your department phone records. The Erin Caldwell call chain."

"Yes," Vance says immediately. "Keep it active."

"Copy."

She hangs up and sits again, staring at the printouts. The pattern is still there. Vance grabs her pen and circles the cluster of names, then she writes one line in the margin, small and precise: **This isn't chaos. This is upkeep.**

She looks up at the bullpen, at the empty chairs, at the scene board tracking the investigation. She knows the system is finally talking and whoever built this has been listening the whole time. Vance reaches for her coffee, takes a sip, and smiles at the heat, two for two ain't bad.

"Okay," she says under her breath, "Show me where you've been hiding."

Shannon makes it to the office with five minutes to spare, the lack of traffic is the only thing she likes about being called in early. She boots up both hers and Ryan's machines, making sure her partner is ready to hit the ground running as soon as he gets through the door. She doesn't wait long, he arrives moments later with an energy drink in his hand and a donut hanging from his mouth.

Shannon eyes his pastry. "Where's mine?"

He shrugs without explanation as he drops into his chair and throws his coat onto the file cabinet.

Her face scrunches. "Rude."

She's already logged into the secure email, pulling documents and opening files. Ryan rolls his chair over without being asked, energy drink in one hand. "Please tell me she finally got something real," he says through his donut.

"Careful what you say," Shannon replies, pointing around the room at dozens of imaginary listening devices. "But yeah, I think she does."

They open documents side by side. Ryan wheels back to his station and pulls raw access data. Shannon builds a visual map, something she can look at without drowning in numbers. Her first pass looks boring, but a picture begins to form by the end.

Ryan squints at his screen. "Okay, so reviewer IDs are there but birth names are anonymized, no big." He stares at a screen full of logs and timestamps, his fingers occasionally touching strings of numbers. "The interaction density is… odd."

Shannon nods. "Yeah. You see that, too?" She highlights a section with her cursor. "Most people drift in and out. The reviewers approve a listing, then disappear for days. Most users skip around without any sort of uniformity or hive clustering. These users are different."

"They almost always post on the same caches," Ryan says slowly. "Like, within minutes of each other. It also looks like they post exclusively on Surveyor caches, like they're shadowing him."

"Or doing damage control," Shannon says.

Ryan turns to her. "You thinking this is some sort of post-event hygiene?"

"I'm thinking pre-emptive," she answers. "Look at the timing."

She zooms in to cascades of activity blooming around each critical cache. They post innocent sounding log entries, making the cache seem fun and harmless, usually very shortly after the FTF log or when someone comments on something disturbing.

"It reads like someone who knows how panic spreads," Ryan says. "And how to stop it before it starts."

Shannon taps the screen where it reads the cache owner's name. "Now cross-reference OverlookLaneCrew."

Ryan does, pulling the account data into a separate pane. "Okay, this is interesting."

The IP history appears in residential nodes, commercial nodes, but through sloppy VPN endpoints. He works his keyboard until the false bounces are eliminated, revealing Overlook's IP address pings from the same location with little variation.

Ryan leans back. "An account this active should move more, shouldn't it?"

"Absofruitly," Shannon frowns. "Plus, it's an old profile and it went dormant for over a year, then suddenly it's active almost daily."

"Yeah," Ryan says. "And not like a normal resurgence. This user isn't finding caches at all, just placing them."

Shannon pulls up the activity timeline again, stretching it across the screen. "Most accounts warm back up. You see a few casual finds, maybe some social noise. This one went straight to precision work."

He scrolls, then stops. "That's not all."

She leans in. "What?"

"The overlaps," he says slowly. "OverlookLaneCrew isn't the only one who did that. At least two of those follower accounts did it too. MapNerd and TrailTempest."

Shannon scans the information on Ryan's screen. "Yeah, they're almost always on top of each other in the log posts."

"Run that location ping on those two." She wags her finger at his IP software. Shannon watches the overlays stack while the screen grows crowded. Lines converge as separate accounts collapse into a single behavioral footprint. "Okay," she says quietly. "That's not right.”

Ryan nods. “They both match what I saw earlier.” He pulls Surveyor’s footprint back into the visualization and drops it over the cluster. The effect is immediate, and the nodes align almost perfectly.

Ryan exhales. “He’s in contact with all of them.”

“I don’t think this is contact,” Shannon corrects. “It looks like shepherding.” They stare at each other as the thought gels into coherence.

Ryan scrolls again. “According to the email Vance sent, Surveyor told her his last approvals happen by eight p.m. and he doesn’t check again until mornings.”

Shannon doesn’t look away from the screen. “What does the data say?”

Ryan pulls up the most recent cache. “Look at the Under the Line cache. Twelve forty-seven a.m. He didn’t approve, but he edited the listing.”

“So he lied,” she says.

“Or he couldn’t sleep,” Ryan offers, then pulls up Hidden Hollow and Where the Path Broke. He shakes his head. “No. He does it a lot.”

They sit with the data for a moment, letting the hum of the lab fill the space. Shannon turns to her monitor and loads each IP address into an active window, then waits for results. The map on her screen lights up and each of the pin locations stack on top of each other. “These addresses,” she says, “they’re all the same residential neighborhood.”

Ryan frowns. “That means they’re all operating from a fixed location.”

“Sure, but multiple accounts in the same place, posting at the same time?” Shannon adds. “That’s not just a neighborhood cookout.”

Ryan pulls data from each of the accounts, but this time his date range reaches back years. He correlates the data for when each account stopped abruptly and what their last known activity was. "Shannon. Look at this."

He highlights a narrow window of data. "OverlookLane's last find was by the cabin," he says.

Shannon straightens. "Which cabin?"

"Dude! How many cabins have you been to lately?" He looks at her dumbfounded. "The one we found with Vance. The Evan kid."

Shannon pulls that file without a word and cross-references it with the IP timestamp. Her mouth goes dry. "There's a bounce," she says quietly. "Not clean, but the same origin pattern shows up here, and here." She highlights two timestamps. "One is from a cache nearby, they logged a find. The other comes from the cabin's digital footprint. Looks like they tried to make a hide, but the cache was rejected on review."

Ryan's voice drops. "So OverlookLaneCrew was at that cabin just before the account went dormant."

She doesn't answer immediately. Instead, she pulls up the reviewer's username from the timeframe. Surveyor. They exchange a look, knowing this is the moment when the work stops being academic. Shannon reaches for the phone. "We need to call Vance."

Vance answers on the first ring. "Talk to me."

Shannon doesn't preamble. "We think the reviewer role isn't incidental, it's operational. Surveyor has been using reviewer access to shape the field, suppress noise, and nudge players."

"Send me everything," Vance says. "And lock this down. I don't want chatter, no leaks. If he's still watching the forums, I don't want him knowing we've caught wind of him."

The call ends.

Ryan leans back, runs a hand through his hair. "So what now?"

Shannon looks at the map again. "Personally," she says, "I feel like we should assume he knows he's losing control."

"People like that," Ryan says quietly, "they don't go quietly."

"No," Shannon agrees. "They escalate." She saves the workspace, drafts a message to Vance, and attaches the modified files.

Detective Mara Vance doesn't open the message right away. She lets it sit in her inbox while she finishes reviewing her notes, leaving her coffee cooled and unfinished. She's learned not to rush moments like this, knowing the data doesn't change just because it waits. Her own paper notes are almost organized enough for her to make sense of it all.

When she finally does turn her attention to the email, the first thing she notices isn't the charts or the attachments, it's the tone of Shannon's notes, which are short and surgical. She opens each file with intention, scrolling slowly through each digital footprint. Those two put together some clean work. This level of detail is why Vance leans on Chesshir and Maddox.

She compares the data with her own notes from the river meeting with Surveyor. Her comments resurface about his posture and the way he'd spoken about the rules as though they were more than simple policy. His mention of last approvals by eight suggested he made no exceptions, which bothers Vance now that she cross-references the timestamp Shannon flagged. Twelve forty-seven a.m. Vance doesn't swear, though the words do form in her chest. "So you lied to me," she murmurs to the empty room.

She scrolls further, pulling up the file on OverlookLaneCrew. She reviews the dormancy, reactivation, and Maddox's notes on the 'precision work without warm-up'. She stops when she hits the cabin reference and steals a glance at the Evan file the clerk brought her the other day. Vance refocuses on the crew account logging a find nearby, then an attempted hide that never made it past review. Just as Maddox pointed out, the account didn't have another point of activity in over a year.

She rubs at her temple, feeling the beginning of a migraine. If Overlook found that cabin odd enough to place a cache at, and if Surveyor denied that cache, then this shows the first stages of control.

Her phone buzzes on the desk, but she ignores it, planning to look after she's done. She pulls up her own meeting transcript, rewinding the memory to the moment she asked Surveyor about his workload. The report shows her the way he generalized instead of answered and the way he framed moderation as burden instead of access. "People who clean up after other people's mistakes," he'd said.

She closes her eyes for a second. This wasn't cleanup, it was curation. Vance opens a fresh document and starts writing a sequence of names, accounts, locations, and times similar to CSU's data, but in a framing that helps her draw lines of connection. On the paper, she sees the quiet chain that doesn't accuse but doesn't let go, she adds this information to the document, carefully placing her notes where they best match the reports. By the time she finishes, there's only one conclusion she's willing to let herself say, the wrong man is sitting in a cell.

She picks up the phone and makes a call to the District Attorney. "Mister Duke," she says when the line connects. "This is Detective Mara Vance from the VSO. I need a few minutes of your time, if you'll permit."

"It's early, Vance." There's a pause. "What've you got?"

"We have reason to believe a reviewer account in the geocache case is being used operationally." She chooses each word to prevent sounding brittle. "We have digital evidence tying that account to multiple scenes and to a number of other accounts operating from the same house."

The DA pauses again, followed by a heavy sigh. "You're asking for another warrant," he says.

"Immediately," Vance replies. "What we originally thought was a lone operator may actually be an organized group and we need to break up this operation."

"I thought you had this guy in lock-up?"

This is the part of the conversation Vance doesn't want to have. "He's in on suspicion, sir." She sticks to facts, avoiding the pressure she received to put a name to the crimes. "The last twenty-four hours provided additional information."

"You were wrong about one suspect, what if you're wrong again?"

Vance doesn't hesitate. "Then I'll own it and accept the consequences due."

"I hope this sloppiness doesn't become a trend. This isn't Halloween and warrants aren't candy." His words and the silence that follows strikes Vance in the sternum. Before she can justify her position, he speaks again, "Send me the report, I assume you need to move on this ASAP."

"Yes, sir." When the call ends, Vance wastes no time. She finalizes the report and emails the DA, marking the correspondence as urgent.

Erin spends another sleepless night on the couch with her laptop balanced on her knees, the screen and a single lamp she forgot to turn off in the bedroom are the only light in her apartment.

She scrolls back through old cache pages, but not the murder-adjacent listings that everyone's already whispering about. She goes years back to dead hides, archived puzzles, and threads that petered out with polite goodbyes and no explanations.

She's not looking for bodies, she's looking for a different voice. Jackalope doesn't show up often. Since Lucia Falls, Erin had assumed TrailWolf was Jackalope, but knowing he couldn't have been behind the Under the Line cache, she realizes she needs to find the real person behind the cryptid. The first thing that strikes her in her search is that there's no solid trace of Jackalope anywhere online, no log posts or hides, no chatter, and aside from recent events, there's no forum presence. When the name does appear, it's usually buried in the comments, and always someone mentioning a username in a reply chain. Jackalope does have a profile link, so she follows it, chasing the rabbit.

There are no find logs, no hides, and no friends, just a profile image. Erin leans closer. It's a photograph of water, a gray lake under a low sky, framed by trees silhouetted in fog. Below it, there is one line of bio text: **For Evan.**

Erin sits back, staring at the blank profile with a find ranking of zero. "Who the hell is Evan?" she asks the empty room.

She searches the image through reverse lookup, but nothing clean comes back. The shape of the shoreline nags at her, she recognizes the curve of the bank and rise of rock on one side, but from where? She pulls up satellite images and starts cross-referencing lakes within driving distance, letting instinct do the first pass.

She pulls her notebook closer without her consciously deciding to grab it. She finds the page where she wrote the name **Jackalope** in the center of a page. Below it, she writes **Evan**. She doesn't know who Evan is yet, but she knows this much, no one builds a myth around a stranger.

Her phone vibrates on the table. Vance's name fills the screen. Erin answers on the third ring. "Hey."

"I wanted to check in," Vance says. Her tone is controlled and careful, like always. "TrailWolf's out. We don't have enough to hold him."

Erin swallows. "Okay."

"You don't sound surprised."

"He's already been online," Erin explains. "I didn't figure he could do that from a cell."

"So, you're on the caching forums?"

Erin stalls. "It was a push notification on my phone."

"Erin," Vance adds, her tone becomes stern, "if you're digging right now, I need you to tell me."

Erin looks at the lake on her screen. "I'm just… reading," she says. It's not a lie.

"Alright. Reading isn't against the law yet." Vance tries to sound pleasant. "Just stay away from anything that is."

After the call ends, Erin doesn't move for a long moment. There was more to the detective's check-in that Erin didn't hear, but she felt it. She prints and pins the image of the lake to her board, dead center on the map.

Erin is still logged in when the message arrives. The forums are restless again, threads stacking up in the background static. She hasn't joined any of it, she's learned better than that. The notification doesn't come through the forum, it comes through her inbox.

From: Surveyor

The name alone catches Erin's attention. When she does open it, the tone is polite and measured, friendly with assumed cooperation.

Hi Erin. I saw your recent activity on Under the Line. I understand emotions are running high, but I wanted to clarify a few things about how reviewer actions work, especially during active investigations. Sometimes posts made in good faith can complicate matters for people you don't intend to involve. For this reason, I am going to delete your message.

Erin doesn't move. Her eyes track each sentence slowly, deliberately. The message feels off, moderators don't usually provide responses this detailed.

If you're looking for context or guidance moving forward, I'm happy to help where I can. It's important to keep things constructive. The system works best when everyone trusts the process.

The message reads as kind, but the simple correction feels invasive. He doesn't mention any of her wording in the log directly. He doesn't mention bodies or police activity. He doesn't even mention rules.

Erin leans back in the cushion, letting her weight shift from her spine to her heels. She thinks about the timing, about how quickly moderators disabled this cache and about how long it took for a reviewer to respond to her comment, the comment she made calling Jackalope out specifically.

She types a reply but deletes it, then types another and deletes that too. She keeps thinking about the one time she tried defending herself on the message boards and how disastrous the fallout from that was. Anything reactive would give him purchase, something to adjust against. She chooses to leave Surveyor without a reply and closes the message instead.

Erin suddenly doesn't feel chased, she feels managed, and that frightens her more than anything that's tried to scare her so far.

Chapter 29: Already Logged

TrailWolf is released at 9:17 in the morning. They give his phone back last, and when he turns it on, the screen lights up with a backlog of notifications he doesn't open yet. He signs two forms, nods to a deputy who won't meet his eyes, and steps outside into a morning that looks just as dreary as every other Pacific Northwest morning he's ever stepped into.

He calls a friend and gets a ride to where he was arrested, back to his truck. He is glad they were honest at release that it wasn't towed, but he had anticipated a boot. He's also thankful there isn't one. Someone even folded his parking receipt under the wiper so it wouldn't blow away. He stands there for a moment, the keys in his hand, taking in the freedom and the forest.

When he finally starts the engine, the radio kicks on mid-song and he shuts it off immediately, preferring not to hear the sound of people. He drives home on side roads instead of the highway. At a four-way stop, a patrol car rolls through ahead of him without slowing. The deputy inside doesn't look over and TrailWolf watches the cruiser recede anyway, counting the seconds until it disappears.

At home, the house smells stale with a faint odor of old garbage. He drops his keys in the ceramic bowl by the door and flinches at the noise. He stands in the entryway, pulling his jacket off, trying to remember what the next normal thing is supposed to be. He needs breakfast or a shower, something ordinary.

Before he moves, he checks his phone. The forums are split clean down the middle, half the posts are performative apologies, and the other half never mentions his name but carries the suggestion of him. He reads threads about "false accusations," threads about "being careful who you trust." There's a new post titled *Patterns Don't Lie* that he stares at without opening. He scrolls past messages from people he hasn't talked to in years, some supportive and some curious. He notices who hasn't reached out at all, one name in particular, and that absence irritates him more than he will admit. She owes him an apology, not that he'd accept it.

He tosses the phone onto the couch and heads for the spare room where his gear lives, feeling a sense of peace surrounded by it, but also a stab of bitterness at how it all feels a little tainted. He kneels to retie a loose lace, then stops, fingers resting uselessly on the knot. He isn't relieved to be out, just bitter he was hauled in. Being cleared doesn't feel like innocence restored, the forums reminded him of that. It just feels like being put back on the board.

He doesn't shower and can't find his appetite, so he falls onto his couch, relishing the comfort of the cushions. His phone buzzes again with another notification, this time it's a cache alert. He stares at it before looking at the details. The coordinates are unfamiliar, but the placement nags at him, a tug at his sternum he hasn't felt since…

He exhales slowly and locks the phone without closing the app. When he finally moves again, it's to pull his pack fully open and start checking his kit, piece by piece, knowing he's going to need it, whether he wants to or not. In the back of his mind, a truth settles that he doesn't want to believe. Whoever did this didn't want him gone, they wanted him at the center.

Elsewhere, Mark refreshes a webpage. He doesn't enjoy reading the forums anymore, but he keeps the tabs current, keeps an eye open. His eyes slide past the posts, ignoring the clutter. They are full of outrage, theories, and amateur forensics. It's just noise, and he's learned online noise never matters.

His phone is face down on the table when it vibrates. He waits a full five seconds before flipping it over, not ready to deal with what he knows is coming. It is a text from a number without a name, but not a stranger: *You did well yesterday. She's still moving, but slower. We may need to adjust.*

Mark's throat tightens, and he hesitates before typing: *You said she'd back off.*

The other number doesn't respond immediately. No triple dots to suggest typing. Mark waits, holding back the burn to lash out. Finally, text appears: *She will, but not yet. She needs to believe she's choosing this.*

Mark rubs a hand over his face and stands, pacing the narrow length of his kitchen. The place feels like it's shrinking around him. He types a response, saying the words aloud: *This wasn't the deal. You said it would stop after the first one.*

Another vibration hits his phone: *Promises are for people who don't understand momentum. Remember, this was never about stopping her. It was about keeping her inside the pattern.*

Mark stops pacing and speaks as he types. "You don't get to decide that," he mutters, then catches himself. He doesn't hit send. He scrolls back through the earlier messages, the ones that came weeks ago. Helpful at first. Directional:

You'll want to approach from the south.

She's faster than she looks.

If you get there second, wait.

At the time, it felt like guidance from someone who understood the game better than he did. It was supposed to help Mark build a connection with a girl he liked, now he's too far into the trap, too dirty, to get free. His phone buzzes again from the same number: *TrailWolf is out.*

Mark sits down hard in the chair. That wasn't supposed to happen yet. He knew it would, eventually, but not now, not with everything else in motion. He types before he can stop himself: *That complicates things.*

Only if you let it, the reply comes back almost immediately. *He's *predictable. He always has been.*

Mark's jaw tightens when he reads 'predictable'. That word comes up more than he likes. He wants out, and he's ready to call the bluff and walk away. Hopefully he can salvage his life with minimal damage. His phone lights up with another message before he can talk himself out of this: *Next stage will go live soon. Rimrock is watching.*

Mark stares at the screen until the words blur. "You said this wasn't about her," he whispers to the empty room while he types again.

The response takes longer this time. When it comes, it's shorter: *It's always been about who listens.*

Mark slaps the phone down like it might burn him and stands again. He goes to the window and looks out at the street, the parked cars, the ordinary afternoon. For a moment, he imagines walking away, deleting the app, throwing the phone into the river. Instead, he checks his pack. Beneath the fear and the doubt, something else has taken root in Mark. If this really is about choice, then Jackalope has been making his decisions this whole time.

TrailWolf showers, letting the water drum against his shoulders until his skin stops prickling. When he steps out, the mirror is fogged and his reflection looks unfamiliar, displaced. He dries off, dresses, and eats half a protein bar, forcing each swallow past the building nausea.

Only then does he sit down and open his phone again. The cache page is still there, patiently waiting for him to come back. This is a multi-cache, a hide with at least two stages, a scavenger hunt within a scavenger hunt. He clicks on the coordinates which opens the map. He zooms the map out, then back in, checking scale, orientation, and access points. There is a lake, and the pin for the cache is on a small island maybe three hundred feet from the highway. Rimrock Lake.

He hadn't planned on thinking about that place again. He hadn't planned on thinking about anything today beyond staying out of the way and letting the noise burn itself out, but there are places you leave, and places that leave something in you. This place is far from Vancouver, much further than his designated notification radius, so why was it coming through to him?

He scrolls through the cache details. The language is clean, sparse, and deliberate. There is no bravado and no typical geocache hide theatrics. It reads to be obeyed without saying so: **This placement is intentional. Access is straightforward if you respect posted boundaries and conditions. Do not rush the approach. Do not attempt retrieval from unsafe angles. This cache is meant to be found, not forced. If you arrive and feel uncertain, you are early. Step back and reassess.**

TrailWolf locks the phone and sets it down on the desk, palms flat on either side of it. He stares at the wall, counting his breaths, trying to tell himself this is coincidence and not design, but he knows the truth. He reaches for his pack again and wonders if she's also seen it.

Across town, Mark hasn't moved. His phone sits on the table where he left it. He stands at the sink, hands braced on the counter, staring at the reflection of the window instead of his own face, trying in vain to pretend nothing happened. Rimrock. That wasn't supposed to be today. He checks the time, then the forums, then the map again, as if the coordinates might tell him it's all a big joke.

They don't. His phone buzzes once more: *You don't need to rush. Let them come to it.*

Mark types back slowly, each word measured: *You said this would end.*

The reply comes almost instantly: *That's exactly what's happening.*

Mark swallows as he scrolls back through the message thread again, farther than before, past the point where he usually stops himself. He sees the first time Jackalope reached out. The way it had been framed as concern, as pattern recognition. As someone older in the game offering perspective. *You don't want to be first here. Let the trail breathe. Sometimes the mistake is going too fast.*

He sees it now for the conditioning it is, the soft authority. Jackalope started by giving the right advice that always positioned him just close enough to be useful and never far enough to be clean.

Mark closes his eyes, damning himself, then starts to reply. "I told you I was done," he says aloud to the phone, his thumbs scolding the keyboard one letter at a time, then sends the message.

The phone vibrates a response: *You are. This is just the last alignment.*

Mark grits his teeth at the word, alignment. He thinks of Erin, and how she looked at him in the coffee shop. She was angry and she was scared, but she was also measuring him. He hates that she looks at him differently now, and hates more that she's right. Mark picks up his pack and checks it, then grabs his phone and pulls up her number. He stares at her name, his stomach tying into knots.

TrailWolf loads his pack into his truck, climbs in, and fires up the engine. He sits there, his hands gripping the wheel, watching the trees sway in the light breeze. He searches for any reason why he shouldn't drive north to the lake, any reason at all. He checks his phone again, there are no messages, no more excuses.

He thinks about the last two weeks, about how the game has felt more like survival, how easily he was removed from the board, and how quickly he was put back. TrailWolf opens the map one last time and drops a pin, not on the cache itself, but on the nearest access point. The place someone would wait if they didn't want to be seen arriving first.

Chapter 30: Puzzle Cache

Morning arrives with the same colors it has brought all week, with low gray clouds and a thin mist that never really commits to rain. Vance stands under the liftgate of an unmarked SUV with her coat collar up and her hands empty. She knows holding anything right now would show that she's shaking, and that won't help the team.

The neighborhood is quiet. Identical houses curve along the street with trimmed lawns and HOA-approved landscaping still clinging to autumn color. A basketball hoop stands over a closed garage three doors down. Porch lights remain on from the night before on nearly half the houses.

No home here looks like it deserves what's about to happen. Most of the police vehicles are parked out of sight, tucked around the bend or staged a street over. A single armored SWAT truck sits farther back near the intersection. Black-clad figures move with practiced economy, their helmets pulled down and rifles slung. A deputy steps around the vehicle and speaks with a tone low enough only she can hear him, holding the warrant packet. "Got your papers."

"It's signed?" she asks.

"Yep, Duke pushed it through," the deputy says. "All systems go."

Vance nods and takes the packet. Behind her, vehicles settle into place and deputies begin blocking roads. On the other side of the barricades, Vance spots two Clark County units, two DNR rigs, and the cybercrime van that looks too new to belong in this sting. They pull in last, headlights cutting through mist. Shannon Chesshir climbs out first, already opening the side door and collecting gear. Ryan Maddox follows with the camera bag slung across his body, scanning the neighborhood.

Tenner steps up beside Vance, his shoulders tight and his gaze stuck to the street number, then up to the windows, half expecting a face to appear and vanish. "This is it?" he asks, voice low.

Vance doesn't answer right away, she knows he's just filling awkward silence.

The house looks normal. The curtains are drawn on all windows except one room upstairs. It's painfully ordinary. She flips the packet open, checks the address again, her own way of filling the silence. This is the residence of OverlookLaneCrew, the account name sitting in her mind above legal names. She damns herself for letting the culture of this silly game affect her processes. The file photo is a happy family, hiking and smiling. She closes the packet and tucks it under her arm. "This is it."

On her phone, a notification stack waits, all the stuff she refused to look at earlier. The most recent is from her man in Jail Operations. The message preview tells her TrailWolf is out, released at 9:17. She doesn't open any of it.

Vance keys her radio once. "We do this like we're serving papers. Two deputies with Detective Tenner and me. Team two in back. SWAT in ready position. All other units on standby. We do this quiet if we can but be ready to get loud if we have to."

A few short acknowledgments click back. She looks down the line of units, then back at the front door. There is a potted plant on the right side of each porch step and just before the door is a welcome mat that says something bland and cheerful. Everything about this house screams domestic grandparents.

She feels the pressure headache she's been ignoring tightening behind her eyes, and she can't push back the DA telling her not to mess this up. "Positions," she says.

Tenner is the first to move and the entry team falls in behind him. Vance follows closely behind, carrying the warrant packet, calm because she has no choice but to be. Two deputies take up the rear, each visibly resisting the urge to rest their hands on their pistols. They reach the porch and Tenner raises his hand. Vance watches the door, expecting it to open on its own. Tenner knocks once, firm and professional. "Sheriff's Office," he calls. "Search warrant."

The sound carries down the street, and one deputy looks at the neighboring homes. The other side of the door is quiet, there are no footsteps, no voices, not even the hollow shuffle of someone shifting weight on the other side of the door. Tenner waits before knocking again. "Sheriff's Office," Tenner repeats, louder this time. "Open the door."

Still nothing. He looks toward the edge of the property at the SWAT lead, who gives a subtle nod and taps one of his men on the shoulder. The breacher reaches the door as team one steps to the side and swings the tool with trained precision. The strike is controlled and effective, landing just next to the knob. The door gives with a sharp crack that echoes across the street, then swings inward on its hinges. No alarm sounds, and there's no shouting or sudden movement. Disturbed dust dances in the light of morning rays.

Vance taps her radio. "We have breach, all units move."

The entry team flows inside, black shapes breaking into open doorways, muzzles sweeping corners, boots playing a rhythm against the floor. Tenner goes with them while Vance stops at the threshold, just outside. The air inside smells normal, lived-in, filtered through new carpet and old wood. Whatever she was bracing for, isn't there.

"Rear team moving," comes over the radio.

Vance glances through the front window as another SWAT element ghosts along the side yard, disappearing toward the backyard, covering exits that no one is using.

"Ground is clear," a voice calls from inside.

Moments after, another voice calls, "Second floor clear."

The movement inside pauses. Tenner, standing at the base of the stairs, looks to Vance. "Mara, this doesn't look good."

Vance steps in once she's sure no one will be running out. She tracks pairs of shoes sitting by the door, four pairs aligned with care.

Her radio cracks, "Garage clear."

Another voice follows, "Shed clear."

The living room opens up ahead of her. There's a blanket folded over the back of the couch, a mug in the cup holder of a recliner, but nothing questionable. There is no television noise, no music, just a ticking grandfather clock on the far wall. Framed photos line the mantel next to the clock that show the lived story of a family of four. School photos of a young boy and girl, a family portrait likely taken at a department store, various outdoor activities, including all of them at a trailhead, arms slung around each other. The same two kids in separate frames, older now, grinning through braces in one, holding up a fish in the other. One frame has been knocked slightly crooked by the entry team, the smiling faces still tilted toward each other. These are not the faces of murderers.

From deeper in the house, a voice cuts in, crisp and controlled. "Locked basement door. Two operators in position."

Over the radio, the same voice issues, "Exterior, watch sublevel windows." Other units confirm.

Vance rounds the corner to the hall where two members of SWAT stand angled out, rifles steady, bodies squared to a threat that hasn't materialized. One of the men leans in, eyes tracing the doorframe, then gives a short shake of his head.

Vance motions CSU to enter and take over. Ryan crouches at the threshold, gloved fingers testing the knob, then the frame. He checks the hinge pins, the strike plate, the seams. Everything is intact and he finds no wires, no secondary tension, and no additional weight on the door. Whoever locked it wanted it to stay locked. "It looks clean, but it's locked," he says quietly.

Tenner looks to Vance and she nods Ryan to open it. He grins and produces a small kit, pulling tools out with precise care. He wastes no time working on the lock, and it gives with a soft click. He steps back, motioning to the knob, still smiling. "You guys can kick it down now, if you want."

The operator nearest the handle rolls his eyes and eases the door open an inch, then another. His partner leans in, using the muzzle of his rifle to finish the job.

Cold air spills out, bringing a coppery stench with it. SWAT steps in, crowding the doorway, aimed down the stairs. "We've got a body," one of them says.

He flicks on the basement light. The room at the bottom of the stairs is small, utility-sized with a concrete floor. Shelves along one wall are stocked with cleaning supplies, storage bins, and some tools. The body of a man is seated in the center of the room, his wrists bound behind the chair so tightly his hands have gone dark, and his ankles are secured the same way. His shoulders are slumped forward at an angle that suggests exertion. The skin has taken on a muted, waxy look. His face is a bloody mess. One eye is nearly swollen closed and the other holds a wide bruise. There are patterned contusions along his chest and upper arms, and bruising rings his neck, deeper on one side than the other.

Ryan steps in just far enough to confirm what his nose already told him, but he refuses to touch the body. "Adult," he says. "Male. Cause is obviously deliberate," he adds. "I'll call the coroner."

Vance stands at the top of the stairs, hands braced lightly on the railing, forcing herself to catalog what she's seeing instead of what it implies. She clocks the restraints, the symmetry, the absence of blood spatter anywhere in the room. The floor beneath the chair is clean, and there is no blood pool like the victim at the Hazel Dell scene. This man was tortured, but the act was methodical and done with a brutal care.

Ryan glances back up. His expression doesn't change, but his voice drops another register. "I could be wrong, but it looks like he also suffered from prolonged asphyxiation," he says. "He was allowed to recover multiple times, from the look of it."

Shannon has been quiet until now, camera already up, not shooting the body but capturing the room around it. "Look at the supplies," she says quietly. "Nothing's out of place. There's no spills, and all the labels are facing outward."

She shifts, framing the chair, then the floor beneath it, then the wall behind. "The unsub cleaned throughout the process," she adds, pointing to the concrete floor. "You can see the different rings for each time right here."

One member of SWAT leans into Vance and asks, "What are these two not trained to do?"

"In a small department, people have to wear many hats." She shrugs. "Plus, they have a knack for the work I don't see often."

The radio comes alive again, this time from the team upstairs. "We've got a 10-72, second bedroom on the right."

Shannon takes one last photo of the doorway itself, showing the frame intact and the hinges untouched. "You collect in the basement," she says to Ryan, already moving. "I can hit the second floor."

Ryan nods with no argument, and Shannon moves upstairs, taking the stairs two at a time. Vance follows half a step behind, close enough to hear her breath. As they climb, photos follow them up the wall. School portraits in cheap frames. Two kids age year by year, the smiles change. The upstairs hallway narrows, and the ceiling pressing down lower than the floor below, and doors line the corridor. A SWAT operator stands off to the side, his weapon angled down now, and posture softened, but he remains threat ready. Another leans over the railing, taking in deep breaths through his nose.

Shannon doesn't go straight in, she looks at the threshold first. The carpet fibers are undisturbed except for the boot prints from the breach team. She raises the camera and documents the doorway before stepping across it. The room is small, a guest room maybe, with neutral paint. The bed is neatly made, and the sheet corners are pulled tight with hospital precision. An old cedar trunk sits at the foot of the bed, the kind meant for blankets and seasonal clothes. The lid is open wide and clear plastic has been cut and fitted inside, taped down at the corners, fashioned as a liner.

The body is packed inside the chest. The dismemberment was done with purpose. Limbs are tucked and bent, separated cleanly from the torso and stacked to make room. The head is still attached but fully bent sideways against the curve of the chest, skin at the throat darkened and uneven. The smell is more than decay, it is iron, sweat, and that sour note of fear that never had a chance to dissipate. No blood is visible outside the container.

"She was alive for part of it," Shannon says quietly, covering her nose and mouth with the back of her glove as she continues to work. She moves around the trunk, documenting the liner, the compression points, and the way the plastic bows inward where the body presses back. "Hard to tell how much she endured without an autopsy."

The nightstand sits untouched beside the bed, holding a lamp and a book titled **The Cask of Amontillado** which is open face-down, to mark a place that won't be returned to. A framed photo sits beside the lamp, turned slightly away from the bed. The woman in it is laughing with one arm around the boy and her other hand pulling a smaller child close against her side. Shannon photographs it last. She doesn't comment on it, but Vance does, "Where are these kids?"

From the hallway behind them, a voice says quietly, "We've got another one."

"Damn me for asking."

The last door at the end of the hallway opens onto a smaller room, painted blue with posters on the wall of dinosaurs, skateboarders, and the Oregon Zoo. Glow-in-the-dark stars and planets speckle the ceiling. A small desk watches out the window from the corner of the room, cluttered with markers and half-finished homework. A shelf of action figures arranged in careful rows, some missing pieces, all facing forward like they're ready for play.

A toy chest sits beneath the window on the adjacent wall. Plastic and bright but scratched along the edges from years of use. One officer stands next to it, pointing but not looking. The lid is closed and Shannon stops short. She kneels beside the chest, fingers pushing the side, feeling the weight through the plastic. "It's heavier than it should be," she says.

Vance steps into the room and stands beside Shannon. She takes in the shelf of toys, the glow-in-the-dark stars, and the bed made the way a child makes it when they're in a hurry. She huffs, trying to push it out of her mind and taps Shannon's shoulder. "Go ahead."

Shannon unlatches the lid and lifts it just enough to look inside. The stench is acrid and sweet, trapped too long without airing. She closes the lid again and the room goes quiet. "There's another liner," she says, voice steady and professional. "Same thing as the trunk."

Vance rests a hand on Shannon's shoulder, anchoring the CSU Tech, then grabs the latch of the lid and lifts it open, staring at the tangle of contorted flesh. "Dammit. The boy." She closes the lid. "We're still missing the girl."

A member of the team behind her swallows hard as Vance straightens and turns slightly. "Seal the room," she says to him. "No one else is to come in here unless CSU needs them." She turns back to Shannon. "Chesshir, I want this entire room documented exactly as found."

She turns to the men at the doorway and commands, "Show me

the daughter's room."

Shannon photographs the details of the chest, the lid, the body, even the fingerprints smeared into the plastic where small hands once pushed it open without fear.

The girl's bedroom is at the end of the hall. The door is half open, and the room is darker than the others, with the curtains pulled just enough to keep the streetlight out. It's a mess. Clothes are draped over the back of a chair. Posters crowd the walls, emo bands and handwritten lyrics are taped up alongside photos of friends. A mirror above the dresser is lined with stickers and notes. The bed is empty and the sheets are tangled. The pillow is missing the case and stuffed animals are shoved aside.

Vance stands in the doorway and lets the absence register. "She's not here," she says.

The radio on SWAT's shoulder comes to life. "Lieutenant. You need to see the garage." Vance looks at the officer waiting in the door. She gestures for him to follow, and they move downstairs to the garage entry, joined by Ryan as he comes up from the basement.

The garage smells different than the rest of the house. It is cold and oily with a faint tang of rubber and concrete. An SUV takes up the center of the space and pegboard walls hold meticulously organized tools. A bike leans against a stack of plastic storage bins labeled in marker. *Camping. Christmas. Clothes.* A chest freezer sits against the far wall of the garage, white and unremarkable, a thin layer of frost blooming along the rim of the lid. It hums softly, steady and patient, flanked by two deputies.

Vance steps closer and Ryan joins her without comment. She reaches out and lifts the lid. Cold spills out with a cloud of fog. The top layer is frozen food. Boxed dinners stacked neatly, one on top of the other. A few brands repeat, and ice crystals cling to the cardboard where condensation has frozen and refrozen. They are organized like so much of the rest of the house.

Ryan lifts the first box and sets it aside, then another and another. Vance knows what's coming by the look on the face of the deputy next to her. Ryan sets dinners aside on the workbench, maintaining the stack order. Beneath the fourth layer is the girl, folded to fit the space. Her hair is stiff with ice and her skin is pale blue, her torture frozen in place. Dark marks ring her wrists and throat, deeper where the cold hasn't erased them yet.

No one speaks. Ryan makes a noise in his throat and closes the lid slowly. The hum resumes, still steady, still patient, but now almost a little remorseful.

"This isn't a network, it was one person," Vance says, looking at the freezer. "Assimilating their life. Sleeping here, eating meals next to the victims." She stares at the stack of dinners now sitting on the workbench, their serving suggestions smiling up at her. She lets it all settle before finishing, "This wasn't just a murder site. It was a house stolen. Lives taken over."

Another call comes over the radio from the other side of the house. "I've got a room off the dining area," one of the deputies reports. "Looks like a home office." It hadn't rated attention during the sweep as there was no movement or obvious threat. Now, with the house secured, it reads differently. The den is small and windowless. The family photos are still present but faced down. The furniture is minimal and deliberate with a desk centered against the wall.

Shannon appears next to Vance and Ryan at the doorway, camera already up, having finished sealing the boy's room. She doesn't speak, none of them do.

The desk holds three cell phones laid out in a precise row, powered off and face down, just like the family. Each has a printed label on the back: **MapNerd**, **TrailTempest**, and **Surveyor**. Beside them, a laptop sits open, and the screen is dark, but the laptop is still warm. A second laptop rests next to it, this one is on a cooling pad.

Ryan wakes the laptop. A login screen appears with the username **OverlookLaneCrew**. The desk has a notebook littered with cacher IDs, Vance recognizes many of the usernames.

Ryan logs into the active laptop with a press of the space bar. "I was expecting a password." He immediately begins sorting through the File Explorer and the open windows. "Detective, this is the hub."

He taps at the screen, pointing to a long forum thread, pausing briefly on each username from the phones on the desk. "All of these accounts were being posted from, right here."

Vance steps fully inside and lets her eyes trace the system of control. There are binders filled with printouts of various geocaches, schedules taped to the wall next to printed maps, and Polaroids, hundreds of them. She finds a carving on the edge of the desk, the profile of a horned rabbit, near the Surveyor phone.

"Jackalope," Shannon mutters.

"Surveyor," Vance corrects.

"He didn't just take their names," Shannon says, nearly reaching out to touch it. "He took their lives and kept using them."

Vance nods. "He keeps their voices alive in posts, messages, cache logs. He lets the world think they're still out there. No one realizes they're talking to ghosts."

A deputy in the room clears his throat. "You're not going to like this." He closes the door, revealing a slip of paper pinned to the backside.

Vance steps closer, reading the neat handwriting. *You were close. If you want a shard of truth, you should check TrailSister's living room.*

"He's been in her house," she says.

Under the writing is a stamp with the same small silhouette of a jackalope. She taps on the door, careful not to touch the paper as she stares at Shannon. "Make sure this gets immediate analysis."

The room seems to constrict around her, and everything clicks into focus all at once. The shoes by the door, the bodies, the digital operations where he has been pulling strings. Their arrival wasn't accidental, this is completion in motion.

In that instant, the scale shifts and she knows this crime scene isn't where she needs to be. She swings the door open and bursts into the hall, her voice already carrying, "CSU stays to process." She hits the front door. "SWAT maintains perimeter. Nobody clears out until I say so."

Then she turns to Tenner who is still thick in coordination with two members of SWAT on the front lawn. "We've gotta move. Secure two units," she says. "Send them to recon Caldwell's apartment." Tenner doesn't ask why, he just moves.

They head for the cruiser while Tenner barks orders through the radio. Vance turns the key and the engine sounds the countdown. Erin is next.

Chapter 31: Cache And Dash

Vance doesn't turn on the siren, she leaves the warning work to the pair of squad cars ahead of her. The windshield wipers keep time with her thoughts, steady and relentless, and the city slides past in gray fragments as storefronts and intersections blur into one long corridor of wet pavement. She keeps one hand on the wheel and the other resting near the radio, ready for it to tell her bad news. Tenner rides shotgun in silence, monitoring dispatch in case he finds a hint of what might be coming.

Erin Caldwell's apartment complex is surprisingly quiet when they reach it, considering how many people live so close together. Rows of identical units make up the large complex, outlined by parking spaces in tight, efficient rows, most of them filled. A shared trash enclosure sits near the curb with its gate half open. One bin is pulled out farther than the others, and a black bag is slumped against the side.

Vance parks half a unit down. "Tell the units to circle the perimeter before finding their position," she says. "We need eyes on suspicious activity, but don't want to spook the neighbors."

The detectives move on foot, their reflections ghosting across windows as they pass. Vance watches the building the entire time, cataloging what she can from the outside. The apartments are calm, with no signs of broken windows or forced entry at Erin's place. Tenner takes the lead at the porch, pressing against the door without knocking, but he hears nothing. Vance steps up beside him, gesturing for him to stand back. She gives a firm knock. "Erin," she calls. "It's Detective Vance."

Erin opens the door almost immediately, standing in jeans and a hoodie with her hair pulled back. She looks from Vance to Tenner, confusion already sharpening her expression. "Oh, detective" she says, "I see you brought company this time."

Vance doesn't answer immediately, instead she looks past Erin into the house. There's a half-folded blanket on the couch, women's shoes by the door, and a mug on the table. What Vance doesn't see is chaos, there's nothing out of place. She finds a moment of relief before reminding herself that Jackalope has been here.

"Erin," Vance says in her-police issued level tone. "We need to come inside."

Erin hesitates, then steps back, letting the door swing open. "Detective, are you going to tell me what's going on?" she asks, trying for casual and missing by a mile.

Vance watches Erin's hands as she speaks for tremors or nonverbal warnings. She seems fine, but something isn't right. Vance steps inside first, just far enough to clear the doorway, and Tenner follows, turning slightly as the door closes behind them. A tote bag rests against the wall, ready for action. Vance thumbs at it. "Going for a geocache today?"

"No, I just haven't put it away." Erin watches the detective's eyebrow peak. "I think it's still legal to not clean up my own home."

Vance doesn't acknowledge the sarcasm. "Has anyone been here today?"

Erin shakes her head. "No. I've been home alone all morning."

Tenner stays near the door, angled just enough to watch the hall through the peephole. Vance remains in the living room with Erin, eyes working, cataloging the space the way she always does. In front of the couch, the coffee table is a cluttered mess with notebooks and a laptop. The coffee mug is nearly full.

Erin catches the detective's glance and smiles. "Do you want some? I'd be happy to pour another cup."

"No," Vance says. "I'm good."

She shifts her attention to the wall between the hallway and the kitchen. Erin's caching board is cleaner than her last visit, but still active with notes and pins. The caches aren't random this time, the only ones still marked are the ones connected to the investigation, and the notes are no longer filled with hobbyist whimsy, just pertinent details.

"You've cleared a bit of the board out," Vance says. "Trying to quit the game?"

"That's kind of the point, right?" Erin shrugs. "You wanted me to back up, so I am."

Tenner walks into the apartment, leaving his post at the door. He studies the coffee table without touching anything. Erin's notebook sits closed on a messy stack of papers. Under the edge of it, something catches light that shouldn't. He doesn't change posture, but he does reach into his pocket and pulls out a pen. "Ms. Caldwell," he says, calm. "What's this on your table?"

She follows his attention. "It's just my journal," she says dismissively. "I like to write stuff down, it helps me think."

Tenner nods like it makes sense, then leans in just enough to slide the pen under the notebook's edge, lifting the cover a fraction of an inch. The mirror shard glints from the light of the lamp and the back of the notebook reflects in its surface. "How about this?"

Erin's breath goes shallow. "That's nothing," she says quickly as her nonchalance evaporates. "I broke my stupid mirror in the bathroom a couple weeks ago. I meant to throw it out."

Vance looks at the shard, then to Erin. "When did you break the mirror?" she asks.

"I don't know. A while ago."

"How long is a while?"

Erin's jaw tightens. "Why does this matter?"

Vance steps closer to the coffee table now, examining the broken glass on her approach. "Because that piece doesn't look like it came from a bathroom accident."

Erin laughs once, sharp. "You're telling me you can tell that just by looking at it?"

"What I'm saying," Vance says, "is that people don't accidentally leave broken glass lying around their house."

The ticking clock on the wall is the only sound filling the silence. Erin glances toward the kitchen, then toward the hallway, checking exits on instinct. "This is insane. You show up unannounced, start digging through my stuff, and suddenly I'm a suspect?"

"No one said that," Vance says. "But I need you to be honest with me."

Erin's hands curl into fists. "I am being honest."

Vance's voice softens. "Erin, we need to move you for a bit, somewhere safe, just until we sort this out."

Erin's face drains. "Move me where?"

"Protective custody," Vance says.

"No. I'm not doing that," Erin says.

Tenner shifts, sensing Erin's caginess. "Erin, nobody's trying to…"

"No," she cuts in, her eyes are locked on Vance. "You don't understand. If I leave, I can't finish…" She stops, realizing she's said too much.

"Finish what?" Vance asks.

Erin's gaze drops to the coffee table, to her notebook and the sliver of mirror. "You're too late," Erin says, bolting toward the table. She snatches the notebook, knocking the mug hard enough to spill coffee on Tenner's shoes, forcing him to jump back. The shard skids across the table and hits the floor. Tenner refocuses and lunges for Erin but misses.

She slings the tote bag over her shoulder in one smooth motion, grabs her keys, and flies through the door before either of them can grab her. By the time Tenner yanks the door open, she's already sprinting down the walkway, shoes slapping wet concrete.

"We have a runner," Vance says into her radio as she moves, voice tight but controlled. "Adult female with a backpack, running west."

Outside, tires squeal as one of the patrol units peels out of its idle. Vance stands in the doorway for half a second longer, eyes on the room Erin left behind. Next to the coffee table, the mirror shard rests in the open. She knows she can't touch it without keying in the proper channels, so she pulls her phone out and takes a picture, giving her something she can come back for through the proper channels.

Rain coats the pavement, making the concrete dark. Erin cuts left on instinct, her bag thudding against her hip as she runs. She doesn't look back. Her car is three rows down, nose-in, tucked beside a pickup with a cracked taillight. She fumbles the key and swears under her breath, then gets it into the lock. The door yanks open and she throws herself inside, slamming it shut as her foot kicks down on the brake. The engine turns over rough, then catches, roaring to life.

Erin throws the car into reverse. In the rearview mirror, she sees a deputy at the end of her building's walkway and another farther back, cutting between parked cars, both are headed her way with hands on their weapons. She slams into drive, her tires squeal, and the bumper clears the pickup by inches. She snaps the wheel hard, fishtailing before correcting. The car surges forward toward the exit.

Her phone vibrates, but she barely notices.

She hits the stop sign at the edge of the lot, barely slowing and turns wide onto the street. A horn blares on her blind side. Rain streaks across the windshield, pushed away by wipers snapping back and forth in frantic rhythm.

The phone vibrates again. She steals a glance as she blows

through a stop sign. It's a text from Mark with a preview beneath his name: *If you've never trusted a thing I've said before…*

Her throat tightens. She ignores the phone and floors it, cutting a sharp right onto Mill Plain, nearly sideswiping a city bus. She takes the first turn without signaling, then another, doubling back through side streets she knows by memory, gripping the wheel, her hands white with fear.

In her mirror, flashing lights bloom briefly at the far end of the block, then vanish behind a corner. Erin swallows hard, knowing she's going to pay for this terrible decision, but not as much as when they confiscate the shard. She should have gotten rid of that damn thing the night she found it.

Her phone buzzes again, refusing to shut up. She doesn't bother looking at it. She accelerates, jumping onto 136th, then 9th. She's a rat in a maze and she doesn't know which way is out, but she knows she needs to go north.

The apartment feels skewed the second Erin is gone. The door hangs open, letting the rain in to puddle at the threshold. The mirror shard lies where it skidded to rest beside the coffee table. Radios chatter, calling Erin's direction before admitting they lost her. Outside the apartment, Vance motions the returning deputy to the door.

"Secure this apartment," she commands. "Nobody is allowed in or out unless I clear it. Start an entry log."

Tenner waits for the deputy to take position at the door before addressing Vance. "Mara, that piece of mirror. Is that what I think it is?"

"Yeah," she says, shaking her head. "We've got probable cause and exigency. This place needs to stay frozen until a warrant clears and CSU can process."

Tenner pulls out his department phone and captures his own photographs of the shard, the scattered papers on the table, and the corkboard without further disturbing anything in the apartment. Vance stares at the empty space Erin left behind, knowing she didn't just run from police, she's running toward something.

"Lieutenant," one of the uniforms says, carefully. "Dispatch has the ATL out from the pursuit, you want it countywide?"

"Yes." Vance shakes her head, still processing Erin's decisions. "Make sure they know she's an endangered witness with possible involvement." Calling her a witness surprises him, but she doesn't explain it.

A second officer tries for more. "Lieutenant, if we call her, maybe a welfare check…"

"No. We don't tip the board," Vance says with finality. "If Jackalope is watching, the fastest way to get Erin killed is to light her up like a flare."

"Tenner, make sure CSU is ready to go as soon as we've got the judge," Vance continues. "They need to do a full sweep. I want every surface, every device, every fiber logged. If she hid a murder weapon, who knows what the hell else we're going to find."

She steps back into the rain, coat already dampening at the shoulders. The complex stays quiet and Vance can't tell whether the tenants are oblivious to everything that just happened or if they're hiding behind curtains until danger passes. "Tenner, ride with me. Dispatch can keep the cell warrant warm, for now we try finding her the old-fashioned way."

Erin doesn't stop driving until the city thins out and the streets start to feel unfamiliar. She pulls into a turnout beside a closed nursery, kills the engine, and sits with her forehead pasted against the steering wheel until her breathing evens out.

Her phone buzzes again and she flips it over with a shaky hand. Damn Mark and his four missed messages. She opens them:

If you've never trusted a thing I've said before, please just trust me now.

Do not go to Rimrock.

It isn't safe.

Please.

Erin scowls at the warning. He knew, he's known this whole time. She scrolls back farther, reading the earlier chain. Every cache number, all the half-finished theories, it was all a pattern she didn't want to see. The way the dates stack, the way he didn't offer information but was quick to pull it from her.

She exhales and opens a new message, but not to Mark. She finds Vance in her contact list: *Rimrock Lake. That's where this goes next. I can't explain it all in a text, but you'll see it if you watch the cache listings. He's using the site to move us. I'll be ahead of you. Please don't try to stop me.*

She hesitates, then adds one more line: *I'm not running from you.*

She sends it before she can rethink it, figuring this is the third stupid thing she's going to pay for today. Maybe Mark was right, maybe she is stupid.

Rimrock Lake isn't nearby, and she knows that. She pulls back onto the road, angling toward I-5 after the 205 merge, then north toward Rimrock Lake. She knows it is the right way out of Vancouver, and the first step in a drive that will take hours, if she isn't caught first. What she doesn't know is how much time she's already lost, or what she's driving toward.

Chapter 32: Multi-Cache

By the time Erin reaches Rimrock Lake, the caffeine has stopped working and the adrenaline has died, leaving her with little more than doubts and the realization she has no good way out of any of this. She pulls off Highway 12 near the small store and boat launch on the north side of the lake. The store is closed, its windows are dark and a large sign says something about Friday. The empty lot tells her the recreationists are gone until the weekend. She brings her car to a stop just before the vacant boat ramp.

She looks out through the windshield. Rimrock Lake stretches long and dark beside the road, steel-blue under a washed-out sky. Pines crowd the shoreline. She checks the cache page again, already knowing what it says.

New cache published. 11:25 a.m.

Multi-cache.

Cache owner: Jackalope

Reviewer: Surveyor

She could read it for the first time or a dozen, but each time, her heart speeds up. This isn't OverlookLaneCrew. Jackalope isn't hiding behind a group handle this time, he's standing out in the open, watching to see who shows up. The timing is wrong as well. He posts at 5:14 and always has, so why daylight, why now? Why is she looking for sorrow at three in the afternoon?

She locks her phone and sits a second longer, counting her breaths, aware of how much ground she's already covered today and how much is still ahead of her. She steps out of the car. The air is colder than she anticipated, lake-fed and sharp. She pulls her jacket tighter and looks east, following the faint bend of shoreline where the map pin sits just offshore. A small island breaks the surface of the water there, barely more than a rocky outcrop, but much larger than the Under the Line cache. The map even has a name for it, *Island Chair*.

Erin unlocks her phone again, giving her thumb a moment to hover before scrolling the cache page. She tells herself she's checking details, the distance, even terrain. What she's really doing is bracing for what lies ahead.

The cache description is clean and almost polite. Jackalope gives enough information to move, but not enough to feel safe doing it: *This is a multi-stage cache. Terrain and conditions matter, prepare accordingly.*

That line could have come from any responsible cache owner. The next sentence is what stabs her nerves: *Truth can only be found by moving forward.*

The OverlookLaneCrew caches were mostly void of information beyond the basics. This cache description is almost a riddle by itself, and it gives Erin a moment of pause to wonder about the legitimacy. Except that Mark actually told her to stay away. She scrolls further: *This cache is not about speed, it is about arrival. Speed gets attention. Arrival decides what you keep.*

The last line sits alone, separated from the rest by a blank space, to be witnessed without distraction: *Take care where you stand.*

Jackalope isn't hiding instructions in coordinates or ciphers anymore. He's speaking plainly, trusting that the people who matter will hear what's underneath. She takes a screenshot of the cache description and opens a message to Vance, attaching the picture: *North side of Rimrock on Highway 12. Look for Island Chair.*

She looks up from her phone to the island. From this angle it looks insignificant, something you could dismiss if you weren't looking for it. Her family has passed by it many times over the years, always on their way somewhere else, but never stopping. She remembers when they were kids, Danny once said he wanted to go to the small island. He joked that he would conquer it and make it his own private country.

Jackalope didn't choose this place for the view, he chose it because it makes people commit before they understand what they've agreed to. She climbs back into her car and closes the door, knowing if she tried to reach it from here, she would need a boat. This is the part of 'prepare accordingly' Jackalope meant. The parking pin is listed for this boat ramp, but the real first step must be closer.

She travels east out of the lot and parks farther down the road where the shoulder widens just enough to pull over without obstructing traffic. This is the closest she can get by car, so she gets out and surveys the island, the road, and even the trees behind her. There's no sign of life, except for one vehicle on the far side of the lot which seems strangely familiar, though she can't place it.

Erin opens the trunk and the smell of old leaves and damp nylon rises up, reminding her of the simpler times when this was still a game. This part she knows how to do, readying herself for a geocache, the preparation is part of her muscle memory. It gives her hands something useful to focus on. She checks the pack, finding her rope, the multitool her dad gave her, a first-aid kit, and an extra change of clothes in a plastic grocery bag, which is a small relief she takes. The water is going to be cold and if this is the first stop, she's got a long evening ahead.

She digs deeper and at the bottom of the pack is Danny's knife, resting where she put it after her last outing. She doesn't take it out, just seeing the shape is enough to bring her back to the way he used to flip it in his hand like it was nothing, grinning when their mom told him to stop. He'd said it made him feel prepared, like he could handle whatever showed up. She presses her thumb lightly against the hilt and whispers, "I know."

Erin closes the pack with a soft zip and slings it over one shoulder, feeling the familiar pull settle against her back. She locks the car and walks toward the lake, stopping at the top of the ridge where the ground drops away more sharply than it looked from the road. It isn't far, maybe twenty feet, but far enough to break something if she slips. There's no trail, no helpful rut between bushes, just loose dirt, pine needles, and rock that shifts under her weight when she tests the ledge with the toe of her boot.

Erin knows if she hesitates any longer, she will talk herself out of it. She turns sideways and starts down, half-sliding with one hand out for balance and the other holding trunks and exposed roots as she goes. Dirt crumbles beneath her boots and she drops the last few feet hard, catching herself on one knee. The impact jars up through her leg and settles into a dull ache she knows is going to give her problems later.

At the bottom, the shoreline is narrow and uneven without a sandy beach, just water lapping quietly against stone. She shrugs off her pack and sets it down above the waterline, then pulls off her boots and socks, tucking them against a rock where they won't float away, then drops her phone in her right boot. The ground is cold against her bare feet and grit sticks to her skin. The lake looks calm from a distance, but up close, it tells a different story.

She steps in and the cold grips her enough to steal her breath. The shock climbs to her chest and for a second her body rebels, locking her muscles.

"Okay," she mutters, forcing the word out through clenched teeth.

She wades deeper and the water rises to her knees, then her waist. Her feet will soon lose connection, so she pushes off before she chooses to turn around. The water closes over her, and the cold becomes a full body burn that demands all of her attention. She kicks and strokes, keeping her head up, reminding herself to keep moving.

Dead Coordinates

The island doesn't seem to get any closer until she's found solid ground again. The dark line of rock rises out of the water, steeper and less forgiving than it looked from the shore. She scrapes her palms against stone as she reaches for it, fingers slipping on slick rocks before they find purchase. Her knee bangs hard against the rock and she hisses, hauling herself up out of the water. A swelling of blood mixes with the water on her leg, thinning it immediately.

Erin stays crouched, hands braced on the rock, chest heaving as the cold settles deeper. She rubs her arms and legs, encouraging her blood to flow again and finding warmth in the friction. Behind her, the shoreline already looks farther away than it should, and she realizes she isn't even half done with this stage.

The island is smaller than it looked from shore. Once she's up on it, there's nowhere to go but up. It's just stone and sky and the sound of her own breathing. She straightens slowly, muscles protesting from the cold, and begins to climb the earthy tower. The surface for each foothold is slanted in places where erosion has chewed at it over the years. Lichen slicks the stone in pale patches. She tests each step before trusting it. Erin climbs the solid stone to the top of the rock outcropping.

Near the center of the flat of the island top sits an abandoned bench, its wood bleached and worn smooth by years of sun and rain, and one leg is braced with a flat stone someone shoved underneath to keep it from tipping. The grain of the seat is split and silvered from exposure. Beside the bench, a twisted pine leans toward the water, its roots gripping at cracks in the rock, refusing to let go. Its needles whisper in the breeze.

Erin turns in a slow circle, scanning the island for any evidence of human contamination on this natural formation other than the bench. There is no obvious container and no fake rocks, nothing that stands out. The bench is made of simple wood with no place for a hidden compartment and nothing fastened to it. Jackalope wouldn't be obvious anyway. She lets the moment stretch, feeling the false calm press in, thick and tempting. This would be the place to sit down and catch her breath, to pretend this is just another find, another box tucked somewhere clever, but she doesn't.

Instead, she moves toward the tree, following the lines where root meets stone, where its shadow gathers before falling off the precipice. Her fingers trail along the rock face until they catch on metal, cool and solid beneath a thin film of moisture. Half-hidden behind the pine, wedged into a natural pocket in the rock on the cliff face, sits the hide. It is fitted carefully where the stone curves inward. She stops, letting the tree steady her as she looks down. The fall wouldn't be far, maybe twenty feet, but the landing on the jagged rocks below could be fatal.

She crouches, wrapping one leg around the small tree, and pulls the container free with both hands. The ammo can has more weight to it than she expected. She brings it to the flat, and the latch gives with a soft click that echoes across the lake. The logbook is damp, not soaked or ruined, but just enough to wrinkle the paper beneath her fingers when she opens the cover. A newly placed cache with a proper seal shouldn't be like this. It should be dry, clean, pristine. This one already feels used.

The book is blank except for one line on the first page. *TrailWolf*. His signature sits near the top of the page, neat and unmistakable. He's already been here and he didn't just tag and go, he was here long enough to leave a clean mark and close the book properly afterward. Long enough to breathe the same air.

Erin is not surprised, not really. Still, seeing his handle here collapses distance in a way that pulls this hunt tighter, she isn't the only prey anymore. She looks out toward the boat dock, at the lone vehicle in the lot.

Beneath the logbook are two laminated cards, placed in a small tray. Her name, not her geocache user ID, is printed across the top one. The sight of it sends a small, sharp pulse through her chest. This isn't a message meant to be shared or misunderstood, this is for her alone. Jackalope isn't speaking to the community anymore, he's narrowed his audience.

The message is short and controlled. It doesn't threaten, it simply explains, leaving her to supply the rest herself: *Follow the high ground. Don't take the easy descent. Some mistakes only happen when someone looks for the shortcut. Next coordinates:* ***46.655214, -121.167111***

Erin reads it again, slower, feeling the weight of what isn't said. The phrasing isn't instructional so much as corrective. Jackalope isn't telling her what to do, he's telling her what not to repeat.

Her hands tremble as she lifts the second card to reveal Mark's name printed the same way with the same coordinates. The message beneath it is shorter, stranger: *You always arrive when it's already happening. This time, decide what you do when you get there.*

She knows there were three cards and that TrailWolf's card is gone. The implication of the named cards presses in, quiet and suffocating. This wasn't a general cache, and it wasn't meant for whoever randomly showed up first. It was selectively published, assigned to three pawns, and distributed in a specific order.

All that's left in the cache are three heavy stones that don't look native to this lake, transplants from another place and another time. Stones that might have pulled an eager cacher over the cliff while extracting the container.

She repeats the coordinates aloud, lodging them into memory. Her hands shake as she slides her card back into place next to Mark's. Every instinct tells her to take the cache, to keep the evidence. She should break the rules and take it with her, but she did that once with the mirror shard. This time, she does what the game demands. She closes the container, reseats it exactly where she found it, and presses it back into the curve of the rock until it sits flush and hidden again. Erin stands, muscles stiff, and takes one last look across the water. From here the shoreline feels unreal. The car is a dark shape tucked against the trees, farther than it should be.

She climbs down the rocks and lowers herself into the water. The second entry is worse, her body recoils and her breath leaves her as the cold clamps down again, more insistent than before. She forces herself forward, her strokes shorter now and less graceful. Every movement sends a dull ache through her shoulders and thighs.

Halfway back, her arms start to burn, the deeper kind that comes with cold and fatigue. She keeps her eyes on the shore, counting strokes to keep her focus on anything other than the pain.

When her feet finally meet stone, relief hits so hard it almost buckles her. She stumbles out of the water and up onto the narrow strip of shore. She braces her hands on her knees as she sucks in air. She peels her waterlogged clothes off, flinching against the breeze. Her fingers are clumsy as she unties the plastic bag from her pack. She pulls on dry clothes, still so numb and shaky that she fumbles the zipper twice before it catches.

While she waits for the blood to return to her toes, she unlocks her phone and opens her text chain with Vance again. The detective hasn't responded, or her first message never went through. She types a new message: *Do not go to Island Chair, this is a multi, the initial cache is a distraction. Track my phone.* She pauses, then types the coordinates for the second cache to be safe.

She shoulders her pack and starts up the embankment without looking back. The climb is more stubborn than the descent. Her boots slip in loose dirt and rocks and her legs tremble as she hauls herself up by exposed roots and low hanging branches. By the time she crests the ridge, her pulse is loud in her ears, each beat sounding like a gunshot. Highway 12 is empty, which is no surprise for this time of day.

Leaning against her trunk, she pulls out her phone and loads the map. The coordinates for the second stage aren't near a road, they never were. They sit north of her, high on the hill, buried in elevation and effort. The forest hugs tight on the far side of the road. Jackalope won't wait for indecision, and neither will she. Erin leaves her car behind and cuts across the road without a glance over her shoulder, entering the tree line.

That's when she hears an engine, distant and indistinct. Then it sharpens, growing louder and faster, unmistakably real. Erin drops low on instinct and peers through branches toward the road. Mark's truck tears past the turnout, aimed straight for her car. She doesn't have time to wait and doesn't have the patience to see him. Instead, she climbs.

Light drops away within a few steps, the canopy is thick enough to swallow the sky overhead. Needles cushion her footfalls, soft but uneven, hiding rocks and roots that catch at her stride when she moves too fast. She adjusts, shortening her pace and letting speed come from consistency.

Part way up the hill, she checks the coordinates once, commits them to memory, then locks the phone and stows it. The hill rises ahead of her, long and patient, challenging her still shivering body and forcing her lungs. TrailWolf took this route as well. The signs are here, a broken fern, mud scraped thin over stone, his momentum is leaving marks.

Behind her, the sound of the road fades, there is no engine now, only wind moving through branches and the quiet, persistent sound of her own movement. Mark will find the island. He'll see the bench. He'll understand enough to follow. TrailWolf is already ahead, carrying the card he took from that container and anything else he didn't want anyone to see.

Erin doesn't slow. She doesn't stop to reassess or second-guess the angle of the climb. Jackalope planned for all of it, and the rules are clear now, even if the reasons aren't. Forward is the only option he's left her. Waiting would be a choice too, and she knows better than to pretend otherwise. As the ground steepens and the trees thin, she feels the structure tighten around her, not quite a trap but a narrowing corridor, with few exits and fewer excuses.

She moves faster. The second stage waits ahead, while behind her the past is catching up, and between the two, Erin makes the only decision that still belongs to her. She keeps going.

Chapter 33: Waypoint

The ground steepens, but Erin doesn't slow, she adjusts, shortening her stride and leaning forward until the slope dictates her posture. The forest closes around her, as the fir and pine crowd together, their lower branches clawing at her pack, testing what she's willing to lose. The trail, if it was ever meant to be one, thins into a natural formation, loosely created by old runoff scars and animal tracks.

Her lungs burn from climbing without rest. She tastes iron at the back of her throat and forces herself to slow her breathing, counting steps. She knows she can't keep stubbornly pushing, so she develops a pattern, eight up, pausing before eight more. The terrain demands her attention as loose rocks shift underfoot, rolling treacherously toward the drop she just climbed from. Roots snake across the ground, ready to twist her ankle.

On the second crest, she checks the coordinates again without stopping, giving her a chance to slow while still making progress. The arrow pulls her higher, angling away from the lake, which is good. High ground was Jackalope's instruction, not the goal. The sound of movement carries through the trees behind her, still farther back but steady. Mark is climbing now, disturbing the forest in a way that tells Erin he's focused on the end game, not the rules. She doesn't look back, doing that would slow her further, and time is already bleeding away.

She veers off the faint track and cuts left, following a contour line instead of the straightest ascent, making her slower up the slope but providing reprieve for her legs. Danny taught her that once, years ago, laughing as she cursed him for dragging her off what looked like a perfectly good trail. "Trails are for people who don't want to think," he'd said. "This is easier for people who pay attention."

Her calf cramps and she stumbles, catching herself on a tree, bark scraping her palm. She swears under her breath, shakes the leg, flexing her toes to the sky as she moves. She has to work through it, stopping isn't an option.

The forest shifts again, thinning to reveal a rock outcrop ahead, holding back the trees around it. The coordinates for the second stage settle, near the center of the clearing. Erin slows at last, feeling the ease of flatter land and knowing stage two won't announce itself. Jackalope wouldn't allow something that simple. She wipes sweat from her eyes, steadies her breathing, and steps into the clearing, already knowing the next instruction will cost her.

The rock formation doesn't tower like the Island Chair landscape, it's a low, jagged rise, fractured where it tried to split before anyone ever stepped foot in this forest. Moss coats the north-facing side in thick, dark patches, while rainwater has carved shallow grooves down its face. Erin circles it once, slow and deliberate, eyes scanning for what doesn't belong or what can be moved. She doesn't touch anything yet.

Jackalope prefers misdirection, and Erin knows if there's an obvious hiding place, it's there to make her commit too early. She crouches and checks the GPS again. The arrow jitters before settling, pointing her closer to the rock's eastern edge where the ground drops away into a narrow ravine choked with ferns and fallen branches. Of course it's there.

She eases down the slope on her heels, grabbing saplings to control her descent. The ravine is ripe with the heady scent of wet earth and damp moss. Sound changes here too, swallowed and reshaped through the landscape. Every movement feels amplified and muted at the same time. At the base of the rock, next to a slab that looks like it fell from above and slid into place naturally, she finds an old metal survey marker stamped with numbers she doesn't recognize, and a triangle etched at its center. Someone has cleared the moss from it recently and the scrape marks are fresh.

She stares at it, wondering if she's focusing on the wrong thing, if this is a distraction to keep her from a container. Erin kneels, presses two fingers to the marker, and waits, but nothing happens. She looks up at the fallen slab and notices the carving in the side of the long stone, shallow, but deliberate. The letters have been cut with patience.

WAIT HERE.

Below it, smaller but just as precise, is another carving.

DO NOT PASS ALONE.

She straightens and looks back up the slope she came down. Ahead of her, the ravine narrows, the ground rising again toward whatever comes next. For the first time since she left the island, Erin doesn't move forward. She shifts her weight, easing the strain in her calves without taking her fingers off the marker. The ravine feels tighter the longer she stands there, and the treetops lean in just enough to make her feel closed in. She checks her phone again, not for cache details, but for acknowledgment from Detective Vance. There's still nothing. She lets out a deflated sigh, but types anyway: *Please tell me you're getting my texts. I'm high above the lake. No road access.*

Sound carries down the ravine, something is moving through the vegetation, pushing through brush. The movement is fast without caring how loud it is. Erin knows it isn't an animal, at least not a wild one. Mark is careless, but he's not cocksure, not that blatantly. It can't be Jackalope, he's worked too hard to build this orchestra to have it ruined, cut short before the crescendo. It's TrailWolf, it has to be. He is advancing in a straight line and stubborn, exactly the way he always does. His movement echoes his bravado.

Erin steps back from the marker and climbs just far enough up the slope to be seen without causing alarm. When TrailWolf breaks through the trees, he looks grizzled. His jacket is unzipped, his breath is ragged, and his eyes are bright with a primal burn. He sees her and stops short, his hands clench at his sides, but all he does is glare. "You waited," he says, almost accusing.

She nods once. "You didn't."

His mouth twitches. "Why would I?"

Erin glances past him, down the path he came from. "You took your card."

His eyes flicker for just a second. "Yeah," he says. "So what? I know where this goes."

"No," Erin says quietly. "You know where you go."

He shifts, agitated, boots scraping against stone. "He's fucking with us. You know that, right?"

"I know," she says. "That's why we're still here."

"No, it's why you're still here." He clenches and unclenches his hands, tensing like he's ready to pounce. "Chasing danger, but acting like a victim. It's what you do."

She sees his anger building and braces herself, but before she can state her case, another sound filters through the trees, this time with a different cadence. The footsteps are lighter and more metered. Erin feels relief that Mark is nearly here. TrailWolf hears it too and his shoulders tense. "Let's just finish this thing, we don't need him."

"We do," Erin says, her tone firmer now, shielding her fear of being alone with TrailWolf. "That's the rule. It's the only way this doesn't end badly."

"You think there's a happy ending in any of this?" He looks at the marker and the carved warning above it. His chest puffs, anger flaring hot and familiar. "Fine, wait for your knight in shining armor. I'm not standing around while…"

"While what?" Erin cuts in. "While the system this psychopath designed actually works? You that eager to run to your death?"

The footsteps draw closer and Mark emerges into view, breathless with sweat darkening the collar of his shirt. Relief flashes across his face when he sees Erin, then confusion when he takes in TrailWolf beside her. The marker between them pinpoints some invisible tension line drawn in the dirt. "What is this?" Mark asks.

Erin steps back toward the survey marker, placing herself deliberately between them. "Stage two," she says. "And it doesn't open unless all three of us are standing here."

Silence settles, thick and uneasy, as the trio wait for someone to move first. Above them, the mountain continues upward. Jackalope isn't rushing them, he's letting the weight of decision settle. Erin now understands the cold and precise nature of Jackalope's game. He isn't testing their endurance, he's squeezing them together, with no way out except forward.

The ravine holds them in place while the stone and earth form a narrow bowl that refuses to let sound escape. Erin can feel the pressure of it in her chest, the sense that whatever gets said here won't stay contained. Jackalope designed this part carefully, the test that forces them forward together or to give the pressure pot of emotions the chance to blow.

Mark breaks the stalemate first. "You didn't call me, you didn't wait," he says to Erin, his eyes filled with a mix of anger and hurt. "You could've gotten hurt."

"I did get hurt," she says. "That's not new."

TrailWolf snorts. "You say that like it's a badge."

Erin turns to him. "And you laugh like pain is optional, but you keep distant from everyone, which tells me you know different."

TrailWolf's mouth opens, then shuts. He finally looks away from her, scanning the slope above them. He mutters quiet enough it would normally go unheard, but the bowl echoes his words, "You're one to talk, bitch."

Mark shifts his weight, uncomfortable but not ready to prove he's always ready to protect Erin. "Whoa, tone it down. We can deal with the problem between you two after this is over. What does the marker say?"

TrailWolf mutters again, loud enough to be heard clearly this time, "Assuming there is an after."

Erin doesn't acknowledge the statement, and she doesn't answer Mark right away. She steps closer to the marker, brushing loose dirt from the stone around it, finding more carved letters. The revealed words are shallow but fresh.

THE PATH OPENS WHEN IT IS TIME.

"It didn't give directions," she says finally. "Not really."

TrailWolf laughs, sharp and humorless. "Of course it didn't."

Mark looks between them. "My card did."

Erin's head snaps up. "What? No it didn't."

Mark hesitates, then pulls a folded laminate card from his pocket. He doesn't offer it, he just holds it up so they can see. Then he turns it over, flashing the back side to them where the note is handwritten. "It says I'm going to arrive when things are happening," he says. "And that I need to decide what to do when I get there."

TrailWolf stiffens. "That's it?"

Mark nods. "And the same coordinates I'm guessing you had."

Erin feels the game growing tighter and more compartmentalized than before. Jackalope is splitting the information just enough to keep them off-balance, providing three cards with three different instructions, and none of them are complete on their own.

TrailWolf's voice drops. "Mine said not to stop."

Of course it did. She doesn't ask to see his card, she doesn't need to. She can already hear the cadence of it in her head, the way Jackalope would phrase it, pushing TrailWolf forward while punishing him for the very instinct at the same time.

"So what," TrailWolf says, tension snapping tight in his shoulders. "We just stand here until he decides we're worthy?"

"No," Mark says. "We stand here until we're together." He looks up the trail, then back down at the ravine, calculating distances.

TrailWolf almost looks afraid. "And if we don't?"

Erin meets his gaze. "Then we never find the next stage."

The wind shifts, carrying the smell of wet pine and stone. The path before them remains hidden, nearly absent. Jackalope isn't forcing them forward, he's daring them to rush, and for once, TrailWolf doesn't. Minutes stretch in the ravine, long enough for Erin's legs to cool and her breath to slow, long enough for the quiet to start chewing at the edges of her thoughts. Both watch Mark, waiting for him to fulfill his part of the game, growing impatient while he scrutinizes the landscape.

The world hasn't stopped and TrailWolf can't stand it. He paces the narrow strip of ground, boots settling in the scree around the settled stone slab. Every few steps, he glances uphill opposite Mark, ready to continue on his own. Erin notices the signs without comment, watching his hands continuing to flex and the way his weight stays pitched forward, already halfway gone. "This is bullshit," he mutters. "He told me not to stop."

"If he did," Erin states, "It was for a reason, but that reason might not apply to this stage. You should just try being patient."

TrailWolf rounds on her. "You don't get to decide what I do."

"No," she says evenly. "But I do get to see the patterns."

Mark steps between them before it can sharpen further. "Look," he says, keeping his voice steady. "If this thing's designed to make us screw it up, fighting isn't helping."

TrailWolf laughs under his breath. "Cute that you say that right before everything goes to hell."

Mark gives TrailWolf a stern glare, but doesn't rise to his words.

He crouches instead, studying the marker again, then the stone above it. His eyes narrow. "This isn't just a stage," he says. "It's a gate."

TrailWolf stops pacing. "So what. We hold hands and chant kumbaya?"

"No," Erin says. She steps forward, stopping just short of the marker. "We acknowledge it."

Mark looks at her. "Acknowledge what?"

"That none of us gets to do this alone," she says. "Not this part."

TrailWolf's mouth twists. "Says who?"

"Jackalope," Erin replies sharply. "He's already proven what happens when people don't listen."

For a moment, Erin thinks TrailWolf is going to bolt anyway, she can almost see it in his shoulders. He's used to solving problems by moving faster than the consequences. She waits, watching until he exhales, long and rough. "Fine," he says. "But if this gets me killed, I'm haunting both of you."

Mark almost smiles. Erin looks down at Mark, at the marker. "LostMarker." She chuckles dryly.

Mark looks up at her when she recites his geocache handle. "What?"

She shakes her head, responding more to her revelation than his question. "It's so obvious it's stupid. That's why you're the key to the second stage."

The marker sits flush with the stone, a dull metal disk no bigger than a coin, stamped and half-worn by weather. Erin steps onto it without ceremony and brings up her compass. The needle wobbles, giving enough movement to make the reading unreliable. She frowns and steps back, trying again and getting the same result. "That's odd." She says, "My needle goes batshit when I step on the marker."

"Big deal, you have bad reception," TrailWolf says immediately. He doesn't bother looking at her compass. He's already moving downslope, putting distance between himself and the other two.

"We're in a shit location for phone GPS."

Mark checks his own reading, then walks a few yards away. "Mine's steady," he says, then hesitates. "No, wait. It just jumped."

Erin adjusts her position and takes another bearing which is worse. TrailWolf drags his own compass out, ready to show them proper usage, but stops and watches the needle on his own compass jolt.

They spread out, each chasing a version of certainty that only makes sense to them alone. TrailWolf circles wide, maneuvering the loose stone. "This is a waste of time," he snaps, pointing straight up the mountain. "I bet you money, if we just head up the hill, we could find the next stage."

Mark crouches, recalibrates, and shakes his head. "The needle shouldn't be this jumpy."

Erin steps back again, looking at her phone. TrailWolf stops moving out of irritation and his feet plant on a flatter patch of ground. Mark straightens slowly, tired of chasing stability. Erin lifts the compass without thinking and the needle settles true. She freezes. For a second she says nothing, afraid the moment will pass if she says anything. "Don't move," she says finally, quiet but sharp. They don't except for TrailWolf's head roll.

She checks the bearing again and it gives the same reading. She points west, "I'm steady that way."

TrailWolf and Mark both check their compasses and all three needles match. Erin looks at the survey marker between them, at the triangle stamped in metal. TrailWolf's impatience took him to one point, while Mark's uncertainty stopped him at another. Erin is standing at the top, finding the right spot through determination. Jackalope didn't hide a cache, he positioned direction through triangulation. Erin lowers the compass, impressed by the ingenuity, and momentarily forgetting Jackalope is a murderer. "That's it," she says. "That's the way to the next stage."

TrailWolf looks up the mountain in the direction he was sure was the answer, then west where all three compass needles point, his anger simmering. Mark looks annoyed as well. Erin realizes this should have been his path to unlock and he's probably beating himself internally for missing his chance. For a moment, none of them move.

TrailWolf lets out a short, humorless breath. "That's bullshit," he says, quietly looking down at the marker. "Standing still shouldn't fix anything."

"It didn't," Mark says. His voice comes out rougher than he means it to. He straightens slowly. "It just showed us that none of us could have done it alone."

TrailWolf scoffs. "Speak for yourself."

Erin doesn't speak. She watches the space between them, the marker, the stones, the way none of them are standing where they wanted to be. The rule has locked into place in her head and she doesn't like it. "He boxed us in," she says finally. "That's all. He was just testing to see if we could come together or if we would let the rules break us."

TrailWolf shoots her a look. "You always got an explanation ready?"

She meets his eyes without blinking. "You always in a hurry to be wrong?"

Mark shifts between them, tension crawling up his spine. "Dammit! Can we not do this here?" He gestures vaguely at the slope ahead. "There's a killer planning god knows what, and you two are bickering like children."

Both Erin and TrailWolf cast angry stares at Mark, but they both know he's not wrong. Ahead, the land pinches into a narrow traverse, steep and exposed. The path only looks reasonable from the new perspective. Erin adjusts the strap of her pack. "Fine, let's go," she says, then continues when she walks by him, "For the record, I hate that you're right."

TrailWolf hesitates just long enough to make it clear he agrees with her, possibly for the first time ever. When he moves, he steps forward hard, boots biting into the dirt. Mark lets out an exasperated breath and follows, frustrated that even when he's the first to act, it still feels like the wrong move.

"Make way for greatness." TrailWolf pushes ahead, cutting Erin off before the incline. She sighs but lets his ego take lead. The reluctant trio climb out of the ravine, each knowing that Jackalope didn't unite them, he simply brought them together tight enough to hurt each other if they stop.

The traverse narrows as they move, the slope dropping away hard on one side and climbing steeply on the other. It isn't a trail so much as a lack of viable options. Erin keeps her weight low, testing each step before she commits, and she hears loose dirt shift under Mark's feet behind her. Ahead, TrailWolf moves fast and recklessly, letting his anger drive him forward.

"Slow down," Mark calls.

TrailWolf doesn't answer, but he reaches a point where an enormous stone taller than the hikers juts out across the path, making him stop anyway. The path thins to a width barely wider than his boot. He plants one hand against the rock, sizing it up. Erin catches up, then Mark. The drop is clean and immediate with no trees to break a fall. The only thing between this reluctant trio and the bottom of the ravine is steep slope and nearly a hundred feet of mountain air.

"This is it?" TrailWolf mutters. "This can't be right. What now, we play rock, paper, scissors to see who jumps and who lives?"

Erin studies the rock face and the angle of its ledge. The ground ahead curves out of sight. She pulls out her compass again, then the card. The words sit there, patient as ever: *Follow the high ground. Don't take the easy descent.*

She looks down at the easy way. Trying to descend looks like the best option, but the sheer cliff on the far side would be impossible to climb back up without gear. That's the mistake. She looks back up at the face above the path and sees it now, faint but real. There's a line of lighter stone where boots have scraped before. The ghost of a path was not meant to be rushed. "We go across," she says.

TrailWolf turns on her. "Across where?"

"There," Mark says, following her gaze and pointing. His voice wavers, then steadies. "See it? We aren't the first ones to try this path."

TrailWolf stares, jaw working. He hates that Mark saw it before him, and hates even more that Erin is already on the move.

"Great," he snaps. "By all means, ladies first. It wouldn't break my heart if you fell."

Erin grunts, but she doesn't respond. She climbs the goat path above TrailWolf, close enough that if either of them slips, neither is walking away. He stiffens, knowing he can't give ground without losing it entirely. His heels press harder into the path, causing the earth to shift beneath him, and he finds purchase by grabbing her leg. For a moment they are locked there, waiting for the ledge to decide whether they can move or if their only way is down. Erin feels the heat of his anger, the question of whether he might pull her down just to prove he can. She meets his eyes, not challenging, but not yielding. For a heartbeat, Erin waits for it, knowing exactly how little effort it would take, but it doesn't come.

She moves slow and precise, forcing him to hold still while she eases past. Her knee brushes his chest and he holds himself rigid, every instinct screaming to reclaim control. When she's clear of his hand, she is shaking, but she's nearly reached the top of the rock.

Behind her, Mark swallows and begins to follow. TrailWolf stops him with an outstretched finger. "Slow your role, boyscout."

He finds leverage on the rocky face behind Erin. "One person at a time and I'm already maxed out on unwanted intimacy for the day."

TrailWolf begins his ascent and Mark waits a moment longer than necessary before climbing. Halfway up, a stone shifts under Erin's foot, stealing her balance. Her stomach lurches and she presses her body against the boulder, knocking the breath from her. Mark freezes and TrailWolf curses as earth slides by him. He reaches up and steadies her foot, giving her enough stability to push off.

They move with new care now, closer than before, each step negotiated by silence and proximity. When they reach the far side, the ground widens just enough to breathe again. Erin straightens slowly, legs shaking. She looks to TrailWolf with an appreciative nod. He rolls his eyes but returns the gesture.

She checks the compass once more, then looks ahead. The route bends upward into thicker trees, climbing into higher and less forgiving terrain.

Chapter 34: Final Coordinates

The three unwilling geocachers step out of the trees onto a broad shelf of exposed stone. Behind them, the forest closes into a wall of fir and cedar. Ahead, the mossy carpet of the forest floor gives way to cracked slabs and wide stretches of bare rock. The shelf runs flat long enough to feel almost safe, until Erin sees where it ends.

The wind is colder up here. Cleaner, carrying the sharp mineral smell of exposed rock and old rain. Miles of mountain stretch out ahead with ridgelines layered into the distance, unbroken by roads, cabins, or power lines. There are no signs of civilization beyond the cliff as far as the eye can see. Her feet slow against the rock.

To the right, half-swallowed by scrub and the broken shoulder of the mountain, stands what remains of an abandoned mining structure. Old timbers, gray with age, lean around a narrow service opening cut into the mountain face, lasting longer than its usefulness.

Rusted hardware clings to the rock where a pulley system once stood. Bolts bite into stone, and a length of old cable hangs slack against the wall, orange with corrosion. Beyond it, a single plank platform extends out from the rock, suspended above the drop. Its boards are weathered thin and silvered by years of rain.

Erin stops cold. On the platform is a wooden chair, fixed in place with rope knotted carefully around the legs and seat, every line pulled tight with patient attention. A hooded figure sits in it, slumped forward with his wrists bound.

Mark gasps beside her, the sound loud enough to be heard over the wind. TrailWolf swears under his breath, "Goddamn."

A figure moves within the shadowed opening of the structure's service entry. Boots scrape against stone and a man steps out into the open, stopping where the waning light of late day washes over him. The head isn't human, but a grotesque rabbit with antlers sweeping back. The eyes are hollow and dark.

Erin thinks of CryptidQueen and her story. She spoke of the jackalope in a way that only makes sense now when she stands face to face with one. Jackalope prances forward three steps, then performs a flourish, ending with his arms stretched out wide. He stands, almost waiting for applause that never comes, then he lifts the mask off his head and stares into the face of the rabbit. "Symbols are only useful when they're precise," he says to the disembodied rabbit, then looks to Erin and the others. "Fear blurs understanding." He sets it on the ground. "We don't need to blur, today is for clarity."

He looks ordinary, much too plain for a man on a mountain ledge, for a murderer playing mind games. His sandy-blond hair is tussled from the mask, and his large brown-rimmed glasses look too large to have fit underneath the rabbit. His windbreaker looks like he picked it for function without regard to style. He could be the man standing in line behind her at a grocery store. He could be the man who nodded once and looked away at a trailhead.

He glances at his watch calm and casual. "5:10," he says. "You're early, I was worried the last stage would have been more of a struggle." He watches them, assessing each cacher. Jackalope smiles softly, pleased they arrived the way he planned. "This is good," he says. "That means we won't have to rush."

No one moves, stunned by Jackalope's theatrics. The wind keeps pushing at them, whispering through the exposed rock, carrying something more with it, a low rhythmic thump that rolls through the basin. The figure in the chair sways slightly from a gust and the plank support creaks where weight shifts. The hood is coarse fabric, pulled low and tied at the throat. Whoever it is isn't struggling, which should be a relief, but it isn't.

TrailWolf stares at the man in the chair and takes a half-step forward. Jackalope notices immediately. "Careful," he says with a mild suggestion. "That edge doesn't forgive enthusiasm."

TrailWolf stops and shifts his weight back onto his heels, but his eyes don't leave the chair. He scans the person instead, noticing his boots first. They are not hiking boots, those are logger boots, worn and muddied.

TrailWolf's hands curl into fists. "That's GhostLogger," he says. The words come out flat and certain.

Mark snaps his head toward him. "What?"

TrailWolf doesn't take his eyes off the large man in the chair. "Those boots. He wears the same damn pair year-round. Says breaking in a new set feels unnatural." He pauses, then his voice drops. "He always says he doesn't bother cleaning them because they'll be dirty again tomorrow."

Jackalope's smile widens just a fraction with approval. "You always did notice details," he says. "Selective, but thorough when it suited you."

Mark follows the line of rope, observing how it is placed to keep the body upright, to keep it facing the drop. There's a second line looped around the back rung of the chair and tied to a remnant of railing, tensioned just enough to prevent tipping. "Jesus," he mutters. "He's going to fall."

Jackalope turns his head, considering the chair. "Maybe," he says. "Imagine waking up like that, feeling the disorientation, the restraint of the ropes, the absolute helplessness. Can you imagine the utter confusion, knowing your center of gravity is already gone?" He gestures vaguely toward the void. "People panic when they wake up confused. Just think about how intense it will be when he sees the ground is over a hundred feet below."

Erin takes a cautious but daring step forward. "What's wrong with you?" she asks, her voice tight. "Let him go."

Jackalope finally looks directly at her. "No," he says, simply.

The word pierces her chest with stern finality. Erin holds his gaze. "What did he ever do to you," she says. "While we're at it, who the hell are you. I don't even know you."

Jackalope considers her, tilting his head slightly, like she's asked an interesting but unnecessary question. "You do though," he says. "You joined my song and continued dancing through it." He makes a pirouette to punctuate his statement.

TrailWolf shifts at the maneuver but doesn't advance, unsure which action would escalate the situation. His breathing is controlled, but only barely. "What do you want?" he asks. "Because this…" He jerks his chin toward the chair. "This isn't a game."

Jackalope's gaze slides back to the platform, to the hooded head tipped slightly forward. "On the contrary," he says. "This is the point where the game becomes honest."

Erin shakes her head once. "You want to talk about honesty," she says. "You pulled me into this. Why?"

His laugh is haunting. "Oh, you thought this was about you?" The humor drains from his face, leaving a cold stare. "You brought yourself to the table when you found Hidden Hollow. That cache was supposed to be for TrailWolf."

Erin and TrailWolf lock eyes, both looking for an answer neither has. Jackalope continues. "This would have all ended with that one cache if he was the first to find, I would have gotten everything I wanted that morning."

TrailWolf turns his attention to Jackalope with the shock of realization that Erin saved his life by beating him to the cache. Jackalope doesn't return the attention, keeping his solely on Erin. "I realized you belonged in this game when you kept moving, even when it would've been easier to stop. So no, this wasn't built for you," he pauses with a grin. "But look how deliciously you fit."

He takes a step closer to the chair, careful not to step onto the platform. He stays just out of reach with his hands still relaxed at his sides. "Nothing happens yet," he adds, almost kindly. "We're waiting."

"For what?" Mark asks.

Jackalope glances at his watch again. "For you," he says. "To decide where you stand."

Mark doesn't respond. The wind keeps worrying at the ropes, making the chair creak with small, irregular complaints.

"Which is it, hero? You don't get to stand on both sides of the fence anymore, which side has greener grass?" Jackalope waits with patience, his hands are loose in an open gesture. He isn't guarding the chair, he doesn't need to. Erin's stare turns to Mark, and the disbelief is only diminished by the sudden anger.

TrailWolf doesn't allow the moment to build. "This is bullshit," he snaps, voice filled with rumble. "You've got my friend tied up over there. You're a twisted bastard and I'm going to beat your ass."

Jackalope's head turns just enough to acknowledge TrailWolf's determined approach. He lifts a finger, pausing the man. "You're assuming the order of operations," he says. "That's been your problem from the start."

TrailWolf laughs, sharp and humorless. "You don't know a goddamn thing about me."

Jackalope's eyes drift to the chair, then snap back. "I know you left Evan because stopping was inconvenient," he says with deliberate measure. "I know you told yourself it wasn't your responsibility. And I know you kept walking. I know you saw him."

TrailWolf's face twists. "Saw who?"

"You don't even remember his name." Jackalope laughs once, thin and broken, without humor. "Of course you don't. He was just some kid on the trail. Something in the way. Something between you and the find."

TrailWolf shakes his head. "What the hell are you talking about?"

"Evan. Michael. Hale." Jackalope steps closer.

"My little brother." His mouth tightens around the words. "He loved this stupid game. He loved the maps, the coordinates, the little plastic treasures people left like promises. He wanted to study wildlife conservation. Fourteen years old, and he was already talking about field journals and habitat corridors and tracking migration patterns like he had the whole world waiting for him."

His hand trembles at his side. He closes them into fists, steeling against the wound. "He was going for The Big One that day."

TrailWolf's eyes grow wide. There, Jackalope sees it. "You remember now."

"No," TrailWolf snaps. "That's not how it happened."

Jackalope doesn't raise his voice. "You watched him go over. You heard him hit. You knew he was down there." Jackalope's composure fractures, just a hair. "And then you looked at your GPS."

TrailWolf backs up half a step. "I went for help."

"You went for the cache."

"No."

"You signed the log."

TrailWolf doesn't move and says nothing.

"You signed the log while my brother was dying in six inches of water." Jackalope's jaw works, muscle jumping beneath the skin. "Then you logged the warning like it was a fucking joke." He recites the log post, tasting each rotten word. "Trail's rough at times. Careful of your footing."

Jackalope's words hit like a shovel and TrailWolf surges forward on pure reflex. Mark grabs his arm, fingers digging in above the elbow. "Don't," he hisses. "We don't really know what's going on right now."

Jackalope looks at Mark with a devious grin. "Actually, you do Mark, don't you," he says more than asks. "Always standing close enough to feel useful, but far enough away to stay clean."

TrailWolf glares as he jerks against Mark's grip. "Get your hands off me."

Mark doesn't. His fingers tighten instead, grounding deeper. "Don't," he says again, but quieter this time, his eyes are almost pleading.

Jackalope lets the moment stretch, he doesn't look at the men locked in resistance. His attention drifts back to the chair, at the hooded head tipped toward the void. "Everyone thinks the worst part is the moment itself," he says. "It isn't, it's after. That's where the damage lives."

"No," TrailWolf snaps. "You don't get to play the victim in that cooked brain of yours. You weren't there. You don't know what happened."

"Evan asked me three times. Three times, because he wanted me there when he found it." Jackalope turns fully. His body tightens but his voice stays level. "I was an adult with a job, paying bills, with no time off. So no, I wasn't there when he slipped. I wasn't there when he hit the rock. But you were," he says. "Alive enough to be helped, but hurt enough to cost you time. You couldn't stomach that a boy could beat you to your precious find."

"That's not how it…"

"You can dress it up however you want. Panic, confusion, bad footing. You said you didn't know how bad it was. But all of that came after." Jackalope snarls. "You made your decision. Everything after that is just lies you tell yourself. Lies you tell others."

TrailWolf goes still, his breath moving sharp through his nose. Erin watches the two locked on each other and feels something cold settle in her chest. She's heard this kind of certainty before, what it sounds like when someone has replayed the same moment so many times it's worn until it lost all meaning except blame. TrailWolf pulls his arm from Mark's grasp but doesn't move.

Jackalope watches the action and slides his attention to Mark, just long enough to pin him. "You held my brother's corpse," he says quietly. "You arrived when there was nothing left to fix. You told my parents there was nothing you could do, and then you went back to work. All search, no rescue."

Mark's jaw locks, but he doesn't look away. "I tried…"

"For a moment, yes," Jackalope continues, "but my brother was gone. My family wasn't, though. You could have given me something, a little compassion. A hint of solace. No, you just went back to your life."

Mark swallows his guilt. "What was I supposed to do?"

"Stay. Not as a medic, but as a human. Consider their pain, our loss." Jackalope says. "You came to us months later when the shock had passed, when our pain finally found your guilt. I never blamed you for not saving him. I blamed you for surviving it."

Mark doesn't argue, he can't. Jackalope's gaze shifts between the men. "At least you showed up, LostMarker" he says the name with bitterness. "Sure, late and clumsy as always." His eyes settle on TrailWolf. "Even in your incompetence, you did more than this bloated worm."

TrailWolf surges again, a raw sound tearing out of him. Erin steps forward without thinking. "Stop," she yells, sharp. It cracks through the air, demanding attention. All three of them look at her.

"This isn't about Jackalope," Erin continues, forcing her voice steady. "Look at where we're standing. He's not guarding the chair. Have you both gotten so wrapped up in yourselves that GhostLogger doesn't even matter?"

Jackalope watches her now with open interest.

"If he wanted GhostLogger dead," she says, "He would be close enough to push him. He didn't just create this elaborate stage to judge us, he wants to put us in our place."

"What place?" Mark asks.

Jackalope answers him with a small gesture of two fingers

tracing the ground in front of the cachers. Erin follows it and sees how the ground tilts inward toward the platform. The route beside them narrows between scrub and the narrowing cliff's edge. Along the ground are three solid slabs of stone where footing holds, everywhere else is loose, threatening to slide. "You don't get to stand wherever you want," Jackalope says. "Gravity decides that. History does the rest."

TrailWolf looks down. His boots are already flirting with bad ground, and the direct path to his bound friend only gets worse. One wrong shift and the mountain will take the choice from him.

"You're a sick bastard," Mark mutters.

Jackalope nods once. "That's fair."

He steps back with open hands, giving them space they cannot use freely. "Nothing happens yet," he says. "But when it does, it will be because one of you decided where to put your weight."

The chair creaks again, and the rope complains. Erin's eyes stay on GhostLogger, the knots holding the chair, and the drop yawning beneath the platform. She sees his orchestration but no longer understands where she fits.

TrailWolf tests the ground in front of him. The rock slopes subtly toward the platform, toward the chair, and also toward the edge. His footing slips on loose stone, causing him to skid half a foot and sending rocks scattering off the edge. He adjusts again, slower this time, keeping his eyes locked on GhostLogger.

Erin scans the ridgeline beyond the platform, and the empty sky beyond. For a moment she thinks she imagined it. Then she sees it again, a speck far off and bright against the gray, moving toward the ledge. She exhales and her pulse steadies with resolve. She looks to Jackalope whose intention is microscopically focused on TrailWolf.

"Hey Jackasslope! If we get to GhostLogger," she says, voice cutting clean through the wind, "what's the insurance?"

TrailWolf freezes and Mark turns sharply toward her. Jackalope doesn't answer right away.

Erin ignores Mark's silent warning. "You've had this staged for a long time," she says. "Every step, every position, every inch of ground. You really expect us to believe the moment we touch him, this all just ends and we all get to skip off into the sunset, holding hands?"

Jackalope's eyes roll skyward, then back to her with a tightness in his expression.

"You're the one who set this trap," she continues. "So, if we all behave the way you want, do we get to walk away…" she gestures at the ravine below, knowing her words are making him boil, "…or did you just plan for it to collapse the second someone moves, so you can justify your pain?"

"That's enough," TrailWolf snaps without looking at her.

Jackalope is fully focused on Erin now. "You were supposed to understand," he says, tapping his chest over his heart. "Danny. That's why you're here. You were supposed to be better than these two buffoons."

Erin's eyes burn hot hearing her brother's name, Jackalope shouldn't know about him. She meets his gaze. "No," she says. "I'm here because you missed something."

Silence snaps tight. Jackalope takes a step toward her. "You think I didn't account for you?" he says. "For a variable? I built my life around this. I built Evan's memory around this. You are the one I expected who would see that. Danny would have seen it."

Erin tenses and Mark shifts closer to her. "Erin, don't. Please."

"Yes, Erin. I know about your brother, I know what happened. Once you entered this, I had to know what kept you moving toward danger," Jackalope continues, his eyes never leaving hers, "And now, after everything I've shown you, after offering to share my catharsis with you, you're denying me and you're standing there asking whether you're safe." His mouth curls into something dark.

"You're not."

Mark shoves off the rock and charges, shoulder down, his momentum carrying him straight at Jackalope.

"Mark!" Erin shouts.

Jackalope pivots on impact, catching Mark's forward motion and redirecting it hard into the rock face beside the platform. Bone cracks against stone. Jackalope drives an elbow down on Mark's spine while Mark slams Jackalope in the ribs with wild fists. Erin lunges, grabbing Mark's jacket, yanking him back before Jackalope can shove him over the ledge. Jackalope shoves her off with a violent shoulder check, sending her stumbling.

"Stay out of it!" Mark yells, already up and swinging again. Jackalope snarls now.

TrailWolf swears and surges forward, ignoring the fray, choosing GhostLogger, leaping from one stable slab to another. The chair jerks and the rope groans as TrailWolf crosses the platform in two strides. The fight behind him becomes noise, Mark's grunt of pain, Erin shouting his name, the scrape of boots on stone. None of it matters. His whole focus has narrowed into the chair.

"Hang on," he says, breath tearing out of him. "I've got you." He grabs the back rung, fingers burning as the rope vibrates beneath his grip. One board falls out from beneath the chair, and it swings enough to make his stomach drop faster than the wood below. He plants one boot on the edge of the platform, tests it, then reaches for the hood.

"Hey," he says, holding the supporting rope. "You're good. I'm here." The fabric is rough under his hands. He pulls and the hood comes away easily and GhostLogger's head lolls forward. His skin is gray, not cold from exposure. His mouth hangs open, jaw slack, and lips tinged blue. His eyes are half-lidded and vacant, unfocused and already starting to cloud. TrailWolf stares at the face he knows by a dozen campfires and a hundred trailheads. The man who argued about hides and terrain ratings. Who laughed loud and ate even louder, who trusted him without question.

"No," he whispers.

He presses two fingers to GhostLogger's neck, desperate, but already knowing. There is no warmth in the skin or pulse underneath. Behind him, the fight slams into the platform hard enough to make it shudder. Jackalope's voice cuts through the chaos, raw now. "He didn't wake up?" he shouts the mockery. "Saving him was never the goal!"

TrailWolf turns. Something inside him breaks loose, clean and total. "You killed him," he roars.

Jackalope turns at the sound of it, blood at his lip, breath heaving as he shoves Mark back with both hands. "He died hours ago. Alone!" he snaps. "Just like Evan did!"

Mark lunges again and Erin holds his jacket, slowing his wild momentum. He still lands a strike on Jackalope who stumbles a step, boots skidding close to the edge.

TrailWolf's vision tunnels while the wind screams in his ears. Evan's fall and Jackalope's accusation come roaring at him all at once. "You brought me here to feel what you felt," he snarls.

"Yes," Jackalope says through the grunts of Mark's attacks. "Now you finally understand."

TrailWolf, burning with pure rage, launches himself off the platform, sending two more pieces of wood to the earth below. He slams into Jackalope with everything he has, throwing wild fists and boots scraping for purchase on ground that hasn't held this many bodies in decades. Erin shouts his name and the collision turns feral.

TrailWolf hits Jackalope with all the fury and mass of his thrown weight, driving him sideways. Jackalope stumbles, grabbing blindly for balance from something that isn't there. The collision jolts through everyone, knocking Mark back and shoving Erin hard into the rock face, breath punched out of her as stone tears at her shoulder.

The two combatants slam each other, their feet flirting with the cliff's edge. Mark lunges to pull TrailWolf back, but he's too late. Jackalope twists, trying to regain footing, knocking Mark to the ground where the platform begins. The ground falls away without warning, causing old planks to groan and release as the dilapidated scaffolding collapses. Mark's heel slips on loose gravel and he windmills, arms flailing and eyes wide with sudden realization.

"Mark!" Erin's voice reaches him, but her grasp doesn't. He goes over backward, disappearing past the collapsed platform's edge. There's no scream, just an echo of the violent scrape of descending wood, followed by a series of cracks against the side of the cliff. Finally, the collapse is silent.

Erin skids to her knees at the edge, hands clawing uselessly in the air. She looks down and sees the distance, the wall of rock, and the endless drop swallowing him whole. His landing is abrupt, crumpling his body in a field of boulders and wood, not far from GhostLogger.

TrailWolf stares, chest heaving and shock draining the color from his face. Jackalope freezes as well, eyes tracking the empty space where Mark was. The mountain absorbs the loss without comment.

Jackalope pivots into the opening Mark's fall created and slams TrailWolf backward toward the edge. TrailWolf stumbles, boots skidding as he's shoved toward open air. Jackalope's grip is iron, fingers locked into fabric and muscle, driving TrailWolf exactly where the ground disappears.

TrailWolf freezes in recognition. Jackalope has him by the front of the jacket, one arm braced, their weight barely balanced. One more shift and gravity will take him to GhostLogger. Jackalope leans in close enough that only TrailWolf can hear him. "This is it," he says, breath ragged now, control finally fraying. "This is the part you pretend you don't remember. This is where you lie to me."

TrailWolf's head rolls back and he stares down at the void yawning beneath him. The mountain waits. "I didn't kill him," TrailWolf says hoarsely. "I didn't push him."

Jackalope's face tightens. Something ugly breaks through the calm. "Thank you," he snarls. "You made the same calculation you're making right now. You decided your footing mattered more than his life."

"That's not…"

"It is," Jackalope snaps, his voice cracking. "You looked down just like that. You saw it all and kept walking."

Erin can't breathe. She sees what Jackalope sees, clear as a knife edge. Evan at the bottom of a ravine with TrailWolf standing above him. She envisions his pause, the choice he makes, and the lie that comes later. She also sees what he doesn't, a helicopter in the distance angling toward the cliff.

TrailWolf doesn't fight back. His hands are open with fingers spread wide. His body is locked between survival and shame. Jackalope presses him closer to the edge, boots dragging, muscles shaking. "Say it," he demands. "Say you chose yourself."

TrailWolf's jaw works and his eyes burn. "I…" The word dies in his throat. This is the moment Jackalope built everything for. The mirror is being held up and the past is dragged screaming into the present.

Erin pulls her pack off, not fully understanding what she's doing until her hand is already inside, fingers ripping past nylon and fabric and memory. The knife is there, Danny's knife. Solid, familiar, and real.

Jackalope feels her approach and turns just enough to register surprise that she's broken the script. "Don't…" he starts.

She drives the blade in hard and low, using instinct over aim. Steel sinks into the left side of his chest, desperate and human.

Jackalope gasps, the sound is small and unimpressive. His grip loosens from TrailWolf's jacket as shock floods his face. Blood darkens his jacket, spreading fast. The broken plank beneath him buckles and he grabs TrailWolf's sleeve. Jackalope drops, pulling TrailWolf with him. TrailWolf hits the ground, the slam of rock against his chest knocking the air from his lungs. Jackalope hangs from his sleeve.

Erin lunges forward and grabs TrailWolf, both hands grabbing wads of jacket, anchoring him against the pull of the edge. Her boots skid and her knees slam into rock. The pain flares white-hot, but she holds.

Jackalope stares down at the empty air beneath him, at Mark's body hundreds of feet below, then at the knife embedded in him. He laughs a short, breathless sound of disbelief. "That wasn't… how it was supposed to go," he says.

Their eyes meet. Jackalope searches TrailWolf's face, frantic now, desperate for something to still make sense. He finds it. TrailWolf isn't ignoring remorse anymore, he's holding on. Jackalope's expression softens just a fraction. "There is hope for you," he says quietly.

He opens his hand, releasing TrailWolf's cuff. His body tips backward and he falls away from Erin and TrailWolf. The moment freezes and he hangs in open air, his eyes closing. Danny's knife stays lodged in his ribs as gravity pulls him down. His fall is silent, swallowed by distance. He makes impact with the ground below, bouncing once before remaining still forever.

Erin collapses against TrailWolf, her forehead pressing against his shoulder and breath coming in ragged pulls. She lets go of his jacket and, for the first time since she was a child, she feels it. Danny is gone and she has finally let him go.

TrailWolf doesn't move. He stares at the empty space where the platform was moments ago, then his eyes measure the drop where a man fell and a debt ended. His face has gone slack in a way Erin recognizes too well, the look of someone who finally understands exactly when they made the wrong choice.

They both lie in silence at the precipice. Then, the distant thrumming of the helicopter bleeds across the mountain. Erin lifts her head slowly, watching the rotors chopping through the air. It circles once, wide and cautious. The pilot is unsure what he's arriving at.

A loudspeaker crackles. "Erin Caldwell," Vance's voice carries, distorted but unmistakable. "This is Detective Vance. We can see you. Stay where you are."

Erin doesn't have the energy to answer and TrailWolf is too dazed to react. The helicopter dips lower, wind blasting dust across the plateau. She leans back against the rock and rests her head against the cool stone, closing her eyes from the swirling dirt as exhaustion crashes over her.

Below, a mountain keeps what it's been given, while above, the machine keeps circling.

Chapter 35: Cache Disabled

The helicopter touches down on a bluff far from the ledge, its rotors chewing at the treetops, but the skids never touch the clearing itself. Vance jumps out, ducking under the blades, with Tenner following closely behind. Over the radio, a distant unit confirms med staging below on Highway 12 and the pilot calls out fuel time. Vance feels the time crunch but has already determined how little any of that matters right now. "Lift when clear if you need," she says into her radio, already sprinting toward the cliff.

The detectives hike in on foot. The trees are thin and the air is crisp. Vance sees where the geocachers passed through the brush to their destination. When the trees finally break, Vance stops, surveying where the ledge opens. She doesn't step into the opening right away. She takes in the scene, the opening to the mine shaft, both Erin and TrailWolf collapsed on the ground, the splintering of rock and wood where the platform was once anchored. The ground nearby shows drag marks where people stumbled, collided, and lost their footing. It's messy. A fight happened here. Vance rests her grip on her service weapon.

Tenner exhales once, slow. "Jesus."

Vance watches Erin walk to the edge, far back enough to breathe, but close enough to peer over the edge. Her jacket is covered in dirt with blood soaking down her sleeve. Her hands hang loose at her sides, fingers stiff, still trying to grab something that's no longer there. TrailWolf is lying at the drop. His arms are dangling over the edge. Vance doesn't see Mark, but she does see broken lines of movement that go right up to the edge and then simply stop. She exhales slowly, grounding herself before she moves any closer.

She lifts her radio but keeps her voice low, contained. "Command," she says. "Detectives Vance and Tenner on foot at the site." She looks once more at Erin, then at the debris near her feet. "I have eyes on two of the hikers."

Her gaze settles back on Erin. "The scene is quiet," Vance adds carefully, "but not secure."

Vance steps forward, careful not to cross what she already knows is the line. "Step careful, Tenner," she says quietly. "Let's be sure of what we're walking into."

Tenner nods without comment. She steps forward, keeping an eye on the service entrance of the mine, and approaches Erin, deliberately angling in from the side instead of straight on, giving her space to register the movement without feeling boxed in. Erin notices the movement and turns to look, eyes focusing slowly, renegotiating distance. She doesn't say anything.

"You hurt?" Vance asks.

Erin blinks, looking down at herself. She holds out her palms, scratched and ripped open. She points to her leg next. The fabric of her pants is torn, showing blood clotted by dirt. She gives Vance a weak nod but says nothing. Vance assesses and lets the silence suffice.

Behind them, Tenner's voice carries through the trees as he updates the scene over his radio. Vance grounds herself on solid rock. "Medical's staged below the ridge," she says. "They'll come up when I say it's clear to move."

Erin swallows. "Mark…"

"I saw from the copter," Vance says gently, cutting the word off before Erin can spiral. She doesn't soften the truth, but she doesn't sharpen it either. "We'll get him."

Erin's shoulders sag and she sobs. Vance lets her be for a moment longer, turning her attention toward TrailWolf. He still hasn't moved. He's breathing, but it's shallow. She crouches next to him.

"Are you hurt?" Vance asks, just loud enough to reach him. He flinches at the sound of her voice, but he doesn't look back. "You're not in trouble right now," she continues. "But I need you to hear me."

He nods once, barely.

"Good," she says. "When you're ready, we'll help you stand."

She looks between the two of them, then back toward the edge. The scene is quiet now. Vance keys her radio again. "Command," she says. "We have two survivors on site. Both are cooperative. No immediate threats on site."

She releases the button and traces the edge of the clearing the way she was taught, letting her eyes work before her feet do. She studies what's left of the platform. The break isn't clean. Stress traveled through wood that had already lived too long past its purpose. A length of rope draped across the cliff tells the same story. She crouches carefully and looks at the rock where the fight turned ugly. She registers the scuff marks, prints of heels being dragged sideways, and handprints smeared in the dirt where someone tried to catch themselves and didn't.

She straightens and looks at Erin again, taking in the woman's damage, both the physical abuse and the way her eyes keep returning to the edge but never linger. "You tried to save him," Vance says quietly.

Erin nods once. Her voice comes rough. "I didn't know what else to do."

Vance accepts that without comment. She steps closer, eyes tracking the scuffed rock near Erin's boots, the disrupted grit, the way one line of movement ends so abruptly. She looks back up at Erin. "How did you stop him?" Vance asks.

Erin hesitates just long enough for the truth to settle into place. "I stabbed him."

Vance doesn't react, she just nods once, absorbing it. "With what?"

Erin glances down at her own hand, not surprised to find it empty. "A knife." She turns her hands over and stares at her bloodied knuckles. "I had my brother's knife."

"Do you still have it?"

Erin shakes her head. "No."

Vance's gaze sharpens slightly. "Where is it?"

"In him," Erin says, pointing to the ledge. "I wasn't trying to kill him. I just needed him to let go."

Vance holds Erin's eyes for a moment longer, then looks past her toward the ledge. Toward the drop below. "Alright," she says quietly. "Then we'll find it."

Erin shudders and sinks to the ground. Her eyes glass up. "I don't need it anymore."

Vance nods again, slower. She doesn't reach for cuffs or a notebook, she reaches for context. She walks the line of movement backward, reconstructing the choices. Where Jackalope stood, where TrailWolf slipped. Where Mark lost footing when the platform gave, at the rock thinning where no one should have been standing to begin with. She stops at the edge.

Down below, the mountain has already taken ownership. It takes a moment for her eyes to adjust. The drop is sheer, broken by ledges and shadow. Far below, three bodies interrupt the natural lines of stone, one more person than she expected. Vance steps back and exhales. "That doesn't line up," she says, mostly to herself.

Tenner, finished with his preliminary check, comes up beside her. "What doesn't?"

She waves him close, keeping her tone low, "We have three bodies down there. Who's the third?"

Tenner peers down the ravine, taking in the wreckage. "I'll call for retrieval."

"Get coordinates ready," Vance replies. "But we need to get these two down the mountain."

She looks at Erin again, then at TrailWolf, who has finally shifted, sitting on his knees, staring at his hands like they betrayed him.

"Looking at these two, I can see nobody came here to kill someone." She pauses. "But everybody paid for being here."

Vance crouches, bringing herself down to Erin's eye level without touching her. It's a practiced move to prevent escalation. "I need you to stay right here," she says. Her voice is neither kind nor cold, just steady. "Don't move, just breathe."

Erin nods, more mechanical than human. Her fingers fumble with rocks and draw lines in the dirt, as if the ground itself has become unreliable.

Vance straightens and turns toward TrailWolf. His eyes are closed and his hands grip the ledge. He's rocking slowly toward the edge and back. "Hey," Vance says. Louder now, but not sharp. "I need you with me." He doesn't answer.

She approaches him slowly, careful with her footing, careful with him. She doesn't touch him at first. She lets her shadow cross his hands. "I need you to sit back from the edge."

TrailWolf swallows. His throat works without producing sound.

"Come on, now." She tilts her body to fill his view, bracing herself on the ledge next to him. "Let's just make a little bit of space right now."

She waves toward flatter ground. He doesn't follow her immediately, peering over the ledge instead. He leans back, bringing his weight to his legs, and his shaking hands come up to his face. She steadies him at the arm, ready for whichever direction he chooses. "Okay, now let's get you somewhere safe."

Vance watches him for a moment longer, then eases him from the ledge. He stands and takes two steps back. She keeps her hold on his arm and keys her radio. "Command," she says. "I'm ready to extract the survivors. One male, one female, both ambulatory but in shock. Terrain is unstable. We are not moving anyone until med is staged and rope is set."

The response crackles back, but Vance doesn't wait for it to finish. She turns TrailWolf away from the edge, walks him to where Erin is still kneeling, and stays with the living. She turns toward the service entrance, knowing she still hasn't fully secured the area.

Erin notices her own breathing change, shallow and uneven. Her hands start to ache with a deep, spreading burn that crawls up her forearms. She flexes her fingers and they don't quite respond the way she expects. She tries to stand despite Vance's instructions to not move. Her balance slips, and she catches herself with one hand. The rock feels colder now and less solid.

Tenner glances over. "Lieutenant."

Vance turns in time to see Erin's shoulders fold inward as the tension finally releases its grip on her spine. Erin presses her palm against her thigh, then winces. She hadn't noticed the pain there yet. Or the scrape along her ribs, or the way her shoulders won't stop shaking.

"Hey," Vance says, moving fast. She drops to one knee, steadying Erin at the elbow. "Hey. You okay?"

Erin nods, but her eyes have gone unfocused. "I didn't mean to…" she starts, then stops. Her jaw tightens and she swallows hard, keeping herself from vomiting. "I didn't mean to. I didn't want any of this."

"I know," Vance says. She doesn't ask what that is. "You don't need to explain anything right now."

TrailWolf makes a sound beside them that doesn't quite qualify as a word. He's curled forward now, elbows on his knees, with his head in his hands. His shoulders jerk once, then again. He doesn't just cry, he folds completely.

The helicopter's thrum deepens high overhead, rotors chopping the air in wide, patient circles. Erin flinches at the noise. She lifts her tear-stained face toward the sky, then drops again just as fast. "They're going to ask questions," she says quietly with certainty. "I have so much to answer for."

"Yes," Vance replies. "Later." Her response is soft, but honest.

She shifts her grip, grounding Erin's elbow more firmly. "Right now, you're going to drink some water when med gets here. You're going to keep breathing and you're going to stay right here with me."

Erin exhales, long and shaky. For the first time since Vance arrived, Erin looks directly at Vance. There's something raw in the aftermath.

"I didn't walk away," Erin says.

Vance holds her gaze. "No," she agrees. "You didn't."

Help Other Readers Discover This Book

If you enjoyed *Dead Coordinates*, the best way to support the story is by helping other readers find it.

Leaving a short review on the platform where you purchased the book, whether it's a few words or a full paragraph, makes a tremendous difference for independent authors. Reviews help new readers decide to give a story a chance.

You can also help by recommending the book to friends, sharing it with fellow readers, or mentioning it online.

Independent authors rely almost entirely on word of mouth. Every review, recommendation, and shared conversation helps keep new stories alive.

Stories travel the same way geocaches do; passed from one curious person to the next. If this one led you somewhere interesting, thank you for helping others find it too.

Thank you for reading, and for being part of the journey.

Acknowledgments

Stories rarely come from a single place.

My thanks to the explorers, puzzle-solvers, and curious wanderers who inspired the spirit of this story. Caching is built on the joy of discovery, the thrill of the hunt, and the quiet satisfaction of finding something hidden in plain sight.

To the readers who continue to follow my work, thank you for walking these strange trails with me.

And to those who believe every set of coordinates leads somewhere interesting… you're probably right.

About the Author

Monsuta writes atmospheric thrillers and speculative fiction that explore the strange spaces where curiosity, obsession, and hidden truths intersect.

His stories often blend mystery, psychological tension, and dark imagination, inviting readers to look a little closer at the things most people walk past.

When he isn't writing, he enjoys exploring unusual roadside attractions, collecting oddities and macabre curiosities, diving into tabletop roleplaying worlds, and chasing ideas that refuse to be caught.

By the date of publication, his geocache record has over 1,200 finds in 21 states and 2 countries. His biggest cache day recorded is 182 finds. He has released 11 trackables into the wild (most of which have gone missing). By the time this book is released, 10 new trackables will become active, each focusing on key characters from this book so you can get the chance to be part of Jackalope's deadly game.

Dead Coordinates is published through **Ink Beyond**, an independent creative imprint dedicated to bold storytelling across genres.